AF615524

WHITE LIGHT

WENDY HALEY

ZEBRA BOOKS
KENSINGTON PUBLISHING CORP.

To Ann LaFarge—for believing

ZEBRA BOOKS are published by

Kensington Publishing Corp.
850 Third Avenue
New York, NY 10022

First Printing: July, 1995

Printed in the United States of America

Prologue

Virginia Beach, Virginia

He lay on the beach, watching the stars twinkle in rainbow colors. The sound of the ocean rolled over him, through him, and it sounded like the beating of his heart.

"Do you like that?" the voice asked.

"Yeah."

A tall shadow moved between him and the stars, and he made a small, discontented sound. "I know," the voice said again. "I'll be going soon. Tell me, Jeffrey. Do you remember last night?"

The stars had been blue. He must have said it aloud, for the shadow seemed to nod.

"Anything else?"

There should be. He had the *feeling* something had happened last night. It crouched in the back of his mind, its breath hot and feral. It held pain and fear, and things that shouldn't be looked at. He shied away from it. He preferred the stars, with their cold, friendly glitter.

"Only the stars," he said. "Blue's my favorite color."

"Good," the voice said.

The shadow moved away. The sound of footsteps was lost in the crash of the surf. Again, that almost-memory tugged at him. Remember. Remember. But it felt dark and heavy, black wings of fear beating in the cringing recesses of his mind. He threw himself away from it. The acid welcomed him, submerging the past, spreading him like butter across the roiling expanse of the present.

His heart beat with the rhythm of the sea, and the stars glittered even more brightly.

Time ended.

Space ended.

He closed his eyes, drifting.

"Hey, you!"

A different voice this time. Harsher, less frightening. He opened his eyes, tried to focus.

"Aw, man, he's loaded," growled another voice. "Come on, kid. Got any ID?"

Cops. He didn't have the power to talk or even raise his head. The world spun as they hauled him to his feet and propped him between them. He felt them digging through his pocket.

"Here's his school ID," one said.

"Got his home phone on it?"

"Yeah." The man sounded tired. "I'm tired of this shit. Kids frying their brains . . ." He drew in his breath with a harsh sound. "What'd you take, son?"

He told them about the stars then. They didn't understand, of course. But at least they stopped asking him questions.

"We'd better get him to the hospital," the first man said. "You want to make the call to his folks?"

"I'll flip you for it."

"Heads."

"Tails. It's your butt, Ed."

"Shit. Take his legs, will you? We're gonna have to carry this puppy. Come on, kid, quit squirming. We're going to get you all fixed up."

He stopped moving, but it was because he could see the stars again, not because they'd asked him to.

All fixed up.

Yeah.

Chapter One

"Your brother's a nut."

Connie stared at her mother for a moment, then looked over at Cullen, the nut in question. He didn't seem to mind. But then, he and Mom always fought. They were just alike, of course; it was only their causes that were different.

"Nice weather we're having," Connie said.

Mom lifted her cup to her mouth, gazing at Connie over the porcelain rim. Age had cast liver spots across the pale, fragile skin of her hands and turned her blond hair silver, but it hadn't had the power to dim her intelligence or iron will. Sandra Balestier Matthias. Southern lady, volunteer for charities and conservative political parties. Her husband, dead more than twenty years now, had called her relentless.

"Don't try to change the subject, Connie," she said. "*You* know how he's been. Save the seals. Save the whales. Save the rainforest, the ozone layer, the pygmy owl—"

"And vote Republican," Cullen said.

Connie opened her mouth to speak.

"You've really gone way out with this one, Cullen," Sandra said. "Psychic powers, crystals, Tarot cards, for God's sake! Cohabiting with spirits—"

"Channeling, Mom."

"Hmph. All for one and one for all."

He smiled again. "That was the Three Musketeers. We say 'All *is* One.' The universal consciousness, you know."

Again, Connie opened her mouth.

"And your wife!" Sandra said. "For ten years I've known her as Penny. Now I'm supposed to call her Phaedra. How pretentious can you be?"

Cullen shrugged. "It means 'bright.' "

"Not in my book," Sandra said.

With a sigh, Connie gathered the coffee cups and took them into the kitchen. It never changed. This was why she'd spent the past fourteen years in Los Angeles. This was why her visits had become shorter and less frequent. If it weren't for her son Jeff, she wouldn't be here now.

She dumped the cups into the sink and turned on the faucet. Bracing her hands wide upon the counter, she watched the steam coil up from the water.

"What's the matter?" Cullen's voice, which seemed to mingle with the sound of the faucet, was smooth, liquid—a politician's voice, or a preacher's.

She turned to face him. Cullen was her twin, but you'd never guess it. He'd inherited the dramatic looks and personality of the Balestiers, complete with the eyes that seemed to change from blue to green to gray, depending on his mood. Connie had grown up the only brunette in a blond family, a throwback to her father's Cherokee great-grandmother.

"Why do you bait her?" she asked.

"It's my family role," he said. "I couldn't stop if I tried. Just like you're the good kid, the practical one who fades into the background when the rest of us start flying high."

"You've been reading psychology books again."

He waggled his eyebrows. "All the better to see you, my dear."

Connie turned back to the sink and started washing the cups. She didn't want Cullen to see her expression; he'd always read her too well. "Jeff was supposed to be here tonight."

"Sandra drives him nuts."

"He hasn't seen me for nearly three months. You'd think he'd make an effort."

"There's no soap in there."

"Huh?"

"You forgot the soap." Reaching around her, Cullen took the sponge out of her hands and turned the water off. "I'm glad you came back, for his sake. He needs you."

"He hates me."

"The kid loves you. It's just that life has gotten too complicated for him, and he doesn't know what to do about it."

"I'm scared, Cullen." She let her breath out in a harsh sigh. "Did he tell you about the Satanism?"

"No."

"He and some of his buddies got caught messing around in a graveyard."

Cullen's brows soared. "Robbing graves?"

"They'd taken a skull and some finger bones . . ." She took a deep breath, remembering her own disbelief, then her terror when she'd realized it was true. Her son. "That's why I sent him here to Derek. To pull him away from that world."

She sighed as Cullen's arms came around her. He knew; he always knew. Closing her eyes, she leaned back against him. He didn't speak, just let her take comfort from him.

"Tell me," she said after a while. "How do you take a kid like that and turn him around?"

"I wish I knew. How's he doing with Derek?"

Her ex. Time had blurred her memory of him. And why shouldn't it? They'd been married for eleven months when they were only eighteen years old. "Derek was sure he'd have him all straightened out in a couple of weeks."

"Ahh, the arrogance of Man."

"He apologized very nicely, thank you."

"And then begged for help."

"In-deed."

Connie straightened. Without needing to be told, Cullen dropped his arms and stepped back. She wrung out the sponge, placed it neatly on the drainer, then turned around. "What are *you* doing, little brother?"

"Haven't you heard of the New Age?"

"I lived in California." She put her hands flat on his chest. "Look, I don't care what religion you worship. But—"

"Why don't you come over tonight and see what we're doing?"

"You and Penny?"

He smiled. "Phaedra, remember? Yeah. And there are a few others who come around fairly regularly."

"What do you do together?"

"Oh, this and that. Hey, why don't you spend the

night, so you won't have to drive back so late? We've got plenty of room."

"Welllll . . ." Connie hesitated, unsure if she had the resources to tackle this tonight. "I've only been in town a few hours, and you know how Mom can be."

"Mom is *always* like that."

She was, she really was. Connie found herself grinning to match her twin's smile of pure unholy delight. She clapped her hand over her mouth to keep the laughter from bubbling up.

Cullen leaned one elbow on the counter. "Do you remember the time she dressed us up in those awful velvet things to impress the senator when he came to lunch?"

"You had those cute . . ." Connie fought for control of her voice, ". . . shorts and little white knee-highs—"

"And you puked strawberry shortcake all over his shoes."

That set them both off. They laughed until the tears came, until Connie had to hold onto her brother's arm to keep from sliding to the floor.

"Oh, God," Cullen gasped. "I missed you, sis."

She wrapped her arms around him, and for a moment it seemed as though they were six years old again. The Matthias twins. Walking in lockstep, finishing each other's sentences, sharing triumphs and troubles and punishments.

"Hey, you two." Mom's voice came from the doorway.

Without breaking the embrace, Connie glanced over her shoulder. "I've decided to spend the night at Cullen's," she said.

Emotion flickered across Sandra's face, but she

suppressed it before Connie could figure out what it was. "That's nice. The two of you have a lot more than hugs to catch up on."

"You don't mind?" Connie asked, surprised to have gotten off so easily.

"Well, actually, it *would* give me a chance to attend Nathan Moore's fundraising party at the Omni." She smoothed a lock of hair back from her forehead. "What shall I wear, Cullen? The beige suit or the green?"

"The green, of course," he said, without breaking a smile. "For money."

"You never change," she retorted. Turning, she disappeared into the dining room.

"Neither do you," Connie said under her breath.

Cullen's house perched atop the dunes like a seagull ready to take flight. A stunning, modern sweep of a house, its white walls reflected the searing colors of the sunset. Beyond it lay the bay, quicksilver-smooth in the breathless twilight calm.

"Wow," Connie said.

"A feast for the eyes and the spirit," her twin agreed, swinging her suitcase out of the trunk of her Grand Am. "Come on, sis. Come see my world."

Connie slipped her shoes off before following him toward the house. The hot sand scoured the soles of her feet, a visceral flesh-memory of childhood. She and Cullen had spent their summers on the beach, building great castles in the sand as the sun baked them Indian-brown.

"Remember Charlie Diaz?" she asked.

"How could I forget?" The fading sun turned his blond hair the color of old blood, an image that didn't sit well with his buoyant good looks. "Old Charlie used to chase you up and down the beach for hours, trying to rub sand in your hair. Looking back on it, I think he had a crush on you."

"Hmmm. Did he have a crush on you, too? I seem to recall him burying you up to your neck in sand and leaving me to dig you out."

"That was meanness."

"What's the difference?"

"One is for love, one for hate."

She snorted. "With men, it's one and the same."

"So young to be so cynical. There are nice men out there."

"Sure. But the only one I know is my brother."

He ruffled her straight black hair, a familiar gesture from their childhood. "You know, I always wished I had your coloring."

"You're kidding. I always felt like an oddball with all the pale, hulking Matthiases."

"There you go. We're all the same, except for you. The Indian princess."

Astonishing, Connie thought. Here, all she'd wanted was to be like everyone else, and what did Cullen want? To be the one who was different.

He unlocked the front door and swung it open, inviting her in with a dramatic sweep of his arm. Stepping into the foyer was like stepping into a cathedral; the room was awash with multicolored light from a three-story bank of stained-glass windows. A stark white staircase curved up from the ground floor, soaring from landing to landing and wrapped with sleek black banisters.

"Advertising must be more profitable than I thought," Connie said.

"I'm good at what I do." He dropped the suitcase

with a thump. "Penny!" Then he winked at Connie and shouted, "Phaedra! Connie's here."

A door opened at the far end of the foyer, and a woman came into the room. A *glissando* of music should have accompanied her. Tall and willowy, with the long, graceful neck of a ballerina, Penny—Phaedra—was still the most beautiful woman Connie had ever seen. Her burnished mahogany hair was pulled back in a neat chignon, giving the honors to flawless bone structure and skin that glowed like mother-of-pearl. She lent impossible elegance to a yellow cotton sundress.

"Connie," she said, coming forward to take Connie's hands in hers. "How nice to see you again!"

Her eyelashes caught the light as she turned toward her husband; Connie could have sworn they were an inch long, and without the help of mascara.

"Cullen, darling, why don't you take your sister's things upstairs and then join us outside? The sunset is gorgeous."

"So are you."

"I'm just an old married woman."

He brushed the back of his hand lightly down his wife's cheek, a gesture of such tenderness that Connie felt her own throat tighten. And after ten years of marriage . . .

"I'm so glad you decided to come to our firewalk," Phaedra said.

Connie's gaze focused on her brother. "I didn't know you were firewalking tonight," she said, hoping her thoughts were adequately conveyed by her eyes.

"Didn't I mention it?" Total innocence.

"Somehow it escaped your attention." *You shit.*

Apparently unaware of the undercurrents of

emotion, Phaedra said, "Have you ever been to one, Connie?"

She didn't look away from Cullen. "This is my first."

"Oh, you'll love it." Phaedra looped her arm in Connie's. "Everyone's already here. Come on out and I'll introduce you."

Connie shot a last glare at Cullen over her shoulder as she let Phaedra lead her toward the inner door. He knew, damn him, that she wasn't comfortable with this stuff. But she forgot her brother's perfidy the moment she walked into the next room.

This was obviously the core of the house. Islands of grouped sofas and chairs were scattered across the pale oak floor, the colors of the fabric adding warmth and intimacy to the huge room. A stone fireplace occupied one whole wall. But the focal point wasn't inside at all; the bayside wall was made of glass, a dramatic sweep of sand and sky that took the breath away. French doors led to the deck outside, which stretched toward the water at odd, slightly disturbing angles that seemed to thrust the observer straight toward the bay.

Five people sat at a table on the deck, all facing west to watch the sun retreat in a burst of violent color.

"Hi, everyone," Phaedra called. "I've got a surprise for you tonight." She looped her arm in Connie's and drew her nearer. "These are our closest friends. I'm sure you'll come to love them as much as we do."

Connie studied each person as Phaedra introduced them. Philip and Evvie Wahlfield were the oldest, somewhere in their fifties. He stood to shake hands, a medium-sized man just going to flab. His wife was as tall as he, broader in the shoulder, narrower in the hips, and had a grip that made Connie wince. She pegged them as eager, earnest, and credulous.

Next were Amy Cortez and her teenage daughter, Lynn—both blond, suntanned, and slim. The mother had the restless, unfulfilled eyes of someone eternally searching for something but never finding it, the daughter the look of a kid who'd been dragged along for the ride so many times she'd passed beyond boredom.

Hamilton Liu was the most interesting. He seemed to be somewhere in his twenties, but possessed the calm serenity of someone much older. He'd drawn back his straight black hair in a ponytail which sharpened his fine-boned Asian features.

"Look! There it goes," Evvie Wahlfield said.

Connie turned toward her in time to see the sun disappear beneath the horizon. A last wash of scarlet flickered over the sky, then faded to violet. The dock looked like a stilt-legged centipede striding a quicksilver sea.

And then darkness fell, rushing across the land to quell the water. The sound of the wavelets lapping the beach seemed louder now. Connie looked at the rapt faces around her, feeling a kinship she'd never expected. *No wonder they believe in magic.*

But they didn't, not really. They believed in themselves. *All is One.*

Something moved out there in the darkness, startling her. A moment later a man climbed the bayside stairs onto the deck. His features were only half-visible in the dimness, but everything female in Connie came to point like a good hunting dog. It was the way he moved—elegantly, economically, yet with an intriguing sense of power.

"Ah, John, you're back," Phaedra said, stretching one arm out to him. "Come meet Cullen's sister."

"In the dark?"

Phaedra walked back to the house. A moment later, light bloomed all around the deck—not from above, as Connie'd expected, but from below. It was a gentle illumination, almost as kind as the moonlight.

Connie got her first good look at the newcomer. He might be a half-head taller than she, maybe a little more, and he had the sleek, slim lines of a long-distance runner. She might have thought him ordinary, if it hadn't been for his eyes. Long and slightly tilted, they were the same soft, pale blue of the sky at daybreak. She felt his gaze sink deep and had the peculiar feeling that he saw things no one else ever had.

"So you're Connie," he said. "I've heard a lot about you."

"I deny it all."

He smiled. "You'd be a fool to do that."

Phaedra came to stand beside him. She was a little taller than he. "This is John Bruycker, our resident psychic."

"Then why did you need the lights on?" Connie asked, without intending to.

His smile widened, bracketing his mouth with creases she liked a lot. "It's cats who see in the dark, not psychics."

"John is our channeler," Phaedra said.

Oh, God. "I'm afraid I—"

"Don't believe in channeling?" John finished for her.

"—don't know anything about it. And am not sure I want to."

"At least you're honest about it."

She returned his smile. "But wrong?"

"That depends on one's point of view."

Hearing the door open behind her, she turned to see Cullen come out of the house. He'd changed into a tee shirt and a pair of tan shorts, and the blond hairs on his arms and legs shone gold in the light.

"I see you've met everybody, Connie," he said. "Ready for the firewalk?"

"I'm ready to watch."

He glanced up at John. "She doesn't trust herself."

"I trust myself fine," she retorted. "It's the coals I don't trust."

"Come on, everyone," Phaedra said, spreading her arms in an encompassing gesture. "Let's get to it. Hamilton, is the fire ready?"

"Should be," the young man replied. "I've been nursing it for hours."

"Let's go, then. Everyone got their flashlights?"

Connie found herself walking between her brother and John Bruycker. She was nervous, more nervous than she should have been. The golden ovals of light from the flashlights were tiny pockets of reality in the ocean-scented darkness, and she felt cast adrift in a world she didn't recognize.

She tensed. Instead of dropping her hand, as Cullen would have done, John tightened his grip. He stroked his thumb across her knuckles, a gesture that should have been innocent, but which felt overly intimate.

"The two of you are something else," he said. "It's like you augment each other. Don't you feel it, Cullen?"

"I feel it. So does Connie."

She pulled her hand away. "Stop it, you two. You're giving me the creeps."

"And you're radiating a hell of a lot of anger, uncertainty, fear—all negative emotions," John said. "It doesn't have to be that way."

Connie had had enough. "Give me your flashlight, Cullen. I'm going back to the house."

"John, it's time to stop," he said, without relinquishing the flashlight.

"Okay. Sorry, Connie. I'll try to be good."

They fell silent. The rasp of their shoes upon the sand seemed loud in the absence of voices. Ahead, the firefly darts of the flashlight beams stopped, resolving into the general ruddy glow of a smoldering fire.

The others made space for them as they came up to the bed of coals tucked away in the lee of a dune. The embers had been raked into a lane fifteen or twenty feet long and glowed a dusky red beneath a gray coating of ash. Connie could feel the heat of them on her feet and shins even as the cooler breeze from the bay plucked at her hair.

"Have a seat, everybody," Cullen said.

The others obeyed. Connie watched in some awe as her brother raised his arms in what might have been a benediction. The dynamics of the group obviously revolved around him. And for a moment, with the glow illuminating his face from below, he looked larger than life.

A leader. Charismatic in the sheer force of his personality, compelling because of the intensity of his belief.

"He wouldn't bother with this himself," John Bruycker said softly, sinking down on Connie's right. "But Phaedra really gets off on firewalking, and so do a couple of the others."

"Flashlights," Cullen said.

The cessation of light was sudden and profound, and it seemed for a moment that darkness had settled over the group like a great winged creature. Then the deeper glow of the coals took over. Cullen stepped closer, his face a mask of orange-red light and indigo shadows.

"We have to conquer fear," he said. His words had the feel of a chant; the others nodded as though they'd heard it many times. "Throw the fear away, take charge of yourselves and your lives."

Phaedra took up the chant. "The fire is healing. Take it in, feel it, let it flow."

Suddenly the scene seemed to take a half-turn to the left. It seemed a primitive ceremony, humankind invoking the power of fire to keep the night at bay.

Imagination's working overtime. Logic, of course, told her that. But here, with the darkness hovering at her back, logic didn't seem much of a shield. A shiver ran cold fingers up her spine.

Absently, she rubbed her arms. It wasn't until John laid his hand on hers that she realized what she was doing.

"Does it bother you that much?" he whispered beneath the chanting.

She glanced at him. "Do you have siblings?"

"A sister. We're not close."

"Cullen and I are twins. Not alike in most things,

but we're close in a way no one but a twin can understand. All my life, that's been a constant. But I don't know this aspect of Cullen, and that bothers me."

"No one knows him better than you. And all you have to do is follow where he leads."

"Maybe I don't like his world."

"Maybe you're just afraid."

"I can accept that."

He canted a smile at her. Connie refused to react; pulling her knees up, she wrapped her arms around her legs and tried to watch objectively.

Philip Wahlfield shed his shoes and socks and stood up. Without hesitation, without a trace of fear on his face, he stepped onto the coals and walked smoothly and quickly to the other end. Evvie went next. Amy and Lynn Cortez went together, arms linked. Hamilton Liu followed more slowly.

Then Phaedra stepped out onto the coals. Her eyes were rapt with pleasure.

Hoo, boy! Connie thought. In a way, however, it was fascinating.

Cullen made it all look good. He strode the lane of red-hot embers unpretentiously, but his face was that of a man who truly believed. But then, Cullen had always believed. With all the passion in his dramatic Balestier soul, he believed.

"Aren't you going?" she asked, turning to John Bruycker.

"Of course." He smiled. "Aren't you?"

"Are you kidding?"

His eyes delved deep, much too deep for comfort, as he rose to his feet in a lithe movement. "Sometimes it's good to be reckless," he said. "It can set you free."

"There's a time and a place for recklessness. And this isn't it."

"Will you know it when it comes?"

She tilted her head back to see him better. "I hope so."

John Bruycker moved across the coals with the cool detachment of one who'd done it so many times it had ceased to be remarkable. Connie watched him, fascinated by the way he moved, and also by the way he kept his gaze on her while he did it.

Suddenly, some sixth sense drew her attention to a point beyond him. A figure appeared at the edge of the light, so suddenly that it seemed to have materialized out of the darkness.

Her breath went out with a harsh sound. "Jeff," she whispered.

He'd grown in three months—in height and in defiance. He had his dad's tawny hair and the changeable Balestier eyes. A good combination, one he might do justice to when he got older. Just now he was a little too thin, a little too dirty, and a lot too hard to be very endearing.

Except to his mother. She loved him, dirt and prickles and all. Enough so that her breath caught on something sharp and barbed at the sight of him.

"Hello, Jeff," she said.

"Hi, Mom."

He studied her, his gaze stark and enigmatic. Some of the night remained in his eyes—whether mood or memory, she couldn't tell. He wanted something. What, she didn't know.

Despair darkened her joy at seeing him. They still

couldn't connect; she'd given birth to him, raised him, loved him, but she no longer understood him. She watched the awareness of it come into his face, saw his withdrawal.

For a moment, she thought he was going to turn and walk away. The intention lay in his eyes. Then he stepped out onto the coals and walked straight toward her.

Chapter Two

Connie held her breath until Jeff sat down beside her. Then she picked his feet up one at a time and examined them. Not a single blister. Plenty of dirt, though.

"When was the last time you wore shoes?" she asked.

"Good opening line, Mom."

She studied this almost-man who was her son. His adult features were beginning to show through the softer flesh of childhood; he had Derek's stubborn jaw and her high cheekbones, with a flare of dark eyebrows that were all Balestier. She wanted to hug him, but the set of his shoulders told her it wouldn't be received well. So she merely set his foot back down on the sand and brushed the grit from her hands.

"How did you get here?" she asked.

"I hitched a ride with some guys I know."

What guys? Who are they and what do they do? Are they going to pick you up later so you can run the streets with them? Why didn't you meet me at my mother's, like you were supposed to?

Three months ago, she would have asked all

those questions. And he'd have given her one of those infuriating teenage smirks and walked away. She was wiser now.

"So, how have you been?" she asked.

"Fine."

"How are you getting along with your dad?"

"Fine."

Liar, she thought. Derek hadn't had any more luck with him than she had, which was why he'd swallowed his pride and asked for help. But this was a fragile moment. His lie couldn't shatter it, only her reaction to it. *T'ain't fair.* But then, it never was.

To her relief, Cullen came to sit with them. "Hey, Jeff."

"Hey. Didn't get Mom out on the coals tonight, did you?"

"How would you know?"

"I'm psychic."

"She also has her shoes and socks on."

Almost, Jeff smiled. "You owe me five bucks."

"Right you are." Pulling a thin sheaf of folded bills out of his pocket, Cullen peeled off a five and handed it to the boy.

Not for the first time, Connie wished she had Cullen's gift for people. But then, getting along with other people's kids was easy; it was getting along with your own that was hard.

"Where are you staying, Mom?"

Jeff's question took her off guard. "Tonight I'll be here. But first thing tomorrow I'll be looking for an apartment."

"One or two bedrooms?"

She glanced up at Cullen, saw a warning in his eyes. "Why, Jeff?"

"I want to move back in with you."

That, from the kid who'd screamed "I hate you. I wish you were dead!" the last time they'd been together.

"I'm not free to make that decision on my own," she said. "Your dad has some say in it."

"It's my life," he protested.

"Not 'til you're eighteen." It was an automatic parental response. She couldn't stop it any more than she could have stopped breathing.

His face tightened. "Same old shit, right, Mom?"

"Yes," she agreed, suddenly weary of it all. "Same old shit."

Jeff lunged to his feet. He glared down at Connie, his hands clenching and unclenching. "I'm out of here."

"Come on, Jeff. Wait a minute," Cullen said. "Why don't we all get together tomorrow and talk about this?"

"Fuck you," the boy snarled.

He stalked off. The darkness gobbled him up the moment he stepped away from the dune. Connie half-rose, then sank back down. She managed to control the urge to rush after him; Jeff wasn't the only one who'd changed in the past months.

"Well, fuck you, too," Cullen muttered.

Connie turned to look at him, absurdly pleased to see that he was still human enough to respond childishly. "But he's just a kid," she said. "And life is just a little complicated right now."

"There's nothing worse than having your own platitudes come back to haunt you."

She raked her hair back, pulling it taut enough to hurt. "I don't know what to do anymore."

"Maybe there's nothing you *can* do."

"Nothing right, anyway."

"He knows you love him. In time, he'll come back."

"Will he?" All her fear crystallized in those two words. A mother's terror at anticipated loss, her concern for the safety of a son who knew no caution.

Instead of trying to comfort her, Cullen seemed to go somewhere else. Oh, he still sat here beside her. But it was obvious from his eyes that he'd unplugged from the real world and was wandering somewhere deep inside himself. For a moment, he looked like a stranger.

Then he blinked, and suddenly her brother returned. "I'm sorry, Connie. I was thinking."

She drew her legs up and rested her chin on her knees. The coals were beginning to lose their smoldering red color, but they were still hot enough to be felt at this distance. The warmth wasn't comforting.

"Cullen," she said, pointing toward the coals and the people clustered around them, "don't you think this is kind of—"

"Weird?"

"Yeah."

His eyes caught the light in a moist sheen. "I've always been different. Saw things other people didn't, felt things others didn't seem to notice. You know, Connie. You were the one who taught me how to hide them."

"Me?" she asked, honestly astonished.

"Sure. You moved through the world with such practical ease, blending your colors to fit the acceptable norm."

"Cullen, that's nuts."

"Is it?" He smiled at her, a grin at once knowing and sympathetic. Then he leaned back on his elbows and stared at the sullenly glowing coals. "I never fit, sis. Until I found this, and these people. This is the only world where I can really be myself and not be labeled weird. I've been exploring myself. And finding things that astound me, things that had been shadows all my life but are now coming into the light."

She studied his profile, the long, fine line of his nose, the dramatic sweep of cheekbone and jaw, the eyes that held passion and certitude. *No wonder they come here to be with him.*

And she remembered the dreamy boy he'd been. All her life, she'd thought being a twin had set him apart. Now she realized it had been Cullen himself. He'd been too gentle, too spiritual ever to be a "man's man."

"I'm glad you're back," he said. "I need you."

She, who'd been thinking about certitude and serenity, stiffened in surprise. "What's the matter?"

He turned to face her. For a moment she thought he was going to spill something important, but then he shrugged and said, "It's just that things haven't . . . felt right lately. Sort of like something is pressing on me, crowding me."

"Good God, Cullen," she said, exasperated. "How can I help you? I don't even believe in that stuff!"

"Just be there for me."

"We're always there for each other."

"True." He took her hand, splayed his out, palm up, beneath hers. "All for one and one for all."

She couldn't help but laugh. "Mom never changes."

"No, she doesn't. But I've come to treasure her stubbornness; it's something that can be counted on." Slowly he curled his fingers so that he was cupping her hand. "Connie, I'm worried about Jeff."

"Why?" she whispered.

"I've never let him firewalk. But he did it like he's been doing it all his life. Like it was nothing."

Her breath suddenly seemed thin, without sustenance. "Someone else?"

"Maybe. Or maybe he just doesn't care whether he burns himself or not."

"You don't think it's the Satanism again—"

"I'll talk to him, Connie."

She wanted so badly for Jeff to come to *her*. Why couldn't he see it? Why couldn't they ever come to common ground somewhere? Too exhausted in mind and spirit to answer Cullen for a moment, she leaned back and just let her gaze drift.

John Bruycker seemed almost to materialize out of the darkness at the other side of the coals. Connie noted it, along with her surprise that she hadn't noticed when he'd left. But then, her brain seemed to move on a different track when Jeff was around. Connie-the-mother as opposed to Connie-the-person.

Bruycker sat down beside Amy Cortez, leaned over to whisper something in her ear. She laughed, unmistakable longing on her face. He didn't seem to return her emotion; a moment later he leaned the other way to say something to Evvie Wahlfield, and his manner didn't change in the least.

Suddenly, Connie's gaze shifted to Hamilton Liu. He sat a little apart from the others, his legs folded in the lotus position. The smoldering light lay in slabs on his face, stark upward slashes at cheekbones and brow. With a start, she realized he was staring at her. Studying. Assessing. Had been for some time. Instead of looking away, as someone else might have, he smiled at her.

"Why is that man staring at me?" she asked.

"Hamilton?" Cullen threaded his fingers with hers. "He's fascinated with our being twins. He says there's a special relationship between twins, and that you and I must share some aspects of spirituality on a level no one else could."

"Boy, was *he* wrong."

"He was once a twin. His brother died when they were seven years old; rode his bike out in front of a car. Hamilton says he can feel him sometimes."

Connie determinedly kept her gaze away from Hamilton Liu, but she knew he was still staring at her. And suddenly she'd had enough. Disengaging her hand from Cullen's, she stood up. "I'm going to bed. We can talk in the morning."

"Meet me on the beach at dawn. I want to share the sunrise with you."

"Don't you have to go to work in the morning?"

He looked up at her, his eyelashes catching the light in a whorl of bronze and gold. "I don't need much sleep these days. Besides, I find it an uplifting experience: sunset tonight, dawn tomorrow. Death and rebirth."

"I need sleep more than uplifting. Let's make it brunch."

"Brunch is plebeian."

"Brunch is sane."

He sighed. "All right, brunch."

She looked past him at the house. It seemed to float in an island of soft yellow light, in welcome contrast to the hovering darkness all around. She started toward it, needing to be enclosed in the solid reality of four square walls.

"Connie!"

She paused, glancing at Cullen over her shoulder. He rose to his feet, a lithe uncoiling of muscles. Looping his arm around her, he held her tightly for a moment. Connie wrapped her arms around him as hot tears prickled the insides of her eyelids.

"Okay?" he murmured.

"Okay."

"Want me to walk you back?"

"I'd like to be alone right now," she said.

"How will you know which room is yours?"

She smiled at him in a brief, irrepressible bout of humor. "I'll know."

Connie woke at dawn. With a groan, she buried her face in her pillow and tried to make consciousness go away. And failed miserably.

"Damn it, Cullen."

If she believed in such things, she might have thought he'd placed the suggestion to awaken in her mind. She flung the covers aside and reached for her clothes. Since she obviously wasn't going to get any more sleep, she might as well indulge Cullen in his daybreak madness. Remembering how blustery autumn mornings could be on the water, she pulled on a sweater.

Horizontal bars of mauve and turquoise stained the horizon by the time she got downstairs. The tall oceanside windows seemed to pull the light in and paint the pale walls with it. Connie paused for a moment to admire the effect, then opened the French doors and stepped outside.

The air had the tangy bite of an early autumn day. The cool salt breeze plunged into her lungs, waking her as coffee never could. She took another deep breath, reveling in the sharp visceral memory it evoked. Home. Until now, she hadn't realized how much she'd missed this. Fourteen years in California, and she'd never gotten used to facing west to look out over the ocean.

She walked west along the edge of the water. Seagulls coasted overhead, wings canted on the wind, greedy dark eyes watching for a handout. Shielding her eyes against the growing light, she looked up and down the beach. No Cullen.

"If you're back in that house asleep, I'll . . ." Her voice trailed off as she spotted something dark on the sand a few hundred yards farther west.

She couldn't tell what it was. But after she'd walked a short distance closer, it resolved itself into the figure of a man, feet toward her. He lay on his back, unmoving. The breeze lifted his hair, scattering blond strands to catch the light.

"Cullen?" she called.

He'd probably fallen asleep. Sure, that was it. But something cold and hard bloomed in her chest, and her footsteps quickened. The gulls followed her as though tugged on the line of her anxiety.

"Cullen?" No answer. "Cullen!"

Her shout was overloud in the early morning silence. She started to run. The sand dragged at her feet, making each step slow and heavy, as though she were running through a nightmare.

She could see his face now. His eyes were open, staring blindly up at the sky, and the only color in his skin that lent by the sunrise. The marvelous blue-green-gray pupils were shrouded now, almost hidden beneath a milky film.

Connie's heartbeat pounded in her ears, dimming

the sound of the ocean and the taunting screech of the gulls. This couldn't be real. It *couldn't.*

"It's a trance," she panted, dropping to her knees beside him. "It's a trance, or something . . . Cullen . . . *Cullen.*"

But the howling emptiness in her soul told her otherwise. From the moment of conception they'd been together. Even a continent's distance hadn't parted them, not really. All her life, he'd been her partner, her ally, her constant companion. No matter how bad things had gotten, there was always Cullen.

"Oh, God," she whimpered.

Her hand shook violently as she reached to test for his pulse. He'd gone cold. She had to force herself to breathe, force her lungs to contract around air that seemed stiff and solid.

She wanted to look away; she wanted to run. But her precise accountant's mind clicked away like an automatic camera, recording images that would haunt her as long as she lived. A stab wound marked the center of his bare chest. An eighth of an inch wide, an inch long, such a small thing to take a man's life. Dried blood marked a path from it down his side and turned the sand beneath him dark. Not much blood, but enough.

"Cullen," she said. "Oh, Cullen."

His arms were stretched wide, his fingertips touching a pair of fat black candles. Another candle had been thrust into the sand at his head, two more at his feet. They made up the points of a pentagram that had been carved into the sand around him. No footprints except hers marred the sand—none.

The thump of her heart was louder now. She

closed her eyes against a world that had begun to spin.

And still her damned logical mind wouldn't stop working. Adding. Computing.

Pentagram.

Black candles.

Jeff.

Not my son. Not this. She looked at the candles, the pentagram, the slit marring the skin of Cullen's chest. And her mother's heart took over then, twisting the answer. Jeff had problems, sure. She could accept his capacity to lie, cheat, even steal. But not this.

Not unless he told her. Not unless she could look in his eyes and see her brother's murder there would she believe.

"I'll talk to him," Cullen had said. *When? Last night?*

She smoothed the bright hair back from her brother's forehead. It still felt alive, smooth, pale strands sliding across her palm. As her soul howled in loss and loneliness, she leaned down and kissed his cheek.

Then she straightened. Pulling the candles from the sand, she set them to one side and started brushing the pentagram out of existence.

"See, Cullen," she said in a voice that seemed to echo in her chest, "I've got to make a decision. Jeff got caught with this kind of stuff before. If I leave it here, the police are going to blame him immediately. So leaving it is an irrevocable choice. But if I take it, I can always give it back later. That's a reversible choice. I've got to talk to Jeff, little brother, before I do what can't be undone."

She took off her sweater and rolled the candles

carefully in it. Then she sat in vigil beside her brother. Distantly she heard the crash of the waves, the high, harsh cries of the seagulls. But her attention remained focused on something much smaller, much closer. Grains of sand. The wind pushed them along, slowly and steadily, tiny particles moving, tumbling. Creating new patterns, erasing the old.

Until she sat in a sea of pristine sand seemingly untouched by man. And Cullen beside her, cold in the bright sunlight.

Chapter Three

Connie sat on one of the sofas in Cullen's living room, studying the police detective as he walked toward her. Everything about him was square: jaw, body, even the cut of his iron-gray hair. He had big, wet-looking Latin eyes whose gentleness she didn't trust at all.

"Ms. Matthias?" Even his voice had a squareness to it. It was the voice of a man who knew exactly who he was and why he did things. "I'm Detective Joseph D'Amato." He held his badge up; light flashed off the metal shield. "Homicide, Virginia Beach police department. I have a few questions to ask you."

Connie nodded. He slid into the loveseat opposite and fixed her with a deceptively unassuming gaze. She wasn't deceived.

Catching movement from the corner of her eye, she turned to see John Bruycker enter through the French doors. He came toward her, moving with the fluid grace she'd come to associate with him. But a uniformed policeman stepped in front of him, motioning him to a seat at the far end of the room.

"Do you know Mr. Bruycker?" D'Amato asked.

Connie swung around again. She'd almost forgotten the detective. Strange, she thought, how Bruycker claimed her attention so thoroughly. Star quality: Cullen had had it.

"I met him last night for the first time," she said. "But I'm grateful for his help this morning. If he hadn't come by when he had, I don't know what I would have done with Penny."

"Pretty upset, was she?"

Connie flinched from the memory of Penny throwing herself on Cullen's body, her own attempts to pull the distraught woman away. John had come upon the scene and had merely plucked Penny up and carried her up to the house.

"She was hysterical," Connie said. "Said a lot of things about wanting to die with him. That's when we called the doctor. She's sedated now, and should stay that way for a while."

Connie envied her; tears, even hysterics, would have been easier to bear than this hollowness inside. Cullen had taken too much with him when he died. Only now did she realize how much of her laughter had been tied up in his.

D'Amato took a notebook from his pocket and flipped it open. "I understand you found the body?"

"Yes."

"What time was this?"

She made a vague gesture with her hand. "Dawn, a few minutes after. I don't know the exact time."

"Dawn was approximately 6:30 today," he said, making a notation. "You told the officer your brother was dead when you got there."

"He was cold." So was she. She rubbed her arms, then dropped her hands when she caught D'Amato watching her. "And his . . . his eyes were filmy."

"I know this is hard for you. Your brother—"

"My twin brother." Something stirred in the wasteland of her being. Outrage, perhaps. It made words bubble up, rash and irresistible, words she would never have spoken to a stranger. "Are you a twin, detective?"

"No. I—"

"Something in me died with him. I can't even cry, it hurts so much."

He studied her for a moment, then nodded. "I'm sorry. But I can't let that interfere with my job, and right now I've got to ask you these questions."

"I know." She let her breath out slowly, reining herself in. "My brother is . . . was younger than me by seven minutes. He has a degree in marketing, and works . . . worked at Lazarus Advertising for the past four years. Before that he was with the Brenner Group. He and Penny were married for ten years, no children—"

"I've got her name down here as Phaedra."

"Yeah, well, that's new."

His brows went up.

"It means 'bright,' " Connie volunteered.

D'Amato's eyes didn't change. "What do you do for a living, Ms. Matthias?"

"I'm an accountant, formerly of the firm of Cabrol, Smith, and Pollard in Los Angeles."

"And now?"

"I just moved back. I'll probably hook up with a firm here once I get my license endorsed here in Virginia."

"Children?"

"One." She controlled the urge to explain too much. "Jeffrey Dean Matthias. Fourteen, lives with his father at 451 Savin Court."

"When did you arrive?"

"Yesterday." She tried to smile, felt it twist. "Some homecoming, huh?"

"Yeah. Did you see anything unusual on the beach this morning?"

"Isn't a dead brother unusual enough?" There was a ragged edge to her voice that bothered her.

It bothered D'Amato, too; a small, vertical line appeared between his heavy brows. "Look, Ms. Matthias, I know this is hard for you. But the crime scene has been badly compromised, and I'd like to pick your brain while your memory is fresh. You're the only one who saw things as they were."

She took a deep breath, controlling the ebb and flow of her emotions. "I'll try. He was lying with his head pointing north, feet south. His arms were outspread."

"Palms up or down?"

"Up. There were no footprints in the sand around him."

"None?"

She shook her head. "It was pretty windy. I sat beside Cullen for a while, and when I got up again, my own footprints were gone."

"How long did you sit there?"

"I . . . don't know."

He checked his notes again. "It says here that the call to 911 was made at 7:14. Now, if you found him at or near dawn, then you must have sat there for close to three-quarters of an hour. Does that sound right to you?"

"Nothing sounds right." Then she sighed. "Something just . . . clicked off in me, I guess. I don't remember much except looking at Cullen and feeling the wind blowing in my face. And then, well, there didn't seem to be much of a need to rush."

He wasn't going anywhere.

The thought was reflected in D'Amato's eyes. She had the impression that he might have smiled if it hadn't been her brother who'd died.

"What made you get up and go in the house?"

"I don't know. I just did."

"Is that when you told your sister-in-law?"

"No. I called the police, then went upstairs to wake her up." *And hide the candles.*

"Do you know anything about your brother's activities after the, ah," he consulted his notes, "fire-walking?"

"No. He said he planned to watch the sun come up and invited me to join him. I said it was too early for me."

"But you went anyway."

"I woke up at dawn. I don't know why, but I couldn't get back to sleep, so I decided to go anyway. You're not . . . you don't think I woke up because he was dying, do you?"

"That would be Mr. Bruycker's department, wouldn't it?" D'Amato's gaze remained steady, unreadable. "In my opinion, he died several hours before dawn."

The flesh of her palm seemed to retain the memory of the coolness of Cullen's skin. She rubbed her hand along her jeans, but the eerie feeling remained.

"Tell me what happened during the evening," he said.

"Just the facts?"

"Just everything."

She gave him her memories of the evening, her impressions of Cullen's group, her own resistance to the firewalking. A memorable night, followed by a dawn she wished she could forget.

"You've got a good eye for detail," D'Amato said when she finished. "What was your brother wearing?"

"Wearing?" She noticed that her hands were moving more than they should, so she clasped them in her lap and stared at them to make them stay. "Let's see. Shorts and a knit shirt, sandals that he took off to firewalk. Ah, the shorts were khaki-colored, and the shirt was blue, one of those pocket . . ." Startled by her own recollection of Cullen's cold bare chest, she looked up at D'Amato. "Where is the shirt?"

"We didn't find it."

"Why would someone take it?"

"I wish I knew," he said. "Why did you leave the gathering early last night?"

"Well, to be honest, I was uncomfortable with all the psychic stuff. I'm an accountant. I deal in reality."

His brows went up. "Facts and figures?"

"Sure. Don't you?"

"Homicide is all too real," he said. "Ms. Matthias, do you have any idea why someone would kill your brother?"

She shook her head. "Cullen is . . . was a good person. He cared, and he got along with people. I don't know anyone he's ever hurt, anyone who might hold a grudge against him."

"There are other motives besides revenge."

Connie spread her hands, thinking about black candles and pentagrams. *Jeff, oh, Jeff!* "I can't help you there."

D'Amato sat back and studied her. His eyes were

much too bland. Frantically, she cast back over what she'd said, searching for anything that might not ring true.

"Is there anything else you can think of, Ms. Matthias?"

She sat there for a moment, feeling as though her omissions were painted across her forehead. "Not at the moment."

D'Amato closed his notebook slowly, riffling the pages with his thumb. She knew the gesture, had used it herself in times when things hadn't quite added up but she couldn't decide where.

A hunch—common to spiritual folks, accountants, and of course, policemen.

"Well," he said, "I've got everything I need right now. I'll be back tomorrow to talk to your sister-in-law."

"My brother . . . when can we have him?"

He slid the notebook into his pocket. "After the autopsy, we'll give you a call."

Autopsy. Reality. Cold, hard facts. They weren't right for Cullen, who'd been so vibrantly alive, and whose sense of wonder had been as deep and honest as faith.

Connie watched D'Amato as he walked away. His tread was firm and solid, the set of his shoulders resolute. He'd come away with a doubt, a small, nagging pea under the mattress; being the man he was, he'd keep worrying at it until he found it.

Not Jeff.

Turning, she walked back to the sofa where John Bruycker sat. A game of solitaire was spread out across the coffee table in front of him, but his gaze was focused on her, not the cards. She had the same unnerving feeling that he saw a lot more than she would have shown him.

"How did it go?" he asked.

"He asked a lot of questions I had no answer for," she said.

"Tell me about it. His partner had me cornered for more than a half-hour. Names, dates, places, doctors, lawyers, Indian chiefs. You name it, they wanted it."

"It's their job. And I want Cullen's killer found."

Not Jeff. Not Jeff.

"Cullen was a good man. No, more than that. He had vision. And he brought us together to share that vision. When he died, we were cheated of something very important."

Connie hugged herself. Yes, Cullen had taken something important when he died, but it wasn't any esoteric belief. It was the man himself, with his joy and laughter, that she ached for.

Bruycker's eyes changed. Turned softer and deeper with a sympathy she almost couldn't bear to see. Abruptly, he stood up and came around the table to take her hands in his. "Why don't you let it out, Connie? It won't hurt so much then."

"Yes, it will," she said.

"I'm sorry, Connie."

"Yeah, well . . . thanks for helping me with Penny . . . Phaedra."

She started to turn away, but he didn't release her hands. Her gaze shot up to his. "To be honest with you, I'm more concerned about you than Phaedra. She let her grief out. And she has us. But you won't allow yourself any of that, Connie."

"So?"

"So I worry." His hands slid up her wrists. "He

was your twin, a closer bond, may I say, even than marriage. Yet you were the one who kept your head during Phaedra's crisis, you were the one who called the police and your mother and Cullen's boss."

"It needed to be done."

"No one's strong enough to take something like this without leaning a little. You might try it."

It was the sort of thing Cullen might have said. It would have brought tears to her eyes had she possessed the capacity to cry. Still Bruycker held her gaze. He wanted too much for her, and from her. He wanted to comfort her, not realizing that walking and talking had ceased to be automatic for her; she functioned only by concentrating. If she let go of herself for a moment, she was sure she'd explode in a million pieces.

She finally looked away, her glance moving here, there, anywhere but on those intense blue eyes. It finally alighted on the coffee table, and she realized the cards were not those of a regular deck. And the game certainly wasn't solitaire.

"What's that?" she asked.

"The Tarot, of course."

"Of course."

He smiled, bending to scoop the cards into his hands. Still smiling, he shuffled them. She couldn't help watching his hands. Long-fingered, graceful, they moved with a practiced economy.

"Don't worry," he said. "I'm not going to ask you to sit for a reading. I'm only learning, anyway; Hamilton is our expert. You ought to let him do you sometime. It never hurts to know the future."

She turned away. "My future is all too clear."

* * *

Connie parked in front of her ex-husband's house. It wasn't what she'd expected from the mercurial man, Derek Valle, she'd married: a neat brick ranch, complete with hedges and flowerbeds and, most bizarre of all, a wooden duck and five ducklings caught in mid-waddle across the lawn.

"Too weird," she muttered.

She heard the music the moment she stepped out of her car. Even with all the windows closed, the raw violence of the heavy metal seemed to make the air vibrate.

The front door was unlocked—a good thing, because Jeff wasn't about to hear the doorbell through that din. Connie walked straight in. She followed the music down the hall, her temper getting hotter the closer she got.

A poster of Cindy Crawford adorned the outside of Jeff's door. The subliminal vibration of the bass made Cindy seem as though she were about to step down from the picture. Connie put her hand on the doorknob. The brass seemed almost warm, and the thump of the music perceivable in the metal itself.

Connie swung the door open, meeting a blast of sound so dense it made her chest tighten. Jeff, who'd been lying on his bed, scrambled to his feet. His hair hadn't been combed, and he wore only a pair of ragged jeans that looked as though a dog had chewed them. His ribs were clearly visible beneath the skin. Bruises marred his shoulders, arms, and chest.

She crossed hei arms over her chest and waited while he turned the stereo off. Mother and son stared at each other. The sudden silence was almost as deafening as the music had been.

"You're supposed to be in school."

He made a furtive gesture. "I wasn't feeling too good this morning. Dad called the school—"

"I've already talked to him," she said. "He said he waited to go to work until you got on the bus. What did you do, Jeff? Get off at the next stop?"

"Look—"

"Your dad will be home in a little while to deal with you."

"Mom—"

"Sit down. I've got something more important to talk to you about than playing hooky from school."

That clearly astonished him. He sat.

"Where'd you get those bruises?" she asked.

"Is that what you wanted to talk about?"

"No. Where'd you get them?"

He shrugged. "Moshing."

"What's that?"

His lips curved in a smile that was old-man cynical, too hard in his young face. "You know, you go to some straight-edge concert and everybody just gets into it."

"Gets into what?"

"Banging into each other. You just shove and move and the music seems to beat inside your head and chest and it's like hitting outer space."

A lot of things hovered at the back of Connie's throat, the first of which was laughter. But she had the feeling that once she started, she'd never be able to stop, so she held tight to them all.

Her son looked back at her with that blank, infuriating gaze she'd seen so often in the past few years. The Teflon kid, she used to call him. Nothing stuck, nothing stayed, nothing marred that impenetrable finish. It made her feel brutal. Partly because she hurt so much, partly because she wanted to reach him so badly.

"Cullen was killed early this morning," she said.

And was rewarded and shamed by his sudden, shocked intake of breath. "Killed?"

"Somebody stabbed him. I found him on the beach."

His eyes cleared, and she caught a glimpse of something raw and powerful. With a shock that stunned her to her toes, she realized it wasn't grief, but fear. Fear. It stared out of her son's eyes, a stark, black, soul-searing terror that made her own soul twist with horror.

Then it seemed as though a door closed, leaving him as slick and untouched as he'd been before.

"What have you done?" she whispered. "Oh, what have you done?"

His face went from white to red to white again. "What did you say?"

"There was a pentagram cut into the sand around him," she said. "And five black candles at the points."

"So?"

Rage bloomed in her, ran in hot little spurts through her veins. "Whatever you know, you'd better tell me."

"What makes you think I know anything?"

"Gee, how many people do I know who play around with black candles and pentagrams?"

He snatched a tee shirt up from the floor, turning away to pull it over his head with a belated modesty that only infuriated her more. Taking him by the shoulders, she spun him around to face her. A small corner of her mind registered just how far she had to reach up to do it.

"Don't touch me!" he shouted. "I'm surprised you didn't just send the cops over here."

"I messed with the crime scene so the police *wouldn't* come looking for you. And that, smartass, goes against everything I believe. Why do you think I did it? Because you're my son! And because I wanted to give you a chance to tell me the truth for a change!"

"Oh, too cool."

Connie knew she was walking the edge, running on the hot fuel of emotions she didn't know she'd possessed. Some was anger; but some, too, was terror as deep and dark as that lurking behind Jeff's facade. Fear for her son, who only seemed to know how to hurt himself, and fear *of* him, because she no longer knew him.

"No more games, Jeff. If you know something, you'd better tell me now."

"I don't know shit." His face twisted, a gut-wrenching parody of the sweet-natured little boy he'd been just a few years ago. "You didn't come here to help me. You just wanted to accuse me yourself." His voice went up in a mocking imitation of female tones. It cracked on the high notes, but there was nothing funny about it. "See what you've done, you bad boy? You messed up once, and now see what's happened? And now dear Mother has to set her standards aside to protect you. Well, you can stick that sanctimonious shit!"

"Sanctimonious!" She lost it—really, truly lost it. "I found my brother dead this morning, and I'm supposed to be concerned about your *feelings?*"

"Well, why don't you turn me in then? Yoo-hoo, Officer, I've got a suspect for you."

"Maybe it would teach you a lesson!"

"Maybe it would teach me fucking nothing except never to talk to you again!"

Connie could feel him quivering beneath her hands. And she knew in that moment that her son wanted to hit her. "Go ahead," she said. "What's left?"

He tore out of her grasp, then shoved past her and ran down the hall. A moment later the front door slammed with a force that echoed through the house.

Connie stood still, feeling as though her heart had been plucked out of her chest. Then she sank to her knees. Sobs seemed to well up from a place deep inside her, and every one hurt. She didn't cry easily. Never had.

Cool, logical Connie Matthias, the one who dwelled so determinedly in the real world, wanted in this moment only to check out. Reality hurt too damn much.

"Help me," she sobbed. "Help me."

But there was no escape for her, no answers and no respite. So she sat on the grungy floor of Jeff's room, crying for her brother, for her son, and for herself.

Chapter Four

Connie sat at a table at the Ocean Tavern's big window, regretting that she'd agreed to come to lunch with her mother and Penny. It had been a quiet, awkward meal; even shared loss hadn't been enough to bring them together.

"I just can't make myself believe he's gone," Penny said, abruptly opening a subject they'd been avoiding until now. "Every time I open a door I expect to see him standing there."

Sandra slashed her crabcakes into jagged little pieces. "I can't stand the thought of what the police are doing to him. It's a disgrace, the lack of dignity in the whole process. I want my son to be properly buried, not lying on some cold . . ." She broke off abruptly, that image apparently too vivid even for her.

"Cullen wanted to be cremated," Penny's face had turned the color of her ivory suit.

"Cremated." The word was as flat as Sandra's voice.

"And then he wanted his ashes scattered over the ocean he loved so well."

"There's a place for him in the family plot," Sandra said. "Five generations of Matthiases are buried there."

"Do we have to argue about it now?" Penny asked. "Please, Sandra. I can't do this right now."

The older woman hesitated, eyes glittering, then nodded.

"I've found an apartment," Connie said, hoping to change the direction of the conversation. "I can move in next week."

"Why not a house?" Sandra asked.

"What do I need with a house?"

"Jeffrey—"

"Jeff lives with his dad." Connie didn't want to think about the possibility that Jeff wouldn't come live with her if his life depended on it. And after the other morning . . .

"How did he take the news of Cullen's death?" Penny asked, sparing her the rest of the thought.

Connie shrugged. "Jeff's reactions aren't always comfortable to the rest of us."

"He didn't care?" Sandra demanded.

"I wouldn't say that, Mom." Absently, Connie lined the silverware up neatly alongside her plate. "It's just that if you're looking for comfort, Jeff's the wrong place to find it. But I know he cared for his uncle—"

"He loved Cullen," Penny said. "Jeff didn't relate to his father or—forgive me, Connie—his mother, but he and Cullen used to talk for hours."

It hurt more than Connie would have expected. She hated the jealousy that stabbed with cold-edged intensity into her guts. Logic told her she should be glad that Jeff had found one adult in whom to confide, but in her heart, where it seemed to really count, *she* wanted to be the one.

I've lost them both.

"Connie, are you all right?" Penny asked. "You've got the strangest look on your face."

Abruptly, Connie pushed her half-full plate away and motioned to the waiter. "This was a mistake. I'm sorry; I shouldn't have come here today."

"We're all grieving," Sandra said.

Connie swung around to the older woman. How typically Sandra, she thought: *Face the music, kiddo; life is tough, and you've got to be tough to get through it.* The very truth of it infuriated her. A lot of things hovered at the tip of her tongue, things that had been simmering for years. But she swallowed them as she'd always done, knowing the price she'd pay wouldn't be worth a few moments' satisfaction.

"Let's all go for a stroll on the boardwalk," Penny said. "It will do us good to get a little fresh air."

Sandra raised her hand in an imperious gesture. The approaching waiter veered toward her immediately. "I'll take the check, young man," she said.

"Sorry," Connie said, smoothly plucking it from his hand. "My treat."

It was a small victory, but sweet nonetheless, and it almost made up for the things she'd chosen not to say.

Outside, they found the boardwalk all but deserted. It was a fitful kind of day; sunny one moment, windy and clouded the next. Surfers dotted the choppy waves, their boards bright dots of color on the slate-blue water. A sailboat lay at anchor out beyond the surf, its sails furled and quiescent. Off to the right, the irregular rocky outline of a jetty spurred far out into the sea, aiming its dark, pointing finger straight toward the midday sun.

They walked quietly for a few minutes, letting the wind scour the effects of the previous conversation away. Connie watched the surfers bobbing on the waves, wishing the silence could continue. It couldn't, of course; her mother had never been comfortable with quiet.

"It's getting so I wait until the tourists are all gone before I come down here," Sandra said a moment later. "Did you know, Connie, that the police have installed video cameras on some of the light poles?"

"Isn't that illegal?" she asked in surprise.

Sandra shrugged. "It's a public street. Anybody can watch anybody—even the police."

"If it helps stop drugs getting to the kids, I'm all for it," Connie said.

"Cullen hated the idea," Penny said. "He said it sounded like Big Brother had come to watch over us."

Abruptly, Sandra turned to look out over the ocean. Connie had never seen her shoulders sag at such an angle, or seen so many shadows in her eyes.

"Mom," she murmured.

"He was my son," Sandra said. A vast sort of outrage creased her face, or perhaps a mother's disbelief that she'd ever have to see her child's death.

Connie laid her hands on the older woman's shoulders, achingly aware of the fragility of the bones beneath her palms. "We all loved him, Mom."

Feeling resistance beneath her hands, Connie let them fall. Her mother had never been comfortable with physical affection, and less so with her daughter than with Cullen. Connie didn't know if it had always been that way; her father had died so long ago that she couldn't remember how her parents had been together. But now, when a little affection might have warmed that cold, empty place inside her, she wished it had been different.

Penny reached up and took off her hat. Her hair shone mahogany in the sun, a bright touch of color against the unremitting ivory of her clothing. Black would have seemed less funereal. "It would be better if you could cry, Sandra."

"Good God, Penny! Is that what you call grief?" the old woman countered. "Weep buckets and then spend twenty-four hours under sedation?"

"It's 'Phaedra' now, Sandra."

"Right." Sandra's tone turned crisp and dry. "You know, Penny, if Cullen hadn't been into that New Age crap, he'd have been sleeping in his bed like a normal person instead of communing with nature on the beach."

"Are you blaming me?" Penny asked.

"I'm blaming that ridiculous . . . stuff. He was so bound up in it that he forgot caution."

"His beliefs had nothing to do with it," Penny said. "It was a cosmic accident . . . just being in the wrong place at the wrong time."

"Cosmic?" Sandra's lips thinned.

Penny stared down at the older woman. She looked chic and cool and utterly composed, until Connie noticed tears glistening on her cheeks.

"Please don't—" she began.

"He was my husband." Penny sobbed, her words and tone and pain so similar to Sandra's that it was uncanny.

And he was my brother. Connie stopped and put

her arms around her sister-in-law. Penny leaned against her, that lovely swan neck drooping so that her head rested on Connie's shoulder. It was a theatrical gesture. Had the tears not been so real, Connie might have felt like a stage prop.

She glanced at her mother, stiffening when she saw true rage in the older woman's eyes. The emotion was so raw that she looked away from it, preferring the comforting imperturbability of sand and water and sky. It occurred to her that Sandra had never had Cullen alone, really. First his twin and then his wife had taken the premier place in his life, leaving Sandra eternally on the outside.

Connie started to reach out, to gather her mother in whether she wanted it or not. Then a slash of yellow in the spray off the jetty caught her eye. Her attention sharpened. The color disappeared, reappeared, then disappeared again. Then, for a single, fragmented moment, Connie saw a man's hand rise out of the spray to grapple one of the rocks with a desperation she could see even at this distance. Then it fell away, sliding beneath the surface.

"Someone's in trouble at the jetty," she said, pulling away from Penny's clinging arms. "Mom, call for help. I'm going to see if there's anything I can do."

Still weeping, Penny turned toward Sandra. The old woman fended her off. "Be careful, Connie," she said. Turning away with a briskness that belied her years, she headed for the street above.

Connie ran down the boardwalk, then jumped down to the sand and stepped out onto the jetty. Her feet seemed to know which rocks were best; she and Cullen had played here—against the rules, of course—all the years of their childhood. Perhaps more quickly than was prudent, she made her way toward the sea end of the jetty.

Her shoes slipped and slithered on the wet rock, and the footing got worse the farther she went. The waves seemed to chew at the jetty with renewed violence, as though angry that she'd invaded their territory. She dropped to her knees above the spot where she'd seen the man. The water foamed and gibbered, defying her attempts to see into its depths.

"Damn," she muttered.

She glanced up to see if help was coming. A clot of people had formed on the boardwalk, but they weren't doing anything but pointing. Farther away down the beach, she saw one of the police ATVs churning through the sand toward her. But he'd be too late. Maybe it was already too late.

A faraway shout caught her attention. Looking up, she saw one of the surfers gesticulate urgently, then point to something farther along the jetty. She stepped from one rock to another, working her way toward the spot he'd indicated.

Something yellow rolled to the surface there beside the jetty. Even as she watched, the waves pulled it under again. Fear and exertion made her breath rasp and her pulse do a triphammer dance behind her eyes as she made her way down to the water line. There, algae made the rocks as slippery as though they were covered with ice.

Her feet skidded, and she lost some skin braking herself with her hands. She came to a stop on a rounded boulder, where the waves soaked her jeans and sucked avidly at her feet. Crouching, she plunged her arms into the water.

Nothing. She tried again, leaning so far over that her blouse belled out into the water. Her hand grazed something. With a galvanic effort, she plunged her arm deeper and got a better feel. She didn't know if it was hair or fabric, but clenched her fingers in it and yanked upward. It weighed a ton. She felt the strain in her bowed back, the quivering, overtaxed muscles of her arms and shoulders.

It had to be him. It had to.

"Come on," she gritted. "Come on."

The waves fought her. Retreating, they tugged heavily at her burden; advancing, they pushed her back against the rocks. Setting her feet more securely, she started to work with the water, pulling as they advanced, maintaining when they retreated.

Slowly and surely, it came up . . . *he* came up. She'd wound her hands in the back of his shirt; his arms and legs splayed limply, his hair floating like seaweed in the water.

Strangely, she never once doubted that she'd get him out. Behind the haze of exertion, her mind clicked away steadily, tallying the time that had elapsed since she'd seen his hand, estimating his chances for survival, planning what she'd do once she got him out of the water.

And then something jerked him down, sharply and powerfully, and pulled her right off the rock.

She plunged into the water in a welter of bubbles. Unable to see a thing in the murky blackness, she had no choice but to wait until her downward movement slowed and her natural buoyancy took over. Then she started to kick toward the surface. Once, she touched something that felt like an arm. But her own movement pushed it away from her, and she lost it in the dark oblivion of the water.

She had no idea how far down she'd gone, how far she had to swim to reach the surface. Nothing seemed to be happening fast, except that her air was running out. Every kick depleted it more. Her lungs compressed, started to burn.

Panic and you're dead.

The thought kept her from flailing blindly and exhausting the slim reserves she still had. She had no idea where she was any more; for all she could tell, she was swimming straight for the bottom. Then she noticed a vague lightening of the water above her. She strove toward the source, pushing until the burning of her lungs spread through the rest of her body.

Something smashed into her back with stunning force. Her breath went out in a long hard grunt, pale dancing bubbles carrying her life away. She reached for them as though to bring them back.

No! Oh, God, no!

She tried to follow those fast-disappearing bubbles. Her kicking feet hit something hard behind her, sending her spinning out of control through the murk.

And then she ran out of time. Her air was gone, her strength with it. The water seemed heavier now, wrapping around her like thick, dark velvet.

Cool. Silent.

Water rushed into her mouth and nose. It didn't hurt. Didn't even frighten her.

I thought it would be harder.

She drifted away.

Chapter Five

Connie became aware of the gritty feel of sand beneath her cheek. With awareness came discomfort . . . lots of it. Her chest felt as though someone were sitting on it, and her throat burned salt-raw.

"She's coming around," someone said.

Her brain seemed to be swimming around her skull in unconnected pieces. She pulled them in, striving for some sort of order.

"How . . . ?" she croaked.

"Some surfer pulled you out."

The voice was male, and it sounded stressed and breathless. It took an absurd amount of effort for Connie to lift her head high enough to see him. She registered a police officer, young, wholesome-looking, and dripping water onto the sand as he crouched beside her. Then her neck muscles gave out, and she let her head fall back down.

"What about that guy?" she asked.

"We're looking for him," he said.

No hope lightened his voice. It had been too long. Tears traced a warm path down her face. She licked her lips, got more sand than salt.

"I had him," she said. "For a second, I had him."

The cop moved into her field of view. "Was he alive then?"

"I . . . don't know. Close enough, maybe."

"Can you give me a description?"

"Yellow shirt, dark hair . . . I never saw his face."

"What about build?"

"Uh-uh." Her eyes drifted closed, somehow feeling as heavy as her chest.

"Did you see him fall in?"

She shook her head. "That's it. Sorry."

"Young man, can't you see that she's in no condition to be questioned?"

That voice she knew. Mom. Connie managed to roll over onto her back to see Sandra standing, arms akimbo, glaring at the officer. Phaedra stood a half-yard behind Sandra. Her clothes made her seem part of the beach, separate only because of that burnished hair.

"I'm all right, Mom," Connie said.

"Of course you aren't. An ambulance is on the way."

That got Connie's head up again. "I don't need an ambulance. I just swallowed a little salt water, that's all."

"Don't be an idiot."

"There's nothing worse than being too weak to fight you," Connie retorted. "Damn . . . if I could just sit up, I'd get my breath back. Officer, would you mind giving me a hand?"

He slid his arm around her shoulders to support her as she levered herself higher. Her lungs eased somewhat, but that only made her aware of a number of other pains. She flexed her arm, assessing the damage, and almost yelped.

"You cut your elbow on the rocks," the cop said.

"I've got a temporary bandage on it, but you're going to need stitches. Couple of other places, too."

"And then you're coming home with me," Sandra said. "You're going to rest, take your medicine, and do what you're told."

Always cool and calm and take-charge, Connie thought. Most mothers would have been hysterical, but not Sandra. Not even losing one child and almost losing the other shook that determined composure.

But it seemed to comfort Penny, who stayed close to the older woman. It should have comforted Connie. But she'd seen too much of it in her mother and in herself, and right now it made her feel as though she'd slipped beneath the water again.

"Are you all right, ma'am?" the cop asked.

Connie drew a breath that sounded suspiciously like a sob. She held it, not daring to take another until she got herself under control. "Yeah," she said at last. "I'm okay."

Then she turned to watch the men who swarmed the jetty in search of the missing man. They worked steadily, but without the urgency of men who thought they had a chance of saving a life. An EMS boat bobbed at anchor near the jetty. From time to time the dark, seal-sleek heads of two divers broke the surface nearby.

"Maybe you shouldn't watch this," the cop said.

"I have to."

He didn't argue. Maybe he understood how she felt. Maybe he was just being nice. Either way, she was grateful that he didn't argue.

"They can't see anything down there," she said.

She could feel his arm move as he shrugged. "They'll feel their way. Those guys are good."

"Do they get a lot of . . . practice?" Penny asked. Her voice sounded blurred. Connie glanced over her shoulder, frowning when she saw how pale her sister-in-law's face had become. She understood. This death—a stranger's death—should have been remote. But it wasn't, not to her, not to Penny. This one burned along the nerves, stark reminder of Cullen's.

Abruptly, Penny turned and walked away, wobbling a little as her high heels sank into the sand.

"You'd better go with her, Mom," Connie said. "She doesn't look too good."

Sandra hesitated. Her gaze went from Connie to Penny and back again. For a moment, Connie thought she was going to refuse. Then she hurried after her daughter-in-law.

Connie turned back toward the jetty just in time to see one of the divers break the surface, gesticulating that he'd found something. The men on the rocks moved closer as both divers went down together.

She watched. She waited. Clouds sent shadows scudding across the beach, swift as birds of prey. One darted across her legs, bringing coolness to her wet skin. She flinched away from it. The breeze plucked at the sand, rasping the grains against each other with a sound that seemed to sink straight into her bones. Just like yesterday.

Cullen, oh, Cullen.

She didn't think she'd ever love the beach again. If the officer hadn't been holding her, she might have jumped up and run screaming for the street. Her heartbeat drowned out the sound of the waves, enclosing her in a cocoon of pulse and grief and visceral loss.

The divers came up again, holding the drowned man between them. His shirt floated around him, a bright splash of yellow on the dark water. The men in the boat leaned over, grasping him beneath the elbow, and hauled him over the side. He would have looked alive except for the total laxness of his body.

"I had him," she said again. "I was pulling him up, and then it seemed as though something grabbed him from beneath and jerked him down."

"Funny things happen to the water around a jetty," her companion said.

"I had him. He shouldn't be dead."

"Lady, not one person in ten would have gone out there the way you did. But sometimes no matter what you do, there just isn't a happy ending. You tried, and that's got to be enough."

Yeah. Sure. But Cullen had left a gaping hole in her world, and it wasn't enough. Maybe it never would be again.

Stitched, bandaged, medicated, and finally, mercifully, rid of sand, Connie lay on her mother's sofa and waited for the painkillers to start working.

She rolled over onto her side and looked around Sandra's determinedly Colonial family room. Except for new slipcovers on the sofa and loveseat, it hadn't changed in fourteen years. The family portraits—Dad in his army uniform, Connie's and Cullen's first-grade, sixth-grade, graduation, and wedding pictures—all hung in the same places. The pictures of Jeff as a baby, a dimpled toddler, a scowling preteen, however, were more of a reminder than Connie wanted to deal with right now, so she picked up the remote and flicked through the afternoon's television offerings. Soap opera. Talk show. Soap opera. *Sesame Street.*

"Nada," she muttered, turning the TV off.

The phone rang. Sandra's voice speared out from the back of the house. "Get that, will you?"

Connie didn't want to talk to anyone. She lay there counting the rings, hoping the caller would give up before she had to move. Nine rings. Ten. Whoever it was, he or she was determined. She reached, groaning, and plucked the receiver from the cradle. "Hello?"

"Connie?"

She knew that voice. Rough but never shaggy, medium-deep, with hints of interesting things underlying the straight, almost formal tone. Funny, she'd forgotten to remember what he looked like, how he walked, but she'd never managed to forget his voice. "Hello, Derek."

"What did you say to Jeff yesterday?"

"I told him about Cullen," she said, adding because she simply couldn't resist, "As I told you I was going to do."

"How did he take it?"

Something cold tapped her on the shoulder. "Why don't you know?"

"Because I haven't seen him."

"Not since yesterday?" She drew her breath in sharply. "Why didn't you *tell* me?"

"Because it's nothing new," he retorted. "Weren't you the one who told me he'd been climbing out his window to party with his friends for a couple of years now? What makes you think he's been doing anything different here?"

"But—"

"So why is there a problem, Connie?"

She should have lied. But she'd never been a good liar, and Derek had never been slow on the uptake; while she was debating what to say, he jumped to the correct conclusion. Damn him.

"You had a fight," he said.

"We had a fight. Yes."

"Christ." He let his breath out with an explosive hiss. "How could Cullen's death have been something to fight over?"

Tell him. It's only right. But Derek had always been impulsive and a bit hot-tempered, and she wasn't sure how he'd react. She needed time to think this through, time to decide what to do and how to do it without complicating the issue.

"It isn't your concern," she said.

"Of course it's my concern, damn it!" His struggle to keep his temper was obvious, even over the phone. "Look, Connie. I've been running myself crazy trying to keep some kind of sanity in that kid's life. If something threatens that, don't you think I have a right to know?"

"Yes," she said. Truth. "But this has nothing to do with you. Jeff and I had a disagreement, that's all." A half-truth. A not-quite-lie. She didn't think it would work.

"Then why are you worried?"

"I'm worried whenever Jeff is out of my sight."

"Don't bullshit me, Connie."

He wanted a fight. At another time, she would have been glad to accommodate him. But the painkillers were beginning to kick in, and she just didn't have the juice for it. "I've had a hell of a day, and I don't want to fight with you right now."

"Tough."

She sighed. "Derek—"

"You're a lousy liar, always have been. Something's wrong. I'm not going to let up until I find out what it is."

"Somehow, talking to you always reminds me why I divorced you."

That one hit; the pause at the other end told her that. "I thought you didn't have the energy to fight," he said after a moment.

"I'm not fighting. Just stating facts."

"Good old practical Connie."

She sighed. "Do you have any idea where Jeff hangs out?"

"Hangs," Derek said.

"Huh?"

"People don't hang out anymore. They 'hang.' Don't you listen to the kids' slang?"

"Not if I can help it. Do you have any idea where he might be?"

He laughed, but it had a bitter ring to it. "What are you going to do, Connie? Grab him by the ear and haul him home? That'll really get the communication going."

"I have to go now," she said, slowly and distinctly. "I have to find my son."

"You're not going anywhere," Sandra said.

Connie opened her eyes, surprised because she hadn't realized she'd closed them. Sandra wore a navy silk dress with gold buttons and looked as coolly elegant as though she'd stepped right off the pages of *Cosmopolitan.* While Connie was still staring, the older woman plucked the phone out of her hands.

"That's Derek, I suppose," she said.

Connie nodded. Sandra pulled off her right earring and put the receiver to her ear. "Derek, Connie nearly drowned today. Yes, drowned. She's in no condition to argue with you. And she's certainly not in any condition to run the streets looking for Jeffrey."

"Stop interfering, Mom," Connie snapped. "I don't intend to just sit here while Jeff's God knows where, doing God knows what."

"I understand perfectly," Sandra said. "Go ahead, get up."

Connie started to rise. But a powerful wave of drowsiness crashed over her, weighing her body and fuzzing her mind, and she sank back to the sofa. "I have to go," she said. Even that sounded fuzzy.

Sandra looked very pleased with herself as she returned to her conversation with Derek. "Why didn't she tell you she'd been hurt? From what I heard, Derek, you didn't give her much chance. Remember that old saying about attracting more bees with honey than with vinegar? Yes, I know I'm interfering. I'm her mother, and I get to."

"Give me the phone," Connie hissed, stung to effectiveness by outrage.

Sandra ignored her. "No, she wasn't badly hurt, just seventeen stitches and a mild case of shock. Yes, seventeen. Of course I'll tell her." She hung up.

"Mom!"

"He said to tell you he was sorry you're hurt and that he'll go out and look for Jeffrey himself. And that he'll call you tomorrow when you're feeling well enough to continue the argument."

"I could have handled him now." Connie yawned, blunting the effectiveness of the statement.

"I'm sure you could." Sandra snapped her earring back on. "Jeffrey's taken off again, I assume?"

"We had a fight."

"He fights with everyone."

Not like this. "I've got to learn not to let him get to me. But he starts with that attitude and I just get so damn mad . . ." She yawned again.

"Well, Derek's going to be out looking for him, so you don't have to worry. That boy's streetwise. He's safer out there than *you'd* be."

Connie shook her head, not to refute that statement, but to struggle against the encroaching drowsiness. "He's my son," she said.

"I know about sons." Sandra's voice turned brittle. "I've got a committee meeting and then a dinner. I won't be back until late."

Connie, abruptly realizing she'd been staring at the insides of her eyelids again, forced her eyes open. "Always full of sympathy, aren't you?"

"I give what I have."

"You don't have much, then."

She shouldn't have said that; even as the words were being spoken she regretted them. But she'd passed into a state of reduced control, where the mouth let things out the mind would rather have kept hidden.

"Well," Sandra said, slipping on a pale gray coat that nearly matched her hair, "I'd better get going. I put your medication on the end table behind you."

She turned away. The door closed quietly behind her, leaving Connie alone in a room that seemed smaller and lonelier than she'd have liked. *I've never been so mean to another human being.*

She felt astonished with herself for saying what

she had, guilty because she should have known better.

But she wasn't sorry. And the velvet cloak of oblivion wrapped her more tightly with every heartbeat, blunting even the guilt.

Chapter Six

The doorbell woke Connie. She was disoriented for a moment; night had fallen, leaving the room dark except for the meager illumination from the back porch light. Groaning, she rolled over and burrowed her face into the pillow.

Nine-fifteen. She'd been asleep nearly six hours, then. The painkillers had worn off, and she felt as though she'd been run over by a train.

Insistently, the bell chimed again.

"Go away," she muttered.

It rang one more time, then fell silent. With a sigh, she reached for the painkillers. The pill bottle slithered away from her, rolled across the table, and fell to the floor on the opposite side.

"Damn it." Every muscle protested as she stood up.

She shuffled around the table and bent to pick up the bottle. Pain lanced through her elbow, making her swear and fumble. The bottle disappeared beneath the sofa. It took her a ridiculous amount of time and effort to get down on her hands and knees. The bottle lay just beyond reach, its smooth plastic sides reflecting the light.

"This is definitely my lucky day," she muttered. "Now, where the hell might Mom keep a yardstick?"

Footsteps crackled in the pine mulch of the flowerbed outside. *Crunch, crunch, pause* . . . as though the walker stopped from time to time to see if anyone were watching. Her gaze shifted to the back door. No security there; Mom had replaced the big sliding glass door with French doors. Glass everywhere.

It's only Mom. Mom would have come in the front door. And even if she had, for some unknown reason, come to the back, she would have known to use the slate stepping-stone path. So would Jeff. Connie remembered her mother telling her about some recent burglaries in the neighborhood.

Adrenaline pumped through her, erasing the pain of cuts and bruises. *Crunch, crunch, pause.* Listen. Her pulse throbbed in a staccato rhythm that got faster and wilder with every footstep.

She crouched in the lee of the sofa, tracking the intruder's path. A man's firm tread, no hesitation now. He must be right outside the side window. She peered around the side of the sofa, saw a silhouette behind the curtains.

She slid on her hands and knees toward the opposite end of the sofa, and the phone. The footsteps resumed. They moved along the back of the house, then up onto the porch. She saw a man's shadowy form outside the French doors. The doorknob turned.

She lunged for the phone, pulling it off the table and onto the floor in front of her with a crash that seemed to echo in her bones.

The man outside tugged at the knob, making the

door rattle. She went down on her knees in a bone-cracking slide, scrabbling along the floor for the elusive receiver.

"Connie?" His voice was familiar, oh, familiar.

She rose to her feet, relief making her knees wobble. No burglar, then, just her imagination running away with her. She let the receiver drop to the floor, and the dial tone seemed unnaturally loud in the quiet room.

"Connie?" he called again. "It's John Bruycker. Are you in there?"

It took her a moment to get her voice working. "I'm . . . in here. Yes."

"I heard something fall. Are you okay?"

She rose to her feet. The pain rushed back along with her breath, and she held herself carefully as she walked toward the door, as though she'd break.

"I'm okay," she called. "Just a second and I'll let you in."

Needing the normalcy of bright light, she switched on the lamp along the way. She unlocked the door, swung it open.

"I thought you were a prowler," she said.

"I rang the doorbell."

"You walked through the flowerbed. I could hear your footsteps in the mulch."

"Hey, you really were scared," he said. "You look like you've seen a ghost."

She retreated from that one. "What are you doing here?"

"Scaring you, apparently."

"That's not the right answer."

He studied her for a moment, then stepped around her and picked the phone up off the floor. The dial tone cut off in mid-hum, leaving the room in silence. John set the phone back on the table before turning to look at her. His eyes revealed nothing of what might be going on behind them. "Phaedra told me your mother was going out tonight, so I dropped by to see if you needed anything." Then he smiled. "Is that the right answer?"

She nearly said no. But tonight wasn't a night to be alone, so she closed the door and locked it. "Maybe."

"Well, that's a start. Why so jumpy tonight, Connie?"

"I don't know."

He didn't believe her, obviously. But he also had sense enough not to push. She felt suddenly awkward beneath that too-penetrating gaze. Her emotions were raw, off-balance.

"Well," he said at last, "is there anything you would like me to do? I'm at your service; no job too big or too small."

Her brain lurched into gear. "You could get my pills out from under the sofa."

He crouched to look. It was a relief to be freed from those eyes.

"Are you going to use your psychic powers?" she asked.

John glanced up briefly, still inscrutable. Then he slid the sofa a couple of feet to one side, retrieved the pills, and returned the sofa to its original position.

"I would have used a yardstick," she said.

He sat back on his heels. "It's the usual solution."

"Which you don't like?"

"This was more direct. I'm a direct sort of person. Like you, Connie." He glanced at the label and whistled softly. "This stuff will knock you for a loop. Pretty stout for a little bruising."

Connie didn't know why she did what she did; it was pure impulse, too sudden and strong to be ignored. Half-turning away from him, she pulled up her sweatshirt and showed him her back.

Something very raw came into his eyes. He got to his feet with a smooth surging movement and came to her. Holding the shirt with one hand, he let the fingertips of the other drift down her battered skin. Goosebumps followed the path of his hand.

"Did I say a little bruising?" he asked.

"Could have been worse."

"What exactly happened?"

"Didn't Penny tell you?" she asked.

"She told me you'd had an accident and had gotten cut and bruised. That's all. She's under a lot of stress right now, Connie. You can't blame her for not being more accurate."

"I don't blame her. Look, I'd like to take a pill, if you don't mind."

"Sure. But let me fix you some herb tea to take with it."

His hand drifted back up her spine, to a place that wasn't bruised. Connie found her adrenaline level going up again, but not from fear. "I don't like herb tea," she said.

"You'll like mine," he said.

Gently he pulled her shirt down again. She watched him as he headed for the kitchen. He moved like a dancer, or like a cat; economically, gracefully, with a leashed power that might be intriguing to release. Not the sort of man she usually found attractive. She liked them tamer, less unpredictable. But she watched him until he disappeared around the corner, and something new and unexpected coiled within her. Life, maybe. Almost lost, then snatched back at the last moment. Maybe that had raised this rampant little beast inside her, making her reckless enough to like his difference.

Whoa, girl. He's just come to make you herb tea.

The phone rang, jolting her out of her reverie. She went to answer it. "Hello?"

"Just checking," Sandra said. "Are you all right?"

"I'm fine, Mom."

"Are you sure? I'm feeling a little guilty about leaving you alone so long."

"I'm a big girl," Connie said. Her voice sounded drier than she intended. "Besides, I'm not alone."

"Penny came by? I hoped she would."

Connie sighed. "No, not Penny. It's John Bruycker, a friend of Cullen's."

"Not one of those . . . New Age people?"

"He's making herb tea."

Sandra hesitated a moment, then said, "Maybe I'd better come home early."

"No," Connie said. "Don't."

Another, longer hesitation. "Well, all right. But I won't be later than twelve-thirty or one o'clock."

"Have fun," Connie said.

She hung up. The smell of tea brought her around to find John setting a cup and saucer on an end table. "I took your name in vain," she said.

"I heard. It didn't sound as though your mother was happy about me being here."

"Mom thought Cullen was a little nuts about this New Age thing, and I'm afraid she put all his friends in the nut category with him."

"What about you?"

She shrugged. "I think all humanity is nuts."

"I'd laugh if I thought you were joking." He pointed to the sofa. "Take a load off."

She eased into the seat gingerly. He handed her the tea and watched with mock solicitousness while she took a sip. A strange taste, part floral, part herbal. She set it aside.

"You don't like it?" he asked.

"Not really."

He handed her the bottle of pills. "Do you like those?"

"Not really."

"Why don't you wait a while before taking them, then?" he asked. "I'd like to talk to you, not watch you sleep."

"I'm really a bitch when I hurt."

His smile wasn't entirely nice. "I won't say the obvious comeback to that one. Why don't we make a deal? I'll distract you with my witty conversation, and the moment I get boring, you can take your pill."

"All right." She set the bottle down on the end table. "What do you want to talk about?"

"Myself, of course. Don't all men?"

"*I'm* supposed to be the bitchy one," she said.

He laughed. "You do have a sense of humor! All right. Let's talk about the biggest issue between us. That which is known as New Age."

"I'm not feeling well enough to debate philosophies with you tonight."

"Come on, Connie. Give. Is there anything you like about me?" Moving his arms in an emcompassing gesture, he amended, "Us."

She shifted position, trying to find a spot that didn't hurt. "It's not you. Or any of the people I've met. Individually, I've liked them all," she said. "Maybe it's because I'm not a particularly creative thinker; all this karma and humanism and crystal stuff just hits a raw edge with me."

"A lot of things hit a raw edge with you."

"Not always," she said, surprising herself by smiling. "As you said, there are times when I even have a sense of humor."

"That's in your eyes. And your mouth."

The way he said "mouth" was silkily intimate. She retreated again, leaning back against the pillow and tucking her feet under her. Not because she minded the intimacy; she just wanted time to assess it and her reaction to it.

"I can see the wheels turning now," he said.

"They always turn," she replied.

"Adding and subtracting? Or maybe judging?"

"Does that bother you?"

He shook his head. "But I think you're selling yourself short; you couldn't be Cullen's twin and not have some capacity for faith."

"I have tons of faith. I never doubt that the sun will come up in the morning, and I'm reasonably sure this sofa won't fall apart beneath me—"

"Semantics."

"I never discuss politics or religion."

He smiled. "Even with friends?"

"Especially not with friends."

She waited for him to reply. But he seemed willing to let her slide out of it. She knew, however, that he wouldn't always do so. He was not the kind of man who took no for an answer, or accepted even a partial answer. And it was equally obvious that he intended to know her . . . better. If she chose to let him, she'd have to walk a fine line between what he'd want from her and what she was willing to give. She had the feeling he'd want quite a lot. Daunting, but in a way, intriguing.

"You know," John said, "you're a lot more complicated than Cullen is . . . was."

"You've got to be kidding."

He sat down in the middle of the sofa, not close enough to be encroaching, not far enough away to seem uninterested. "Cullen was just . . . out there. If he liked you, he liked you. No deep divination there—he just did. He welcomed everybody. Come on in, make yourself at home, be my friend. Sometimes he was disappointed, sometimes he got hurt. That, too, was right there for everyone to see. I found it unusual for a man to be so open."

"Cullen shone like the sun," she said, truly astonishing herself.

John stared at her for a long, tight moment. Then he moved toward her in a smooth glide, slipping his hand behind her neck to draw her up for a kiss. She thought about retreating again, briefly, but tossed it away, along with her natural caution. Hell, he was warm, she was willing, and it just felt good to be alive. Also, he was very good at what he did; her mind catalogued this automatically while her body did all the things it was supposed to do.

She gasped for air when he broke the kiss. He crouched over her, his hair mussed from her hands, his breath coming as fast as hers. Something wild raged in his eyes, and it seemed to pull at her, demanding things she wouldn't have believed she could give. Now, looking up at him, she thought she might.

He put his hands on her waist. A simple caress, but the intensity of his eyes made it seem much more. She arched her back as he slid his hands higher.

"Ouch!" she hissed, as her injured elbow hit the back of the sofa. Pain exploded up her arm, surged in red rivulets through her brain.

"Sorry," he said. "Connie, I'm sorry."

"Give me a minute," she gasped.

He sank his hands into her hair, his fingers threading through to her scalp. Slowly, he massaged her. The pain abated in time with his motions.

"Mmmm, that feels good," she said.

"Relax." He moved down to her neck, his fingers slipping beneath the neck of her shirt. "You're wound up like a spring."

"My brother died."

She didn't know why she said that. It didn't seem absurd, however, with this man's hands on her. Neither did the tears that ran down her cheeks. John leaned forward and fitted his mouth to hers. The kiss tasted of salt and heat, life and death and loss and joy all at once.

"I wanted to do this the minute I saw you," he said, when they came up for air again. "But damn, Connie. I don't know where to touch you so I won't hurt you."

"You'd better look, then. So you'll know all the right spots."

He levered her to a sitting position and gently pulled her sweatshirt off. Tossing it over his shoulder, he sat back on his heels and studied her. "Wow," he said.

"Pretty beat up, huh?"

"I wasn't talking about the bruises." His eyes were feral. If his hands hadn't been so gentle, she might have been frightened of them. "Those spots I won't be able to touch tonight," he said, "we'll save for later."

Warm as she was, she shivered. He excited her. She'd never been looked at quite so hungrily by a man, even the ones who'd loved her.

He ran his fingertips up the outside of her arm, avoiding the bandage, then over her shoulder and down to her wrist. Had he touched her breast, he couldn't have aroused her more.

"Did that hurt?" he asked.

"Uh-uh." She wanted him to do it again. It must have shown in her eyes, for he did. With his mouth.

"Are you always so . . . leisurely about sex?" she asked.

"Only when it counts."

"Does it count now?"

He laid her back against the pillow and untied the drawstring of her sweatpants. "What does that practical accountant's mind of yours tell you?"

"Hmmm." She raised her hips to help him slip the pants off. "It's telling me that thinking maybe isn't the right thing to do right now. And that I should be glad that only one of us is bruised."

"Huh?"

"I get to touch you all I want." She wasn't reticent at all about undressing him, just greedy. It seemed the self-controlled Connie Matthias had turned into someone entirely different tonight. "And I don't give a damn about saving anything for later."

He came to kiss her again. Skin against skin, and all heat. She hardly felt the bruises anymore; mind and body, she was so powerfully tuned to him that a bomb might have gone off and she wouldn't have felt it.

Whatever it was, it was good. *He* was good. Something in her began to heal there in his arms. It didn't replace Cullen; nothing would. But it was a start.

"Trust me," John whispered against her mouth. "Let me have it all, Connie. Everything. You have to."

"I have to," she repeated. Maybe only for tonight. But she had to.

Chapter Seven

Jeff peered down the street at his dad's house. The porch light and living room light were on, which meant no one was home. He leaned forward, trying to wipe the smoke film from the inside of the windshield.

"You're makin' it worse," Tick said from the back seat.

"Man, I can't see shit through here."

The driver laughed. Jeff didn't know this guy; Tick picked him up somewhere, got him to drive them over here. He hadn't said a word yet, just gave that weird laugh every once in a while, and not always when something was funny.

"Your dad home?" Tick asked.

"It's cool," Jeff said. "You can let me off here."

"You're gonna get some real shit when the old man gets home."

Jeff shrugged. He swung the door open and got out, then leaned back in and looked at Tick. "You wanna come in, man?"

"Nah." Tick's face was too pale here under the street light. Weird greenish smudges surrounded his eyes, and with those bony shoulders and too-big hands, he looked like some kind of ghost. "Me and Steve are gonna party some more. See you later, man."

He oozed into the front seat and reached over to slam the door. The car roared off down the street. Jeff didn't want to be alone right now; even taking his dad's shit might be better than being alone.

The shrubbery held the shadows close around the house. If he stared at them too long, they started to move. Dark, squirmy things seemed to lurk there. He shook his head. Shouldn't have smoked that last one.

He walked around to the back of the garage, where he'd fixed the lock on the window so he could get in anytime. Man, Dad didn't know shit; Mom would have had that window fixed a month ago and started looking for the next escape route. He'd had a hard time staying ahead of her.

Dad believed in trust. Shit.

Raising the window, he wriggled inside. A faint scent of oil tinged the quiet air of the garage. He caught sight of the fishing pole Uncle Cullen had given him for his birthday last year. He looked away hastily, not wanting to think about Cullen. Or of the look in Mom's eyes when she'd asked him about the candles.

He headed for the house, walking a straight line, one foot in front of the other, as though something might grab him if he strayed. The kitchen was too brightly lit. He blinked, trying to accustom his eyes to the light.

"Hey, Jeff."

He froze. The voice came from the living room, floating out of the darkness and wrapping around him like a big, thick blanket. "Hey," he said.

"Come on in. We've got to talk."

Jeff didn't want to talk. His mind hung back, but his feet obeyed the command. His eyes stung as they tried to adjust to the change in light. The man sat in the loveseat in front of the big picture window, his head and shoulders silhouetted against the backlit curtain.

Mingled fear and anticipation ran in hot currents through Jeff's veins. He'd never made the mistake of thinking this guy was his friend. But then, maybe that was best; some of the guys he'd trusted had burned him.

"How did you get in here?" he asked, hating the way his voice cracked on the last word.

"I have a key, Jeff," the man said.

"How—?"

"You gave it to me, remember?"

Jeff shook his head.

"Of course you did," the man said. "But then, you don't remember much these days, do you?"

"I remember enough." Sullenly.

"Do you remember the night your uncle died?"

No. "Yes."

The man's teeth caught the light as he smiled. "Oh? Then you remember that we were together."

"For a while."

"I gave you something nice to try."

Jeff began a gesture, aborted it as though it might tell the man too much about him. "I was totally fucked for about twelve hours, like you knew I'd be."

"*You* came to *me,* asking for it," the man said. "Don't you remember where you were? What you did?"

"What do you friggin' want from me?"

"You told me you couldn't stay, that you had to meet your uncle. Do you remember that, Jeff?"

Something banged on the inside of Jeff's chest. After a moment, he realized it was his heart. His mind spun frantically, trying to grasp what had happened to him. It had all gone wrong. Everything. The darkness seemed to press around him, choking him, pulling at him until he felt as though he was about to fly into a million pieces.

"How the shit should I know?" he screamed. "I don't know nothin' about nothin'!"

"Easy, boy."

The man rose, came further into the light. He was smiling, and his eyes seemed almost kind. Almost. Jeff retreated, his breath coming so hard and fast it made him dizzy. "Stay away from me!"

"Don't get crazy on me," the man said. "I know you didn't mean to do it."

"Do what?" he almost whimpered. Please, God!

"Nothing, Jeff. Nothing."

Fear pounded his brain, shot spikes through his veins. He couldn't remember. He couldn't. He'd found himself in his room the next morning, feeling like he'd been to Mars and back, and he couldn't remember anything.

He started to cry. His brain curled around itself, not wanting to look, to see, to know. What he'd done.

"Take it easy," the man said again. "Come on, let me take you out for some ice cream or something."

Ice cream. Like he was some little kid with a bruised knee, whose hurt could be fixed with something sweet and cold. Jesus, God.

But he let the man drape an arm around his

shoulders and lead him outside. Because he didn't want to be alone.

Nothing lurked in the shadows this time; the monsters were all inside him. *They* knew. They knew what he'd been doing during those lost hours when his uncle had been killed.

"I'm parked over here," the man said, leading him toward a dark blue Taurus parked a little way down the street.

Jeff only nodded. Fixed up. Yeah, he could use that. The man would see to it. Maybe he could get the friggin' stars to change color again.

Light ran over the smooth metal skin of the car, picking up tiny metallic glints buried in the paint. The vehicle seemed to get bigger and bigger as Jeff got closer, the man's arm heavier on his shoulders.

"Don't worry about a thing," the man said. His eyes reflected the street lights oddly. "I'll help you remember everything that happened."

Panic closed Jeff's throat. He could hear the beat of his own heart, the sound his blood made as it rushed through his veins. He stood impaled by his own terror as the man unlocked the passenger door and swung it open.

"Hop in," the man said.

It felt as though a bomb went off in Jeff's head. He tore out of the man's grasp and ran. Blindly, frantically, jumping hedges, tearing through flower-beds, banging into trees and lamp posts with painful force.

He could hear the man coming behind him, running fast and silent. The silence was what frightened him the most. He pushed himself harder, running until he thought his chest would burst. And still the man came after him.

Finally, a measure of reason speared through the panic, and he slid into the shadows beneath a huge, spreading azalea in somebody's back yard. He crouched in the dirt like an animal, his breath coming in audible pants.

Stop. He'll hear you, he'll hear you.

He forced his breathing into control, pressed himself yet closer to the ground as the man came around the corner of the house nearest him. He watched the way the man stood, peering into the shadows, his head thrust forward as though he was sniffing the air.

This is crazy, to be so scared. He's just some guy. Tell him you don't want his help. Tell him to go away and leave you alone.

He couldn't. He didn't know why he couldn't. But terror closed his throat and pressed him deeper into the shadows.

"I know you're close," the man called softly. "You might as well come out; you can't hide forever."

Don't move. Don't. Don't.

"Come on, Jeff. We have to talk. You have to remember what you did. It's important."

Jeff closed his eyes. He couldn't have done . . . that. But from the time the stuff had kicked in, he'd lost the whole night. He didn't know. Oh, man, he just didn't know.

"Jeff!" the man called. "Come out. You don't have to do this alone. I'll help you."

He wasn't big, or even threatening. He even sounded like he really wanted to help. But something held Jeff silent beneath the bush, breathing in the peaty smell of the dirt beneath his cheek. Maybe it was all the shit he'd smoked earlier; maybe it was the fact that he didn't want to remember what had happened that night.

Suddenly a light came on in the house, drawing Jeff's gaze. when he looked away again, the man had gone. The car's engine purred to life, soft in the velvet darkness. A moment later the twin spears of headlights slid down the street, then disappeared as the vehicle turned the corner.

An outside light went on, pushing Jeff farther beneath the bush. Then a fat guy opened the door and stepped out onto the back porch. Hair stuck out in clumps from the neck of his tee shirt, fugitive, maybe, from his bald skull. His wife, wearing curlers and even more fat, came out behind him.

"Do you see anything, Hank?" she asked.

"Nah. Probably those goddamn kids again. Next time I'm gonna call the police. You hear that, you little bastards?" he called in a bass growl that probably rattled the glass in the neighbors' windows. "You better hope I call the cops and not shoot your butts myself."

They went back inside. Jeff flinched as the door banged shut with a crash. After a while the light went out in the house.

Still, he waited. The night ticked away in time with his heart; cricket song and the soft rustle of the branches were all he heard. The Taurus didn't come back.

Finally, he eased out of his hiding place and headed for home. Just a quick in-and-out, time enough to pick up some clothes and the money his father kept stashed at the back of his underwear drawer.

* * *

The mid-morning sun hung overhead as Connie drove out to her new apartment, a quarter of a big, old farmhouse in what had once been rural Virginia Beach; now, it was a half-mile away from the interstate. The house had been carved into apartments sometime in the fifties. Perfect, if you didn't mind fifties bathrooms and kitchens, which she didn't. Not when the rooms were big and airy, and a wooden swing hung in the corner of the wide front porch.

Her landlord, who occupied one of the ground-floor apartments, came out in time to open her car door for her.

"Mornin'," he said.

"Morning, Mr. Ranke. Great day, isn't it?"

"It's a fine day," he replied, leading the way up to the porch. "Hey, did you hurt yourself?"

She reached up to touch the bruise beside her eyebrow. "I had a little accident yesterday. Just some bumps."

"Can't be too careful these days."

He was a small, wiry man, made even more wiry by age. As she followed him up the inside stairway, she saw that he'd combed his hair back to cover his bald spot. He seemed nice enough, and she had the feeling he knew everything that went on in his domain. She wondered what he'd think of John Bruycker.

"Another girl lives in the apartment next to yours," he said. "Sherrie's a wild one. New boyfriend every other month or so. But she's a good kid. You got a boyfriend, Ms. Matthias?"

"Connie. And if I say yes, will I be a good kid, too?"

He laughed. "Know any pretty ladies to fix me up with? I'm looking for a rich widow."

Connie considered her mother, then decided against it. It was awfully tempting, though. "Sorry, Mr. Ranke."

"Oh, well." He unlocked the door and pushed it open, then stepped back to let her go in ahead of him.

The apartment had been freshly painted—white on white—and the beautiful old oak floor gleamed like butter in the sunlight.

"It looks great," she said.

"That polyurethane did real good. I'm glad you talked me out of carpet."

"Is it dry?"

"Sure."

She walked into one of the sunbeams, watching the dust motes swirl around her like tiny golden fireflies. *Cullen would have loved this.* Then, *Cullen's dead.* The sunlight seemed to dim all of a sudden, and she shivered.

"When's your furniture coming?" Ranke asked.

"The day after tomorrow," she said, adding, "at least, I assume so. Enough so that I'm going to the grocery store now and stock the refrigerator."

"You eat meat?"

"Yeah," she said, surprised. "Why?"

"Only thing I can't stand is a vegetarian."

She turned to look at him. "Why?"

"I'm suspicious of anybody who can eat that tofu stuff. You know what that is?"

"Mr. Ranke, I lived in California." He looked so stricken that she laughed. "But I assure you that I don't eat tofu."

"Whew. Scared me for a minute. Anything else you need?"

"No." She stood for a moment, waiting to see if the golden feeling would come back. It didn't. With a sigh, she turned toward the door. "Thanks for doing the floors for me. I appreciate it."

"Hey, we're like family here," he said. "We want everyone to be happy."

Maybe if my brother wasn't dead . . . but she merely smiled at him, accepting the key he held out.

"Honk when you get back," he said. "I'll help you carry the groceries up."

"Thanks," she said.

When she returned, however, he was waiting on the porch. With Derek. They had the air of a couple of old school buddies shooting the breeze; Mr. Ranke sat on the swing, arms spread out across the back, and Derek sat on the top step with his long legs stretched out in front of him.

He rose as she came up the steps. She hadn't seen him close up in years, just glimpses of him in the car when he dropped Jeff off. He hadn't changed much. Still tall and rangy, still with those not-quite-put-together features that women never seemed to find ugly. The tawny hair had receded a bit at his temples, but the body looked as fit and hard as it had at eighteen.

"Hello, Derek."

"Hi, Connie."

He stood looking down at her, his hands thrust into the pockets of his jeans. For a moment, she was beset with memories. They'd put a lot of anger and passion into their brief marriage. Highs and lows, ups and downs. It had been too much for her.

"How'd you find me?" she asked.

"Your mother gave me the address."

Mr. Ranke unfolded himself from the swing and came to stand beside Derek. "This the boyfriend?" he asked.

She looked at him. "Ex-husband."

"Oops."

From the look on his face, he thought she'd made a mistake. *You marry him, then.* Shifting her gaze from him to Derek, she said, "Come upstairs. And bring a couple of bags with you."

"Killing two birds with one stone?" he asked.

"Yeah."

She walked upstairs ahead of him, overly conscious of his gaze. Was he looking at her rear end, or was he looking at her back, picking a good place in which to stick a knife? It took considerable will power not to turn around.

He set the bags on the counter and went to close the door. She would have preferred less privacy. To keep from looking at him, she busied herself putting the groceries away.

"Jeff came home last night," he said.

Her breath went out in a long sigh. "Good. What did he say about—"

"He came in while I was out looking for him." Derek's voice turned harsh. "He took some money I'd been keeping in my drawer for emergencies, then left again."

She dropped the egg carton. It opened when it hit, sending shards of shell and bright yolks sliding across the tile floor.

"How much money?" she asked.

Derek took her by the shoulders and set her aside, then bent and began cleaning up the mess. "Almost four hundred dollars. How long can a kid live on the street with that much?"

Too long, too long. Connie watched his long-fingered hands as he scooped the eggs back into the carton.

"I've spent two nights cruising Virginia Beach and Ocean View looking for that kid," he said. "I drove up every alley, talked to anyone who'd talk back. I haven't slept, haven't eaten a decent meal in two days."

"What do you want me to say, Derek? That I'm glad you went looking for him, and that I'm grateful? Okay, I am."

He glanced up at her. "When I got home this morning, I found someone waiting for me. Do you know Detective D'Amato?"

"Yes."

"He asked a bunch of questions about Jeff. He also said that Cullen was killed with a knife about six inches long, an inch wide, and with a blade that tapered from one-eighth of an inch to one thirty-second of an inch at the edge. Kind of like a hunting knife."

She closed her eyes, seeing the wound in Cullen's chest. Seeing the knife, watching it go in . . .

"Connie!"

With a start, she opened her eyes and looked at Derek. He crouched on the floor, but there was nothing subservient in his position; those golden-brown eyes blazed with anger. "After D'Amato left, I went out into the garage to check my hunting equipment. And do you know what I found?"

She curled in and around herself, wishing she could make him disappear. Wishing she could make the whole world disappear.

He reached up and grasped her wrist. It didn't hurt; it only made her feel trapped. "My hunting knife is gone, Connie. I saw it there a month ago, but now it's gone."

"He's my son," she whispered.

"He's my son, too!" Fury etched his face, turned his voice savage. "I'm going to have to tell D'Amato—"

"No!" she cried. "Don't!"

"Why not?"

"Because . . ." She tried to finish. But she couldn't.

"Why not, Connie?"

Reaching over, she tried to pry his hand from her wrist. But he caught her free hand, too, pulling her to her knees in front of him. "Talk."

"What are you going to do?" she asked. "Pluck my fingernails out one by one, or maybe burn me with a cigarette?"

His eyes changed. With a muttered curse, he let go of her. "I quit smoking two years ago."

"Good for you." She braced her hands on her knees, wishing she knew the right words to make him go away. "Now, tell me where he might be hanging out."

"Tell me why you don't want me to go to the police."

"I can't."

"Why the hell not? Don't you think I love him as much as you do? Don't you think I want the best for him, too?"

"What's the best for him, Derek? Putting him in jail? Will locking him up somewhere solve his problems?"

His eyes narrowed. "Maybe."

"I can't do that. And I'm not going to let you do it."

"Come on! Are you going to let him kill himself, maybe, or . . ." He broke off abruptly, his face showing the words he hadn't been able to say.

Or kill somebody else.

"I've got to go," she said, getting slowly to her feet.

"We're not finished, damn it!"

"Yes, we are."

He rose, stood towering over her. "It never changes, does it? We can never talk, just fight."

"Hey, why the hell are you blaming me? It takes two to fight, and you're doing your full share."

"Sure. You drive me nuts. I see you looking at me with those eyes that show that little calculator going on inside your head, adding, subtracting—"

"And coming up short."

His mouth thinned. "You know something you're not telling me. You know something you're not telling D'Amato. He knows it. And that's not a man who's going to give up until he finds out. Better think real hard, Connie. If Jeff's done something he shouldn't have, you're not going to be able to protect him, no matter how hard you try."

She turned away. "Goodbye, Derek."

"Connie." He caught her by the arm. Although his grip was gentle, his hand closed directly on her cut elbow. She cried out involuntarily.

His eyes narrowed. He pulled her sleeve up and inspected the bandage. "Seventeen stitches," he muttered. "Where else are you hurt?"

"Nowhere."

"Is that why you're walking like an old woman?"

"Maybe I just *feel* like an old woman."

She turned away again, and this time he let her go. As she paused to open the door, he called her name.

"What?" she asked without turning around.

"Your mother will tell me what happened," he said. "She's always liked me, you know."

"She liked Richard Nixon, too."

Neither of them laughed. After a moment, she headed downstairs. Slamming into her car, she peeled rubber on the way out the drive.

Chapter Eight

Connie walked along one of the upper bay streets in Ocean View's East End. She didn't remember which number; she'd walked so many of these short north-south streets that she'd forgotten to keep track. Houses here were a far cry from the pleasant homes in the city's other sections.

A short distance ahead, she spotted a group of kids leaning against a convenience store's graffiti-marked wall. Just the ticket, she thought, heading toward them. They glanced up as she approached. Some looked like they'd just hit the streets yesterday. Some looked like they'd been there forever, with their old, old eyes in thin young faces. They were the ones who'd never go home.

Not my son.

She walked up to them, breasting her way through a palpable wall of suspicion. Pulling a picture of Jeff out of her pocket, she held it up.

"Have any of you seen this boy?" she asked, for perhaps the thousandth time today.

They all shook their heads, eyes revealing nothing.

"I'm not a cop," she said. "I'm his mother."

Their eyes didn't change. Cop, mother, adult . . . she was still the enemy.

"Never seen him," one of the boys said. He might have been sixteen or seventeen under the dirt and hair. His breath stank, even at this distance.

"If you do, would you tell him to come home? Tell him we can work it all out, if only he'll come home."

"I said we don't know him."

"Then can you tell me the name of someone else who might be able to help me?"

The boy laughed. "Lady, do we look like social workers or somethin'?"

With a sigh, she turned away. It was always like this. She'd walked the streets for hours, showing the photo, asking questions, leaving her message with anyone who'd talk to her. But these kids lived in a world far removed from hers, and she wasn't sure she'd reached them at all.

Then she swung back around. These were kids, most of them not much older than Jeff. And there were so many of them out here, living in packs, sleeping rolled together in those rundown cottages . . . *if* they were lucky enough to have the money for rent.

"Have you thought about calling home?" she asked.

That got their attention. Before anyone could protest, she continued, "Even if home isn't a place you can go, there are shelters and things. They'll help you."

They turned away from her. She knew she'd been saying the same things they'd heard from adults too many times. So young, she thought. So young, so tough, so hopeless.

"Hey, lady," the boy called.

Hope welled in her mind. "Yes?"

"You got any money?" His teeth showed yellow when he smiled.

"You got any information about my son?" she shot back.

He pushed away from the wall and walked toward her. Two of the other boys came with him. The rest just watched; the fresh faces showing fear, the others apathy.

Connie gauged the distance to the convenience store's entrance, discarded the idea. She might be able to outrun them. Then again, maybe not. As they spread out around her, even that option disappeared.

The moment stretched interminably; almost-danger, the smell of fear on the air. Then Connie reached into her pocket, took out the ten-dollar bill she'd put there, and held it out to him.

"That's all I have," she said.

He took it. Thrusting it into his pocket, he looked her over as though assessing her fear. Then he turned and walked away. The others followed one by one, like soiled little pearls on a string.

Grit crunched behind her. Whirling, she saw a car pull up to the curb behind her. The driver pushed his door open and stood up. She blinked, recognizing him. Hamilton Liu. The afternoon sun seemed to strike sparks in his black hair.

"Connie? Are you all right?"

"I'm fine."

Under the circumstances, the statement seemed absurd. Hamilton had the grace not to comment on that, however, so she didn't, either.

"You're not planning on hanging around here, are you?" he asked.

"Hanging," she said. "The term nowadays is hanging."

"Right. I'll walk you back to your car."

"Ah, it's back on Tidewater Drive."

"Uh-huh." He propped his elbows on top of his car. "Then I'll drive you. This isn't a good place for a lady alone after dark."

Connie considered refusing. But she also realized that walking the streets like this wasn't fast enough or thorough enough. So she nodded. "Thanks."

He came around to open the passenger door for her. They were almost the same height, she noted. His hands were finer and more graceful than hers, a novel experience for a small woman.

The interior of the car was plain, ordinary beige, but it smelled of something exotic. Apricots, maybe, with a hint of cinnamon and sandalwood. The scent grew stronger when Hamilton got into the car, and she realized it was the man, not the machine.

"What are you doing here?" she asked.

"Just passing through. I couldn't believe my eyes when I saw you out here, and did a quick U-turn to come back around. Did you get lost?"

"Sort of."

Again, he didn't press, just started the car and did a crisp turn to head west, away from the amphibious base. She watched his profile as he drove. He didn't look to be solely Chinese; surely there were some other ethnic goups in his ancestry somewhere.

"My mother is French-Canadian," he said.

As she sat there gaping at him, he shot her a look from the corner of his eye and said, "Everyone asks, sooner or later. I figured I'd save you the trouble."

"I thought you were going to say you'd read my mind."

He smiled. "John said you were uncomfortable with our belief system."

"I didn't realize I was a topic of conversation."

"Of course we're interested in you," Hamilton said. "You're Cullen's twin."

Right now, she had no intention of getting into a discussion of twinness. Especially with someone else who'd lost a twin. She was holding together with the proverbial bubble gum and baling wire, and simply didn't have the resources for it.

So she retreated inside, pulling the hatches in behind her. Outside, the sun went down. It was a violent sunset, blood-red and fiery orange, barred with razor-edged indigo clouds.

Hamilton reached over to switch on his headlights. The growing darkness blurred the hard edges, making the cottages seem not quite so run-down. But she knew what lay behind those soft violet shadows. And those kids . . . dropped out, tuned out, set adrift from a world they couldn't seem to find a place in. Cullen had felt like that: disconnected. Somehow, he'd managed to find somewhere to fit.

"Most people rush to fill the silence," her companion said.

She turned back to him, found him looking at her with speculation in his eyes. "Most people watch the road when they drive."

"I'm watching," he said. "You're looking for Jeff, aren't you?"

Her breath went out in a long sigh. "You slid that one right in there, didn't you?"

"Had to. You're not easy to talk to when you've got your guard up."

"You know my son."

He nodded. "We've talked some. I guess it's because I'm closer to his age than anybody in the group except for Lynn, and she never bothered with him. But I can't say Jeff and I were friends; he never let me get close enough for that. Did he run away because of Cullen's death?"

Things were coming so fast she was having trouble batting them away. "I didn't say he ran away, Hamilton."

"Why else were you down here?" he asked.

"Turn here," she said.

He swung the car around the corner, those slim, graceful hands moving smoothly over the steering wheel. A perceptive man, this one. The most dangerous kind; it would take a better liar than her to fool him.

"I know you've got no reason to trust me," he said. "But I knew something was bothering Cullen. If he'd tell anyone, he'd tell you. Had he—"

"Foreseen his death? Hardly. He said something 'felt' wrong. Hardly a vision of his imminent demise. And with all you psychic types around, how come nobody told him to stay off the beach that night?"

"It doesn't work that way, Connie."

"Then what the hell good is it?" Her voice was ugly with bitterness; she would have taken that too-revealing tone, if not the words, back. She was glad it had gotten too dark for him to see her expression.

"Cullen was special," he said. "From the moment we got together, he was the focus of our group. All the talent, all the needs and wants revolved around him."

"What are you saying?"

"I'm saying that Cullen was a powerful force in our lives, Connie. If anyone wanted to strike at our group, the logical target would have been him."

She turned away, unsure she had proper control of her expression. "You think he was killed because someone wanted to break up your group? Say, someone with a different philosophy?"

"Is it so incredible?"

"Ye-es, it is." Her head was beginning to throb. She rubbed her temples with her fingertips. "Look, Hamilton. Maybe you folks have a 'belief system' a little out of the ordinary. But who else cares, really?"

"Somebody did."

Or maybe Cullen had just run into the wrong person at the wrong time. Somebody who liked rituals and black candles—and needed someone's life to whet the grindstone. She clenched and unclenched her hands for a while, until Hamilton reached over and stopped her.

"You're tearing yourself up," he said. "I wish you'd let me help."

"Then look into your crystal ball and tell me who killed my brother." His silence shamed her. After a moment, she said, "I'm sorry. You didn't deserve that."

"Maybe I did." He stopped for a traffic light. In profile, his eyes looked like elongated triangles. "We let Cullen be our mentor. We warmed ourselves at his fire, fed on his spirit and his enthusiasm. And when he needed us, none of us could help him. He was so happy when you came back, Connie. Maybe because you were the one person *he* could lean on."

He let go of her hands, and she was able to breathe again. "Who do you think killed him?" she asked. She didn't know why she'd asked that question; it had come, unbidden and powerful, and her mouth had obeyed.

"I don't know. But I think it was someone he knew; Cullen read people well, and I don't think he'd have allowed a stranger with murder on his mind to just walk up and . . ."

"And just stick a knife in," she finished. Baldly. Brutally. The words seemed to etch themselves into her soul. But she couldn't help but bring Hamilton's thought to the logical conclusion: not only did Cullen know the killer, he trusted him. Her heart tried to squeeze itself into a tight little ball.

"You don't spare yourself anything, do you?"

That was too close, an intimacy of thought she wasn't willing to share with anyone but Cullen. "My car's over here, on the right," she said.

He sighed, then swung the car to the curb behind her Grand Am. She pushed her door open and got out. The night air ran cool over her skin. She took a deep breath, then leaned back in the car and studied Hamilton. He let her, that massive serenity of his absorbing even this close scrutiny. She wondered how much of it was real.

"Thanks for the ride," she said.

"I want to help you, Connie. You can't run from yourself forever; sooner or later, you'll have to look in that dark place inside you."

He knows.

The overhead light turned his skin the color of old ivory and cast golden glints in his obsidian eyes.

For a moment she thought she saw her own face reflected in their depths.

"Think about it," he said. "We have an awful lot in common."

It took a conscious effort for her to take her hand off the door handle.

"Less," she said, "than you think."

Connie drove back to her mother's house. She hoped Sandra would be away at one of her meetings; she felt as thin and ragged as an old pair of pantyhose.

The outside of the house had remained as unchanged as the inside. Occasionally, the color of the trim had changed from white to beige and back again; now, with vinyl siding in place, even that would remain the same. It was almost as though time had stopped for Sandra Matthias.

"It must be a gift," Connie said aloud.

Cullen had been the butterfly. All his life, he'd been metamorphosing from one thing to another: boy to man, college student to marketing whiz, Episcopalian to New Age mystic.

Her vision blurred. She licked her lips, tasted salt. "Damn it, not now," she muttered, steering with one hand as she swiped at her eyes with the other.

The car lurched as the right front tire scraped the curb. She corrected. Overcorrected. The tears kept coming. She'd never thought it could hurt so much to cry. Finally, the car bumbled to a stop against the curb.

"Why?" she sobbed, slamming the heels of her hand on the steering wheel to punctuate each word, "why, why, why?"

Someone opened her door, reaching past her rigid arms to turn the car off. "Connie."

She knew the voice, knew the arms that went around her. Leaning her head against John's chest, she struggled to bring her emotions under control.

"Don't fight it," he said.

Somehow, he wriggled into the seat with her. She didn't know how he managed it, didn't care; it felt too good to be held. He talked to her. For a while she was crying too hard to understand what he said, but the sound of his voice comforted her more than she would have believed.

For a brief, precious moment, life had become simple. She found the pain in her chest easing. Enough to speak, enough to register the understanding in his eyes.

"I'm okay now," she said, after a shuddering breath. "I probably scared the hell out of you."

"I'm glad you finally let go." Emotion put a ragged edge on his voice. His arms tightened, almost-pain against her bruised back, but she welcomed it.

"How did you know I needed you?"

"I was the one who needed *you,*" he said. "And I had every intention of sitting on your doorstep until you got home."

She didn't question the miracle of it. If this was the only good thing to come out of this tragedy, then she'd be a fool not to accept it for what it was.

The pressure of the steering wheel against her hip turned her attention to the fact that she was very uncomfortable. It must be worse for John; he'd gotten himself intimately acquainted with the gear shift. But first things first. Reaching up, she sank her hands into his hair and brought his face to hers.

The kiss was long and sweet, part passion, part

gratitude, part aching memories, and part awakening. He made her feel alive in a way she'd never experienced before: wild and a little reckless, as though her senses had slid into a higher gear. Her emotions had become more sharply defined—pleasure and pain, grief and joy, and all the things in between.

She was the one who broke the kiss. She had the feeling that he'd sunk deep, and wasn't about to come up until she let him. "Thank you," she said.

"You're welcome." He studied her for a moment, his eyes restless with a need she understood very well. Then he smiled. "Now that that's settled, can we get out of this car while I can still call myself a man?"

She raised her wrist and checked her watch. Eight-thirty. Mom would be home about nine. "Instead, why don't you crawl into that seat so we can go somewhere else?"

"Have you eaten?"

"Not yet. But I—"

"There's a great restaurant a few blocks away from my house. After dinner, I can show you my etchings."

"A feast for the eyes?"

"There are some things better left to the sense of touch."

"Touché."

"I'm very witty when I want something as badly as I want you," he said.

She ran her fingertips along the curve of his full lower lip. Somebody shivered; she didn't know who. Maybe both. "I don't know why you want me at all. I'm not spiritual, I don't believe in crystals or reincarnation or karma, and right now I've got a big, aching hole where my heart used to be. There are times when I feel like I died on that beach with Cullen."

"Then why did you cry out when I loved you last night? Why do your eyes turn hot when I do this?" His hands moved lower, making her feel very much alive.

"I like that," she whispered.

"I know."

She shifted, restless in the confinement. "I'm hungry, John."

"Yeah. Me, too. Ooh, ah!" That came as he extricated himself from the gear shift. "Maybe we should just grab some fast food on the way home."

"You promised me dinner."

"I'll suck your toes."

He probably meant it. Still, she hadn't found anything he did that she *didn't* like. Or didn't do. And then reserved, practical Connie came up with the most astonishing statement of her life: "You can suck my toes at the restaurant."

She watched it hit, sink deep, then explode again in the depths of his eyes. Desire, raw and dark and uncontrolled. He stared back at her, letting her see it all. Tonight would be unpredictable. He might be gentle, like he was last night. And then again, maybe not. For the first time in her life, she found the unknown exciting.

Better than firewalking.

She smiled at him, accepting the challenge.

"Put the car in gear," he said. *"Now."*

Chapter Nine

The big grandfather clock read 2:40 when Connie slipped into her mother's house. The Colonial ambiance was less welcoming in the wee hours of the morning, something of chastisement in the broad, clean lines of the furniture.

Why are you sneaking around? God knows you're old enough to have an affair without worrying about what your mommy thinks.

A floorboard creaked loudly under her foot. Connie cringed. Why was it, she wondered, that people never worried about sneaking around if they'd stayed late at a church dance? Stay out late having sex, now, and even the floorboards shrieked the sin to the world.

"I got your message," Sandra said from the dark hallway. "Did you have a good time?"

Connie had to struggle to keep from smiling. Oh, yes, she'd had fun. "Hi, Mom. You didn't have to wait up."

"I didn't. The phone rang a minute ago, but I couldn't get to it in time. Why don't you check the machine?"

With a sigh, Connie headed for the kitchen. The

light on the answering machine blinked at her like a malevolent red eye. She hit play.

"Mom. It's me." Jeff's voice sounded blurred, off-kilter. Connie didn't want to think why. "I heard you were looking for me. Look . . . I'm with friends, okay? I got a place to stay and enough money for food. But I'm not coming home."

He paused after the last word, as if he'd almost said something else. It might have been "ever." But Connie's heart whispered "yet," for she couldn't bear anything else. Then the machine clicked off, leaving her in silence.

"That's not good enough, Jeff," she said.

"Let him go."

Connie turned to look at her mother. Sandra stood in the doorway, her hair backlit by the lamp in the foyer. They were much alike, the two of them, small and slim and straight. But inside, there were worlds of difference. Now, after hearing that comment, Connie thought perhaps those differences were too big ever to be reconciled.

"That's a hell of a thing to say, Mom."

"Someone needs to say it," Sandra said. "He's lost. Maybe in a couple of years he'll come to his senses—"

"He's fifteen years old," Connie said. "I can't just turn my back on him no matter what . . ." She couldn't finish. The thought was too awful, her own suspicion a monstrous thing for a mother to have.

"He's got the Balestier wildness."

"Well, screw the Balestiers," Connie snarled. "They're ruining my life and my son's life."

Sandra switched on the overhead light. The sudden fluorescent brightness blinded Connie for a moment. Then her eyes adjusted, and she faced her mother across the oak and tile efficiency of the kitchen. Something hard and cold lay in the older woman's eyes: retribution, perhaps, or merely disdain. Anger would have been easier to see.

"It's come full circle," she said. "After all this time."

"What do you mean?" Connie asked.

"You drove me crazy. Pregnant at seventeen, married at eighteen, divorced at nineteen. And then you ran off to California—"

"I went to college, Mom. And then I settled down to earn a living for me and my son."

"Well, Cullen never grew up. Like a little boy, he ran from one toy to the next, one game to the next. He and Penny didn't have a molecule of sense between them."

Connie felt her hands begin to clench. With an effort, she relaxed them. "Is there a point to this?"

"Oh, yes." Sandra took a deep breath, and Connie knew it was going to be bad. "You didn't do badly; the only price I paid for that pregnancy was your college tuition. But I bailed Cullen out of a hundred scrapes, even used my connections to bring him business at the agency. Life was smooth for Cullen; handsome, popular, intelligent, and a good talker, he never really understood the real world. I wonder what he thinks of his 'all is one' theory now."

"I see." Connie folded her arms over her chest. "So I should let my fifteen-year-old son run the streets and maybe burn his brain out on drugs so that he can learn to understand the real world."

"As if you could stop him."

"I have to try."

"Is that why you were out screwing that weird friend of Cullen's?"

Ah, Connie thought. Now we're getting to it. "I'm long past the age when I have to justify my personal life to you."

"Oh, yes. I'm sure there are a number of thirty-three-year old fools out there."

"John is a nice man."

"How would you know? You met him all of three days ago."

"Come on, Mom; give me credit for having some sense."

Sandra's mouth compressed. "What is it that attracted you to him, Connie? Is it his skill with crystal balls?"

"Maybe he just shows me a little compassion," Connie said, more heat in her voice than the situation warranted. "Maybe he just offers some comfort."

"*I* think he's the proverbial forbidden fruit. The accountant and the psychic; the practical and the visionary. Or maybe he's your only link to Cullen's world."

That was just a little too close for comfort. Connie opened her mouth to retort, then closed it again. This was how all Sandra's and Cullen's arguments began. She'd goad him to quivering outrage, then puncture his arguments, belittle his beliefs and criticize his friends. Cullen, always passionate, fell for it every time.

Years ago, Connie had found an easier way. Now, in the face of having to take up Cullen's role, she fell back into the old gambit: be calm, be practical, be the adult.

"This really has you torqued, Mom," she said. "What is it about John that bothers you so much?"

"Let's get past the fact that he's not at all the sort of man I'd consider suitable. It's the timing I hate."

Fair enough. "Because Cullen died."

"Yes," Sandra said. "Because Cullen died."

Connie raked her hands through her hair. "Yes, the timing is bad. I admit it. And maybe John isn't even the 'right' man; it's way too soon to know that. But he makes me feel alive, Mom. He puts something into that deep, empty place Cullen's death left in my soul. It doesn't take away from the grief; it just makes it bearable."

"How nice for you." Sandra's tone turned ugly. "Did you stop to consider that if you'd spent a little more time with your brother during the past fifteen years, you might not have that deep, empty place to deal with? And maybe it's not grief you're feeling, but guilt. And you're dashing into a mad fling with this man so that you won't have to think about it?"

That hit, and it hurt. More than it should have; but, unfair as it was, it paralleled Connie's feelings too well. If only, if only . . . realizing that she'd drawn her clenched fists up to her chest as though to stem the tide of her pain, she dropped them to her sides. "I wish I could be surprised that you'd say something like that."

"I have always been honest with you children."

"Right." The words seemed to scrape Connie's throat raw as she forced them upward. "Then why don't you say the rest?"

"What rest?"

"That you wish it had been me who had died."

It sat, flat and ugly, in the air between them. Connie watched her mother's eyes, looking for hurt, looking for denial. But it seemed as though a shutter had banged down behind those lovely chameleon irises, closing Sandra in her own private world. Connie had seen that look often. It signaled "Keep out," "Don't touch." And it always hurt. Always.

"Foolish of me to think that Cullen's death might bring us a little closer," Connie said. Driving the spike a little deeper into her own bitterness.

"I've given what I could."

"You said that before."

"And you said that wasn't a hell of a lot." Sandra's voice was as neutral as her eyes. "Whatever, it isn't enough for you."

"I guess not."

They stood looking at each other. It was so quiet that Connie could hear the faint ticking of the grandfather clock in the hall. Maybe each was waiting for the other to break the silence.

But maybe it didn't matter. Maybe everything had already been said.

A bit jerkily, like a machine left unoiled too long, Sandra started walking toward her. Connie didn't know whether it was to strike her or hug her; either would have hurt. Brushing past her as though she were a stranger, Sandra went to the desk and opened the top drawer.

"Here," she said, thrusting a piece of paper into Connie's hands. "Cullen's lawyer called. He wants you to call him back first thing in the morning."

Without another word, without a change in expression, she turned and walked out. Connie would rather have been slapped.

* * *

"Have a seat, Ms. Matthias," the lawyer said.

Connie chose one of the leather chairs that sat in front of his desk and studied him as he settled down opposite her. Rich Drayton had the poise and graying hair of a man nearing fifty, but his smooth baby face made him seem younger. His gray eyes were coolly calculating as he met her gaze.

"I'm very sorry about your brother," he said.

She inclined her head, accepting the statement. "I must admit I'm confused, Mr. Drayton. Why did you contact me?"

"Because you're the executrix of Cullen's estate, and it's my job to hand the will over to you."

"Executrix?" This she didn't want.

"Why are you surprised, Ms. Matthias?"

"I'm not surprised, exactly. I . . . to tell you the truth, this isn't a job I'm looking forward to."

Drayton wiped an invisible speck of dust from the desk in front of him. Except for the phone, the polished oak surface was empty. Connie wondered if the man was really so neat, or if he scurried around madly to stuff stacks of paper in his closet before appointments. It was a disturbingly Cullen-ish thought, and she pushed it away hastily.

He studied her for a moment as if to see whether she'd rush to fill the gap in the conversation. She clasped her hands in her lap and waited for him to tire of it.

"There isn't going to be much of a job with this estate," he said at last.

"What do you mean?"

Reaching into his drawer, he pulled out a manila envelope and placed it on the desk. Then he pushed it across to her. Connie, feeling as though she'd made an irretrievable mistake, took the will out and started reading.

Once she glanced up at Drayton and said, "Why don't you guys write something in clear, easy-to-understand language?"

He smiled. "I did."

"Well, numbers are my language. Where's the . . . oh, right, here they are." She read the list of bequests. Then she read it again. "This doesn't make sense."

"Why not?"

"The estate shows assets of just over twenty thousand dollars. There's a life insurance policy for fifty thousand . . . but that's it."

"Yes, that's true."

"That house they're living in has got to be worth a half a million dollars," Connie said. "They've got the best furniture money can buy, and I assure you, my sister-in-law dresses well. They drive a Mercedes."

"You can lease a house, a car, and furniture."

Connie balanced the papers on her palms as though weighing them. "Do you know what my brother made a year?"

"In the neighborhood of thirty thousand dollars. But I understand that he cut his hours sharply this last year, so that figure will no doubt be considerably less."

Her brain kept adding figures and coming up short. *What's the monthly lease for a house like that? And for a Mercedes?* "Do you know if he had a safety deposit box?"

Drayton shook his head. "I'm sure his wife does."

"Are you her lawyer, too?"

His eyes narrowed as he registered her question. "No. Is there a problem?"

"Only with me." She slid the will back into the envelope, then put it into her purse. Rising, she shook hands with the lawyer. "Thank you, Mr. Drayton."

He held her hand and her gaze a moment longer than necessary. "You'll contact me if you happen to come across anything . . . of interest?"

"Why?" she asked, honestly surprised.

"I liked your brother."

"Most people did."

"One person," he said, "obviously did not."

He released her hand. She turned and walked out of his staid, elegant office, letting the door swing closed with a restrained *snick.* The secretary gave her a practiced smile as she left.

What had begun as an overcast day had turned to rain. Big, fat drops made splotches on the sidewalk. Connie held her purse overhead to shield her suit from the wetness.

"Hey!" a man called. "Miss Matthias!"

She turned toward the voice. Detective D'Amato waved at her from beside a dark Ford sedan parked haphazardly beside the curb. Connie's insides congealed. But she had no choice but to walk toward him.

"Morning, Detective," she said.

"I'd like to talk to you for a minute." He thrust his thumb toward the passenger door. "Why don't we get out of the rain?"

As if she had a choice. She got into the car, half-turning toward him as he slid into the driver's seat.

"How did you know I was here?" she asked.

"Did you think I was tailing you or something?"

He snorted. "I called your house. Your mother told me where you were."

"Oh."

"Did the lawyer have anything interesting to tell you?"

She looked him over. He didn't really expect her to tell him, she saw, but she had the feeling that not doing so would tell him nearly as much. "He gave me Cullen's will."

"You're executrix?"

"Yes."

"I'd like to see that will."

Connie considered that. The document didn't seem to contain anything that might put Jeff at risk. Equally, however, she simply didn't know enough to be sure. She felt as though she were walking a tightrope over quicksand: fall one way and you're dead, fall the other and you're equally dead. Or your son. "Why do you want to see it?"

"Well, it's this way," he said, raking his thumbnail along his jaw. "If your brother had been the victim of a drive-by shooting, say, I wouldn't think a will would have any bearing on his case. But I've got a guy who was loved by friends and family, who had a nice lifestyle, but who ended up murdered. It doesn't add up. Obviously, there's a fly in the ointment somewhere, or he'd still be walking around, loved by friends and family. And I've got to dig into all aspects of your brother's life if I'm gonna find it."

Connie, thinking about the beautiful house and car and furniture Cullen didn't own, nodded. She and D'Amato were after the same thing: information. But their goals weren't the same: he wanted to wind up the case, and she wanted to protect her son.

Even if . . . the thought was unbearable, so she pushed it aside.

"Look, Detective," she said, "the family hasn't even had a chance to see this will. I can't let you see it without talking to them first."

His eyes didn't change, but she knew he didn't believe her. "When can you let me know?"

"When I talk to my family."

He fell silent then, and she let her gaze drift to the rain-streaked windshield. It hadn't been washed in a while; the drops made sinuous muddy paths down the glass. She grimaced inwardly; it seemed like a long time since she'd had a clear view of anything.

"Look, Detective. I'm facing a family war when I get back. My mother wants to bury Cullen in the Matthias plot, but my sister-in-law insists he wanted to be cremated, his ashes cast out over the water. I'm going to be caught in the middle. And quite frankly, I don't have the resources for it."

"Do you care how it's done?" he asked.

The question surprised her. She didn't know why he'd asked it, or if he gave a damn what she said. "In the ground or floating on the Atlantic, it just doesn't matter. He's gone."

D'Amato nodded. "He didn't specify his preference in the will?"

"Believe me," she said, "the will presents more problems than it solves."

"Now, *that* I believe."

She met his dark gaze squarely. For once, she was glad she didn't have those too-expressive Balestier eyes. "When can we have Cullen back?" she asked.

"We notified your sister this morning. The funeral home will pick him up this afternoon."

"So you've got . . ." she took a deep breath, "everything you need from him?"

Speculation came into his eyes. "Do you want to know?"

"No. But I've got to know."

"He was stabbed with a long, sharp object, most likely a knife. It severed his aorta, and he died almost instantly. We think he was killed where you found him."

"Somebody walked up to him, took out a knife, and just . . ." She made a short, stabbing movement with her right hand.

"Right."

Someone he knew. It had to be. Someone he knew. Someone he trusted. What would it have been like to welcome a friend and then see the knife?

Maybe he hadn't even seen it. Maybe death had come as a surprise. A sudden pain, a swift cessation of thought. In her mind's eye, she saw the motion, saw the flash of moonlight on metal. Impact. Jolting, brutal, cold. A tearing pain in her chest, the breath not coming, no matter how hard she tried . . .

"Ms. Matthias."

D'Amato's voice jerked her back to reality. She sucked in air with a shuddering breath, the edges of that vision still hammering at her mind.

"Ms. Matthias," he said again.

She looked at him, saw that he was holding out a box of tissues. Realizing that her fists were clenched, she forced them to relax. Her nails left half-moons in her palms.

"Wipe your face," he said.

Her hand trembled as she raised it to her cheek and found tears. "I . . . don't know what happened there."

"Looked to me like your imagination was working overtime," he said.

Imagination: a safe explanation for something that had seemed so much more. "I suppose you don't have much use for imagination in your line of work."

"It's bad for the case, worse for the digestion."

D'Amato didn't smile. If it was a joke, he didn't find it any more amusing than she did. She reached out and took the tissues from him.

He leaned his forearm on top of the steering wheel and stared out at the rain-wet street. Her crying didn't seem to bother him. In a way, it didn't seem to register with him at all. Maybe he'd become immune to such things.

Her tears dried in the face of such arid insensibility. "Is there anything else, Detective D'Amato?"

"Actually, yes. I'd very much like to talk to your son."

She folded the wet tissue into a square, then a triangle, then another, smaller, triangle. "Jeff lives with his father. Have you spoken to Derek about it?"

"This morning. He says the boy came home around midnight the night your brother was killed and was home the rest of the night."

She hadn't expected that. "Well, there you go."

"I want to talk to the boy. Have you seen him or spoken to him since the night of the murder?"

"He called me just last night, as a matter of fact," she said, grateful to be able to tell the truth—for a change. "Ah, he said he was out with friends and that I wasn't to worry—"

"Why would you worry?"

"Mothers do."

D'Amato regarded her with his flat black gaze, his thumbnail scraping along his jaw in a gesture she realized was habitual. "When did he run away?"

She let her breath out in a long sigh. It couldn't be hidden any longer; the more she and Derek put the cops off, the more they were going to want to get their hands on Jeff.

"He ran the night after Cullen died," she said.

"Do you know why?"

"He's been on the edge of it for a long time. This thing with Cullen . . ." She forced the tissue into a still smaller triangle. It tore, and she tossed it into the trash pouch hanging from the dashboard. "He and Cullen were pretty close. My brother did well with kids. He connected with Jeff in a way he couldn't with Derek and me anymore."

"It happens," he said, pushing the washer button with an idleness that didn't fool her at all. "He's run away before this."

He's already contacted the Los Angeles police. The ground had just gotten a whole lot shakier. "Yes. Twice. That's why I sent him here to his father, hoping maybe a man could do more with him."

"Has he been doing drugs?"

"I don't know."

He didn't believe her, she knew. In his place, she wouldn't have, either. Even if it had been true. He regarded her steadily, and it was all she could do not to fidget like a guilty schoolkid. That damned Anglo-Saxon conscience of hers!

"Do you have a recent photo of your son?" he asked.

They had to look for him. Of course. "Why didn't you ask his father?"

"He had only snapshots, none of which was very good."

Connie stared at him for a moment, considering refusal. Then she pulled her purse into her lap and took out the photo she'd used in her search the day before. It wasn't a flattering picture of Jeff, but it was an accurate one. He didn't meet the camera's eye any more than he did hers these days; it had caught his sullen, uncompromising expression with painful accuracy.

After a moment, she handed it to D'Amato. He studied it for a while, then thrust it into the inside pocket of his jacket. "Thanks. I'll see that you get it back when I'm finished with it."

"Do you have children, Detective?"

His brows went up. "Three girls. Seventeen, fourteen, and ten."

"Are they good kids?"

"I think so."

"Do you *know?"*

"What do you mean?"

She zipped her purse closed. "I mean, do you follow them every moment of every day? Do you know for certain they're not smoking cigarettes or drinking a beer at a friend's house, or that the oldest one is sleeping with her boyfriend?"

"More of your imagination?"

Connie was pleased to hear an edge of annoyance in his voice. Good. "Probably," she said. "But unless you're with your kids every moment of every day, you can't know for sure. And you can't open up their heads and look in to see what tempts them—even if they don't do whatever it is. It's damn hard being a parent these days."

"Not for my kids. They walk the straight and narrow, believe me."

She pushed the door open and got out into the rain. Leaning in for a moment, she said, "I hope you never find out otherwise, Detective."

Chapter Ten

"Of course Cullen should be buried in the Matthias plot," Sandra said.

"Except, that isn't what he wanted," Penny said.

"Then why didn't he say so in his will?"

"Maybe he didn't feel he had to."

Sandra uncrossed her slim, elegant legs and leaned forward to place her teacup on the coffee table. She fit the rich but refined tone of Cullen's house, her neat red suit a bright contrast against the calm earthen tones of the beach house's great room. "You will not convince me, Penny."

"I don't know what to do," the younger woman said. Her hands shook as she reached up to smooth her hair.

Connie sighed. She'd badgered Sandra into this meeting here in the hopes of giving Penny a fighting chance. It didn't look as though it had done any good.

As though divining her thoughts, Sandra swung around to face her. "What do *you* think, Connie?"

"I'd rather remain neutral, if you don't mind."

"I do mind."

With another sigh, Connie set her own cup aside.

The time had come to decide her feelings. Did she want Penny to win because she thought Cullen wanted the cremation, or did she merely want to see Sandra beaten?

"Actually," she said, "I don't think Cullen would mind either way."

"That's a cop-out," Sandra said. "What do *you* say?"

"I'd like to see Cullen with the family," she said, thoroughly surprising herself. From the look on Sandra's face, it surprised her, too.

"Oh, all right!" Penny said. "It's not worth fighting about anymore. Cullen's dead, and nothing else matters."

She started to cry. Connie went to her, slipping her arm around her to offer what little comfort she could. She hadn't wanted to give her opinion; hadn't even been aware she had an opinion. But somehow, it seemed as though she could hold Cullen just a bit closer if he were in the graveyard.

"I'm sorry," she said.

Penny just shook her head. Sandra leaned forward to offer a dainty lace-trimmed handkerchief. Penny took it as though she didn't quite know what to do with it.

"You see, Penny," Sandra said. "Tradition is very important in our family. Whatever absurdities Cullen may have gotten into in the past year or so, he was and always *will* be a Matthias."

Connie looked up. "Gee, Mom, could you be just a little more pompous?"

The doorbell rang, fortunately. Actually, Connie thought, "rang" was an inaccurate word for that sound. The bell was a mellow chime that resonated with rich timbre, its tones proclaiming that this was a rich man's house.

Only Cullen wasn't; hadn't been.

She rose. "Do you want me to get it?"

"No, thanks." Penny dabbed at her cheeks, then got to her feet with less grace than usual.

Connie watched her until she disappeared into the foyer. "You know, Mom, you could have some sympathy for her. She's lost her husband, and now she isn't even going to get to bury him the way she wanted."

"She has the option to insist," Sandra said.

"But she won't, as you very well know."

"No Balestier would have given up the fight."

Connie rolled her eyes upward. "You make that sound like a virtue."

Sandra opened her mouth to say something but closed it again as Penny came back into the room with John Bruycker and Hamilton Liu. John walked straight toward the sofa, pausing to brush his fingertips down Connie's arm.

"I'm glad to meet you at last, Mrs. Matthias," he said, offering his hand to Sandra. "I've heard a lot about you."

"And I you." Her gaze darted past him to fasten on Hamilton Liu.

"Hamilton is our resident scholar," Penny said.

"Indeed?" Sandra's eyes looked more green than blue just then. "In what field?"

"He just got his master's in philosophy this year," John said. "He graduated *magna cum laude* from Berkeley."

Hamilton ducked his head. "My minor was in Eastern religion."

Connie wondered if he knew just how useless

Sandra would consider his studies. Perhaps he did; there was a spark in those dark, shielded eyes that might have been amusement.

"And what was your relationship to my son?" Sandra asked.

"We were kindred souls, Mrs. Matthias."

"Who'd like some tea?" Penny asked, just a little too loudly.

Sandra's machine-gun gaze never flickered. "Does your kindred soul tell you who murdered my son?"

"No," he said.

"Then I must say, it wasn't very useful."

He smiled. "Your daughter said the same thing yesterday."

"Then that is one thing on which she and I agree." Sandra's expression was one of crisp finality as she rose to her feet. "I'd best be going."

"But we haven't finished with the will," Penny protested.

"Obviously, this isn't a good time for you. Not with guests to entertain."

Penny put her hand on Hamilton's shoulder. "But John and Hamilton are just like family."

"Not my family," Sandra said, with a gentleness unmatched by her eyes. "But feel free to continue when I'm gone."

Somehow, she seemed larger than she was, Connie thought. So had Cullen. Two of a kind, just a half-turn apart. If anyone was the kindred spirit here, it was Sandra. Then she turned and walked out, leaving the rest of them in a sort of stunned silence.

"Wow," Hamilton said after a moment. "Is she always like that?"

Connie grimaced. "Unfortunately."

"She's in great pain," John said. "Maybe more than any of us."

Maybe. But Connie knew her mother would wall it away as she'd done all her life, and just keep on with her volunteering, her campaigning, and her parties. After a while, the wall would become part of her natural boundaries and she'd forget anything existed on the other side.

With a shrug, Connie went on. No one had ever been able to change Sandra; no one ever would. "Are you sure you want to go over the will now, Penny?"

"Let's get it over with. And it's 'Phaedra.' "

Connie was beginning to empathize with her mother's obdurate refusal to use the new name. But instead of saying anything, she went back to her seat on the sofa and pulled the will out of her purse. John sat down beside her at a noncommittal distance; close enough to be friendly, far enough away not to encroach. Hamilton took Penny's arm and sat her down in the chair, then perched on the arm beside her.

"Okay," Connie said. "Cullen left everything to his wife. That includes the savings account, which is approximately twenty thousand dollars, the checking account in the amount of one thousand, twelve dollars and seventy-eight cents—"

"You did your homework," Hamilton said.

She shot him a glance. "I'm an accountant." Without looking at the document, she continued, "and finally, his insurance policy for fifty thousand dollars. Unfortunately, that won't be paid until there's been some resolution about his death."

"But . . ." Penny blinked rapidly, and Connie

braced herself for more tears. "How am I supposed to live without it?"

"Try to manage on the twenty thousand," Connie said.

"But for how long?" Penny asked.

Connie spread her hands. "Ask Detective D'Amato. I suppose you can talk to a lawyer about dealing with the insurance company, but the guy I talked to this afternoon didn't seem willing to bend. Your best bet right now would be to tighten your belt and try to make the money go as far as you can make it. Maybe the owners of the house will let you out of the lease, considering the circumstances."

"This house belongs to Philip and Evvie," Hamilton said.

"Cullen leased it from them?" John asked.

"Actually, they just let him use it. No money ever changed hands."

It was Connie's turn to blink. Not from tears, however; from astonishment. "They had, like, an extra five-hundred-thousand-dollar house lying around?"

"Well, yes." Hamilton ran his hands through his straight blue-black hair. "They're very wealthy. This is only one of several homes they own here and elsewhere."

A whole vista sprang into existence in Connie's mind, a landscape paved with money and booby-trapped with greed. It didn't necessarily change the situation, but mix people and dollars and . . . "How do you know so much about it, Hamilton?"

"I've known them for years. They're friends of my family's and even lent me the money for my college education. Very generous people. I only hope I live long enough to pay them back."

Connie folded the will neatly and thrust it back into her purse. "The Mercedes is theirs, too?"

Hamilton nodded.

"I knew about the car," Penny said. "But I thought Cullen was paying them for the use of the house."

Connie stared at her incredulously. "How could you not know a thing like that?"

"Cullen never bothered me with money matters."

Connie's thoughts must have been showing on her face, because Penny's tone became defensive. "Not everyone has your interest in numbers, Connie. My husband was a good provider and he was always generous with me, so as long as he wanted to handle the financial things, I was willing to let him."

With a mental throwing-up-of-hands, Connie turned back to Hamilton. "Did you introduce the Wahlfields to Cullen?"

He nodded. "They've always been interested in the mystical. When I met Cullen, I knew I'd found the real thing. As soon as they spoke to him, they knew it, too. Letting him use the house benefited all of us. Many forces abide in this spot, things Cullen could feel and tap into."

A spasm of pain brought Connie's gaze to her hands. They'd tightened on her purse until the knuckles stood out in pale ridges beneath the skin. Aware that John was looking at them, too, she forced herself to relax.

"We know you don't believe any of this," Hamilton said. "But Cullen did. Cullen *lived* it."

She felt trapped beneath their regard. Surging to her feet, she started pacing along the edge of the carpet. "Why did you pick Cullen as your leader?"

"We didn't pick him," John said. "It just happened. We centered around him, around what he was—"

"And especially around what he would be," Hamilton said.

John nodded. "We're very diverse people, you know; only someone of Cullen's talent could have brought us together and forged us into a cohesive whole."

"Will they want the house back?" Penny asked.

The men swung around to her, obviously thrown by the question. "Who?" John asked.

Fear shone in Penny's eyes and bleached her face from ivory to chalk. For the first time, she looked her age. "What am I going to do if they want the house back?"

"I wouldn't worry—" John began.

"Cullen said he'd always take care of me," Penny said, a wild, lost note creeping into her voice. "Now he's gone and everything is falling apart. Our lives were so beautiful. How many couples can say they adored each other after ten years? How many can share the spiritual and the physical the way we did? We had it all. And now it's all been taken away."

She paused for breath, and this time Hamilton tried to stem the tide. "Phaedra, you can't—"

"I can, I can," she said, in that same lost voice. "I can't bear to leave. This was *our* place. I used to sleep secure with his arms around me, secure that our future would always be shared. Now I sleep alone. I have no future, no home, no one to dream with." She raised her hands, and they fluttered like graceful white birds as she smoothed her hair back. "If I leave here, I'll lose him completely. I don't think I could stand that. Oh, God, maybe they'll sell the house, and Cullen will have no one but strangers—"

"Penny!" Connie said loudly.

The other woman let her breath out in a gasp, staring as though she'd just awakened from a nightmare. Then she started to cry, great, gulping sobs that sounded like they'd come from deep in her soul. Hamilton put his arm around her shoulders. She half-turned, burying her face against his chest. His eyes blazed raw with sympathy.

Catching his gaze, Connie thrust her thumb toward the stairs. He nodded. Somehow he managed to slide down from the chair arm without dislodging Penny, then pulled her up with him and led her out.

"Well, *that* went well," John said.

"Maybe we should call her doctor."

He spread his hands. "Her sedatives are upstairs; other than those, I don't think there's anything a doctor can do to help her. Cullen was her life, you know. It's going to take time for her to find another reason to live."

"Jeez."

With a smile that was a bit more sharp-edged than usual, he rose and went to her. "You'd never let a man take over your life so completely, would you?"

"I can't imagine I would."

He didn't touch her. In a way, it would've been easier if he had; the demand would have been physical instead of emotional. There was no escaping the need in his eyes, or the awareness that her own need matched his. She felt her nostrils flare, a betrayal she wouldn't have made if she could have helped it.

"You've got something interesting running

around in that sharp little mind of yours. I can almost see the wheels turning. Want to share?"

"Uh-uh. I just have this way of sliding everything into its proper slot, and a minute ago all the slots changed."

"You mean the Wahlfields."

She nodded. "Did you know they owned this house?"

"No. None of us did, other than Cullen; I'm convinced of that."

"Except Hamilton Liu."

"Except Hamilton," he agreed. "I wonder why he never said anything about it."

So did Connie. With a touch of lightness she didn't feel, she said, "One thing for sure: if you tell him a secret, it'll stay a secret."

"I wonder if the Wahlfields will want their house back."

"That's not my business," Connie said. "Even if they do, Cullen may not have left a fortune, but he left enough to give Penny a pretty good start."

"You mean a job?" His lips quirked as though he didn't quite dare smile at the idea. "Can you see Phaedra working behind a cash register?"

"Maybe not. But Penny Draper worked for a living before she married Cullen, and if I'm not mistaken, she has a BA in English."

"Or maybe she'll convince Hamilton to talk to them about letting her stay here. He can be very persuasive."

A subtle touch of disapproval colored his voice. So subtle, in fact, that Connie might have missed it if she hadn't known him as well as she had.

You've only known him a few days, idiot.

True enough. But they'd come together in the

tragedy of Cullen's death, and that had broken down the barriers she normally kept up. Her feelings for him were deeply primal, as visceral and compelling as anything she'd ever experienced. A not entirely comfortable feeling, but one she didn't want to give up.

"I wish it was summer," he said.

Startled, she looked up at him. "Huh?"

"I'd like to sail away with you for a couple of months to someplace where I could drown you with attention. Just for a while, I'd like that oh-so-rational mind of yours focused only on me."

"Don't hold your breath."

His voice dropped to a whisper. "What if I made love to you the whole time?"

"I might be awed," she said. "But never stupefied."

"I'd like to see you let go," he murmured. "Really, truly let go."

"I thought I let go last night."

He smiled. "That was sex. People hide behind the physical, especially you, Ms. Accountant. Most men are satisfied with that."

"Why aren't you?"

"Because it isn't enough. In your own way, you're as deep as Cullen, and vastly more complex. No straightforwardness there; it's all twists and turns and different levels, and all designed to protect you. There's a whole world in you that you haven't let me see. And I want it."

She stared at him, disturbed by what he thought he saw in her. Most of her wanted to draw back. But a small, treacherous part of her found it exciting to be thought so deep and devious and mysterious. She hated that part, that Achilles heel of the soul.

"If that is inside me—" She held up her hand to stop him from protesting. *"If* that is in me, then it belongs only to me."

"Are you sure?" he asked softly.

He moved closer. Although he still didn't touch her, she could feel him, feel his warmth, his need. She didn't want to be like this. But she also loved walking the edge, taking the risk that he might take something she'd rather keep for herself. It put substance into the emptiness Cullen had left in her and kept the darkness at bay.

His eyes seemed to suck her in, wrap her up and pull her under.

She'd already survived drowning once.

"Yes," she said, breasting the tide. "I'm sure."

He reached out, sifting his fingers through her hair. It wasn't an imperative touch, merely a memory of what had been and a promise of what was to be. "Cullen used to show us pictures of you. There was one taken in California, on the beach. I didn't know why, then, but that picture hit me like a ton of bricks. Your hair was blowing in the wind and looked like an iridescent black curtain against the sky."

Connie closed her eyes against the demand in his. "It's just plain black, John. No magic there."

"That's where you're wrong. Cullen called you the 'Indian Princess,' said you looked just like your great-grandma."

"Great-*great*-grandmother," she corrected automatically.

"Are you like her in other ways?"

She opened her eyes. "She was a child on the Trail of Tears. Her mother died during the trek, and her father a short time later."

"That's one hell of a family story."

"She never told it," Connie said. "Dad came across it in some old family papers."

John looked genuinely astonished. "Why didn't she?"

"She'd survived. And maybe to her, that was enough."

"There has to be more than just surviving."

"Sometimes there is, sometimes not."

"You don't frighten me, Connie."

It was her turn for astonishment. "Why would I?"

"Isn't that what you do, intimidate every guy who tries to get close to you?"

"I don't—"

"You do."

"I let you suck my toes," she said.

He drew his breath in, a harsh sound of surprise and, judging from his eyes, remembrance. "It's a beginning."

"So don't expect the brass ring when the ride's hardly started."

"Setting limits?"

"I have a feeling that's going to be a necessity with you."

He curved his fingers around the back of her skull with brief but definite pressure, then let his hand slide away from her hair. "Like Cullen, I recognize no limitations."

Connie blinked through a sudden refraction of tears. "Cullen found his limitations, though, didn't he?"

He didn't answer. She retrieved her purse, then headed toward the foyer.

"I want to see you tonight," he said.

"Why?"

"Because I want to."

No other answer would have compelled her. And still inside her was that terrible empty place that might swallow her whole if it weren't for him. Her skin prickled with a sudden chill at the thought of being left alone with nothing but that.

She wanted him, maybe too much. Why him? Because he kept the coldness away, and that, even for a few hours, was precious. So she swung back around to look at him. For a moment, she thought she might drown in his eyes. Damn.

"I'll be at the new place, unpacking," she said.

Chapter Eleven

The sun shone brightly the day of Cullen's funeral. Connie stood between her mother and Penny and watched the light strike metal-flake sparks on the coffin. The wind blew cool against her face, bringing her an overwhelming smell of roses from the funeral bouquets. Cullen hadn't liked roses.

She shifted focus to the people who stood at the other side of the coffin. John looked very dramatic with his coat flapping around him and his dark hair flaring on the wind. The Wahlfields' faces were slick with tears, in stark contrast to Hamilton Liu's impassiveness. Amy Cortez and her daughter looked as though they didn't quite know what to do with their faces and were waiting for someone to tell them. Connie couldn't understand what Cullen had seen in these two; mother and daughter seemed equally unformed, equally unsure of their place in the world.

Behind them stood a number of other people who had known Cullen: co-workers, college friends, a newspaperman quietly taking pictures. Connie spotted Detective D'Amato off to one side. His hair looked like iron filings in the uncompromising light.

Even Derek had come. It shouldn't have surprised her; Cullen had gotten along with her ex-husband as well as he had everyone else. Derek looked lean and rangy in his dark suit, and definitely uncomfortable. He joined D'Amato, obviously feeling unwelcome in the circle of more intimate mourners.

Her attention flicked back to the minister as he began the "Ashes to ashes, dust to dust" part, and found herself flinching away from it. Not Cullen. Her breath started to come hard and fast. She tried to hold it back, but it seemed to be tied into her grief and not under her control at all.

Sandra reached over and took her hand in a grip that made her gasp. "Don't embarrass me," she whispered.

The outrageousness of it steadied Connie. With anyone but Sandra, she might have been surprised. But Sandra was Sandra, and propriety was probably her only support just now. So Connie squeezed back as hard as she could, and the two of them stood locked in pain as they watched Cullen's friends come to lay flowers atop his coffin.

Once, she shot a glance at Penny. Her black suit stole the color from her face, making it look garish beneath the fashionable hat and veil. But, fortified with Valium, she seemed to be holding up well enough. Her lips moved. Connie thought she said, "Goodbye, Cullen."

It was too much. Connie had to look away, lest the tightness in her chest expand and choke her. Her gaze skittered over the coffin, rested for a moment on John. He stared back, the desire to comfort her plain on his face. But his raw emotion was too much to bear right now, and so she shifted yet again.

And found herself looking at her son. She went

very still. He'd cut his hair, and the change in appearance was startling. Her gaze cut to D'Amato. He huddled over a portable phone, his shoulders shielding his actions from the crowd. All he had to do was look up. She didn't think the haircut would fool him.

She looked again at her son. The sacrificial lamb in her brother's slaughter.

Not yet. Not on D'Amato's terms, but on hers.

Get out of here!

Derek stepped into her field of view. He carried a rose for Cullen's coffin, but his gaze was on her. Urgent. Imperative. She knew he'd seen Jeff, too. And she knew what he wanted.

She had to do it; no one else could.

With a cry, she let herself fall backward. Locked as they were, Sandra had no choice but to go down with her.

"Look out!" Derek shouted. "She's fainted!"

The ground hit Connie hard in the back, driving most of her breath away. Then Sandra's elbow landed in her midriff, and she almost *did* faint.

She wanted nothing more than to curl up around her belly, but forced herself to lie still. Even with her eyes closed, she knew it was John who reached her first. He slipped his hand behind her head, apparently feeling for a wound.

"Ohhh," she moaned, letting her eyes flutter open. "What happened?"

"You fainted."

Peering faces made a background for John's. Derek's was not among them. For once, she was glad he was quick on the uptake. She let John lever her to a sitting position. Penny was nowhere to be seen; probably Hamilton had spirited her away.

Sandra, however, had stayed. Although her face was composed, she hadn't smoothed her tumbled white hair.

"Sorry, Mom," Connie said. "Are you all right?"

"Right enough. You?"

Connie nodded. Then D'Amato pushed through the crowd, blocking her view of her mother, and went down on one knee beside her.

"You okay, Miss Matthias?" he asked. "I can call for an ambulance."

"No, thanks. I'm fine, really. I just feel kind of stupid, falling over like that."

With a grunt, D'Amato got to his feet. He stood for a moment looking down at Connie with eyes that seemed to look straight through her. "You know, for a minute there I thought you'd seen a ghost."

"If there's a ghost here," she said, "it's only somebody's guilty conscience."

He smiled. "Nothing truer."

"Help me up, John," she said.

Bruises on bruises, she thought, wincing as she flexed her muscles. Oh, well. It was worth it. She watched D'Amato walk away, his square body as unambiguous as his stride.

"Come on," John said. "I'll take you home."

She shook her head. "Not today; there's something I've got to do." He looked like he was about to protest, and she laid her hand over his mouth. "Come by later."

His eyes were reluctant; but he nodded, acquiescing. She let her hand linger on his mouth for a moment, then turned and hurried after D'Amato. "Hey! Detective!"

D'Amato ground to a halt, then turned to watch

her as she came up. "Pretty spry for someone who just fainted," he said.

"I've never fainted before," she replied. "How is one supposed to act?"

"Fall into your hero's arms," he growled.

"Gee, Sergeant, I didn't know you had such romantic ideas."

"My wife is training me."

"I've got the will. Do you want me to read it to you while you drive me home?"

He absorbed the shift with impressive aplomb. "Absolutely."

Holding out his arm in a mockingly gallant gesture, he led her to his car. He even opened the door for her.

Connie didn't speak until he'd pulled away from the curb. "Are you shocked?" she asked.

"Let's say surprised."

"Why? Don't people cooperate in your investigations?"

"Not generally, no."

D'Amato accelerated smoothly onto the interstate, his blunt-fingered hands sure upon the wheel. Connie waited for him to ask directions, then abruptly realized he didn't need any.

"I only moved in yesterday," she said.

He shot her an enigmatic glance with those long-lashed Latin eyes. "We like to keep up on things."

She stared at him for a moment, contemplating the ramifications of that, then pulled the will out of her purse and started to read.

He interrupted once to ask, "Your brother didn't own that house? Who the hell does it belong to, then?"

"The Wahlfields."

"The older couple? Jesus Christ."

She finished reading. He sat for a while, his face, even in profile, intensely curious. She knew he, too, saw a whole new vista enfolding.

"Very interesting," he said at last.

"I thought you might find it so."

"Of course. That's why you decided to give it to me."

Her hands felt suddenly cold, her fingers stiff as she folded the will and put it back in her purse. "I don't know what you mean."

He shot her another glance. "Sure you do."

Using her fingers, Connie tried to rake her hair into some semblance of order. "I expect solving a murder is kind of like a jigsaw puzzle. You have to have all the pieces to put it together."

"That's sort of true," he said. "But I don't need all the pieces."

"Just enough to convict?"

"That's the way the system works, Ms. Matthias. Beyond reasonable doubt."

Black candles and pentagrams surely fell into the category "beyond reasonable doubt." Connie shifted back so that she wasn't quite facing him.

"Have you talked to the Wahlfields?" she asked.

"Only superficially."

"You mean they weren't directly under suspicion like the rest of us?"

He smiled, a quick slash of a grin that had little humor in it. "It's my job to suspect."

"Only not rich, elderly eccentrics?"

"What the hell do you want from me?" he growled.

"I want you to see that this is a whole lot more

complicated than it seems. And that there is more than one possible scenario for my brother's death."

"Why do you want me to think that, Ms. Matthias?"

She let her breath out in a sigh of exasperation. "Talking to you is like walking through a snake pit."

"That's my job, too."

"Do you have a favorite candidate for murderer?"

The question didn't seem to faze him at all. "I do."

"Who is it?"

He turned his head to look at her, ignoring the road long enough for her to get nervous. "I can't tell you that."

"Why not?"

"You know too much as it is."

That got her adrenaline surging. "What do you mean by that?"

"You haven't told me the truth. Or all of it."

"Psychic ability, Detective?" She was glad her voice didn't shake.

"Policeman's gut," he shot back. "Now, I also sense that you're a straight-up person, and that this lack of truth bothers you. I work on motivations a lot: what made this guy want to kill this other guy? Was it money or drugs, or maybe a woman? So when I look at you, I wonder what your motivation might be for holding back."

There were a lot of possible answers to that, all of which were dangerous for Jeff. "Better try the psychic ability next time, Detective. Your gut is wrong." She glanced out the side window, registered a familiar storefront. "My street's coming up at the next light."

"I know."

He didn't ask any more questions and she didn't volunteer any information. The air in the car was thick with tension. Connie was very glad when D'Amato pulled to a stop in front of the old farmhouse.

"Thanks for the ride." She swung the door open, sure now of escape.

"Ms. Matthias." He laid his arm over the back of the seat and leaned toward her. "You're smart enough to realize that you might be protecting your brother's killer. If it were me, I'd be having some trouble sleeping at night."

"What makes you think I sleep?" She didn't like the savagery in her voice, liked even less that he heard it, too.

"Goodnight," he said. "Pleasant dreams."

His tires squealed as he drove away. Connie was left with the dubious satisfaction of knowing she'd gotten to him almost as much as he'd gotten to her.

Am I wrong?

He's my son.

But am I wrong?

There were no answers, and there was certainly no logic. And since the sunlight was too bright and cheerful for her mood, she turned and went inside.

"Hey, Connie!" Mr. Ranke called, stopping her with her foot on the bottom step.

She turned to see her landlord come out of his apartment. Derek came out behind him. She could tell by his eyes that he hadn't caught up with Jeff.

"You've got company," the older man said. "Ex-husband."

"Come on up, Derek," she said. "Thanks, Mr. Ranke."

"I like the old buzzard," Derek said, when they were out of earshot.

"I do, too," she said. "He helped me move furniture around."

"I thought you'd have the boyfriend do that."

She paused, glancing over her shoulder at him. "I want the boyfriend for other things."

"Oooh," he said. "Nasty, aren't we?"

"Derek, do you want to end this conversation right here?"

Some of the heat left his eyes. "I'm sorry. I was out of line, I guess."

"You guessed right."

"Truce?"

She sighed, feeling somehow that she was making a mistake. "Okay. Truce."

Her furniture looked good in the apartment, the southwest-print sofa and loveseat bright splashes of color against the pale oak flooring. She'd always been spare when it came to furnishings; other than the sofa and loveseat, a few modern floor lamps, the coffee table, and a trio of bookcases on the far wall, only space dominated the room. Maybe someday she'd bring some plants in to enjoy the sun.

Derek seemed ill at ease in her apartment, cruising around touching one knickknack or another while she made coffee. That was fair enough; shc was ill at easc having him here.

"Jeff got away," she said.

"Yeah. I couldn't actually run after him without attracting D'Amato's attention. By the way, that was a great fainting act."

"I've acquired a lot of new skills due to Jeff. Fainting, lying to the police—things like that."

He turned abruptly and sat down on the sofa. Wriggling out of his jacket, he tossed it carelessly on the cushion beside him. Never a fashion plate, Derek Valle. But the sunlight burnished his hair and cast buttery gleams over his face, erasing the lines and softening the long jaw. For a moment, he looked like the impulsive, passionate kid she'd loved so desperately and disastrously all those years ago.

Not an image she wanted to see. So she turned to the prosaic business of pouring coffee. "Do you still take your coffee black?" she asked.

"Yeah. Do you still tart yours up with a half-pound of sugar and enough cream to clog your arteries?"

"It's my one vice."

She poured two mugs, one black, one pale and sweet, and carried them out to the living room.

"Thanks," he said. "I'm half blind from lack of sleep."

"That makes two guilty consciences," she muttered.

"What?"

"Nothing." She sat in the loveseat opposite him and spent some time stirring her coffee while she got her thoughts in order. "Thanks for helping me out today."

"He's my son, too."

"Yeah. Sometimes that's hard for me to remember."

He took a long draught of coffee. "Why don't we agree to trust each other, Connie? For his sake."

Setting her cup down, she studied him. Trust was

a fragile thing with Jeff's fate in the balance. "Why did you tell the police that Jeff came home early the night Cullen died?"

"Because it seemed important to you that the police not think he wasn't home. And whatever differences we've had in the past, I know you love that boy and would do anything to protect him."

"Even lie to the police."

He spread his hands. "What's a lie when it's your son?"

She let her breath out in a long sigh. It had been an act of faith for this man, one for which he could expect little reward. And it demanded trust from her.

"Okay, Derek." Leaning forward, she set her mug on the coffee table. "When I found Cullen, he lay at the center of a pentagram, and there were black candles at his head, his hands, and his feet."

Derek's breath went out with a *whoosh,* and for a moment he looked like a man who'd been punched in the stomach. "Oh, God. Satanism."

"Right. Now, what do you think D'Amato would do if he found out that Jeff had been picked up for stealing skulls from a graveyard for some ritual he and his buddies had cooked up?"

"He'd have his case all locked up."

"And the rest of Jeff's life would be spent either in prison or in a hospital for the criminally insane."

He raked his hands through his hair, a gesture that was viscerally familiar even after all these years. "Big trouble, Connie."

"Yeah."

"Do you think Jeff did it?"

She went very still, her being coiled around that question. "Do I think my son killed my brother?"

"Yeah."

Echoes of pain roughened his voice. She understood it, for it was her pain. "That's a hell of a question."

"I've got to know. *You've* got to know."

"What?"

"Whether we're protecting him because he's innocent, or because he's our son."

She rose with a surge that sent the loveseat sliding back a few inches. Striding to the window, she stared down at the neatly mown lawn. Dust motes swirled around her, tiny worldlets cast upon a sea of light. She felt cold, even here in the sun.

"Mr. Ranke sure takes good care of this place," she said.

"Yes, he does. And he watches over his tenants pretty good, too."

She held her hand out, palm up, and watched as a speck of dust settled on it. "You've changed, Derek. When we were married, you'd never have let me slide away from the issue like that."

"That was fifteen years ago," he said. "We've both changed. Back then, you'd have gone cold and silent on me, then shut yourself away into some world of your own."

"I was silent now."

"Not the same. There's a difference between taking time to think and shutting someone else out of your life."

She turned, placing her back against the glass, and studied this man to whom she'd been married so briefly. There were gold flecks in his hazel eyes. She'd forgotten that. "How long were you married to Mary?"

"Four years. How long were you with Brandon?"

"Seven and a half years."

He grimaced. "You lasted longer than I did."

"What do you think happened? With Jeff, I mean."

"I don't know."

She tried to rub warmth into her arms. "We used to be so innocent at that age. Life was so much simpler than it is now."

"Maybe for you, Connie. But I came close to running away so many times I forget to count."

She stared at him in astonishment. "Why?"

"Dad used to drink a lot. When he did, he'd beat us kids . . . just because. Sunday afternoons were the worst."

Connie ducked her head, digesting this startling information. She'd always liked her father-in-law; sometimes, more than she'd liked her husband. "He seemed like such a nice guy."

"He was to the outside world. He saved the other stuff for his family."

"Why didn't you tell me?"

"It wasn't the kind of thing you go around telling."

"Come on, Derek. Not even your wife?"

He lifted one shoulder, let it fall. "Okay, I should have. But I was eighteen years old, trying damn hard to be a man. The one example I had, I didn't want to follow. So I screwed up a lot."

We were too young, she thought. We needed too much, both of us, and didn't have the resources to give it. What a waste. "Jeff hated Brandon."

"We're even there. Did you know he used to hang up on me when I called?"

"*I* used to hang up on you."

"But you always let me talk to Jeff, even if you

had him call me back after you hung up on me. Brandon didn't."

She nodded, accepting the truth of it. "Brandon was a prick, no doubt about it. I'm sorry."

"Me, too. For a lot of things."

With an abrupt movement, she pushed away from the window and went to sit down again. "Your father beat you, but neither of us has laid a hand on Jeff. I tried to balance love and discipline, and I can't say I can criticize your fairness with him. But it just seems as though he started spinning away from me, and the harder I try to reel him in, the faster he goes."

"Maybe he just got lost. It happens."

"Not to my son," she said. "Not without a fight."

Derek leaned forward, reaching across the coffee table to tilt her face into the light. "You don't think he did it."

At another time, she might have drawn away. But those hazel eyes reflected everything she was feeling, and she needed to be able to share this with someone who had almost as much to lose as she did. "I gave him life," she said. "I raised him. I watched him take his first step, heard his first word, helped him ride a bike for the first time."

"Does that mean he isn't capable of killing another human being?"

"It should." *Oh, it should.*

He sighed, a harsh sound. "Sometimes I think logic isn't all it's cracked up to be."

"You don't think he did it?"

"Ah, Connie." With a harsh sigh, he let go of her and sat back. "Everywhere I look, I see the words 'not my son.' My hunting knife is missing, I say 'not my son.' I hear Jeff puking his guts out in the toilet the morning after the murder, and I say 'not my son.' "

"You're talking about faith. I've never been good with that."

"Yeah, I know. Good old facts and figures."

"They're more dependable."

"Not always." He leaned forward again. "Look, I'm a firefighter, not a philosopher. But there've been times when the only way out of a burning building wasn't the logical one. When it's life or death, I listen to my instinct. Or impulse or blind faith, or whatever you want to call it. It's saved my life more than once."

For one brief, terrible moment, Connie thought he was going to touch her again. She put up her hands in mute protest; contact just now might have shattered her. Slowly, he curled his hands into fists and held them propped on his knees. "Look, Connie, you can't straddle the fence on this one. You have to decide what you believe. Did Jeff do it, or didn't he? We can't help him, really help him, until you do."

She wanted to look away from those intense hazel eyes but couldn't. He wanted as much from her as John did. No, demanded. And because it involved her son, the risk was so much greater.

The unexpected knock on her door nearly sent her bolting out of her seat. But it also broke the brimming tension in the room, releasing her, for the moment at least, from Derek's gaze.

"Excuse me," she said, rising to answer the door.

And found John waiting on the other side. She hesitated, overly conscious of Derek behind her, then stepped aside. "Come in."

He obeyed, but stopped short when he saw Derek. "Ah, I think I came at a bad time."

"No, it's all right," she said. "Derek, John. John, Derek."

"The boyfriend," Derek said.

John strode forward, hand outstretched. He was several inches shorter than Derek, but she found herself watching him almost exclusively. His eyes were noncommittal, the set of his shoulders less so. Derek rose to meet him, and the two men shook hands with the gingerliness of males who hadn't yet decided who was top dog.

Men! Connie thought. No wonder teenage boys were such a mess.

The men stared into each other's eyes, assessing, challenging. "And you are . . . ?" John asked.

"The ex-husband."

"Oh," John said, visibly relaxing. "Jeff."

"Right." Derek swept his jacket up from the sofa and stepped toward the door. He paused for a moment to look down at Connie, his gaze hooded. "We've got some more to talk about . . . as soon as you're able."

"I'll call you tomorrow."

"Fine. Thanks for the coffee."

He brushed past her and went out. She heard him call goodbye to Mr. Ranke, then the sound of an engine as he drove off. With a sigh, she closed the door and turned to face John.

"Was it bad?" he asked.

"Jeff's run away."

"Ah, Connie, I'm sorry. Do you know why?"

She ought to tell him. He'd understand. Looking into his pale, beautiful eyes, she saw that he *wanted* to understand. But Jeff was not his son. Strange as it was, no one but Derek could share this pain; no one loved Jeff as much as she and Derek.

"No," she said. "I don't know why. Jeff has had a lot of problems in the past couple of years, and it's only getting worse."

He came to her then, folding her against him. She leaned her cheek against his shirt, listening to the strong, steady beat of his heart. He smelled like the sun-tinged outdoors. Slowly, warmth seeped into her skin, taking some of the chill off the icy knot in her chest.

"I'm sorry," he said. "I wish there were something I could do."

"There is." She laid her hand flat against his chest. "Just hold me. Keep me warm. Just for a while, make me forget."

"Jeff?"

"Everything," she said. "Everything."

Chapter Twelve

Jeff woke alone. The rankness of too many bodies and too few baths still filled the one-room cottage, punctuated by the flat oregano smell of stale pizza.

"Hey, where did everybody go?" he mumbled.

He felt like shit this morning . . . afternoon, he amended, glancing at the clock beside the bed. Christ. With a groan, he stumbled into the bathroom to pee.

Suddenly, Tick's face appeared in the window behind the toilet. Jeff reeled backward, spraying urine all over the bathroom. The other boy rapped urgently on the glass.

Avoiding the dribbles, Jeff went to raise the window. Fresh air surged into the room, bringing everything in clearer focus than he would have liked. Tick looked like the walking dead: pale skinny face, eyes sunk in blue-black shadows, hair lying in limp clumps along his cheeks.

"You oughta eat something," Jeff said.

"No shit." Tick swiped his nose with his sleeve. "The cops are lookin' for you, man. C'mon."

"Fuck." Panic rose like thick paste in Jeff's throat. His hands shook as he searched his pockets for money. He came up with a ten and maybe a half-dozen ones. "Where's my money?"

"We bought that crack, remember?"

Vaguely. Real vaguely. "Two hundred dollars' worth?"

"There were nine of us, man. Now, come on. The cop just went into the place next door. You gonna wait until he's got a view clear up your asshole?"

Jeff ran into the other room and scrabbled around until he found his shoes. Snatching his backpack, he slung it over his shoulders and tore outside. Tick hustled around the corner of the building, grabbed his arm, and led him down toward the beach. The sand sucked at their feet as they ran, and it didn't take long for Tick to start slowing down.

Jeff glanced over his shoulder in time to see a man go into the cottage he'd just vacated, then come out again a minute later and scan the surrounding area. "Come on," he panted, tugging on Tick's arm. "We gotta get out of here."

"Hey, you kids!" a man called behind them. "Wait up, I want to talk to you!"

Jeff started running up toward the road. If they could make it across, they'd be able to lose the guy in the neighborhood on the other side. A few steps behind him, Tick was blowing hard, his feet foundering in the sand. Jeff reached back and caught him by the shirt, hauling him along with the strength of terror. He didn't want the cops. They'd throw him in a cell, ask him questions about Uncle Cullen . . . "Come on, Tick!" he gasped.

Tires screeched behind them as they pelted across the road. They ran through one yard, changed direction, then ran through two more before Jeff pulled his companion into the shelter of someone's hedge. A dark car sped past, its engine hooting like the guy was really punching it.

"Oh, God," Tick gasped, clutching his chest with both hands, "I think I'm gonna have a heart attack."

"Shut up," Jeff said, as the car came back the other way. "He's going."

They waited a while longer. When the cop didn't come back, they dared to crawl out of their hiding place at last. Jeff skinned out of the backpack and let it drop to the ground. Unzipping it, he pulled out a couple of sweatshirts.

"Put this on," he said, tossing one to Tick.

"What for?"

"They're bound to call in a description. That won't be for a kid wearing a Redskins' sweatshirt, will it?"

"Hey, cool." Tick slipped it on over his own shirt.

Jeff slipped the other shirt on, then added a baseball cap that said, "Firefighters like it hot." "We'd better split up for a while. They're looking for two of us."

"Okay. When do you want to meet up again?"

"Just after dark, in St. Mary's Cemetery."

"Fuck. I hate cemeteries."

Jeff slipped the backpack on again and adjusted his hat lower down on his forehead. "Wait outside the gate if you're scared."

"I'm not scared."

"Whatever. Look, man, we'd better get going. Thanks for comin' by to warn me." Reaching into his pocket, he pulled out the ten and gave it to Tick. "Get yourself something to eat. You look like friggin' Dracula."

Tick giggled. "See you later."

Jeff took off, leaving his friend still laughing behind him. Man, Tick didn't get it at all. This was serious. Maybe Mom had told the cops about the pentagram and the candles. Probably.

He looked down at his hands, trying to imagine them holding a knife, trying to imagine driving it into his uncle's chest. Closing his fist, he brought it down in a sharp stabbing motion. Just to see what it felt like. Was it familiar?

"I don't know," he muttered. "I don't know."

The houses seemed to stare at him with empty glass eyes. Watching him. Judging him. Fucking suburbia. But just for a second, he felt a pang of homesickness. Just for a second, he wished life would become normal again. Clean sheets, clean clothes, a place that was safe. A place where cops didn't come around looking for him.

"Shit," he said, louder this time. "Want your mommy back, huh? Well, your mommy thinks you murdered her brother."

Better wish for something real: like having his two hundred bucks back. If he hadn't bought the crack, he could have bought a bus ticket back to California. He could have stayed with Benny; Benny would have helped him.

Sure. Benny had told the police that robbing the graves had been Jeff's idea. It hadn't, but who'd believe it? Not Mom.

He spent most of the day moving around, not daring to drop in at the usual hangouts because of the police. Dinner took most of his money. With the rest, he bought some Jolt . . . for the jolt. He was down to change now.

The sun turned orange and then red, but for all its

fiery color, didn't seem to put much heat on the street. He pulled his jacket out of his backpack and pulled it on, wishing once again that he hadn't spent that two hundred dollars. Tonight was going to be a bitch.

Someone honked softly. Glancing over his shoulder, he saw the blue Taurus. He considered running. But his feet hurt, he was broke, and his terror the other night had been pure paranoia. So caution, not flight, was the ticket.

The car matched his pace. The driver's window rolled down with electric smoothness, and then he saw the man's face, a white blur in the shadowy inside of the car. Sunglasses bisected the pale face.

"Hi, Jeff."

He stopped. The car stopped.

"Feeling better tonight?" the man asked.

"Yeah."

"I was only trying to help you, you know."

Jeff shrugged, wishing he remembered why he'd been so afraid. Right now, he only felt cold and tired. "I guess so. I'd been smokin'."

"I understand. Do you want a ride somewhere?"

"Not home." Warily.

"Did I say home?" The man smiled. "Wherever you want, of course."

Jeff walked toward the car. The lock clicked upward to let him in, clicked downward again once he'd settled into the seat. He kept his backpack on his lap.

"Are you doing okay?" the man asked.

"I can take care of myself."

"I never doubted it." The man eased out into traffic. "Where to?"

"St. Mary's Cemetery."

Eyebrows rose above the sunglasses. "Are you planning to sleep there?"

"Nah. I'm meeting somebody."

"Do you need money?"

Jeff made a furtive movement of surprise. "Yeah. Enough to get me back to California."

"Sorry, but I don't have that much with me." Reaching into his pocket, the man pulled out his wallet and took out three twenties. Tossing them onto the backpack, he then added a small square of paper. "How's that?"

Jeff stared at the paper. A small, dark dot marked its center. So innocent-looking. Reaching out, he closed his fist around it. "Thanks."

"Go ahead. I don't mind."

Bringing it to his mouth, he thrust his tongue forward. It stuck to the moistness, and he brought it into his mouth. Chewed. Swallowed. He'd stepped onto the roller coaster.

"Why don't I pick up something for you to eat?" the man said. "You won't feel like it later. Then I'll drop you off."

Jeff nodded. Now that he'd taken the irrevocable step, he had only to slide along. The man pulled through a Burger King drive-through, came out the other end with a bag of cheeseburgers and onion rings.

"I gotta go now," Jeff said, glancing at the dashboard clock. "I'm supposed to meet a guy."

The man remained silent during the drivc to the cemetery. Pulling up to the curb, he released the door locks and waited for Jeff to get out.

"You be careful, now," he called, as Jeff headed toward the gate. "You don't want to be walking around too much once that stuff hits."

"No, man," Jeff said over his shoulder. "I'll just fly."

He watched the Taurus pull away and finally disappear around the corner. Then he wriggled through an opening in the gate and entered the cemetery. Tick was nowhere around. And the stuff was beginning to hit him, sending wild little corkscrews rushing through his system. Straight lines began to curve.

Jeff sat down on a gravestone. Right now, he didn't care whether Tick came or not.

Awareness came back in the form of crickets chirping. Jeff rolled over, huddling in the predawn chill, and abruptly realized that the back of his clothes were wet with dew.

The colors were gone.

He sat up, impelled more by discomfort than an urge to move. The graveyard had turned spooky, threads of mist curling among the headstones in the best horror-movie tradition. It was nothing compared to the crap roiling around inside him; he was bottoming out but good. It took a couple of tries to get to his feet.

"Ohhh, man," he groaned, throwing his arms wide in a bone-popping stretch.

Then he checked his pocket, found that the sixty bucks was still there. He slid the bills between his palms, feeling the crispness of paper. Coffee would be good. Food . . . he checked the mood of his insides, decided food could wait.

The breeze picked up, chilling him through his damp clothes and signaling that it was time to go. He started walking. Twigs crackled underfoot, sounding like gunshots in the stillness. An owl hooted behind him, startling him.

"Shit," he muttered.

Something grabbed him by the legs. He leaped backward only to be pulled off balance. He crashed to the ground with enough force to drive his breath out. Instinctively he kicked out, connected with something that gave off a metallic bong. The smell of crushed flowers rose like murder on the air.

He crouched on all fours, panting like a dog on a summer afternoon. An urn. God, only an urn.

His chest heaving, he got to his feet. He kicked at the urn with a savagery that sent it spinning off among the gravestones. Shit. This was really getting to him. Well, there was nothing better than the squeaky-clean normalcy of a McDonald's to bring a guy back to reality. He jerked the collar of his jacket higher and resumed walking.

And went down again. On something soft.

He scrabbled back, terrified that he'd landed on a new grave. Then he saw it. Him. Tick.

His friend lay on his back, arms spread wide. The hilt of a knife protruded from his chest.

Jeff forced himself to breathe. In. Out. In. Out. It hurt every time. Dew had collected on Tick's face, glittering like diamonds against the chalk-white skin. Jeff couldn't stop looking at his open mouth. It looked like a deep black pit, and as he stared at it, he could almost see movement.

With a shudder, Jeff scrubbed his sleeve across his mouth. He'd have puked if there'd been anything in his stomach. He took a couple of deep breaths, then a couple more, as he tried to understand what had happened. Two of them: Tick . . . Uncle Cullen . . .

and one knife. Jeff didn't know why he thought that knife had killed them both, but he did. It had to be.

Because it was Dad's knife. The one that had disappeared from the garage. The one he couldn't remember taking, couldn't remember *not* taking.

"Jesus," he said.

He didn't remember. He didn't even remember whether he'd awakened in the same place he'd gone to sleep in. Didn't remember seeing Tick. And damn well didn't know how the knife had gotten here.

Maybe he only knew certain things at certain times.

Slowly he reached out and took hold of the hilt. Slowly he pulled it free. It came out easily. His teeth chattered as he wiped it on Tick's shirt. Over and over, like a barber stropping his razor.

Realizing at last what he was doing, Jeff scuttled on all fours away from the body. Away, away, away. He took the knife with him.

The day dawned bright and sunny, and warmer than it should have been this time of year. Just the kind of day to bring people outside. Connie decided to try East Ocean View again. But with a system this time: taking a map, she divided the area into quadrants. Armed with the map and another picture of Jeff, she headed out to her car.

She faltered just for a moment when she saw Derek leaning against her car. He looked like he'd been there for a while.

"What are you doing here?" she asked.

"Waiting for you. We need to talk, Connie."

Brushing past him, she opened the car door and

tossed her purse inside. "I'm on my way out," she said.

"Do you mind if I ask where you're going?"

"Yes." After a moment, she sighed and turned to face him. "I'm going to look for Jeff."

"I spent most of the night doing that."

"Yeah? Well, I'll spend the day doing it."

He plucked the map out of her hand. Jeff's picture fluttered to the ground; they both ignored it. She restrained the urge to tap her foot while Derek examined her handiwork.

"Very efficient," he said finally, handing it back.

"Yeah, well, that's my specialty. Organization."

"So I remember. You're too early."

"Huh?"

"It's eight o'clock in the morning. Do you remember a time when Jeff voluntarily got up before noon? Not only that, chances are he'll be down at the beach, where the action is."

She folded the map along its original creases. "What did you have in mind?"

"Let me take you out for breakfast. Afterward, we can look for him together."

"Don't you need to go to work?"

"Not until tomorrow."

"Then don't you need to sleep?"

"Who sleeps?"

That, more than anything, made her decision. "Okay. Get in the car."

"Let me drive." He pointed toward a white Toyota that had long since seen better days. "I traded with a friend of mine for a while. Jeff knows both our cars; he'll run if he knows it's us."

She hesitated, not liking the loss of control it would mean. But he had a point. "All right."

His driving hadn't changed appreciably in the past fifteen years; more than once, she found herself pressing an imaginary brake pedal. Old, impatient Derek. Old, practical Connie.

"I didn't think you'd be alone this morning," he said.

She pressed the invisible brake pedal to the floor. "What business is it of yours?"

"It must have been Mr. Ranke."

"Spending the night?"

"Come on," Derek said. "I was married to you, remember? And I know that an alert landlord is bound to reawaken all those old-fashioned instincts your mother drilled into you from the time you were born."

Connie regarded him from under her lashes. Then she smiled. "He sucks my toes."

"Mr. Ranke?"

"Uh-uh."

He glanced over at her, a quick flash of hazel eyes. "He doesn't bother you like I do."

"*Nobody* bothers me like you do." Still, she couldn't help remembering the times when it had been passion, not anger, driving them. It had been good then—young and hot and reckless. Come to think of it, maybe that explained John's attraction; he stirred those old juices, touched that vein of youth she'd almost forgotten.

"You're not supposed to be thinking about one man when you're with another," Derek said.

"You're not a man," she retorted. "You're my ex-husband."

"I'm *so* flattered."

She snapped the map open, holding it like a barrier between them. "I suggest we start at Sixteenth and Bay and work our way east. I met some kids around there who, while they didn't admit they knew Jeff, didn't exactly deny it, either. And he called me not too long after I talked to them."

"Okay."

He didn't say anything more, but she didn't have to be a psychic to know what he was thinking. She'd hardly thought of anything else since he'd left yesterday. Even John, with his considerable skills at distraction, hadn't been able to turn her away from it.

"All right," she said, slamming the map down onto her thighs. "We're back to the faith thing."

He nodded.

"I've never been big on faith, at least, the unconditional kind. Jeff's my son. I love him more than anything on this earth."

"But—"

"But you should have seen his face when I asked him about the candles, Derek. First there was this great wash of fear, like he remembered something so scary it made him sick. Then he went blank on me. No emotion. He's always loved Cullen—or so I thought. Sometimes I tell myself that I want him to be innocent so badly for my own sake. I mean, most parents blame themselves when their child screws up, but we're talking murder here."

"Premeditated."

She nodded. "He had to bring the candles and the knife. He had to walk up to Cullen, smile, say something, maybe, and then . . ." Again she made that short sharp stabbing motion that seemed to drive straight through to her heart.

"Not my son."

Connie flinched from it because her own heart

said it with such frightening certainty. "He's my son, too."

"Then act like it."

The brutality of it staggered her. And the truth. Her breath turned shallow and hard. "That's not fair."

"No, it's not," he said. "But there are times when you simply have to believe because nothing else makes any sense."

"How easy for you to say." She was painfully aware that her voice had gone up both in pitch and in volume, but she was unable to do anything about it. "Everything has always been black and white to you. Never a compromise, never any middle ground. Derek's way or no way."

"You're making an assumption on fifteen-year-old facts."

"Some things never change."

"And you have? Connie the Right. Your logic is always the best, even if the other guy happens to be working with completely different parameters."

"Parameters?" she repeated. "Whose parameters say that murder isn't wrong?"

With a wrench that flung her against her seatbelt, Derek pulled over to the curb and slammed the car into park.

"Okay, that's it," he snarled. "I'm not going to let you fuck me around this time, Connie. You always do this. Anytime you don't want to deal with something, you talk yourself and the other guy into a corner. And then you go 'round and 'round until you hardly recognize your own name anymore."

She released her seatbelt. "This was a mistake. We can't be together five minutes without fighting—"

"Decide!" He grabbed her upper arm in a grip that numbed it to the elbow.

"You're hurting me!"

"I'll rip your fucking arm off. *Decide!"*

"I don't have to decide. I just have to find Jeff!"

"Wrong again," Derek said. His voice was as implacable as his hand. "Because when your son looks into your eyes, he's going to know what you think. You're not going to be able to straddle the fence."

"And I'm not going to be able to lie."

"And if you *don't* believe in him, you'll lose him completely. Lack of faith, Connie. He might take it from Sandra, he might even take it from me, but not from you. Of all the people in the world, *you* have to believe in him."

She twisted her arm, hurting herself but not budging him at all. "It's easy for you to say," she said. "You don't know . . . you didn't see his face—"

"Then turn him in to D'Amato and be done with it."

"I can't!" The words ripped out of her unbidden. She drew her breath in with a sharp sound of surprise, feeling as though she'd stripped her soul bare. Judging from the triumph in Derek's eyes, she had.

"Well, there it is," he said. "You can't. Think it through. The truth doesn't change, it doesn't stretch to fit the situation. It's there inside you. All you have to do is say it."

"I—"

"Say it!"

"All right!" she screamed. "I can't believe he's guilty! Everything's right there, pointing to him. But in my heart, where it really counts, I can't believe it. Because if he isn't innocent, I don't think I could live with it." Pain beat behind her eyes. "But that's not faith. Not the kind you're talking about."

"Jesus, Connie." With a visible effort, Derek unclenched his hand from her arm. "It doesn't have to be so complicated. As long as you believe in him, even for those reasons, that's what matters."

"What about you?"

He reached across her and pulled her seat belt back into place. "Faith's always been a little easier for me than for you. But maybe between the two of us, we'll have enough to save our son."

Chapter Thirteen

"I told you everyone would be at the beach," Derek said.

Connie registered the heat of the sun-warmed boardwalk beneath her feet as she looked out over the Atlantic. The jetty hulked above a sea that was almost glass-smooth today. The water caught the sunlight in brief impressionist flashes, and the horizon line was so clear-cut it almost hurt the eyes. Below, the sand teemed with bodies: some old, some young, some slim, some not so slim. All, however, were spread out and basted, sucking up a last few rays.

"No sign of Jeff," she said.

"The kids come and go like bees. But I think you're right about Jeff preferring to hang out on Sixteenth Street instead of down here. More action." Derek shaded his eyes with his hand, casting a spiky shadow across his face as he looked toward the jetty. "This is where it happened, isn't it?"

She bent her head, letting her hair fall forward. "What?"

"The drowning. Someone else's and almost yours."

"So you got it out of Mom."

"Did you think I wouldn't?" After a moment he added, "You did good, Connie. Not many people would have taken the risk. You might not believe it, but your mother is very proud of you."

It meant more than it should have. So she just nodded and watched the horizon. It hurt her eyes. She was aware that Derek studied her for a while before turning his attention to the beach again.

"Beautiful morning, isn't it?" D'Amato's voice came from behind them.

Connie turned, aware that Derek matched her movement. D'Amato had doffed his suit jacket. His sleeves were rolled up, exposing forearms furred with long, dark hair. With his casual air and liquid Latin eyes, he looked as innocently dangerous as a sleeping rattlesnake.

"Are you following me, Detective?" Connie asked.

He smiled. "Not at all. Apparently we just had the same idea: on such a beautiful day, it's likely that a runaway kid would end up on the beach."

"We haven't seen him," Derek said.

"I have," D'Amato said. "At least one of the surveillance cameras did."

Connie took a step toward him. "Was he all right? How did he look? Was anyone else with him?"

"You're hurting my arm," D'Amato said.

Startled, she looked down to see that her hand was indeed clamped on the detective's forearm. She let go. Her fingernails left half-moon depressions in his skin. "Sorry about that."

D'Amato shrugged, his gaze going over her head to Derek. "Is she always this intense?"

"I'm the ex-husband, remember?"

"Talk, Detective," Connie said.

"Your son looked all right."

She let her breath out slowly, surprised that she'd been holding it.

"He ran from one of our men yesterday," D'Amato continued. "He'd spent the night in a cabin off Bayside Avenue with a pack of other kids. We found two empty tequila bottles in the trash can and residue of crack cocaine on the table. Your son's into some hard stuff."

Connie felt Derek's hands come down on her shoulders. She needed the support to answer. "I know," she said. "We want to bring him home, Detective. We want to help him."

"And I want to talk to him," D'Amato said.

"I'm sure your investigation doesn't hinge on one fifteen-year-old boy."

"Maybe it does, Ms. Matthias. He intrigues me, what with his disappearance just when I need to see him." His eyes were bland, but he ran his thumbnail along his jaw in that gesture Connie was becoming much too familiar with. "Did I mention that we found some black wax beneath the fingernails of Cullen's left hand?"

"No," Connie said. "You didn't." The world had taken on a terrible sort of clarity, as though every line, every color clamored for her attention.

"Well, we did." Again that thumbnail scratched audibly. "Strange, isn't it? Not many people use black candles."

Connie couldn't think of anything to say that wouldn't make things worse. The silence dragged on for a long, uncomfortable moment. Then

D'Amato clasped his hands behind his back and rocked back and forth on his heels.

"See, folks," he said, "I've got some real problems with this case, the worst being the people involved. We've got self-styled psychics, firewalkers, crystal-gazers, and Tarot readers. One of them wanted to do my goddamn astrological chart. The only thing missing is a witch on a broom, and maybe a Satanist."

Connie didn't think that last was accidental. She didn't trust her voice, so she looked at Derek, hoping he'd see her plea for help.

"So, Detective," he said, "with all the talent available in that group, you'd think they could come up with an answer to why Cullen was murdered."

"Oh, they did," the detective replied. "The prevailing theory blames karma. Your sister-in-law, however, thinks your brother was some kind of martyr to the cause, so to speak—"

"Any reason for that?" Derek asked. "Threatening letters, phone calls?"

"She said there had been some letters, cranks saying he'd become the devil's tool. It got especially bad after the newspaper did an article on their firewalking." D'Amato's implacable gaze moved to Connie. "And didn't you say your brother 'felt' something wrong?"

"Yeah."

"Well, there you go. Personally, I'd like to chalk it up to karma. But my boss, now, he's a Presbyterian. He's not going to go for the karma thing. So, although it's as inconvenient as hell, I've got to bring him something a little more concrete."

"Everyone's a comic," Derek muttered.

"What about the others?" Connie asked. "Haven't you investigated them?"

"Sure," D'Amato said. "Nobody has a record, nobody seemed to have any feelings except love and respect for your brother, nobody seemed to have been on the beach at the time of the murder. Nobody seemed to have anything to gain from his death. Apparently the group worked well together; no apparent jealousy among the members, no, ah, swapping around of the women—"

"New Age doesn't mean hedonist, Detective," Connie said.

"I didn't say it did, Ms. Matthias. But you've got to remember that first and foremost, your brother was a man. A human being. And so are the rest of them. Whatever their beliefs, they still have the weaknesses and vices that make them human."

"Greed, power, jealousy, sex," she said, ticking them off on her fingers.

"And sometimes, just plain foolishness," he countered.

"Do people kill for that?" Derek asked.

D'Amato grinned. "You'd be surprised. A discussion turned into an argument, an argument turned into murder. Everybody's sorry when it's over."

"I'm a light sleeper," Connie said. "I'd have heard an argument."

The detective bobbed his head, a gesture that neither affirmed nor denied. "So here's what we've got: your brother was a popular guy. He led the group, but it was an informal thing, more because they wanted him to than anything else. He was a thinker, a spiritual sort of guy. He didn't seem to worry much about money, but then, with the Wahlfields bankrolling him, he didn't have to. Right now, I can't find a rational motive for anyone wanting to kill him."

His eyes were secretive, watchful. Connie knew he was playing her, gauging her reactions, poking just to see what he could get.

"Since I can't find answers in the rational," he continued, "I have no choice but to look at the non-rational aspects of it. There's plenty to choose from: New Age mumbo-jumbo. People writing hate mail because your brother has gone public with his personal philosophy. Add some black wax beneath a dead man's fingernails, and we've got a veritable witches' cauldron."

Connie grimaced. "Really, Detective. Your metaphors are something else."

"Yeah, well," D'Amato said. "Maybe they believe in karma, too."

"Metaphors?" she asked, startled.

"Whatever. And speaking of karma . . . if you hear from your son, you ought to try to get him to turn himself in before *his* catches up with him."

"Do you think we're out here because he trusts us?" Connie asked. "He ran away from home, remember?"

D'Amato studied her, his face impassive. "I remember a lot of things, Ms. Matthias—chief of which is that this case smells like week-old bait, and I don't like people stirring the mess."

"We're not trying to interfere with you," Derek said. "We only want to help our son."

"The time may come when that becomes a conflict of interest," D'Amato said.

Derek's lips thinned. "Not to us."

"You're walking on thin ice, Valle."

"And you're harassing us."

A hot spark of anger flared in D'Amato's eyes. He took a step forward, and Connie found herself hemmed between the two men. She resisted the pressure of Derek's hands, urging her to step aside.

"Ooooh," she said. "Are we going to bark and growl now?"

D'Amato blinked. Then some of the tension went out of his shoulders. "If I were you, I wouldn't try getting the boy out of town."

"We don't have him to try," Connie said.

The detective's implacable gaze shifted to her. "Maybe not. But you *do* have something I want, don't you?"

"I don't know what you're talking about."

"Think about it real hard, Ms. Matthias. You're taking a big risk. In the long run, it may cost you more than you want to pay."

He kept her gaze for a heartbeat more, then stared at Derek for a long, hard moment. Connie thought she could hear her pulse beating in the frozen silence.

Then, with an abrupt, angry movement, D'Amato swung on his heel and walked away.

"Gee, that went well," Derek said.

Connie stepped forward, away from his hands. "Somehow, he doesn't seem like the kind of guy who gets emotional about his cases."

"He was pretty emotional a minute ago. I thought he was going to sock me."

"This is getting to him. It's probably a lot more comfortable dealing with the normal drug-related killing or wife-shoots-husband, husband-shoots-wife scenario."

"I can't say I blame him."

Connie closed her eyes against a sudden upwelling of memory. But it came anyway, playing on the stage of her mind: Cullen, lying so still and cold, she sitting beside him with the black candles in her lap. The possibility of Jeff's guilt, the stark, simple fact of Cullen's death—it all seemed so wrong, so awful, that it shouldn't have been real. The sound of the waves was inside her and outside her and seemed to lap at her soul. It grew louder and louder, claiming more of her even as she tried to push it away.

She gasped as Derek's hand fell heavily on her shoulder. Opening her eyes, she found him staring at her in obvious concern. "Are you all right?" he asked.

"Yeah." Reaching up, she pressed her fingertips against her temples. "I was remembering something."

"Let's get off the beach."

He dropped his hand from her shoulder to her elbow. His grip was light and undemanding, so she let him draw her toward the parking lot. Her mind worked steadily beneath the veil of silence, churning the stew of D'Amato, Jeff, Cullen and murder. When the decision came, it was as clear as one of Penny's quartz crystals.

"We've got to do more," she said.

"About Jeff?"

She nodded. "If he didn't kill Cullen, then someone else did."

"It's not your job to find out."

"It's not only Jeff. You see, I've got to square things. I took the candles, so I've got to get D'Amato something else."

"You're out of your mind."

"Maybe. And maybe a little craziness is what you need to see into this situation."

Derek turned his head to study her. For a moment, he looked so much like Jeff that her heart turned over. "Somehow, I think you're about to have a spiritual epiphany."

"You *do* have your good points," she said, surprised that he'd followed her thought processes so well.

"You used to think so."

"Hmmm. But your mind seems to have finally caught up with your hormones," she countered. "Now look. Jeff's the perfect candidate to take the rap for this: young, snarly, with a past that matches the way Cullen was killed. If I were D'Amato, I'm not sure I'd look any farther, either. Unless somebody gave me something else to think about." The breeze kicked up, flicking her hair across her face. She dragged it back with her free hand. "I want that bastard. Not just because he killed my brother. He set me up to think, if only for a while, that my son was capable of murder."

"That's the dramatic Balestier blood talking." He held up one hand, forestalling her retort. "Hey, it's not a criticism. That passion was what attracted me to you in the first place."

"Cullen had the passion, not me," she said.

Derek shot her a glance. "If you believe that, you haven't learned much about yourself in the past fifteen years."

"We're digressing."

"Can't do that," he said, without a hint of a smile. "So, the epiphany."

"I'm feeling the need to explore my brother's beliefs. Maybe it's a way of holding on to him a little while longer, or maybe it's the fact that we were twins that's drawing me in. I want to throw myself into the eddies and currents of his life."

"I like it," Derek said.

"It needs a little refining, but I think you get the general idea."

"What about that guy . . . John. Are you going to tell him what you're doing?"

The sixty-four-thousand-dollar question. She wasn't sure how she felt about John, wasn't sure if trust were something that entered the equation no matter how she felt. "I don't know."

"I don't want you to."

That brought her chin up. "He's helped me a lot."

"He's a stranger. And no matter how much you like the way he sucks your toes, you don't have the right to hand our son's future over to a stranger."

"I'm really sorry I told you about that."

With a harsh, frustrated sound, he pulled away from her. "We're supposed to be working as a partnership here. For the good of our son, remember? And the first time a big decision comes up, you push me right out of the picture."

"I didn't—"

"You did. Come on, Connie. You've got to work with people in decisions that concern them. Didn't two failed marriages teach you anything about compromise?"

That hurt. "You're not being fair," she said. "There were other people involved in those failed marriages."

"Yeah," he growled. "And both of them were just as stupid as you."

Connie stopped walking. He stopped with her,

and they turned in unison to face each other. She opened her mouth to argue with him, ready to battle for anything and everything. Then she took a good look at him. Below the scowl, below the belligerent line of his jaw, he was scared—as scared of losing Jeff as she was.

The realization cooled her temper and closed her mouth. In this one irrevocable way, she and he were kin.

"You're right," she said. "I'm sorry."

She'd never seen him look so surprised. It might have been funny if there'd been any laughter left in her. He stood for a moment looking down at her, then said, "I have a feeling that's just the first of many things we'll be negotiating before this is over."

"That's the nature of partnerships."

"Jesus, Connie. You never give an inch."

"I'm trying," she said. "For fifteen years, you've been the enemy. Now I've got to work with you in a way I've never worked with anyone before. It takes some getting used to."

"Okay." With a sigh, he raked his hands through his hair. Then he gave her a rather lopsided grin. "I guess we've both grown up some. When we were married, neither of us would have budged on that argument."

"We've never had Jeff's future at stake."

"That's not something I'm comfortable gambling with."

"I've never been comfortable gambling at all," she said. "This is more risk than I'd ever be willing to take, given the choice."

Silently, he extended his arm. Silently, she took it.

Another truce. Perhaps as fragile as the others they'd forged for Jeff's sake, but just as necessary.

Derek pulled to a stop in front of Connie's apartment. The afternoon sun laid bars of tangerine light across the yard, and the trees had begun to gather shadows beneath their limbs.

Connie glanced at her companion. His expression had little but grimness to it, and she didn't blame him. They'd spent a day cruising the streets, asking questions, showing Jeff's picture around, and had gotten zip for it.

"What are you going to do now?" she asked.

"I've got to get some sleep. I feel like I've been chewed up and spat out."

"The day wasn't a total loss. You almost got to punch D'Amato in the nose."

"Was that a joke?"

"Are my jokes so bad that you have to ask?"

He dragged his hand down his face. "I'm too tired to keep up with you. Tomorrow, how about we start our search after dark? I think Jeff may be lying low during the day. And I think we ought to give the Diamond Springs area a try."

She nodded, trying to banish the sudden vision of Jeff running through the darkness, terror on his face as he fled an amorphous pursuer. Despite the vivid light all around her, she shivered.

"Invite me in," Derek said.

"Why?"

"I want to see those candles."

Connie reached up to rub the back of her neck, where the tiny hairs had risen in involuntary response. "I haven't looked at them since . . . the day of the murder."

With a sigh, Derek shook his head. He turned the car off and came around to open her door. The wind skirled along the ground, pushing some fallen leaves around her ankles. She flinched from the touch.

"You've really got the jitters," he said, taking her hand. His palm was warm against hers. "Are you sure you're okay?"

"I . . . it's just that Cullen's death seems less, ah, remote today." She held her free hand out in front of her. The light made her skin look brittle, the slight tremor more obvious. "And I thought I was further along."

"It's grief, Connie. You don't get over it in a few days; you're just throwing off the numbness."

"I don't want to feel it."

"Come on," he said, tugging her toward the house. "A cup of coffee will do you good."

Leaves crackled underfoot as they walked. Ahead, the house sat square and comforting amid its nest of azaleas. The porch swing creaked softly.

"Is that you, Mr. Ranke?" she called.

He stood up and moved into the light. "Sure is. I see you've got the ex-husband with you."

"Hey, Henry," Derek said.

"You shoulda come fishing with me this morning. I caught some real pretty ones."

"Sorry. Had some chores to tend to."

The older man's gaze dropped to their joined hands. "That don't look much like a chore, son."

" 'Night, Mr. Ranke," she said firmly.

She pulled away from Derek to lead the way upstairs. "It's a hell of a thing when your landlord knows more about your business than you do."

"Henry's an observant fellow."

"Tell me about it," she said.

"Why didn't you set Mr. Ranke straight? About us, I mean?"

"I suppose I could say something like, 'I'm not really with him, Mr. Ranke. We're just trying to find our runaway son before the police pick him up and charge him with murder.' "

"It would have gotten a reaction, I'll tell you that."

"Besides, after watching my neighbor Sherrie in action, he probably thinks my dating both a boyfriend and an ex-husband is pretty tame stuff."

"This Sherrie must be something else."

"I'll introduce you," she said, unlocking the door.

Inside, the last daylight washed through the living room, gilding everything it touched. A beautiful time of day, she thought, one last, glorious flare of color before night closed in. Even as she registered it, the light began to fade. Violet shadows crouched outside the window, rife with movement. They drew her.

She laid her hand on the cool glass and stared out over the darkening lawn. The big old azaleas clustered tightly around the trees, their leaves flashing pale undersides as the breeze riffled their branches.

Movement caught her eye, brought her pressing close to the window. Then she spotted a black-on-black shadow against one of the towering loblolly pines. Human shaped against the straight up-and-down of the trunks.

He's watching me.

"Derek," she said, without turning away. "Somebody's out there. No, don't come here, he'll see you."

"Is it Jeff?"

"Can't tell."

"Keep him watching. I'm going down."

She could hear him moving toward the door. Probably on his hands and knees. A moment later, she heard the door open, then quiet, rapid footsteps on the stairs.

And then, between one blink and the next, the shadow disappeared. "Damn," she muttered.

Derek came into view then, Mr. Ranke a few feet behind him. The two men quartered the yard thoroughly, the beam of Mr. Ranke's flashlight bringing oval-shaped patches of vegetation into bright relief. They found nothing, however; in a few minutes they headed back to the house.

Connie stood at the window, wondering if it had been her imagination. Maybe. But it had seemed so real, that man-shaped shadow.

Ask Cullen about reality. You're exhausted, body, mind and soul, and you wonder why you're seeing suspicious shadows? Next you're going to start thinking you're as psychic as the rest of them.

"Connie?"

Derek's voice brought her swinging around. He took her by the arm and drew her away from the window. "We didn't find anything, not even footprints, and the ground beneath those trees is pretty soft. Are you sure you saw someone standing there?"

"No," she said. "I'm not sure. It must have been my imagination working overtime. And don't start with the 'you ought to take it easier' crap."

"Did I say anything?"

"No, but you thought it."

"The only thing I'm thinking is that we both need a cup of coffee." He went into the kitchen and started going through her cabinets. Noisily. "Why don't you get those candles?"

She headed for the bedroom. The walls had been painted a pale terra cotta to complement the bold modern colors of her bedspread. Now, in the gathering dusk, the color looked like dried blood.

The last of the daylight faded. She switched the light on and the room returned to normal. Jitters, all right, and bad.

With a sigh, she pulled a stool over to the closet. She'd hidden the candles in a box and put the box in the back of the uppermost shelf. She didn't know why. Yes, she did; one always buried the worst secret in the deepest, darkest place one could find.

"Coffee's ready," Derek called.

Balancing the box on her palms, she carried it out to the kitchen. Derek took it from her and set it on the counter. Pushing their mugs aside, he lifted the candles out one by one. Connie stared at them as though she expected them to leap upon her if she turned her back. Fat, black, and glossy, they squatted spiderlike in the prosaic familiarity of her kitchen.

"I heard that Satanists make their candles from human fat," he said.

Inwardly, she recoiled from it. "I wouldn't know."

He leaned down to examine the candles more closely, but Connie saw him wipe his hands on his jeans. She got an indecent amount of satisfaction from knowing he was bothered, too.

"They've been lit," he said.

"Either they were used for real, or whoever set Jeff up was very thorough. I'm not up on Satanic rituals."

"What about Jeff?"

She spread her hands. "I don't think he was into the real stuff. But he was in a crowd of kids who played around with it. You know, do the most shocking thing you can think of, make the old folks crazy. So one night, he and a buddy got high and pulled a midnight raid on an old graveyard. When the cops picked them up, they found a skull and the bones of a man's right hand, some black candles—"

"Shit."

". . . Some black candles, a shovel and a crowbar, a crucifix made of wood, and twenty-two empty beer bottles."

Derek raked his hands through his hair. "Cripes. You can't fault him for having a sense of drama. Most kids would have just held up the nearest service station and been done with it."

"Are you blaming the Balestier blood again?"

"Nobody in *my* family has any imagination."

She considered a number of replies, none of which would be productive. "I'm going to ignore that. Anyway, if a real true Satanist had been at work here, why would he leave evidence at a murder scene?"

"He wouldn't. Those candles were put there to implicate Jeff. And it would have worked, if you hadn't taken them." Derek sipped at his coffee, studying her over the rim of the mug. "I wonder what he's thinking now?"

"Who?"

"The murderer."

Connie spun her mug between her hands. "He's a

smart guy. The candles were just gravy for him; he knows all he has to do is let the police run through the rest of the possibilities and then come back to Jeff. Once D'Amato gets his hands on that boy, it'll be all over. Hell, he acted so guilty and defiant that even *I* thought he'd done it."

"I don't—"

The phone shrilled. Connie knocked one of the candles over reaching for it. "Hello?"

"Connie." John's dark-velvet voice was low and intimate. "I was worried about you; I've been trying to reach you all day."

"I was out looking for Jeff."

"Oh, God. Any luck?"

"No."

He made a soft sound of distress. "I'm sorry."

"Yeah, me, too." She watched Derek take the mugs over to the sink and rinse them. "What's up?"

"I'm at Phaedra's," he said. "We're having a little get-together in Cullen's honor. Why don't you come out and share it with us?"

"Now?"

"Please come. I need you."

And there it was, the lure he'd always held for her. Desire. Warmth. The simple human comfort of holding and being held, of forgetting, for a short, precious time, anything but passion. She needed it, needed the surcease that went along with it.

"I'll be there as soon as I can," she said.

Derek turned off the water and swung around to look at her. "That was the boyfriend, as Mr. Ranke would say."

"They're having a get-together in Cullen's honor. It'll be a perfect opportunity to get to know the gang a little better."

"Admit it, Connie. It's libido, not intrigue, that's got those fingers tapping."

She glanced down, saw that she was indeed drumming her fingertips on the countertop. Damn him for knowing her so well. "Are you driving tomorrow, or shall I?"

"I will," he said, looking as though he'd like to say a lot more. "Seven o'clock, or do you want to go get something to eat earlier?"

"Seven will be fine."

He headed for the door. Connie crossed her arms over her chest and waited. It didn't take long; he paused with his hand on the knob, then turned around to look at her.

"I knew you couldn't leave without saying it," she said.

"What?"

" 'Have fun.' "

His brows contracted. "Actually, I was going to tell you to be careful."

"Were you really?"

"Yes, really. Only one of us qualifies, either in gender or personality, for the title of bitch."

He slammed the door on the way out, which suited her just fine.

Chapter Fourteen

Connie counted four cars in Penny's driveway. The gang must all be here, then. She parked at the end of the line, but instead of going straight up to the door, she walked past the house to the dunes.

This was Cullen's special place. Here Cullen had lived and loved. Here he'd died. He'd been a gentle, dreamy boy and had grown into a gentle man whose dreams were powerful enough to draw others. He'd found serenity here, and he'd found himself.

But tonight, Nature offered little of serenity. A storm raced toward shore, dousing the moon with thick ballooning clouds. The wind tore at Connie's hair and sent the waves crashing white-tipped to gnaw hungrily at the beach. A lightning bolt snagged across the sky's dark underbelly.

Connie knew she should run for the house. But she stood transfixed by the gravid violence above her. This was herself, this wild realm of sea and sky and looming clouds. Her soul wailed like the wind, churned like the roiling waves. Rain speckled her face, ran like tears down her cheeks and into her mouth. She spread her arms wide as though to ride the storm like a kite.

"Connie!"

John's voice carried only dimly through the wind. She glanced over her shoulder, saw him silhouetted against the French doors. Lightning flared overhead, giving her a clear view of him. His wet hair clung to his skull, making him look sleek and feral, and his pale eyes looked almost luminescent in that searing instant.

She turned more fully toward him and waited.

Another man might have called out again, insisting that she come in from the storm, but not John. He came to her, moving through the rain and wind as though they didn't exist, as though nothing existed but Connie. He knew what she wanted, what she needed. She didn't know how he knew, didn't care.

They came together, melding, as fierce and wild as the elements around them. Sensation dragged Connie deep, deeper, and deeper still. She cried out as he sank his hands into her hair roughly, urgently, responded by digging her nails into his back.

"Connie," he gasped. "God, Connie."

"It's the storm," she whispered.

"No," he said. "It's magic."

He drew her to a spot out of sight of the house. She clung to him, not knowing whether she walked or he carried her, sure only that she had to have this. Tonight. Now. They fell to the sand amid the pelting rain, rolled in a welter of limbs and grit and sluicing water. She straddled him. Taking. Possessing. His skin gleamed in the frantic stormlight; his teeth were bared, his eyes wild as he gave himself up to her. And she, part of the tempest, raging like the wind and the rain and the clamoring pain inside her, drawing him in, drawing him on.

They cried out together with the thunder—and became merely human again. Braced on shaking arms above him, Connie bowed her head as she tried to regain her senses. He lay with his chest heaving, and his fingers gripping her hips so hard that her skin was white beneath them.

"I have never . . ." he paused, drawing a long, shuddering breath, "felt like that before. Never."

"Me, either," she panted.

"I could do this forever." His grip eased, but the curve of his fingers on her hips remained possessive. "Over and over and over, until there was nothing left of either of us."

She raised her head and looked into his eyes. They were glazed with something raw and powerful, something that wanted to consume her. No man had ever demanded this. Fear beat heavily in the back of her mind—not of him; of herself. For some deep, primitive part of her wanted to give in to that demand, to be consumed and to consume.

She'd never been so close to the edge, so near to letting go of everything she'd held so tightly to all her life. She felt stripped bare, both awed and repelled by the violence within her.

Rolling away from him, she retrieved her clothes and started getting dressed. "The storm's getting worse. We'd better get inside."

"What's the matter?" he asked.

"Nothing," she said. "I just want to get in out of the weather."

"I like storms," he said. "Especially when they have such an effect on you."

She tossed his pants to him. "I'm not sure that was me."

"It was you, Connie, every bit of it. Maybe it was

the part you've never allowed to come out before. But we all have something like that in us, something dark and just a little dangerous." She opened her mouth to say something, but he shook his head. "Don't deny it. Not to me. Not now. I like that beast in you, and I'm going to make sure I free it again."

"Don't."

"I've never met anyone like you," he said.

"I'm not sure that's a compliment. You haven't exactly seen me at my best, you know."

"I don't give a damn about the Connie you've built for the rest of the world," he said, his voice blending with the wind, his eyes reflecting the streaking lightning. "I'm talking about the Connie I saw tonight, the dark one, the one you've spent your life denying. It's like riding the whirlwind."

She wrestled her wet pants up her legs, then struggled into her sodden tee shirt. "I'm not like that at all."

"Yes, you are. Someday, I'll prove it to you." He held out his hand. "Come on, let's go in. This is turning into one humdinger of a storm."

Sea and sky had blended into one rain-dark entity, and the wind buffeted them as they ran toward the house. John opened the French door, holding it against the wind, and shooed Connie in ahead of him. He had to put his shoulder to the door to get it closed.

Connie flipped her wet hair back out of her eyes, and found seven surprised-looking people staring at her. Penny was the nearest and most surprised-looking. She seemed tired, but it only made her look more ethereal and lovely. Philip and Evvie sat together on one end of the sofa, Amy and Lynn

Cortez on the other. Hamilton Liu had brought a girl with him, a blonde with beautiful vivid coloring that almost made up for her undistinguised features. They'd curled up together in one of the big overstuffed chairs.

The room was so quiet that Connie could hear the water dripping from her clothes onto the floor. "Hi, everyone," she said.

John stepped closer, mingling his puddle with hers. "Connie, we've got a visitor tonight. This is Margo Gulton-Pratt, a friend of Hamilton's."

"Hi." The girl extracted her arm from the tangle of limbs and waved.

The name struck a spark of memory in Connie's mind, but she couldn't quite chase it down.

"Have you two been swimming?" Philip Walhfield asked, his eyes shining with laughter.

"Actually, we went for a walk," John said. "But it turned out to be one and the same. And before we ruin the floor, we'd better go dry off. Phaedra, do you think you can lend Connie a change of clothes?"

"Of course." Penny got up, moving with little of her usual grace. "And you can use something of Cullen's."

Turning, she headed toward the stairs. Connie followed, impelled by the pressure of John's hand on the small of her back. Penny went into her bedroom and came out a moment later carrying a bundle of clothes.

"Here," she said, handing the clothes to Connie. "You can use the same room you had before." Her face drew taut, and she pressed her lips tightly together before continuing. "John, you just . . . pick what you want."

He took both her hands in his. "Are you sure you're okay with this?"

"They're only clothes."

But her eyes denied the words. Lines bracketed her mouth and creased the fragile skin around her eyes. Connie stood transfixed by the sight of the other woman's pain. Her own welled up inside her, echoing the other, augmented by it.

Penny walked away, leaving Connie smothering in a web of loss and anger at her own helplessness. She should have been able to offer the woman some comfort, even empty words. But she didn't . . . couldn't.

"She's having a hard time," John said softly, his gaze following Penny down the hall.

Connie opened her mouth, forced her voice to work a moment later. "Maybe this get-together isn't such a good idea."

"She needs it. And we need to help her say good-bye."

Connie closed her eyes, fighting the violent up-wash of her own grief. "I don't know if I can do this."

He turned to her. His pupils contracted in the bright light, making his irises look almost crystalline. She could see her reflection in those pale depths.

"What's the matter?"

"He was my brother." There was too much bitterness in her voice. She wrapped her arms around herself as though that might keep her from falling apart. "In a way, I had more of him than Penny ever did. But I was the one who had to make the funeral arrangements. I was the one who had to deal with my mother and take care of Cullen's will. I was the one who had to cope. And now I've got to help Penny say goodbye—"

"Connie." John grasped her by the arms, his hands warm through her sodden clothes.

She bowed her head, unable to bear the weight of what was inside her. "He was my brother," she said again.

"I know."

"Cullen's dead, Jeff's gone, and I can't help either of them."

"Connie, look at me."

She shook her head, but he slid his hand around to the back of her neck and forced her to obey. His eyes didn't hold the sympathy she expected to see, but they held understanding. Not only did he see her pain; he accepted her rage.

He couldn't share it; no one could; but his acceptance might be enough to hold the emptiness at bay. She relaxed beneath his hand, let him pull her against his chest. Slowly, the heat of his body warmed hers.

"There's nothing wrong with taking help from your friends," he said. "Or showing your feelings. You're safe here with us. With me."

She nodded, waiting for tears that wouldn't come. A year ago, a month ago, maybe even a week ago, she might have loved him for what he gave her. Today, however, she was too full of Cullen and Jeff—and yes, herself—to have room for love.

"There's no need for you to do this if you don't want to," he said. "Look, why don't I take you home? Don't worry about your car; we'll pick it up tomorrow."

It would be easier. It would also be defeat. Something in her rejected that; Balestier blood, or maybe just plain, human stubbornness. For somewhere in this mess was retribution for Cullen and salvation for Jeff, and those she had to have.

She raised her head. "I'm all right now."

"Sure?"

"Yeah. Thanks."

He opened his mouth to say something, but she laid her fingers across his lips. "Don't," she said. "I can't take kindness right now."

After a moment, she dropped her hand. When she turned away, he let her go.

Connie sat on the floor, watching the flames dance in the big stone fireplace. She felt alien, out of place. Cullen's friends radiated a calm serenity that seemed almost a mockery of the storm raging outside.

Her gaze drifted to Penny, who sat alone on a sofa, arms and legs arranged in perfect doll-like symmetry. Her eyes glittered in the firelight. Connie couldn't believe the others couldn't see it. Maybe they were too caught up in their own grieving to see how close to the edge Penny now was.

Then John walked into the room and the whole focus shifted. Connie watched avidity come into Amy Cortez's eyes, and pleading come into Penny's. Hamilton Liu's expression didn't change, but the movement of his hand on Margo's hip stilled. Only the Walhfields retained their almost identical expressions of serene beatitude. Maybe it was karma, maybe just money.

It was a thought worthy of D'Amato, and Connie pushed it aside. Cynicism wasn't the ticket tonight.

"I'm glad you could all come out," John said. "Almost like old times, isn't it?"

Philip Walhfield bent his head. His bald spot reflected the overhead light. "Not quite."

"It's not the same," Evvie said. "Not without Cullen."

"What are you trying to say?" Hamilton asked.

"Evvie and I are thinking about doing some traveling. Without Cullen . . ." Philip made a vague gesture with his right hand. "Maybe go to Vail for a while. The winters are so beautiful there."

Connie hugged her knees to her chest and watched the shifting emotions on her companions' faces as they realized what was happening to them.

"You want to leave?" Amy Cortez asked, her voice high and agitated.

"It isn't that we don't love everyone here—"

"Then how can you just take off?" the blond woman demanded. "It affects all of us, you know, not just you and Philip."

"Cullen was such a *positive* force," Evvie said. "For the first time in our lives we felt centered. But now we feel—well, sort of cut loose."

"You want to find another leader," Hamilton said.

Philip took his wife's hand in both of his. "Evvie and I are perennial searchers," he said. "In Cullen, we found a reason to stay. Now that he's gone—"

"But he's *not* gone," John said.

Connie blinked, completely astonished. The others looked as surprised as she felt; if John was using shock methods to get their attention, he'd succeeded.

Propping his hip on the back of the sofa, he met their gazes one by one. "Cullen was the center of this group. He brought us together, melded us with his vision."

"That's what we've been trying to say," Evvie said.

"I understand what you've been trying to say," John said, his eyes gentle. "But why are you assuming that Cullen's death is also the end of this group?"

Evvie cocked her head to one side. "Shouldn't I?"

"We're all part of the world, and the world is part of us," John said. "Cullen's physical self died, but that was only a small part of what he was. His joy, his intelligence, his love for others will continue to exist. That part of him can't die, can't be changed."

Connie felt her shoulders tighten. *Good Lord, why doesn't he just call it a soul?*

He got up. With that smooth economy of movement she so admired in him, he started pacing back and forth in front of his rapt audience. "Remember when we first started jelling as a group? It was so exciting. We were bouncing around like kids in a candy shop, awed by what we were doing. Cullen knew how to fan the flames in us, knew how to help us tap the power we all hold inside us. But it didn't depend on him; he was just the catalyst. And he'd be the first to tell you that."

Pausing in front of the Walhfields, he looked down at them for a dramatic moment of silence. "If you lost your sight, what would you do?"

"I'd learn to use my hearing better," Philip said, enthusiasm lighting his round face.

"Absolutely." John swung away from the older couple to point first at Hamilton Liu and then at Amy and Lynn Cortez. "We have special talents. Because of that, when we came together it was more than just good conversation. We became an entity. Cullen was our sight, but our heart is much more than any one of us. It's all of us."

"Yes," Lynn said.

"We'll keep Cullen with us." A spurt of lightning paled the windows, casting platinum sparks in his eyes. "And we'll learn how to see again."

Tears glittering on her cheeks, Penny held out her hands to the Wahlfields. "We're friends, more than friends. You and Amy and Lynn, Hamilton and John, are my family. Please, don't go."

A tremendous bolt of lightning stabbed down somewhere close, turning the room into an incandescent nightmare for a moment. Thunder shook the house. The lights flickered madly, as though fighting for life, then went out.

Connie got to her feet, conscious that no one else had moved. The firelight seemed to lick at their faces and strike ruddy avid sparks in their eyes. John stood at the fulcrum, looking as sleek and graceful as a cat.

Echoes of the storm rolled through her. She didn't know what to call what she felt for him; lust or love, or maybe obsession. Whatever the tag, it was a powerful thing. She wasn't even sure she liked it, for she might come to depend too much on its ability to fill that emptiness inside her. She felt as though she'd stepped into a world where a whole new set of rules applied, rules she didn't quite understand.

"Does anyone have a flashlight?" she asked.

The charged tension popped like a bubble. But Connie knew a decision had been made; no power on this earth could make the Wahlfields leave now.

John turned to look at her, his mouth curved in a

smile, his eyes as hot as the lightning had been. Then he stretched his hand out, beckoning her. She wanted him so badly it scared her. "Come sit with us, Connie."

She went to him. He pulled her down onto the sofa beside him, in a place where the firelight washed across the fabric.

"We came together tonight to honor our friend," he said. "And to welcome two new friends. We can all feel how brightly Margo glows—"

Yeah, Connie thought, cynicism raising its grizzled head again. She wants Hamilton so badly she's about to burst into flame right there in his lap.

"—and his twin sister." John's fingers curled more tightly around hers. "I hope this isn't making you uncomfortable, Connie. But there's so much of Cullen in you—"

"Cullen and I were nothing alike," she said.

"But you're wrong," Hamilton Liu said. "It would be obvious to you if you weren't so close to it."

"My brother is dead." She'd said the words often enough to be used to them. But she wasn't.

"But he's not gone," Hamilton said, "just changed. You can't see him or hear him, but he's here, all around us. We can feel him most strongly when you're with us."

She felt nothing but the dark, echoing emptiness Cullen had left behind. Hamilton's certainty angered her because she couldn't feel it, couldn't share it. She shook her head.

"Don't you want to touch him again?" Hamilton asked. "You can if you believe you can."

Faith again. It had been easier with Jeff, and a lot

less frightening. "I can't do this," she said, rising to her feet. "I'm sorry, but I just can't."

John got up with her. Laying his hands on her shoulders, he gently turned her to face him. "Don't run from it."

Balestier pride raised its head. "I'm not running. I just don't want to be some kind of, of *conduit* to Cullen. Yes, we were twins. Yes, his death tore something out of me I'll probably never get back. But no, I don't intend to be his subsitute for you people."

"We don't need that from you," John said. "And we wouldn't accept it if you offered."

"Then what the hell *do* you want?"

"Nothing," John said, "but to be your friends."

It seemed so simple and sincere. The Walhfields' faces showed it, Amy and Lynn Cortez showed it, John showed it. Penny had retreated into that stilted, doll-like inertia again and showed nothing but her own pain. Hamilton Liu's hand moved slowly along the curve of Margo's hip—down, up, down . . .

The girl's eyes went soft with arousal, and her pointed little breasts rose and fell beneath her shirt. But Hamilton was looking straight at Connie, his gaze intent, so completely focused on her that he couldn't have been aware of Margo's reactions.

"Give us a chance," Philip Walhfield said. "We cared very much for Cullen. And while we realize your loss was much greater than ours, perhaps we can help one another to heal."

Connie was still looking at Hamilton. So cold, she thought, watching his eyes as he stroked the girl in his lap. So very cold.

And then she remembered where she'd seen the name Gulton-Pratt.

Holy cow, wait 'til Derek hears this!

She looked away swiftly, as though Hamilton might be able to divine her realization through her eyes. She found John staring at her, his face taut and hopeful.

"Come on," he murmured. "Sit down."

Sit down. Learn. Listen. Watch Hamilton drive that girl into a frenzy while he's thinking about something else.

With a sigh, she let John draw her down to the sofa again. She did it for Jeff. Not because she thought they could help her touch Cullen again. Not for that.

Chapter Fifteen

"Phaedra, do you remember the first time we fire-walked together?" Philip Wahlfield asked.

"How could I forget?" Her expression turned dreamy. "It was one of the most special nights of my life. Cullen had been doing it for months, of course, and you and Evvie were old pros. But it was my first time. I was so frightened. But then Cullen started talking about overcoming fear and taking control of my body and my life, and I just . . . did it. And I felt as though I'd battled a pride of lions and won."

"It was like that for me, too," Hamilton said.

Connie, watching Margo's hand slide further down his abdomen, thought he had a tiger by the tail now. "How did Cullen get started?"

"Firewalking?" Penny flinched as another bolt of lightning stabbed down. "He met some guy over in Chesapeake who'd been doing it for years. I mean, he'd been studying the writings of Edgar Cayce and had read everything else he could get his hands on, but that firewalk was his first hands-on experience. He came back that night looking as though he'd touched the moon."

He would, Connie thought. Cullen was a man of absolutes, of revelation, and of change. His life had been a series of great, sweeping metamorphoses. She wondered what would have come after this.

"When's the next time we do it?" Hamilton asked. "Margo's dying to try."

Connie watched the others turn to John. He accepted the decision with a roll of his shoulders. "How about Saturday night?"

Their eagerness both fascinated and repelled Connie. This was something she didn't think she'd ever understand. To walk barefooted across red-hot coals, unburned skin dependent simply on one's believing it wouldn't happen . . .

"Will you come, Connie?" Hamilton asked.

She looked over at him. Once again his eyes were focused on her while his hand moved on Margo's thigh—slowly, as though he was impressing her in his flesh. But no heat lit his dark, triangular eyes.

"I'll come," Connie said.

"It'll set you free," Evvie Walhfield said.

Connie shook her head. Nothing could set her free, except going back in time and making Cullen not be dead anymore. If a few hot coals could make that possible, she'd walk in them, roll in them, *bathe* in them.

The air suddenly seemed too confining. She needed to move, to do something to deflect the silent urging in their eyes. She got up and went to stir the fire, turning her back on the others to watch the sparks be sucked up the flue in a bright cascade.

The conversation continued behind her, fond memories of times she hadn't shared. Old home week. She'd heard it was healthy, this reliving of happy things. It didn't work for her.

John came to her and took the poker out of her hand. "I think it's dead, Connie."

"What? Oh," she said, looking down at the mess she'd made of the fire. "I'll throw another log on."

"I'm beginning to think you were right."

"About what?"

"About this being not such a good idea."

She glanced over her shoulder at Penny, who was laughing at some fond Cullen story. But the tendons stood out sharply in her throat, and her eyes caught the light in a manic animal-glitter.

"I've never seen her like this," John said. "She's very off-balance."

"Who isn't?" With a sigh, she pushed her hair back away from her face. "Look, don't mind me. I'm being a bitch because I'm uncomfortable. This is an aspect of Cullen's life I never expected to share. And to be honest with you, I was prepared not to like the lot of you."

"I hope you've reconsidered."

"You ought to know," she said.

He smiled, an intimate upcurve of lips that warmed her insides as the fire warmed her skin. "And you ought to see yourself in the firelight," he murmured. "Maybe we should cut out early."

"Not a good idea. Penny looks ready to bounce off the walls."

"Hamilton can take care of her. He's done it before."

"Hamilton's got his hands full."

He glanced past her, and his smile broadened. "So he does. Well, back to the trenches," he murmured, holding his hand out to her.

She laid her palm in his, willing to follow, for the

moment. Libido, she thought. Amazing how cooperative it made a person.

As they walked toward the sofa, she caught sight of Amy Cortez's face. She was watching John, and her expression held the same longing Connie had seen before. He didn't seem to notice; maybe he never had. But Connie did. And she also saw the burn of jealousy behind Amy's blue eyes.

So did Lynn. She seemed to curl in on herself, retreating from the sight of her mother's too-obvious emotion.

Instead of finding it disconcerting, Connie found it comforting to know they possessed the usual human frailties. With all the talk of spirituality, self-power, self-determination, et cetera, it was easy to forget these were regular folks. And Amy Cortez had the pinched, frustrated look of a woman who wanted someone very badly and couldn't have him.

Connie saw her struggle to keep from saying anything and also saw her lose the fight a moment before she spoke.

"How did you and John get to be such good friends, Connie?" she asked.

"He came around and offered his friendship," Connie replied.

"Oh. That simple."

"It usually is," John said.

"I think we should open some champagne," Evvie said, smiling the overbright smile of an experienced hostess who sees her guests sliding downhill. "To celebrate our new friends sharing our time tonight."

Philip pushed up from the sofa. "An excellent idea. I've got some in the refrigerator. Come to think of it, we'd better drink it before it gets warm—"

The lights clicked on, leaving them all blinking in the sudden brightness.

"Back to reality," Hamilton said. "Let's go back to the firelight."

"No," Penny's voice was even more falsely bright than Evvie's smile had been. "I don't want to look at the dark right now."

The storm began to abate. Penny sat for a moment, her gaze focused on the rain-streaked windows. Then she sighed and reached up to smooth her hair back from her face. Her hands shook.

"Cullen didn't like storms much," she said.

"No," Philip agreed, his expression turning dreamy. "He always said they awed him, but he preferred to see the sun."

Echoes of thunder rolled through Connie's brain. *I know. I knew him longer than any of you. I knew him better.* As children, she and Cullen had reveled in the storms that had come pounding in off the ocean. They'd clung together, shrieking in delighted terror as the lightning slashed down, turning all the world to fire for brief, glorious moments. But he'd grown out of it, turning more to the serene side of nature. Not she; darker in nature, both more practical and less gentle, she had never been one for serenity.

The beast inside you. The hairs rose on the back of her neck. Sometimes she believed Cullen had gotten all the brightness in their personalities, and she all the darkness.

Maybe that was why she'd opted to be an accountant. She preferred the practical to the spiritual: facts and figures, all manageable, all adhering to easily understood rules. If she surrounded herself with such things, she could contain that darkness, keep it from breaking free and taking over.

She found herself beset with a sudden powerful fear: fear of letting go, fear of losing the little bit of Cullen that still remained to her. She fought to keep her breathing even.

A sudden silence in the room made her look up. The others were watching her with all-too-easily read expressions, and she realized that her face must have betrayed more of her thoughts than she expected.

They believed she'd touched something in herself that frightened her.

They believed it was Cullen.

They believed.

She stood up abruptly, distancing herself from the sudden tension. Then she caught sight of Penny's face, saw something volatile in her eyes.

"Don't stop," Penny whispered. "Don't you feel it?"

"No." *No!*

"You do feel it. You *do.*"

As Connie struggled to think of something, anything, to stop the conversation, Penny rose to her feet with a sudden, jerky movement that startled everyone.

"Why you?"

Connie flinched. "I didn't—"

"You should have seen your face," Penny said, in a voice that had become inflectionless—stark contrast to her raging eyes. "I can't sleep at night. There are times when I can almost touch him, almost hear his voice. But it's like a sheet hangs between us, and it all stays, almost. He hovers at the edge of my vision, and no matter how fast I turn, I just miss seeing him. There are times when I run into a room, thinking I might catch just a glimpse of him before he slips away. And you . . . you have the ability to reach him, and you won't even try."

"Somebody stop her," Lynn Cortez said, the single note of sanity in the frozen silence.

Connie didn't want to do it; she felt brittle, ready to shatter at the slightest touch. But no one else seemed to be able to move. So she forced herself to walk over to Penny, forced herself to lay her hands on the other woman's shoulders. "Penny," she said, "Phaedra. Don't do this to yourself."

"I want him back."

"So do I. But he's dead, and we can't have him back."

"I know he's dead!" Penny shouted.

Connie tightened her grip, trying to use pain to get through where words could not. Her soul twisted with all the things she could see in Penny's face: loss, anger, sorrow, desperation.

The two of them stood locked together, hating the contact, needing it to hold themselves together. The always-rational part of Connie's mind cringed at playing this melodrama in front of an audience, but her emotions were running too high to be stopped. She could feel John's hands on her shoulders, but the pressure seemed remote in the face of her inner pain.

"You were his twin," Penny said. "Of all the people in the world, you know how I feel."

Connie shook her head. There were no glimpses of Cullen at the edges of her vision, no echoes of him in her soul—only normal human memories, the only barrier to the dark, gnawing emptiness where something vital had been torn out. Did she want more? Did she want to be like Penny, constantly looking for what couldn't be there? She shuddered, wanting the answer to be no.

"You could help me," Penny whispered.

"I can't."

"You can."

Something cold twisted in Connie's chest. "He's dead, Penny. No one can talk to him, no one can bring him back."

Penny's lashes drooped, half-hiding eyes that had gone both despairing and sly. "Even John—"

"Even John can't help you," he said.

Connie jerked in surprise as his hands tightened on her shoulders. His touch was meant to be comforting, but she could feel it only remotely; Penny, with those raging, almost-out-of-control eyes, claimed all her attention.

But Penny's gaze had shifted past Connie to John. "I expected more of you."

"I'm only human, Phaedra."

"I won't accept that."

"You have no choice," he said. His voice was gentle, but his grip was not.

Connie felt trapped between the two of them, an unwilling buffer waiting to be drawn into their conflict. When she tried to move away, however, John's fingers tightened, keeping her there.

"Don't do this to yourself, Phaedra," he said. "Cullen has passed on to another state of existence. You can't bring him back to this one."

"But he's here," she said, her chest heaving. "I can feel him all around me. There has to be a reason for it, something important enough to keep him here. What's going to happen to him if I leave?"

"Leave!" Philip Wahlfield said. "My dear girl, where did you get that idea?"

"The house—"

"Sit down, dear. There's something I want to tell you."

Connie relaxed her grip. Penny seemed to flow down out of it, back to her seat on the sofa.

"Connie, John, sit down," Philip said. "All of you need to hear this."

Connie sat down beside Penny. She felt the cushion dip as John took a seat on her other side, but her attention remained on the older couple.

Philip glanced at his wife, who nodded. Then he clasped his hands in his lap, settling forward like a seasoned storyteller. "Months ago, we went to Cullen with a proposition. You see, we wanted him to be free, to be able to pursue his dreams without the cares of a conventional job. So we asked him to let us set up a fund—a trust, so to speak—that would enable him to do that."

Connie retained enough presence of mind to glance at Hamilton. He didn't see her; his gaze was turned inward, toward something only he could see, and it didn't look as though he liked it.

"Cullen wouldn't hear of it," Evvie said. "But Philip is persistent, and if he's blocked in one path, he always tries another. That's when we suggested that we incorporate the group itself. Although Cullen still had serious reservations, he was a bit more receptive to that idea, especially as we were willing to fund a library for the use of all the members. Also, we intended to deed this house to the company."

"Why did my brother have reservations?" Connie asked.

Evvie cleared her throat. "He didn't want to take someone else's money."

Aha, Connie thought. The Walhfields had bumped into that vein of Balestier pride and independence that ran through all the Matthiases. Sometimes to their detriment. Sometimes, she added, looking at Penny's lovely shattered eyes, to the detriment of others.

"Why are you telling us this now?" Hamilton asked.

"Because tonight our commitment to the group is reborn," Philip said. "And we realize that without Cullen's leadership, the group needs more from us than ever before."

"In what way?" Hamilton's voice dropped to a whisper.

"We need that library. We need a place where we can meet, a special place where we can feel free to explore our inner selves. Where else but here? After all, this is our center. And maybe you're right, Phaedra, and something of Cullen exists here for us."

Connie glanced around the group. To give them credit, they actually seemed to be considering the pros and cons.

"I don't know," John said. "If Cullen had reservations about it—"

"What about Phaedra?" Amy asked.

The Walhfields turned in uncanny unison. "Why, Amy, she'd live here just as she always has," Evvie said. "We always intended for her and Cullen to be the caretakers of the house, just as they were caretakers of our spiritual selves. Cullen was supposed to have been president, so Phaedra will have to step into that position."

"I don't know anything about business," Penny protested.

Philip smiled. "But Connie does."

What? Connie's mind reeled. She stared at the older man's placid face in disbelief. "I don't think—"

"You're an accountant, after all," he said. "Cullen told us that if he agreed to heading up the company, he intended for you to handle the financial end."

"But I'm not even—"

"One of us?" John finished for her. "Apparently you are."

Connie looked over at Hamilton Liu. But whatever the young man thought about it, he kept it hidden behind those flat obsidian eyes. "This is a big decision," he said. "I want to think on it and meditate."

"I agree," John said.

Connie cleared her throat. "Before any of you makes a decision, we should take time to study the ramifications. Would you want it set up as an educational foundation, or a religion—"

"Minutiae," Evvie said with a wave of her hand. "If we decide to go with it, we'll find a way to handle the details."

Only the rich, Connie thought, with a mental shake of her head. They could afford not to worry about minutiae because they always had enough to cover things.

Money, money, money. The root of all evil. She wondered if the Wahlfields ever thought about what they had, and what other people might do to get a piece of it. Wise Cullen, for resisting it as long as he had.

She glanced over at Penny, who'd drooped against the back of the sofa. Exhaustion, or maybe relief that she wasn't going to have to move. Or work.

Cynical again, aren't we? But the talk of money had taken the get-together out of the realm of the spiritual and plunked it straight into reality, and Cullen had never seemed farther away.

She liked it that way. It allowed her to push the fanciful aside, square the edges, and set the world back into an easily managed state.

Philip fetched the champagne. Connie only half-listened to the older man's graceful toast to Cullen's memory. She knew John was watching her, knew he wanted her more than ever now that her barriers were firmly in place. Why, she didn't understand. Maybe it was the hunt that appealed to him; certainly no mystery lurked in Amy's adoring eyes.

The lack of understanding didn't bother her, however; that was a man-woman thing, and she'd long ago given up wondering why relationships worked—or didn't. But Hamilton was staring at her, too, and that *did* bother her.

She drank, watching him over the rim of the fluted glass. His eyes looked like black pools, absorbing everything, revealing nothing. Which twin had he been, she wondered—dark or light?

He smiled at her, a subtle curving of lips that was meant only for her. And his hand, separate from his mind, moving in long, slow strokes along Margo's flank.

Independence was all but deserted at 3:00 A.M. Connie drove carefully, aware of the slick asphalt beneath her wheels. The storm had gone muttering off while they'd been in the restaurant, but then fog had rolled in behind it, coiling thick and white in her headlights. She could barely see John's car a hundred yards or so behind her.

The fog had changed Virginia Beach from a bustling city to a shrouded, lonely place. Traffic lights hung disembodied in the mist.

Her mind muttered and churned, adding up the facts and coming up with too little. Where had Cullen come up against the killer? Had he been killed because he didn't want the company, or because he did?

Or had it been spiritual? Leadership of the group, maybe, or a conflict in beliefs?

"I don't believe in martyrdom," she said aloud. "Not in this world."

Ahead of her, the green amorphous glow of the traffic light turned to red. She rolled to a stop. Wondering why; other than John's, there wasn't another car in sight. Ingrained obedience. Cullen would have gone on through.

"Okay," she said. "So let's leave martyrdom behind and look at this logically."

A cynical voice hooted at the back of her mind. *There's no logic in any of it.*

But there was; there had to be. She shared this with D'Amato: a puzzle existed, and although she didn't know what the picture might be, she knew the pieces had to fit together.

Viewed on an emotional level, her experience tonight had been a powerful one. Cullen's friends really seemed to care, really seemed to miss him. Viewed with an intellectual—all right, cynical—perspective, she simply didn't know. Everyone had seemed genuine, from their concern to the less exalted feelings of desire and jealousy. No flaming nuts there, only people who held the range of human emotions and faults.

So who had killed Cullen?

Not one of them seemed to have a motive.

Again, the crime of passion. An argument gone bad, a knife pulled on impulse and wielded without thought. And again, only one good candidate: Jeff.

Not my son.

"Like the good detective says, this thing stinks," she muttered. "I'd like to take a look at Cullen's hate mail."

The light turned green. She accelerated carefully. The road was slick. Just ahead, she saw the glow of headlights set high above the ground—trucks. The glow soon resolved itself into two sets, both barreling down as though afraid the light would turn before they got there.

Something big and dark leaped out of the fog in front of her. With a cry, she wrenched the steering wheel to the left. Her wheels locked up, sending the Grand Am sliding sideways across the pavement.

Headlights speared into the interior, blinding her. Tires shrieked.

Impact. The windshield turned opaque, then disintegrated. Something pale bloomed in front of her face amid shards of shattered plastic.

Then darkness.

Chapter Sixteen

"Connie!"

The voice ran through the corridors of her mind, almost recognized. An important voice. It knew things she wanted to know, offered things she wanted to have. She chased it, grasping desperately for its identity.

"Connie!"

It flitted away from her, teasing, wanting her to follow. She had to.

"Come on, Connie."

She rode up toward the light on the magic carpet of that voice. Finally, she breasted the veil between oblivion and consciousness, rising into a well of pain. Someone touched her cheek gently, an achingly familiar touch that anchored her to the present even as it spun her into the past.

"Cullen!" she gasped.

"It's John, honey."

She opened her eyes, focused with an effort. John. Not Cullen, John. For a moment, she'd thought she could . . . she'd thought Cullen hadn't . . . she shook her head, then squeezed her eyes shut again as agony darted through every synapse.

"Where do you hurt?" John asked again.

"Every . . . where." Even talking hurt. "Get me out."

"Can't. One of the truckers called for help. It won't be long. Hang on, sweetheart."

The car looked like a wad of tinfoil around her; the frame of the windshield had been bent into a sharp vee, and the dashboard all but sat in her lap. Glass and chunks of plastic lay everywhere. The airbag lay deflated on the steering wheel in front of her.

She couldn't move.

Terror beat frantic black wings in her throat. She gritted her teeth, trying to force movement into limbs that felt like cold rubber sticks. Her mind conjured up the picture of the firemen peeling the car away from her, leaving her sitting like a lump of clay, never to move again, trapped inside a body that no longer worked, would never work. *I'd rather die. At least then I'd have Cullen.*

"Easy," John said.

"I can't move." Her teeth started to chatter.

"Connie, look at me."

She forced her eyes open. He reached in through the window and brushed her hair back from her face. His hand came away red, but he didn't seem to notice.

"You can't panic," he said. "You'll only hurt yourself more."

"I can't move."

"Look around you. Take stock of the situation. I can't make you any promises; only God can do that—"

"I didn't think you believed in God."

He smiled. "But you do." His fingertips drifted

lightly down her cheek. "Someday soon we'll talk about it."

Her vision started to get fuzzy. She blinked, forcing herself to clarity again. "Did you see it?"

"The car?"

"Yeah. He didn't have his headlights on."

"No, he didn't."

"You've got to tell the police—"

"I plan to." His mouth set in a grim line. "Now save your strength, Connie. I'll take care of everything else."

The words wouldn't come anymore. She squeezed his hand before she drifted into the darkness again.

Where echoes of Cullen waited . . .

Jeff felt himself falling. He landed on something soft, something that exploded under his hands like a big puffball, sending a wash of black blood squirting over his face. Hands grasped him, pulling at his clothes, scraping jagged nails along his twitching skin.

He flung himself backward, but the hands only tightened their grip. And then he fell. Tick's face floated overhead, blood running from his mouth and nose and eyes. With a shriek, Jeff scrambled away on hands and knees.

Tick's crazy laughter followed him, followed him . . .

"Hey, Jeff, wake up."

A knife in his hands, dripping blood. He'd done something terrible with it. He tried to drop it, but it clung to him as though it had been welded to his skin.

"Jeff!"

He sat bolt upright. The girl rolled off him with a squeal, landing hard on her naked butt.

"Hey!" she cried.

"Sorry." He stared at her pointed little breasts, trying to remember who she was, where he was, and how he'd gotten here.

"You were having one hell of a nightmare," she said.

Memory came back with a rush. Her name was Tammy, she was blond and hot and this was the motel room she and her sister were sharing. They were from Vermont. He'd spent the rest of his money getting them high last night. Now his nerves felt like they'd been flocked, and he couldn't remember if he'd had a good time or not.

"Thanks for waking me up," he said, scrubbing his hands over his face.

"Anytime. That happen to you often?"

He shook his head. "First time."

"Well, it wasn't your first time for something else," she said. "You're a good fuck, Jeffrey."

That was a pleasant thought; it distracted him from things he didn't want to think about. He hoped he'd had as good a time as she had. She got up from the floor and climbed back on the bed. And on him. She was still blond, still hot; he could feel her juices on his belly. His penis was ramrod-straight, quivering against her ass.

"You look a lot younger in the light," she said. "How old did you say you were again?"

"Eighteen." His standard answer to girls; young enough or old enough for almost anybody.

She shifted position, sliding him straight into the furnace. Blood beat in his brain to match the pounding in his groin, and he felt as though the top of his head was about to come off.

"You look like such a kid," she said.

"I'm a hundred years old," he panted.

She lifted up, slammed down. Her lips skinned back from her teeth, and she sank her nails into the skin of his shoulders. Scratched him. Raked him. The black terror of his dream washed through his brain, and he went from almost-coming to limp in one rushing second.

With a cry, he rolled out from under her, dumping her on the floor a second time.

"Hey, what's wrong?" she demanded. "Jeff—"

"I gotta go," he said, ripping his jeans up his legs. "I gotta get out of here."

He didn't answer any of her questions while he finished getting dressed. Grabbing his backpack off the dresser, he flung himself out of the room and tore off down the street.

His teeth chattered as he ran. If he'd had a dime to his name, he'd have called Mom right then and there. It took him several blocks to run out of panic and energy. He slowed to a walk, breathing hard.

Shit, man. One stupid nightmare and you want your mommy.

Realizing he was getting close to the area where the cops had the frigging surveillance cameras, he turned left on Baltic and headed away from the beach.

Time to get back to Ocean View. He slung his backpack over his shoulders. It seemed heavier lately, maybe weighed down by the knife that had killed Tick.

"Shoulda got rid of it," he muttered.

Sure. But he hadn't. Uncle Cullen would have

gone off on a bunch of existential bullshit about guilt and all that other crap. Bunch of shit, Jeff thought. Truth was, he hadn't gotten rid of the knife in the stupid superstitious fear that if he did, it would kill somebody again.

He searched his pockets, came up empty. So was his stomach. So he walked up to a passerby, a fat, older guy with "tourist" written all over him. Jeff smiled his most ingratiating smile, counting on his clean-cut face to work for him.

"Excuse me, sir."

The man slowed, clearly reluctant to be approached. "Yes?"

"I lost my money on the beach, and my mom is going to kill me if I'm not home soon. Could you spare a dollar or two for the bus?"

"Well . . . okay." The man reached into his pocket and pulled out a handful of change. "You ought to be more careful."

"Yes, sir, I know. But I was watching this redheaded girl who was wearing this bathing suit you wouldn't believe, and my mind sort of went on the blink. You know?"

This time the man smiled. "Yes, I do. I'm kind of partial to redheads myself." Dredging a handful of change out of his pocket, he poured it into Jeff's outstretched hand. "Better get home, son."

"Yes, sir. Thanks."

Jeff walked on, counting the coins. Two seventy-five. Not bad. Another dollar or two and he could buy himself a decent breakfast. He scanned the street for his next target.

There we go, he thought, spotting a middle-aged couple who looked like they'd be good for a couple of bucks.

"Excuse me, sir, but—"

"Get outta here, kid," the man growled.

Brooklyn, Jeff though sourly. He was beginning to think New Yorkers didn't have hearts at all.

"Do you need some help, son?"

The voice was male and came from directly behind him. Jeff whirled to face a tough-looking guy about thirty who had the comprehensive, gritty gaze of a cop.

"No, I . . . I've got to go," Jeff gabbled.

He started down the street, half expecting to feel the cold metal embrace of handcuffs. But the guy just fell into step beside him.

"My name's Rick," the man said.

Jeff remained silent. He thought about running, but hell, the guy was in better shape than he was.

"I'm not a cop, you know," Rick said. "I'm from the Redemption Mission."

"I don't believe in religion," Jeff said.

"We don't ask that you do."

"Well, what the hell do you want, then?"

"Only to help you."

Yeah, right. Everyone wanted to help Jeff Valle. He was beginning to regret not running in the beginning. "You looking for a fuck? 'Cause if you are—"

"No, thanks."

That brought Jeff up short. "I wasn't offering."

"Oh. Some do."

"I'm not so bad off that I have to suck somebody's . . . never mind. You're for real, right?"

"Right."

Jeff walked in silence for a moment, trying to digest this unexpected situation. Every so often he glanced at his companion, waiting for him to whip out his Bible and start praying or something.

"You're not one of those people who talk in, like, tongues, are you?" Jeff asked.

Rick laughed. "Actually, I'm one of the people who serve breakfast to those in need. Are you hungry?"

"Starved."

"Then why don't you come with me?"

Jeff considered that. It could be a trap; there were plenty of those around for kids who were out of the loop. But he had two-seventy-five to his name, and a free breakfast now meant dinner later on.

"All right," he said.

Rick led him to a battered station wagon. Jeff got in cautiously, riding with both eyes on the guy and one hand on the door handle.

"Where are we going?" he asked.

"The mission's in Ocean View. Is that a problem?"

Manna from Heaven. Thank the Lord and all that shit. "No."

"How long have you been on the street?" Rick asked.

"Long enough to know what I'm doing."

"You don't sound like you're from here."

"We . . . I moved here from California. Maybe I'll go back."

Rick glanced at him. It was an undemanding sort of glance, nonjudgmental, unthreatening. "You said 'we.' "

"My Mom, okay?"

"Okay."

The man kept his attention on his driving. He didn't seem bothered at all by the silence; Jeff, however, chafed and fretted and tried to think of something to say.

"Nice weather," he finally said.

Rick glanced at him, a noncommittal flash of blue eyes. "Sure is."

End of conversation. Jeff settled back for the rest of the ride, grateful that Rick didn't pry. But the encounter had started something inside him, something that took root and grew. To be safe. Not to worry about the cops, the knife, or his own future. It had been so long since he'd felt safe that he'd almost forgotten what it was like.

The mission occupied a building that had once held a service station in the days when they really serviced cars. A fresh coat of white paint covered the brick. A hand-lettered sign read "Redemption Mission—the Lord will provide. Open every night until 1 A.M. Breakfast served 7–10, dinner 4–7."

Inside, the place smelled like coffee and disinfectant. Two long lines of tables, attended by beat-up metal folding chairs, occupied most of the room. Maybe a dozen people sat in widely spaced seats, most of them alone. Jeff hoped he didn't look as scruffy as they did.

The food was set up buffet-style: pancakes, biscuits, funny-looking scrambled eggs. One of the pans shone with the grease of long-gone sausage. Jeff loaded up. The orange juice tasted like weak Tang. He took two cupfuls.

Rick sat down across from him. "Mind if I join you?"

"You're gonna have to watch me eat."

The man's blue eyes gentled some, and he clasped his hands on the table in front of him. "I'm not going to ask for your name or for anything else you don't want to give me. But if you're in trouble, there are resources—"

"Not for me," Jeff said through a mouthful of food. "What kind of game are you playing? You don't know me, and you sure as hell don't give a shit what happens to me."

"You're right, I don't know you. But I care about all you kids. Black, white, straight or drunk or high, I don't want to see any of you get hurt. And you can get hurt out there."

Jeff crammed another biscuit into his mouth. While he chewed, he studied his companion. The guy seemed sincere enough, without the sappy emotionalism most do-gooders held.

"I'm not going home," he said.

"Is the street better?"

Than jail? Yeah. "I do okay."

Rick heaved a sigh. "How old are you?"

"Eighteen."

"Bullshit."

For some reason, Jeff felt compelled to honesty. "Fifteen."

"You're an innocent." He waved off Jeff's automatic hoot of laughter. "Not like you think. I'm talking about your spirit. You've done nothing to deserve the street, nothing to condemn you to a life of sleeping on the sidewalk and bumming change from strangers."

"I do okay," Jeff said. "I've got friends." *Dead friends.* He pushed that thought aside. "And I haven't had to sleep on the sidewalk."

"It's a downward spiral. You're new, you're at the top of the loop. That'll change. You've got guys who'll shoot you for a dollar, you've got cold weather and bad drugs and AIDS."

"Yeah, so what's your point?"

"You don't have to live like this. Go home."

"Can't."

"Won't, you mean."

Jeff shrugged.

"Do you think your Mom cares about you?" Rick asked.

"Yeah." *She thinks I killed her brother. Fuck,* I *think I killed her brother.*

"What about your father?"

"He's okay. Strict. He'd bust my ass if I went home."

"Somebody's going to bust your ass if you stay on the street."

"Whatever."

Rick studied him for a while. Then he reached into his pocket, pulled out a quarter, and laid it on the table. With his forefinger, he slid it across to Jeff.

"This is my gift to you," he said. "Use it to call home." He raised his hand, forestalling Jeff's protest. "When you're ready. Call. Tell them you're okay if nothing else. Put this someplace where you won't spend it on something else. Oh, and feel free to come by anytime. We've always got coffee and sandwiches between mealtimes."

He got up and went out. Jeff stared after him for a while, then took the quarter and put it in his pocket.

Chapter Seventeen

"What do you think, Doctor?" John asked.

Connie registered his voice in the darkness behind her eyes, but felt no urge to open them. Her thoughts were moving slowly and a bit mistily, and a grind of pain hammered at the top of her head. Besides, if things were really bad, she wanted a chance to get a handle on herself before having to deal with someone else's sympathy.

"All in all," came an unfamiliar female voice, "she's very lucky."

That's what they all say, Connie thought. Then they stare at the afflicted one in silent gratitude that it wasn't them.

The woman spoke again. "Is there family you should call?"

"Hell, I forgot. If you've got a phonebook around, I'd better give her—"

"Do not call my mother." Connie opened her eyes.

John whirled. The doctor had better reflexes, and merely turned. A sharp-faced woman of about fifty with steel-gray hair and flinty eyes, she exuded a reassuring air of capability.

"Did you hear me, John?" Connie asked. "Do not call my mother."

"Why not?"

"Sandra's hard to take at the best of times. Flat on my back and helpless, I'd be dead meat."

"You're never helpless."

The doctor moved closer. Her name tag read "Dr. Maureen Glenn." "I'm Dr. Glenn, Ms. Matthias. How do you feel?"

"My head hurts, my shoulder and ankle hurt . . . hey!" Connie said. "I'm not paralyzed, then!"

With an irrepressible sigh of relief, she levered herself to a sitting position. She didn't mind the pain. Pain was good. Movement was better. Realizing that both John and the doctor were staring at her as though she'd lost her mind, she said, "I couldn't move before."

John opened his mouth a couple of times before anything came out. Then he sort of dived toward her, wrapping his arms around her so hard it hurt. "Is that what you thought? Oh, Connie!"

"You have a very mild concussion," the doctor said. "On top of that, a bruised shoulder and a sprained ankle. Three stitches on a cut just below your hairline. Considering what I was told about the condition of the car, you're a very lucky woman."

"The airbag saved your life," John said. "The firemen said you'd have been hash otherwise."

"You have such a way with words," Connie said.

"I'm quoting."

Connie looked over his shoulder at the window, which was full of golden daylight. She waited to feel something, gratitude for this extra lease of life, maybe, but found nothing but emptiness inside. Maybe she'd used it all up earlier. "Where am I?"

"Virginia Beach General," the doctor said. "You were brought in by ambulance. Do you remember anything about last night?"

With an effort, Connie dredged through her scattered memories. She could remember bits and pieces: sirens and flashing lights, the tortured sound of metal being torn or cut, a sensation of oft-disturbed sleep. And most of all, a voice that sounded like Cullen's.

"I remember this and that," she said. "Nothing detailed, and most of it disconnected."

Dr. Glenn nodded. "Mild shock, normal in these circumstances. Excuse me, Mr. Bruycker. I'd like to examine her." With smooth efficiency, she pulled a pencil light out of her pocket and flashed the beam into Connie's eyes. "Your reactions have returned to normal. Good." She moved to the foot of the bed to make a notation on the chart.

"When can I go home?" Connie asked.

"Are you in a hurry, Ms. Matthias?"

My son is gone, and I've got to find him. "I've got a lot to do. When can I go home?"

Instead of answering her, Dr. Glenn looked at John. "Mr. Bruycker, you said you'd be willing to stay with her for the next twelve hours or so?"

"I believe I asked the question," Connie said.

"Yes, you did." The doctor's gun-metal gaze focused on her. "But with concussions, we want to make sure someone observes the patient to be sure sleep doesn't turn into a coma."

"Don't worry about her," John said. "If she doesn't want me, I'll just call her mother to come sit with her."

"You're really playing dirty now," Connie snarled.

The doctor smiled for the first time, and her face settled into pleasant creases. "I'll see about getting you released, Ms. Matthias."

"Come on," John said. "Let's get you dressed. Although," his hands started to wander, "there are decided advantages to those hospital gowns."

Connie's emptiness evaporated. It was always this way with him; sensuality just under the surface, ready to burst free at any moment. It might not be love, but it made her feel like a whole human being. A small part of her mind whispered that she'd never be whole, that Cullen had taken something that could never be replaced, but sensation soon laid that treacherous little voice to rest. For now, for this moment, she could feel.

She could feel a lot. Soon, she was really, really glad she hadn't been paralyzed. Sensation could be a very good thing. "Maybe we could do a study on the healing effects of sex," she murmured.

"Now? Come to think of it, these beds have some interesting advantages of their own. If we raise it like this—"

"Ahem."

Connie looked up to see Dr. Glenn standing in the doorway. "We . . . didn't expect you back so soon, Doctor," she said, retrieving the fugitive gown and pulling it back up.

"I wanted to warn you about avoiding excess physical exertion," the woman said. Her mouth twitched.

"We'll certainly avoid excess," Connie said.

Dr. Glenn disappeared again. John levered himself up off the bed and went to retrieve Connie's clothes from the closet.

"Let's get out of here," he said. "There's no privacy in hospitals."

"At least she didn't ask to take my temperature."

"That," John said, "would have been obvious to anyone: hot—very, very hot."

Twenty minutes later, they were in his car and heading toward her apartment. The sun had burned the fog away and returned Independence to its normal traffic load. Connie sat stiffly, recoiling inwardly when another vehicle pulled out in front of them.

"Nervous?" John asked.

"Reflex. It'll go away."

He glanced at her, then reached over to lay his hand over hers. "Do you realize how glad I am to still have you with me?"

She ducked her head; if they'd been in bed, she would have known what to do. But now, with her emotions as bruised and off-balance as her body, she couldn't decide how to react. So she merely turned her hand upward and linked her fingers with his. Maybe it was enough, for he smiled.

"Did they find out who was driving that car?" she asked.

He shook his head. "I couldn't see the license plate. Couldn't even tell what color it was, the fog was so thick. All I could tell was that it looked like one of those squarish, high-up things like a Bronco."

Something nagged at the edges of Connie's mind. A near-memory, one that eluded her no matter how hard she tried to grasp it. She remembered a vague shape, then the squeal of tires and the steering wheel hurting her hands as she swerved.

And fear. A lot of fear.

She remained silent until John pulled up in front of the old farmhouse. He came around and helped her out of the car, then scooped her into his arms and carried her toward the house.

"This is embarrassing," she said.

"But more efficient than letting you hobble on that ankle."

Mr. Ranke came out to meet them, brows raised high. "You all get married?"

John's expression remained pleasant, but Connie saw annoyance in his eyes. She smiled a little, realizing he'd had a very intimate and tender scenario all set up in his mind, which Mr. Ranke had just popped like the proverbial bubble.

"No, we didn't get married," she said. "I had a car accident and sprained my ankle."

"So you're okay," the old man said, with a vigorous nod of, she hoped, approval. "The car?"

"Totaled," John said.

"Whoa." Ranke whistled softly through his teeth. "Well, that explains the cop comin' around."

Ice dropped into the pit of Connie's stomach. "What cop?"

"Some cop. He asked if I'd seen you, or if you'd gone somewhere with someone. I told him what I knew, that you'd left alone at seven twenty-three, and that you didn't tell me when you'd be back."

"Seven twenty-three," John repeated. "You're very accurate, Mr. Ranke."

"I watch out for my tenants."

"Do you patrol the perimeter, too?"

The old man's eyes turned hard. "Sure. I learned it in Korea."

"This policeman, Mr. Ranke." Connie's fingers shook a little as she reached up to brush her hair back from her face. "Did he leave his name?"

"Hell, no. Flashed me a badge, then flashed me the questions."

"Did he have gray hair and brown eyes?" she asked. "A square kind of guy, sure of himself?"

"Yeah, that's him."

D'Amato. She studied Mr. Ranke, trying to guess if D'Amato had said anything about Jeff. The old man met her gaze steadily and quite blandly, and she decided not.

"Well, we'd better get upstairs," John said, shifting her in his arms.

"Need help?" Ranke asked.

"I've got her. But if you'd open the door for us—"

The old man snatched the keys and trotted into the house. A line appeared between John's brows.

"I think there was more privacy in the hospital," he said.

"Mr. Ranke's a sweetheart."

He looked down at her and his expression cleared. "I ought to be glad you've got a guardian angel," he said. "You can't be too careful these days."

"No," she said, thinking about that vague, rushing shape that had almost meant her death. "You can't."

"Hey, Jeff!"

It took Jeff a minute to register the voice. Then he

did, and his heart revved: this was the guy who'd driven Tick and him out to his dad's house. He turned around slowly, hunching his shoulders against the wind.

"Hey," he said.

"Remember me? I'm Henry. You and me and Tick partied together."

"Yeah, I remember."

Henry laughed, the same weird giggle that had bothered Jeff before. "You seen Tick anywhere?"

"Ain't seen him in days." The knife seemed to hum in the backpack. "You?"

"Uh-uh. He was supposed to score some PCP for me. You know anything about it?"

Jeff shook his head.

"Man, that little fucker has fifty bucks of my money. I'm going to stomp his balls but good if he's tryin' to fuck me."

"Tick wouldn't do that," Jeff said.

"He better not."

A bubble rose in Jeff's chest. He struggled to contain rage too big for him, rage against what had happened, what was bound to happen in the future. He stared at Henry, hating the blotchy, pimply skin, the mouth that looked as hard and cruel as a shark's. He wanted to smash that mouth. He wanted to hit and hit and never stop until he'd worn out the pain inside himself.

And then he looked into Henry's eyes. There was no anger in those eyes. They were cold, emotionless. A snake's eyes. His own anger curled away like hair held in a flame, and fear rose in its place. He might be capable of hurting someone in anger, in pain, or maybe under the influence, but Henry would do it . . . just because.

Jeff remembered some of the things Rick had said to him earlier today. "You're at the top of the loop, and it's a long way down." Yeah. Looking into Henry's flat, empty gaze, Jeff got a real good view of the bottom.

"You got anything on you?" Henry asked.

"I'm totally broke, man," Jeff said, feeling the two bucks like a death sentence in his pocket.

"You'd better not be fucking with me."

"Fuck with you? Shit, man. I had to go down to the fucking Redemption Mission just to get a fucking cup of coffee."

Henry stared at him for a minute, then nodded and walked away. Jeff went the opposite way, just in case the guy changed his mind. He put a couple of blocks between them before slowing down.

This was too hard, too friggin' hard. Running the streets with money in his pockets and no real troubles was one thing, but doing it broke and hunted and scared was something else. He hadn't figured on this.

He wanted his mother.

You can't go home. They'll put you away for a hundred years, with guys who make Henry look like a fucking altar boy.

But he could talk to her. Maybe she'd thought of a way to help him, maybe not. But if he could just talk to her, he might be able to feel safe for a couple of minutes. He needed that. Maybe she'd even find an out for him; Mom was good at things like that.

He stared longingly at the brightly lit Denny's down the street. There, normal people ate and drank and had conversations. He and Mom used to hit Denny's every Sunday morning until he turned thirteen. Then he didn't want to go, at least with his mother. Too cool. Well, he didn't feel too friggin' cool now.

Pulling his baseball cap down over his eyes, he walked down to the restaurant. It'd be warm in there, and they had a phone. . . . Catching sight of a cop car in the parking lot, he kept on walking. He'd have to give up warmth and normality and the smell of bacon and sausage cooking.

He kept walking. A few blocks farther on, he came to a service station, where a pair of pay phones stood in the illumination from the street light.

"Yeah," he said.

Rick's quarter was warm when he took it out of his pocket. Slipping it into the phone, he dialed his grandmother's number.

"C'mon, Mom, be there," he said. "I don't want to talk to the old biddy."

But it was Sandra who answered. Jeff felt a surge of annoyance when he heard her too-sugary southern-belle accent. She must be waiting for the garden club or the DAR to call.

But he needed her, so he used some charm of his own. "Hey, Grandma."

"Jeffrey." Her indrawn breath was sharp and loud. "Where are you?"

"In town. Is Mom around?"

"Your mother has moved into her own place."

"Can I have her address and phone number?"

"No, you *may* not."

It was his turn to inhale. She'd always been a bitch, but he hadn't expected her to go this far. "So I'll call Information. Thanks for nothing—"

"The number is unlisted."

"Look, Grandma, I know Mom wants to hear from me—"

"There's no bigger fool than a mother," Sandra said. "I should know. But you're not mine, and I'm going to protect my daughter from her own foolishness."

He couldn't believe this was happening. "Hey, look—"

"Don't use that tone of voice with me, young man. You've chosen your life-style, and you didn't once think of your mother while you did it. You wanted nothing to do with her, if I recall. And now that things have gotten hot for you, you want her phone number so she can pull your fat out of the fire like she did so many times in California. Not this time. I've got one piece of advice for you: turn yourself in to the police. Maybe you'll get a lenient judge."

"You can't do this," he hissed, struggling with a flaming uprush of temper.

"And you've got a lot to learn about life, Jeffrey." Her voice was oh-so-reasonable, masking the crabbed little soul beneath. "You've spent a lot of time screaming that no one can tell you what to do. Well, you can't tell us what to do, either. And I do not *choose* to give you my daughter's phone number."

"Hey, listen—"

"If you show up here, I will call the police. If you call here again, I will call the police. Be a man. Stay away from Connie. You've hurt her enough."

Then she hung up on him. He stood there for a moment, clenching the receiver until his hand hurt. "You old bitch," he muttered. "You old bitch!"

Letting the receiver fall, he sat down on the curb

and leaned his face on his knees. He could smell the street, asphalt and dust and a faint reek of garbage. Or maybe the garbagey smell was him.

"Fuck you, Grandma," he moaned. Tears ran down and soaked the grimy denim of his jeans.

Hearing a car coming down the street, he looked up. Cops. Damn. They'd stop for sure if they saw him sitting here. He scrambled to his feet and cut diagonally through the service station parking lot.

And then it came to him: the solution. He could catch a bus over toward the beach, then walk the rest of the way to Cullen's house. Aunt Penny wasn't too bright, but she'd always been decent to him. *She'd* tell him where Mom had gone.

His shoulders straightened. Yeah. And this time, he wasn't gonna take no for an answer.

Chapter Eighteen

Connie woke, aware that John's warmth was missing from the bed beside her. The dying sun had left a trace of blue-violet in the western sky, and the shadows lay thick and cool in the corners of her room.

Her head hurt. But it was manageable now, and after a day of on-again, off-again sexual activity, she couldn't find a reason to give in to the soreness of her body. John was definitely good for her perspective; every time she started to fall into self pity, he gave her something much more fun to think about.

She murmured, "I wonder where my demon lover has gone."

She got out of bed cautiously, then with growing confidence. Actually, she felt pretty good. Maybe she was getting used to being kicked around.

The rest of the apartment was as dark as the bedroom. She started to turn toward the kitchen, but then froze as she saw a shadowy figure sitting on her sofa. Motionless. Silent.

The hairs on the back of her neck lifted. She stood there for a moment, breathing through her nose in sudden panic. Her mind tallied the possibilities: ghost, mass murderer, and worst of all, considering the fact that she was stark naked, Mr. Ranke.

She took a step to the left, toward the phone. The figure, now silhouetted against the lighter rectangle of the window, resolved into the head and shoulders of a man. She knew the sleek lines of that head.

"John?" she whispered.

He didn't answer. Her imagination went into high gear, conjuring images of a knife-wielding murderer creeping into her apartment to take John away from her as he'd taken Cullen.

Crazy. Impossible.

"John?"

No answer. Her breath felt like a solid, icy column in her throat as she limped across the room. She didn't want to go, didn't want to become what she'd become if she had to sit beside the corpse of yet another person she cared about.

His eyes were closed and his chest rose and fell with deep, even breathing. For a moment, she thought her legs would collapse under her. *Thank you, God!*

She switched on the floor lamp. He didn't stir, although the cone of illumination fell across his face. He was as naked as she, his arms and legs wound into an impossible-looking position. Lotus, that was it.

The feeling of creeping dread returned, but for a different reason: this wasn't the John she knew. Oh, the body was the same, the taut lines of his chest and belly and legs as sleekly powerful as a cat's. Connie had touched or tasted every inch of that skin, had experienced with him every physical pleasure that men and women could share. But now, she sensed something strangely asexual about him that almost repelled her.

She waved her hand in front of his face. No reaction. *Oh, God, he's in some kind of trance.* Some atavistic chord in her, perhaps bred by an Episcopalian upbringing, made her reluctant to touch him.

"John," she called softly. "John?"

His eyes opened. But he didn't seem to see her; his gaze remained focused on something inward. Feeling really spooked now, she touched his shoulder.

"Clovis?" he muttered. Then he shuddered, and his eyes returned to normal. "Connie." He reached out to run his hand over her hair. "Your aura is burning high tonight. Cullen must be near."

She slapped his hand away. "What the hell are you doing?"

"I'm sorry if I frightened you." He unwound from the lotus position and spread his arms across the back of the sofa. All of a sudden, he looked like her lover again.

"You scared me," she said.

"Because I was meditating?"

She took a deep breath, let it out. "I'm not used to finding people meditating on my sofa. And then talking about auras."

"You don't believe."

"No."

"Do you ever feel Cullen nearby?"

"No." Only the emptiness.

He studied her, a half-smile curving his mouth. She didn't know what he found in her during that perusal, half hoped she never would.

"I wish you could see yourself through my eyes," he said. "You burn brightly, Connie. Maybe differently than Cullen, but just as bright. Only a few moments ago, I could almost feel him in the room with me. I think he came to you."

"I can't feel anything."

"You won't let yourself feel anything. Cullen was wide open; he didn't know any other way to be. But you . . . you're afraid of feeling anything, in case you feel too much. And if you do that, you might have to step out of that comfortable little world you've built around yourself."

She turned away abruptly, limping into the kitchen to run water into the coffeepot. "Who's Clovis?"

"Clovis?"

"Before you were fully awake, you called out to someone named Clovis."

He didn't answer. With the water running, she didn't know he'd come into the kitchen with her until she felt his arms slide past her. He turned the water off, then swiveled her around to face him.

"Do you know anything about channeling?" he asked.

She tipped her head back to look at him. "Cullen filled me in, or attempted to. I was trying not to listen too hard, so I might not have it exactly. You go into a trance to contact a spirit, or maybe now it's called the higher consciousness, or something. Like the mediums that were so popular in Victorian times."

"Cullen didn't say *that.*"

"Is Clovis your contact?"

"Yes."

"He or she?"

"She." He smiled. "I've always had more of an affinity for women than for men. When Clovis was alive many years ago, she was a healer, a teacher, a woman of great wisdom. I'm lucky that she chose me."

"And what did she tell you just now?"

"That you're the key."

She raised her hand to ward that away. "To what?"

"Cullen had a . . . greatness of spirit. Death can't take that, can't make it less than it was. That spirit still exists around us—"

"Part of the great consciousness?"

"Call it what you want."

"Then call it a soul. I can live with that."

He inclined his head. "Entities—souls, if you prefer—are drawn to those things they once loved. Cullen more than most, since he had a depth of caring that is very rare. I think he loved you more than anyone in the world."

"Not more than Penny."

"Yes. Terrible as it seems, he did. *You* were the one, his twin, his soulmate. Do you know what he said to me that last night of his life? He said now that you'd come home, he'd be whole again."

Connie's throat tightened; John understood her too well, touched those things she wanted to be true. Wanted, at times, so badly it was scary. She shook her head, denying not what he'd said, but what she knew was coming.

"I don't have special dispensation for Cullen's soul," she said. "I'm trying to have an open mind about this, maybe because I need to share, even a little, something of his life." Realizing she'd crossed her arms over her chest, she forced herself to relax. "But it's hard. I've come a long way in just agreeing to handle the group's financial matters."

"Phaedra needs you."

"Hell, she needs Cullen. And she thinks I'm the magic conduit to getting him. It's not healthy, John."

"It's not healthy for you to shut yourself away from those who care about you," he said. "But you do it."

"It's self-preservation."

"It's a waste."

"Of what?" she cried. "I'm a thirty-three-year-old woman with two failed marriages behind me, a kid gone off the deep end, and a brother who's been murdered. If I open myself to the goddamn continuum, I'll probably explode."

"But there's also a chance to be whole, a chance to be more than the sum of your mistakes. It's a risk, Connie. But there's so much to be gained."

She tilted her head back to look at him. "This isn't about Cullen at all, is it?"

He spread his hands. "In a way it is, because without touching him, you'll never come to terms with yourself. You'll never be whole. But I want you whole for me. Nobody else, *me.* Do you think I'd offer to share your careful little soul with another man, even your brother, for anything less?"

"What—"

"I'm in love with you, Connie."

"John—"

He gripped her by the shoulders, pulling her up and closer. "My logical mind tells me I'm going too fast, asking too much when you're still recovering from Cullen's death. But logic doesn't seem to have much to do with my relationship with you. It's kind of like being on a roller coaster—fast and crazy, and just a little frightening. I find myself wanting every little part of you, even those you'd like to keep for yourself. I want more than you're willing to give. More, probably, than is fair."

She stared into his crystal blue eyes, rocked by the power of his declaration. "I don't know what to think—"

"You think too much. Try feeling for a change."

"That's the hard part."

"Yes," he agreed. "The risky part."

"I've never been good with risk." But her body was giving her a different message; the flare of his nostrils showed that he got it loud and clear.

He took her hand and raised it to his mouth. As he sucked her fingertips one by one, she shivered.

"Sometimes you've got no choice but to take the risk," he said.

"There's always a choice," she murmured, maybe because she knew she was fast passing the stage of choosing. To be wanted like this . . .

"Take the step, Connie."

"What step?"

He smiled, transferring her wet finger from his mouth to hers. "Just take a step toward me, so I know you want me."

Now, *that* she could do. "There doesn't seem to be much risk in that."

"You never know."

She took the step. His eyes seemed almost to darken, and she felt as though she'd fallen off a cliff. He read her well, played her even better. While he touched her *here,* kissed her *there,* nothing else mattered. He lifted her legs around his waist. She clung to him, striving, the heat of his body a stark contrast to the cool, impersonal countertop behind her. She'd thought she had already touched the heights with him, but this was better than ever before, the pleasure so intense it almost became pain.

Yes, it was good . . . better than good. It thrilled her body and submerged her mind in a wild, dark torrent of sensation. And yes, she panted and gasped and called out his name when she climaxed. But it didn't touch her soul.

"I love you," he whispered into her ear, as they leaned together, sweating. "I love you."

Connie held him, feeling the beat of his heart against her cheek. Self-contained, once again in control. She knew he wanted her to say it: "I love you, John." She ought to say it; any woman in her right mind would say it, even if it wasn't quite true, in the hopes of making it real someday.

All her life, however, there had been things she'd never been able to give men. So instead of telling him what he wanted to hear, she pulled him down for a kiss.

And all the while, her mind moving clickety-clack, clickety-clack, the serpent in this particular Garden of Eden.

Jeff. Cullen. John, me, John, me. And Clovis. Jesus Christ.

Connie hit the redial button. "For the tenth time," she muttered as it rang and rang. "Damn it, Derek! Are you the only person in the United States without an answering machine?"

She hung up, then leaned close to the mirror to inspect the cut along her hairline. Her skin had already begun to bruise; a couple more hours and she'd look like she was wearing a purple-black headband. She turned her head from side to side, gauging the effect.

"Maybe I should try for bangs." *Nah.* Or as Jeff would say, *Not!* She hadn't worn bangs since the eighth grade, and had kept her hair shoulder-length to avoid the Indian-princess look. She'd have to stay with the bruises.

Someone knocked on the outer door, hard enough to seem demanding. She smoothed her hair back into place. "Coming!"

Her ankle started to throb halfway across the room, and by the time she reached the door she was almost hobbling. It didn't do her mood any good to find Derek outside, looking annoyed.

"It's almost nine o'clock," she said, moving straight on the offensive. "You were supposed to be here at seven."

"What are you worried about? The boyfriend didn't leave until seven-twenty," he said.

She gaped at him. "How . . . oh, Mr. Ranke. Why did he tell you?"

"He likes me."

"And he doesn't like John?"

"He doesn't like anybody who makes cracks about perimeter patrol. Said he wanted to pop John one."

"It wasn't meant to be nasty."

"How do you know?"

"I was there."

He spread his hands. "Better take it up with Mr. Ranke. *I* don't give a shit."

With a sigh of exasperation, she stepped back and motioned him inside.

He came in, closing the door behind him. Something surged in the depths of his hazel eyes. It might have been anger, might equally have been a half-dozen other things. He'd always been better at reading her than she was at reading him.

"I called earlier," he said. "John said you were asleep, that you'd been in a wreck and had a concussion, and that you weren't in any shape to go out."

"I'm the judge of that."

"Agreed. But he wasn't about to let me talk to you, was he?"

She grimaced. "Male territoriality."

"Birds do it, bees do it—"

"And people are supposed to have some sense."

"So you say." His gaze flicked to her bandaged ankle, then to her forehead. "What's next, Connie? A high dive from the Berkeley Bridge?"

"It isn't my fault."

He snorted. "What about the Grand Am?"

"Totaled, or so I heard," she said. "Look. It was just one of those freak accidents. A car came at me out of the fog, and took me completely by surprise. I reacted poorly; chose a Mack truck instead of a storefront."

"Were you able to identify the car?"

"It was a . . ." *Bronco. Say it. Remember it.* She frowned as shadows of cars rolled through her memory. It should be there for the taking. She pulled at it, willing it to come into focus. But the images refused to coalesce, and soon even the shadows slipped away from her.

When she focused on Derek's face again, she saw him studying her with a decidedly odd expression.

"What?" she asked.

"You just sort of trailed away, Connie. Do you know what kind of car it was or not?"

"Not. I . . . was told it was something like a

Bronco. But I can't remember anything but a shadow. You'd think it would be etched in my mind. Living or dying—one of life's big crossroads."

"Or end of the road."

"Hey, that should have been my line," she said.

"How did the meeting go?"

She cocked her head to one side. "You must be psychic."

"Try suspicious."

"That's good enough for me," she said. "The meeting was interesting, to say the least. It seems the Walhfields had been trying to get Cullen to accept their financial support."

"Hell, they'd been doing it for that Liu kid. Might as well add one more."

"Cullen refused."

"Yeah. He would." It was obvious that Derek approved.

"Well, they decided to try a different tack. Incorporate the group."

"Huh?"

"You can incorporate almost anything; seventy-five bucks to the State Corporation Commission, and you're in business. The house would have become the property of the company, and God knows how much cash. The Wahlfields are no pikers; I checked them out, and they're worth just over sixteen million dollars. *Not* counting the real estate."

Derek whistled. "How did Cullen feel about that?"

"He didn't like it."

"Let me guess: the Walhfields resurrected the idea with the others, who think it's great."

"They have to vote. But I expect they'll go for it." She couldn't shake the memory of Hamilton Liu's cold, calculating eyes. She didn't know how deeply he was into the Wahlfields, or how much he'd already gotten; human nature being what it was, she didn't think he'd be happy about sharing.

"If this flies, who's supposed to handle the money?"

"Actually, little old accountant me."

"Holy shit," he breathed.

"I'm Cullen's twin," she said. "How could they possibly exclude me?"

"Cripes." He raked both hands through his hair. "And somebody didn't like having a little old accountant watchdogging the expenditures, maybe. By the way, where was your boyfriend while you were having your accident?"

"Don't look so hopeful, Derek. He was following about thirty yards behind me."

"Damn. I had him pegged as a killer."

"Well, you were wrong. Not, may I add, for the first time in your life?"

"Maybe I just understand someone's motivation for trying to off you. There were times when I could have cheerfully wrung your neck."

"Why didn't you?" She'd meant the question as a joke, but there was an undercurrent in the air that made it not quite so funny.

"You lived too far away," he said.

Connie reached for her jacket. This conversation had gone far enough; she didn't have the resources to pick through the currents of Derek's emotions right now.

"Well, let's go," she said, slipping her arms into

the sleeves with an air of finality she hoped would convey to him.

She didn't. "So who else do you think it was?"

"I think it was an accident."

"I can't let you do this anymore," he said.

" 'Let' doesn't enter into our relationship."

"What relationship?"

"Strained truce." She assessed the thrust of his jaw, then sighed and took a half-step backward. "Look, Derek. I'd risk a hell of a lot more for Jeff's sake."

"Or for revenge."

"For that, too."

He let his breath out slowly. "I don't have much choice, do I?"

"Nope. With or without you, I'm playing this out to the end. My son needs me, whether he knows it or not. And I intend to help him, whether he wants it or not."

"Ask not, and ye shall receive?"

"Amen."

He bowed to her with half-mocking elaborateness. "It shouldn't sound like logic, but it does."

The phone rang, making them both jump. Connie rushed to answer it, knowing Derek would think she did it because it might be John. But she did it because she couldn't stop hoping it might be Jeff. "Come get me, Mom. I want to come home."

She snatched the receiver up. "Hello?"

"Connie, it's John."

Of course it wasn't Jeff. Of course. She looked over at Derek, who'd leaned his elbows on the counter. His shoulders slumped as though something heavy pressed them down. "I can't talk right now, John. I'm on my way out."

"I'm at Phaedra's. Your son came by here tonight."

"Jeff was there?" Everything in her sharpened, focused; glancing at Derek, she saw the match in his eyes. "When? What did he say? How—"

"He beat her up."

"What?"

"He beat her up. Badly."

Connie shook her head, trying to assimilate this new blow. "Is she all right?"

"She's upstairs, resting. The doctor's been out already. He says she'll be okay, although it'll be a while before she looks like her old self."

"Oh, God."

"Connie . . . we had no choice but to call the police. I'm sorry. Phaedra's determined to press charges, and I can't say I blame her."

"I can't either," she said, feeling a hundred years old.

"She wants to see you."

Connie glanced at Derek, whose arms were braced so stiffly that the muscles stood out in striated ridges beneath the skin.

"Tell her we're on our way."

She hung up. Propping her elbows on the counter, she ducked her head and clasped her hands over the back of her neck. "I can't believe this."

"What?" Derek hissed.

"Jeff beat Penny up," she said.

He let his breath out in a long sigh. Then, so suddenly that she jumped, he swung around and punched the wall, clear *through* the plasterboard. They both stared at the wreckage for a moment, then he retrieved her purse and handed it to her.

"Sorry about the mess," he said, the calmness of

his voice only making his eyes scarier. "Tell Mr. Ranke I'll take care of it tomorrow."

Blood spattered his knuckles. He didn't mention it, and neither did she.

Chapter Nineteen

Connie rang the doorbell of the beach house. She glanced at Derek, but his gaze had turned inward, seeking something she didn't think he was going to find.

The door swung open, framing John against the light. "Come on in," he said.

Connie stepped in, conscious of Derek too close behind her. Blood flecked the pale tiles of the foyer, splashed a dark fan across the baseboard.

It hit hard, that image. For it conjured another one: Jeff attacking Penny, pounding her, making her bleed. What had it been like? Had she pleaded with him, fought back? Connie felt as though her stomach were turning inside out.

How could he? It rocked her, this revelation about her son. She'd tried so hard to believe in his innocence, tried so hard to hold it, despite the evidence against him. But if he were capable of this . . . she swallowed hard. Turning to the only person who might understand, she looked at Derek.

His eyes had gone hard and glittery, and a muscle jumped in his cheek. She knew he'd reached bottom. And she had to turn away from it, because her own despair was too great.

"What happened, John?" she asked.

He made a sharp gesture. "The kid just blew, Connie. I wish I could have avoided calling the police, but Phaedra is determined to press charges."

Connie closed her eyes. Poor Penny. Poor Jeff. He'd just dug himself a hole, maybe deeper than something he could ever climb out of. *Where did I go wrong? What did I do that made him turn out so warped?*

"Connie, are you all right?" John asked, taking her by the arm.

"Sure, I'm fine," she said, her voice sounding as defeated as she felt. "I've just found out that my son beats up women, and I'm fucking *fine.*"

"We'd better get some weight off that ankle," John said, tightening his grip.

She shook him off. "I want to see Penny."

"She's resting."

"Now," Derek said.

John looked from her to Derek and back again. Then he sighed. "I was hoping to spare you something."

"You can't," Connie said. "No one can."

Between them, they all but carried her up the stairs. She didn't want to be touched; she felt fragile and flawed, ready to shatter at the slightest provocation. The moment they reached the top, she pulled away from their hands.

"Wait here a second," John said. He opened Penny's door and went in.

Connie leaned against the wall, watching the man who'd once been her husband. He'd retreated inside himself, walling himself, malelike, behind a veil of cool self-control.

The lack of emotion in him annoyed her. She wanted to shock him out of that stolid control; she could face this only if one other human being felt the same despair, the same pain.

Inevitably her gaze was drawn to his battered knuckles. Men, she thought. Men and their anger, men and their violence. Hit something, smash something, and it was all okay because they were angry.

"Don't say it," he said.

"Say what?"

"Like father, like son."

"No," she said. "You only punch other people's walls."

"I didn't expect you to understand."

She shook her head. "Oh, I understand. All too well."

"Damn it, Connie—"

John opened the door and beckoned to them. Connie followed him in, avoiding Derek's hand as he tried to steady her.

Penny lay in a nest of pillows, swathed to the chin in a fluffy blue bathrobe. She hardly looked human at all. The black eye wasn't the worst; that went to the upper lip that lay like an overinflated balloon beneath her nose. As she raised her hands to press an icepack to her mouth, her sleeves fell back to reveal forearms that had been battered purple-black as she'd tried to defend herself.

Connie's breath went out in a gasp. This was worse than she'd expected, worse than she'd imagined. That Jeff could do this to another human being . . . because of her former beauty, this seemed even more a desecration. More monstrous, somehow, to crush an orchid underfoot than a weed. "Penny. Oh, I'm sorry!"

"No . . . not your fault," she said through the icepack. "Not even Jeff's. He was . . . was—"

"High on something," John finished for her. "He didn't know what he was doing."

The doorbell rang. Penny flinched visibly, and John reached out to pat her on the shoulder.

"That'll be Detective D'Amato," he said.

Connie drew in her breath sharply. "You called *Homicide?*"

"I did," Penny said. "I . . . wasn't thinking straight. And his number was right beside the phone. I'm s-sorry, Connie."

With an effort, Connie kept her voice even. "You couldn't help it, Penny. And I'm the one who's sorry."

"What should I do?" John asked.

Connie glanced at Derek, whose face was stark with the knowledge that they'd just lost Jeff; he belonged to D'Amato now. "Go answer the door, John."

He paused in front of her for a moment, his eyes reflecting her pain. But her soul had congealed around her lost son, her lost brother, and there wasn't room for sympathy. She turned her face away.

"Connie," he murmured. "I—"

The doorbell rang again. With a muttered curse, he swung around and headed for the door.

Connie felt Derek's hands come down on her shoulders and realized that she'd begun to list to one side like a ship slowly going down.

"Easy," he said. "We'll get through this."

But it was the sound of feet on the stairs, not his

voice, that made her straighten. D'Amato was like a shark; show any weakness, any sign of a wound, and you were dead meat.

The detective pinned Connie with a long, penetrating look. "I didn't expect to find you here, Ms. Matthias."

"We're family," she replied.

The corners of his mouth turned up in something that wasn't quite a smile. Then he turned his attention to Penny. Connie watched his face change as he tallied what had been done to her.

"Have you seen a doctor?"

"Yes," John said.

"Maybe a hospital would be better."

"No," Penny said. "I want to stay in my own home."

D'Amato studied her for a moment, then shrugged. "Okay, tell me what happened."

"Jeff came to th-the door . . ." Penny paused, touching her grotesquely swollen lip as though to convince it to behave. "It was . . . was about seven. I sh-shouldn't have let him in, but he's just a kid. I had no idea . . . I thought I might be able to convins' him to go home."

"Did he ask for money?" D'Amato asked.

"No."

"Drugs?"

"No. I tried to talk to him, but he didn't make any sense, jus' kept shouting at me."

Connie found pain in every labored word as Penny's poor battered mouth struggled to form the right sounds. *My son did this* . . .

"Did he take anything from the house after he beat you?" D'Amato asked.

Penny stared at him in evident incomprehension,

then turned to John. "I . . . had fifty dollars or so in my purse, but I didn't think to—"

"I did," John said. "The cash is gone. And the house keys."

"Oh, God," Penny gasped. "He'll come back. He said he'd kill me if I called the police."

Connie made a gesture of negation. And despair. Jeff had dug himself a hole tonight. Dug it, climbed in, and pulled the earth in after him.

"I'll call a locksmith as soon as we're finished here," John said. "He won't get back in."

D'Amato's arid gaze lingered on Connie. She bore it, resisted it, resisted the thoughts she knew were going on behind it.

"What exactly did my son say to you, Penny?" she asked.

Penny held out one graceful hand in a gesture of helplessness. "He wasn't making much sense, jus' rambling on about how you didn't believe him, how you never let him have any freedom. He said things about you I can't even repeat—"

"Say them," Connie said.

"Connie—"

"Say them. The detective wants to know."

"I'm afraid so," D'Amato said.

Penny touched her lip again. "He s-said, 'That fucking bitch is going to be sorry for what she's done to me. When I get through with her, she's going to be sorry she was ever fucking born.' "

"He's got that already," Connie said.

"I tried to talk to him," Penny continued. "I tried to calm him down, but he jus' ranted and raved and then he punched me and punched me—" Her voice went up the scale, and for one horrified moment

Connie thought Penny might start screaming—and she along with her.

"Phaedra." John didn't raise his voice, but something in it touched Penny; she took a deep, shuddering breath and some of the wildness drained from her eyes.

"Sorry," she said. "Anyway, I don't think he meant to do this, Detective. He looked like he was high on something."

D'Amato's eyes narrowed. "How so?"

"His . . . his eyes were glazed. Didn't focus right. He kept saying, 'I gotta find a way to get to that bitch.' Over and over, like a chant."

"Like a chant?" D'Amato repeated.

"That's the way it s-sounded to me. Toneless. Like something he'd said so many times it didn't need inflection anymore."

D'Amato nodded, and Connie saw shadows of black candles in his eyes. "Did he say anything else?"

"He . . . said something about Cullen," Penny said, obviously reluctant.

"And what was that?"

Connie felt Derek's hand on her shoulder again, the touch remote, uncomforting.

"He called for my husband," Penny said. "He . . . didn't seem to remember that Cullen was dead."

Derek's fingers tightened spasmodically. They hurt, but Connie hardly felt it. She watched tears well up in Penny's eyes, watched them overflow and spill slow rivulets down her cheeks. The drops slid over the shiny, distended flesh of her swollen mouth, then fell to make irregular dark splotches on the front of her robe.

"Why did he do this to me?" Penny sobbed. "We

were always nice to him, always invited him to our home, sent him Christmas presents every year—"

"Drugs don't care about 'nice,' " D'Amato said.

"We were *family,*" Penny said, as though he hadn't spoken. "We'd have taken him into our group if he'd asked. We could have helped him. I let him into my home, hoping he'd let me help him, and he leaped on me. Hitting and punching, snarling . . . like an animal."

"He wasn't hitting *you,*" Connie said. "He was hitting *me.*"

She held herself stiffly, for to bend would be to break. It must have shown on her face, for John hesitated on his way to comfort Penny—the first indecision she'd ever seen in him. Then he turned and went to her. Taking her by the arm, he led her out into the hall.

"Don't do this to yourself," he said.

"How can I help it? Penny's in there because I failed my son. When he looked into my eyes and asked me if I thought he killed Cullen, I couldn't answer him."

"Phaedra had it easier," he said.

She stared at him, truly astonished. "What are you talking about?"

"Her bruises will go away. But you're beating yourself up psychically, and you're never going to let it heal."

"This was my fault," she said, forcing the words through a throat gone raw with despair.

"No. This isn't your responsibility." He slid his hand around to the back of her neck and pulled her toward him until their chests were touching. "I've called a meeting tomorrow night. We want to join together to ease Phaedra's pain. But you need us more. Please, Connie. Let us help you."

"Is this Clovis talking?"

"Just me . . . the man who loves you."

His eyes were only human. No special powers there, nothing but human emotion. He cared. He'd seen the darkness in her and still wasn't frightened. Slowly she nodded, then let her head fall forward until her forehead rested against his collarbone.

"Will you stay with me tonight?" he murmured into her hair.

"I've got to look for my son."

"And what if you find him?"

His question pulled her upright. Tipping her head back to look into his eyes, she searched within herself for an answer . . . and found nothing.

Footsteps sounded behind her. She turned, saw Derek and D'Amato come into the hallway.

"I want to talk to you and your hus . . . ex-husband, Ms. Matthias," he said. "Downstairs." Jabbing his thumb toward the doorway behind him, he said, "She wants you, Mr. Bruycker."

Connie turned, wobbling a bit on her weak ankle. Derek caught her by one arm, D'Amato by the other.

"Don't touch me," she said.

Derek only tightened his grip. "Shut up."

They carried her down the stairs. She didn't struggle, just held herself stiffly until they set her down on the sofa in the great room.

"How did you hurt yourself?" D'Amato asked.

"Car wreck."

His brows went up. "Are you accident-prone?"

"Only this year. What are you going to do about my son?"

"Arrest him. Your sister-in-law is pressing charges. Think about what her face looked like before you make excuses for him."

She chopped the air with the edge of her hand. "There's no excuse for what he did to Penny."

"And he'll have to pay the price for it," Derek added. "That's a given. Connie was asking about the situation with Cullen."

"Well, that's an interesting question, now," the detective said, scraping his thumbnail along the angle of his jaw. *Scritch, scritch.* "I want to talk to that young man very badly, and the longer I go without talking to him, the more questions I have. On one hand, I have a killing that doesn't seem to make much sense. On the other, I have a kid who's on drugs, who's run away from home, and who seemed to be pretty far away from rational. It doesn't take a rocket scientist to see a connection."

"You've already made up your mind," Derek said.

D'Amato shook his head. "I collect evidence. I match a person to motivation and opportunity, and then I take that to the judge and the jury and let them decide innocence or guilt."

"Then why haven't you investigated the authors of those threatening letters my brother received?" Connie asked.

"But I have. One was from an eighty-four-year-old woman in Smithfield who thought your brother ought to be burned at the stake as a witch; a man who wrote to tell Cullen that he had taken Satan's path and was drawing others with him, and offered to go talk to him so that he could 'find the Lord's way' again; we had several from young women who wanted his help traveling the 'spiritual path' through sex magick—your brother was very photogenic—and one from a man who wanted a face-to-face meeting to offer his services to the group."

"And?" Derek prompted.

"The old woman is all but crippled with arthritis, can't hold a pencil, let alone drive a knife into a man's chest. The redeemer, who lives in South Carolina, was peacefully asleep beside his wife all night. The young women were basically groupies—looking for a thrill with a good-looking man. Their alibis check out. The last guy is a Cullen wannabe, hangs out at the Chrysalis Center where everyone but him seems to know he's a fake." He paused, his gaze stabbing from Connie to Derek and back again. "Don't look so hopeful; he was in a 'group session' the night your brother was killed—all night. And seven people verified it."

"So in your mind, there's only Jeff," Connie said.

"I've been trained not to limit the possibilities, Ms. Matthias. There's always your sister-in-law—"

"Penny?" Connie snorted. "Right."

"She doesn't *seem* to be the type, but then, you never know. And then there's you. You were asleep alone in the house, just like the wife, and you had equal opportunity to sneak out, do the deed, then sneak back in again until it was time to discover the body."

"So nice to know you're being thorough."

"It's my job."

"So do your job and pay a visit to the Wahlfields," she said. "Ask them how much money they were going to funnel into the company they were forming."

D'Amato's heavy brows went up.

"Got your attention, huh?" Connie asked. "Cullen had refused the trust they wanted to set up. So they offered to set up a corporation to handle the needs of the group. Money, Detective. Lots of it."

"What about the black wax, Ms. Matthias?"

"I've got more confidence in plain old human greed than I do in black wax, D'Amato."

"And I have to look at everything."

"No," she said. "You won't look past my son."

"That's not true. I'm trying to keep things in hand, but this case gets screwier and screwier the more I learn about it. Maybe your brother was killed by some religious fanatic who thought he'd strayed from the holy path. Maybe he was killed by some *unreligious* fanatic who thought he hadn't strayed far enough."

"A martyr either way," Derek said.

D'Amato grunted. "Or maybe he was a martyr to your son's drug habit. Plain, everyday murder. Not nearly so glamorous, is it?"

"Don't you see what happened here?" Connie demanded. "My son has been run into a box, and he's trying to fight his way out. Because he's a kid, with no resources and less sense, he's doing everything wrong. He has nowhere to go, nowhere to turn, and he's run away from the only people who will accept him."

"He's a druggie."

"And he's desperate."

"That's the most dangerous kind." The hard glitter of anger faded from the detective's dark Latin eyes, leaving them looking merely tired. "I'm not unsympathetic, Ms. Matthias. I've got kids of my own. I understand. But you're judging him by the wrong standards right now."

"Which are?" Derek prompted.

"Yours. Mine. Society's. He doesn't live by those rules, doesn't run on what you taught him of right and wrong and fair play. All he's interested in is now, this moment, and how he can get his hands on more drugs."

"We won't abandon him," Connie said.

D'Amato glanced from her to Derek and back again. "Is either of you acquainted with a kid known on the streets as Tick?"

"No," Connie said. "Is he a friend of Jeff's?"

"He was. Remember that body I told you we found in St. Mary's Cemetery? Sixteen-year-old Caucasian male, five-five and one-seventeen, brown and brown, HIV positive, so full of PCP and alcohol that he might have died even if he hadn't been stabbed through the heart. The weapon was apparently a broad-bladed knife, possibly a hunting knife. Sound familiar?"

For a moment, Connie couldn't breathe. She clenched her hands into fists until they hurt, using the pain to anchor her in a world that had begun to tilt.

"Your son is violent," D'Amato continued, his voice as unrelenting as his eyes. Connie shrank from this, seeking any crack in the logic. "I'm going to ask you again: do you know where he is?"

"No," Derek said.

"Would you tell me if you knew?"

"Not until I'd hired a lawyer."

The rasp of the detective's thumbnail on his jaw was loud in the suddenly silent room. Then he nodded. "Maybe you'd better get one now. He's going to be charged with assault and battery and anything else I can get him on. We'll find him, and when we do, his butt's mine."

Connie unclenched her hands. "Thanks for the warning."

She and the detective locked gazes. Neither looked away; neither won. Finally she said, "Whatever he did tonight, he's our son. We'll fight for him."

"I'm sure you will." D'Amato turned away. Just as he reached the doorway, however, he turned back around. "I admire your loyalty. It's too bad your son isn't here to see it. But no matter how much you love him, you can't make him into something he's not—good or bad. Remember, Jeffrey Dahmer had parents, too."

With that he left. And although he closed the door softly behind him, the sound of his leaving seemed to echo throughout the house.

Derek looked as though he wanted to punch another wall. Instead, he raked his hands through his hair and went to stare out at the starlit beach.

"You've gained *some* control of that hair-trigger temper," she said.

"Some." He shot her a glance over his shoulder. "It's cost me too much in the past."

"This time *I* was the one who wanted to punch D'Amato's lights out."

"Yeah. But he's only doing his job."

"That I don't mind. It was the Jeffrey Dahmer crack that got me."

Derek's shoulders twitched. "Let's get going. I get the feeling that time's running out for Jeff, and we'd better find him soon."

"I'm half afraid to find him."

"I won't let him hurt you," he said.

"That's not what I'm afraid of."

Their gazes met and locked. She let him have

every raw, raging bit of her anger, her frustration, and her outrage. He accepted them, met them with his own. It wasn't pretty to see or to feel. But it was powerful.

Our son the monster.

"Where'd you leave your purse?" he asked.

"Upstairs."

He turned away.

"Derek?"

He swung around to look at her. Something reckless surged in her, making her say aloud what shouldn't be said.

"Tell me again about faith," she said.

For a moment, she thought he might fling himself at her. "No, Connie," he rasped. "I've got nothing to say about faith anymore. But he's my son. I'm going to find him, and I'm going to find out the truth if I have to—"

"Beat it out of him?" she flung at him.

He walked out. His footsteps rasped on the stairs, heavy, despairing, determined. He had such capacity for pain; he'd force her to face it with him whether she had the resources for it or not.

She clenched her fists again.

Chapter Twenty

Jeff curled miserably in the shadow of a dumpster. The air felt thick, redolent of brine and exhaust and the stink of the garbage. His skin felt too tight, a not-so-flexible membrane holding his guts together. Even so, he found himself dozing off; thirty-four hours without sleep made even this bed tolerable.

He heard himself whimper as images swirled into his mind. Red stars, blue stars, and an incredible rush shooting through his body. His mom, watching him from the other side of the coals, her eyes wide, her mouth open in astonishment as he walked toward her. Her face again as she asked him where he'd been the night Cullen had been killed. Another kind of rush.

He bounced away from that one like a ball in a pinball machine. Then Cullen's face loomed on the horizon. He looked dazzled, as though he'd seen something almost too bright to bear. He smiled at Jeff, opened his mouth to speak.

A hand rose, in it a knife glittering red in the starlight, then slashing down, returning redder than before.

My hand?

Yes.

He held his hands up before him. The stars backlit them, showing shadowy bones within flesh that glowed red and molten. He'd played that game so many times with a flashlight, his mother laughing with him when he'd turned the light up his nose.

His knife. His hand. Cullen, down on the sand in front of him, arms outspread like he was about to make a snow-angel in the sand. Snow angel, sand angel. His eyes fluttering closed, then drifting slowly open as the light went out of him.

He's dead. Look what you did.

The words ran through his head, cutting through his brain and leaving a raw, screaming wound behind. He fought to get away, to leave this dream-that-might-be-a-memory. But it wouldn't let him go.

Help me, help me, help me! Mom!

The knife hovered in front of him. Red, wet, with a wicked glitter of metal behind it. He picked it up. It felt warm in his hand and for a moment seemed to wriggle in greeting. Horror crept into his mind at the feel of it.

He tried to throw it away, but it clung to his palm. As he watched in horrified fascination, it took over. His hand had no choice but to go with it as it lifted, turned. He didn't make a sound as it came nearer, nearer. The point pressed against his chest, into his chest. His breastbone split under the pressure. The knife quivered, gleeful, slid in further, impaled muscle that pumped frantically around it.

It didn't hurt. Jeff looked down at himself, watching as the blood spurted out around the knife. It ran down his belly and pooled in his lap, smoking in the cold air.

Look what you did.

Somebody laughed.

Denial rushed through him in a raw, pounding wave. *Save yourself!* Too late. Too, too late; blood everywhere, on his hands, in his hair, dripping from his mouth. "No!" he screamed, terror giving him a voice. "Nooooooooooo!"

He surged up, hitting his head on the cold steel of the dumpster. Shaking in horror, he looked down at himself. No knife. No blood. *I'm alive. I'm alive!* Shuddering, he buried his face in his hands.

Somebody had laughed.

Not in the dream; when Cullen had died. *Maybe it was me.* He couldn't feel guilt in himself . . . or innocence.

Tick died, too.

Jeff had lost the memory of that death, as well. He didn't understand how he could kill and not remember it. Had it felt good? Had he picked Cullen and Tick because they trusted him, or just because they were there when he needed to do it?

Tears leaked out of his eyes, ran through his fingers to wet the ends of his sleeves. He wanted all this to go away—the killing, the cold, the friggin' dumpsters. He wanted to lie in his bed and be clean and warm and safe. He wanted his mother to love him again.

He wanted to be a kid.

You can't go home ever again. They'll lock you up for a hundred years.

He wasn't sure that might not be better than this. If he paid for his sins, maybe he'd learn to feel something for them. And if he could feel that, maybe he had a chance to be human again. He damn well didn't feel like it now.

"Fuck," he said.

Scrubbing the tears from his face, he pushed up to his feet. Standing gave him a better perspective. He'd come down hard after the crack. Bottomed out; that was why he felt so shitty. He didn't need guilt or innocence, only to get high again.

His hands shook as he reached into his pocket and pulled out the money he'd gotten from Penny. Or whatever she called herself these days . . . Phaedra. What a bunch of shit.

Forty-two bucks. Enough to get high for a while. Jamming the bills back into his pocket, he headed out into the street. He left his backpack behind. Didn't care; that came from a life he'd never have again. Besides, he didn't want the knife any more. It couldn't be trusted.

Time to get high again. He didn't care how; all he knew was that it hurt too much to be straight.

Connie rubbed her eyes, reaching inside for something to get her through the rest of the night. The clock on the dashboard read 2:13.

"Coffee?" Derek asked, offering the thermos.

She shook her head. "It's only giving me the shakes now."

"Want to call it a night?"

"Not yet." She opened the map, trying unsuccessfully to keep it from rattling between her hands. "Turn right here. We haven't been down this way yet."

He spun the wheel. This street ran parallel to the bay, and the wind kicked grit against the windshield. "I can't believe how much this place has run down since we were kids."

"Everything's running down." Connie craned to watch a group of teenagers huddled on the corner. Smoke rose above them, writhing like lost souls in the headlights.

"Should we stop?" Derek asked.

"They look pretty rough," she said. "Sure."

He shot her a glance out of the corner of his eye, then pulled over to the curb. Connie rolled her window down.

"Excuse me," she called. "Could I speak to you for a moment?"

One of the boys sauntered over to the car. He looked to be about sixteen or seventeen, his face thin and sweet-looking beneath a bristle of whiskers. "Lookin' for company, folks?"

"I—" Connie began.

"Don't be shy. For twenty bucks I'll show you a real good time. Don't like boys, try Sylvia over there." He pointed to a skinny blonde. "She'll do you for thirty. Fifteen for a blow job."

"I'm not equipped for blow jobs," Connie said. She held up Jeff's picture. "I'm looking for this boy. His name is Jeff. He's about five-nine, with sandy-colored hair and hazel eyes. Hangs with a guy named Tick."

"You cops?"

Derek leaned over. "If you thought we were, you wouldn't have made that offer. By the way, there's a girl two streets over who'll blow you for ten."

"But we're still paying," Connie said, pulling a twenty out of her pocket. "If you've got anything to say."

"I know Tick," he said, his gaze on the money.

"Ain't seen him in a couple of days. Guy named Henry hangs with him sometimes. Try down at Thrasher's on 30th; he's there most every night."

Connie handed him the bill. "Thanks."

He rejoined the group, and they all turned their backs to the car. Derek pulled away faster than he needed to. She glanced at him, saw a muscle pumping spasmodically in his cheek.

"The kid was trying to shock you," he said.

"I'm not shockable any more."

"Hell, *I* am. As a firefighter, I've seen shit that makes me wonder how the human race survived as long as it has. But some of these kids . . ." He let his breath out in a long sigh. "They ought to be in school, they ought to be cheerleading or playing baseball or shopping the mall, anything but what they're doing. Giving head for a couple of bucks, for Chrissake. Haven't they heard about AIDS?"

"They don't care," Connie said. "They're not thinking of living long enough to die of AIDS."

"I'd rather give Jeff to D'Amato than leave him to this."

She grimaced, hating him for saying it. But after driving around here, seeing the kids who lived in fear and the ones who'd gone beyond it, she knew he was right.

"Do you feel up to this?" he asked.

"My ankle's holding up."

"That wasn't what I asked."

"I'm fine." After a moment, she asked, "What the hell is Thrasher's, anyway?"

"I dunno. I just hope the name has nothing to do with the game."

Fifteen minutes later, they pulled up in front of a long, skinny building wedged between a discount furniture store and a laundromat. A neon sign in the single window gave off its sickly greenish glow. "Thrasher's," with the T sputtering in time to the heavy metal music that made the glass thrum.

"Stay here," Derek said.

"You must have lost your mind."

"Look at that place, Connie. God knows what I'm going to find in there. I don't want to have to watch my back and you, too. Just do what you're told for once."

She opened her mouth to say something else, but closed it again. Fifteen years of living had taught her something, too: it didn't pay to argue with a man whose jaw thrust forward at that angle. She waited until Derek had disappeared inside before getting out of the car.

"Do what I'm told," she muttered.

She paused outside the door to glance up and down the street. It wasn't a nice area; more buildings were empty than not, and several streetlights were dark, allowing shadows to cluster in every nook and cranny.

Something nibbled at the back of her mind, demanding attention. She tried to ignore it.

Someone's watching.

Ridiculous. The shadows hid nothing but the rundown buildings. No one watched. No one cared.

And yet . . . the hair at the back of her neck lifted in pure primordial fear. Here, with the neon blinking behind her head, she stood exposed to the darkness, the prying eyes, the unseen. Her ears deleted the solid thump of the music, focusing instead on the smaller sounds. The wind rolled papers along the pavement, a faint scrabbling sound like the stealthy scrape of claws.

She found herself watching the deeper areas of shadow, waiting for movement.

"Scared of the dark like a kid," she muttered.

No. The kids she'd met tonight were at home with the night. And if she and Derek didn't find Jeff, he'd become just like them. Doing drugs, doing men who liked screwing kids, the younger and fresher, the better . . .

With a shake of her head, she opened the door and stepped inside. The interior of Thrasher's mirrored the exterior: long, skinny, dirty. Video games lined the walls. A black Formica counter bulged into the middle of the room, festooned with cigarette smoke and clusters of potato chip bags.

The music howled, an almost physical force in the room. But the kids paid no attention; they were glued to the video games, plugged into the computer screens like human-shaped microchips. So much for walking into danger; a bomb could have gone off in here and they'd still keep pressing buttons and slamming joysticks around, determined to get a few more points before the final immolation.

Derek was easy to spot as he moved among the kids, stopping briefly at every machine to talk to the players. Some of the kids ignored him; most shook their heads no. Then one boy nodded, and without taking his gaze from the screen in front of him, pointed with his left hand.

Derek eased past the clot of teenagers clustered around the snack bar and approached a tall, dark-haired kid. The boy—Henry, presumably—shook his head when Derek spoke to him. *Nada,* Connie thought. He didn't understand. Hell. But it was going to take more than a shake of the head to put Derek off; he was on a roll tonight, running on anger and fear and a full load of adrenaline. She understood, although she'd rather have talked to the kid herself; all that emotion mixed with testosterone was one evil combination.

"Come on, Derek. Take it easy," she muttered.

He leaned closer to the kid, talking fast beneath the beat of the music. Henry shook his head again, then started to turn away. Derek grabbed him by the shoulder and swung him around. The boy's face turned ugly, and his mouth formed an expletive Connie could see from here.

He jammed his elbow into Derek's chest, then whirled like a halfback and ran straight toward her. Connie leaned her weight on her good ankle and watched him come. He was bigger than she, and moving fast, knocking people out of his way as he ran. Derek was overhauling him, but not quite fast enough.

She stepped to one side, then stuck out her foot as Henry went past. He went down, hitting the floor with a crash she could hear even over the music. Derek pounced on him, grabbed him by the back of the neck, and hauled him to his feet.

"Very nice," he panted.

Connie turned to look at the crowd. Henry didn't seem to have any friends here; other than a few curious glances, no one seemed to give a damn what happened to him.

"As D'Amato would say," she said, "his butt's ours."

"Lemme go!" the kid squealed, his face contorted with rage.

"Take it easy, Henry," Derek said. "We just want to talk to you."

"Fuck you, asshole!"

Derek's hand tightened. "Open the door, Connie."

She obeyed, moving aside as her ex lifted the boy off his feet and hauled him outside. Derek pinned him against the car and patted him down. A moment later he came up with a big pocket knife, which he tossed over his shoulder to Connie.

"You can't do this!" the kid panted. "Fucking cops!"

Derek spun him around, holding him in place with a forearm across the throat. "We're not cops, Henry. We just want to ask you some questions, and if you answer them, we'll let you go. You can get in the car and do it comfortably, or we can continue the conversation right here. What's it going to be?"

"Derek," Connie said, "he can't answer you unless you let him breathe a little."

"Oh."

His arm relaxed a little, and Henry sucked air. "Ready to talk?"

The kid nodded. Grabbing him by the front of his tee shirt, Derek yanked him upright. Connie swung the rear door open. As Henry got in—impelled by Derek's hand between his shoulders—he turned to glare at her.

She locked the door before closing it, then slid into the front seat. Derek joined her. She turned to study Henry, wondering who he was, what he was. He looked to be about seventeen or eighteen. But he was hard, real hard. Where the other kids they'd seen had been edged by fear and disillusionment and despair, he'd been formed another way. Her chest went cold at the thought of Jeff having anything to do with this boy.

"We're looking for this kid," she said, holding up the photo of Jeff. "Some people said you might know him."

"I seen him around." Sullenly.

"Where?"

He crossed his arms over his chest, then jerked when Derek snapped, *"Where?"*

"Around. Here and there. We ain't good buddies or nothin'. Last time I talked to him, I was just lookin' for his friend Tick."

"Tick's dead," Derek said.

Henry's eyes showed only annoyance. "Shit. He had fifty bucks of my money."

"He was murdered," Connie said. "Stabbed."

"So maybe the little fuck took somebody else's money, and they liked it even less than I did."

Looking into his eyes, Connie felt something cold bloom in her chest. This kid was off, way off. He'd have killed Tick himself without a qualm, and he'd keep Jeff from her just for the hell of it.

"What about Jeff?" she asked.

"What about him? I told you everything I know."

She came up on her knees, leaning over the back of the seat to thrust her face close to his. He stank of sweat and beer and unbrushed teeth, but it was his eyes that were the filthiest.

"You're not a very good liar, Henry," she said.

"Hey, fuck you, bitch."

Connie flinched as Derek's hand flashed past her face. He grabbed the boy by the throat, and she watched in a sort of frozen fascination as his hand tightened. There seemed to be a direct correlation between the color of Henry's face and the tension in the tendons in the back of Derek's hand.

She ought to do something. But instinct had

taken over, and hers were running right along with Derek's. This was the chance. One shot, win or lose. Let Henry go, and they might never find Jeff. So she knelt beside the man, watching the boy's face go from pink to red to purple.

Finally she said, "Derek."

"Yeah, I know. I gotta let him breathe."

He eased the pressure, but kept his hand clamped on the boy's neck. Henry, his eyes bulging, drew air in with great, gulping breaths.

"He's crazy, lady, you know that?" he gasped.

"Yes, I know," she said. "And a minute ago, I was 'bitch,' remember?"

He opened his mouth to say something, but then his gaze went to Derek and he closed it again.

Connie leaned her elbows on the back of the seat. "Now, Henry, tell me everything you know about my son."

"Okay, lady. Shit, you people are something else." Moving carefully in Derek's grasp, he slid upward in the seat. "I told you the truth before. I don't know him too good, him and me an Tick got high together once. I seen him a couple of days ago, when I was lookin' for Tick. We talked, he didn't know where Tick was, and that was that."

Not enough, Connie thought. Not nearly enough. At that moment, she didn't know what she was capable of doing; Derek, she knew, was capable of almost anything just now. "That's not going to give me Jeff," she said. "Do better."

"You're as crazy as he is."

"Crazier. And meaner." *Give me my son.*

"Fuck," he said, his shoulders slumping. "It's no skin off my ass. He said he'd been down to some fucking mission, having coffee and donuts with the do-gooders."

"What was the name of the mission?" Derek asked, too softly.

"I don't fucking remember . . ." His eyes bulged as Derek's hand tightened, and he shook his head frantically.

"Talk," Derek said, easing the pressure.

"It's the fucking Redeemer Mission, okay? Shit."

Derek glanced at Connie. She nodded, and he slowly released his grip on the boy's throat. "Okay," he said. "Get out of here."

Henry scrabbled for the lock, then swung the door open and lunged from the car. His footsteps faded rapidly in the distance.

"I'm going to need a bath after this," Connie said.

"Yeah." He leaned past her to close the door. "Put your seatbelt on."

"Will you squeeze my neck if I don't?"

"Hey, look, Connie. Do you think that kid was going to listen to reason?"

"I'm afraid to think anymore."

Then she smiled at him in pure, unholy joy. He stared at her for a moment, obviously taken aback, then put the car in gear.

It was almost dawn when they finally found the mission. Derek parked in front of it, craning to read the sign in the violet dimness.

"*Redemption* Mission, not *Redeemer,*" he said. "Henry isn't quite as smart as he thinks he is."

"Redemption or Redeemer . . . both are pretty remote, as far as that boy is concerned. What time do they open?"

"It says seven, but there's a light on inside. Maybe somebody's cooking."

He got out of the car and came around to open her door. She let him help her out; her ankle felt swollen again under the bandage, pain pounding in rhythm to her heartbeat.

Derek knocked on the front door. "Hello? Anyone in there?"

A moment later the door opened. Connie found herself facing a short, strongly built man whose eyes were both gentle and no-nonsense. "It's a little early," he said, swinging the door open wider, "but you're welcome to some coffee until breakfast is ready."

"We're not here to eat," Derek said. "We're looking for someone."

The man looked them over, then motioned them to take a seat at one of the long tables. "I'm Rick Durillo. Reverend, if you're being formal. You're . . . ?"

"This is Connie Matthias, and I'm Derek Valle. Our son's name is Jeff. He's fifteen years old and we want to take him home."

Rick nodded. "Do you want some coffee before we get started?"

Derek shook his head. "We were told our son came here a short time ago. We've been looking everywhere for him, and so far this has been our only lead." With a sigh, he leaned his elbows on the table. Exhaustion etched deep lines in his face. "He's in big trouble, and we want to help him."

"Do you have a photograph?"

Connie handed it over, watching Rick's face as he studied it. He looked tough and capable, and she thought he'd been in a few scrapes himself. But not now. Serenity lay beneath the toughness, ran deep and warm in his eyes. A very practical sort of do-gooder, she thought.

"He was here the day before yesterday," he said, laying the photo on the table between them. "We talked a little. He looked pretty good, actually. Acted tough, but I think he was scared beneath it. I can't tell you if I reached him or not. If I did, he'll be back."

Connie looked around at the bare, unlovely room, the battered chairs, the plastic spoons and forks and stacks of napkins laid out on the buffet table.

"Jeff doesn't belong on the street," she said.

"None of them do, Ms. Matthias." Just for a moment, his eyes went bleak, and she caught a glimpse of a painful past. Then it went away, leaving the serenity again, and he asked, "Why did Jeff run away?"

Connie met his gaze levelly. "He ran away because I lost faith with him when he needed it most."

"Connie—" Derek began.

"It's the truth."

Rick laid his hand over hers, and she found comfort in the stranger's touch where she might have drawn away from someone she knew.

"Faith is everything," he said.

She looked away, blinking at a sudden misting of tears. "Yeah, well, sometimes reality intrudes. Jeff's a tough kid to deal with. If you see him again—"

"I won't betray his trust." Rick held up one hand, stopping their protest. "The kids come to me because they know that I don't call the police, I don't call anyone they don't want me to call. If I did, they'd never come around again. For some of them, this is the only haven they have from their lives; if I betray them, I can't help them."

It was hard to take that refusal; Connie could see it in Derek's face, too.

"He's our son," she said. "No matter what he's done, we love him."

"I'll make you a promise, Ms. Matthias. If I see him again, I'll do everything in my power to convince him to contact you. I've already planted that seed. We can only hope it will take root."

Connie rose to her feet. Derek came up with her, steadying her when she wobbled on the weak ankle. "Rick . . . if you talk to Jeff, tell him we believe in him."

"I don't see belief in your eyes. And neither will Jeff."

"You might say a couple of prayers for us, Reverend," Derek said. "We could all use a few."

Chapter Twenty-One

"I've seen it, but never thought I'd actually know someone who did it," Derek said.

Connie rolled the car window down, craning to see what had prompted that statement. She found Mr. Ranke mowing the lawn. Not back and forth, but in neat diagonal stripes, first one way, then the opposite. It left the lawn in a green-on-green checkerboard pattern.

"Well," she said. "Now you know."

"Sheesh." He turned the car off, then swiveled in his seat to look at her. "It's been a hell of a night."

"How many laws do you think we broke? Bribery, assault, and let's not forget that red light you ran."

"I used to be a law-abiding citizen."

"Me, too. Well, we can always be glad we didn't stay married long enough to have two kids."

His face tightened, and she realized she'd hit a tender spot.

"I meant it as a joke," she said.

"Did you?"

"Yeah. Come on, Derek. We've been divorced long enough to have developed some objectivity."

He looked his age suddenly, the stark, too-rugged features becoming merely ugly for a moment. "I guess I'm short on objectivity right now."

Connie didn't know what to say; anything would probably be wrong. He'd been off-kilter since he'd come to pick her up last night, and not just in a bad mood. He'd been too cynical, and more aggressive than she'd ever expected to see.

"What's on for tonight?" he asked, giving her a reprieve.

"The group is meeting at Penny's. They're . . . we're going to help her heal. And as John says, maybe me, too."

"Oh, brother," he muttered.

She shrugged. "Whatever. I'd better go in; I'm going to need some sleep if I'm going to deal with those people."

"Stay there," he said, when she opened her door. "I'm coming around to get you."

She would have protested if her ankle hadn't hurt so much. He hauled her out of the car almost gently, then, holding her around the waist, carried her up the sidewalk.

Mr. Ranke stopped the mower to watch. "Did you all get married?" he asked.

"*No,* Mr. Ranke," Connie said. "It's the ankle, you know."

"Sure, I know."

He winked at Derek, then returned to his lawn-mower. The engine roared back to life. Absurdly, Connie found comfort in the noise—familiar every-day sounds of suburban living, so alien to the world she'd left not too long ago.

"Let's go," Derek said.

He carried her upstairs and set her down so she

could unlock the door. To her surprise, he walked in ahead of her. She closed the door behind her, then stood with folded arms and watched him check the bedroom and the big pantry closet.

"Looking for assassins?" she asked.

"Yeah."

The flat honesty of his answer left her nothing to say, so she went to check her answering machine. A waft of cool air from the hole in the wall washed over her as she pressed the playback.

Click. "Connie, it's John. Everyone's supposed to be here around seven. Call me if you need a ride. Call if you need anything. By the way, I dreamed about you last night. You were wearing that black teddy you wore for me the time we—"

"Oops," Connie said, hastily turning the volume down. She didn't have the courage to look at Derek. After counting to ten, she turned the volume back up.

Click. "Connie, this is your mother. Call me, please."

Click. "This is your mother again. It's important that I talk to you."

Click. "Connie, Mother here. I called Penny, hoping she might know where you were. Why didn't you tell me about the accident? And why in God's name didn't you tell me about Jeff beating her? What's wrong with you? Don't you think I might be concerned? Don't you think—" *Beep.*

The machine had cut her off, but Connie just waited for the next message. No one ever got the last word in on Sandra Matthias.

Click. "—I might want to protect myself? That boy might just show up here next. Or there. I want you to call me the *instant* you get home."

The tape rewound, mercifully. Connie turned to find Derek sprawled on the sofa, his head propped on a throw pillow.

"Make yourself comfortable," she said. "I'll check the refrigerator and see what's available."

"Aren't you going to call your mother?"

"I'm too tired to deal with her now."

"She's not as bad as all that."

Connie grimaced. "You're only saying that because she likes you. But Mom has a good side and a bad side. Get on the bad one, and you'll think you walked into a metal shredder."

"You're more like her than you realize."

"Me?" She stared at him in mingled outrage and astonishment. "That's a hell of a thing to say!"

"Sandra's got a lot of good qualities, Connie. She's loyal, determined, terrifyingly organized, and plays a heck of a game of bridge. And she loves her children as fiercely as you love Jeff."

"She pushed me away." Connie clapped her hand over her mouth in horror. That had popped out unplanned and unexpected, and had just stripped her naked in front of him.

Derek raised one tawny brow. "Freudian slip?"

"Stupid slip."

"You're entitled, the way you keep getting knocked in the head."

She smiled at him. Years ago, he'd have pushed her until she walked out in fury. People change, she thought.

"Are you in love with him?" he asked.

Connie felt her mouth drop open. "Who?"

"The guy who sucks your toes."

"What was that, another Freudian slip?"

"Are you in love with him?"

It hadn't been a fair question; she knew it, he knew it. So she walked into the kitchen, ignoring the issue, and he let her.

"Want some breakfast?" she asked. "Coffee and toast and eggs is all I've got."

"Sounds great. No coffee, though; I want to be able to get some sleep this morning."

But when she walked into the living room a few minutes later, plate in hand, she found him already asleep. He looked big and tawny and male lying there on her sofa, and she remembered some of the reasons she'd married him. Most were hormonal, which hadn't translated into a successful marriage, but it had been a wild ride while it had lasted.

Because of that, she let him sleep.

She considered calling her mother . . . and discarded it instantly; the bed seemed to hold out soft, beckoning arms to her.

It took her about ten seconds to prop her foot on a pillow and another ten seconds to fall asleep.

"Are you sure you don't want me to come in with you?" Derek asked.

"No, thanks," she said.

He watched her for a moment, then swiveled to look at the house. "It's a great night for a seance."

Connie leaned back against the headrest. The house sat in a buttery pool of floodlights, looking like a fairy castle against the night sky. But the clouds belled low above it, and fog had begun to drift in off the ocean. A shiver rippled up her spine.

"I don't think they call them seances any more," she said.

"Your hands are shaking."

She closed them into fists. "Knee-jerk reaction; it was foggy the night of the accident."

"Oh," he said. "Is that it?"

"Yes!"

"There's nothing wrong with it," he said. "Considering the circumstances, I think you'd be stupid not to be afraid. Fear leads to caution, and you're going to need caution tonight."

"That's the last thing I need."

He drew in his breath with a hiss. "Yeah. But if I were you, I'd make sure I stayed with the crowd."

She turned to look at him. His face was only half-lit, sharp pale wedges of cheekbone and jaw and nose in violent contrast with the shadows that hid the rest of his features. "It would be kind of suspicious for the murderer to kill me on the same beach where Cullen died, don't you think?"

"Suspicious for anyone but a drug-crazed teenager. You know, bad kid, crazy kid, none of the rules apply."

Maybe they didn't, Connie thought. A strange notion for someone who'd never been comfortable outside the rules. But then, the world had been nuts since this thing had begun, and maybe accepting that was the only way to survive.

"I'll be as careful as I can," she said.

"That's an odd way of putting it."

"It's the only way there is."

"Shit, Connie."

"Are you going back to the mission now?"

He turned, bringing his face more fully into the light. It seemed even more grim than it had been before. "I'd planned on it. Want to come along?"

"This has to be done."

"Why?"

"Have you decided that Jeff is guilty?"

He smiled, but it twisted oddly. "Let's not start on the faith thing again, will you?"

"Connie—"

"I'm not being snide. I know Jeff has dug himself a nice, deep hole. I know he's done some stupid things and some wrong things. But as long as there's the slimmest chance of his innocence, I'm not about to rest. I need to do it for him. And for me; if he's lost, it won't be because I didn't take my best shot."

For a moment, it looked as though he was going to argue. Then he sighed and walked around to open her door. "Come on," he said, holding out his hand.

Connie put her hand in his. He pulled her up and forward, straight against him. She stood stiffly, startled by the unexpected contact.

"Hey," she said.

He stepped back. "Sorry. I was only going to hug you."

"In case you never saw me again?"

"Something like that."

She tipped her head back to look at him. "Derek, I—"

"It was only a hug, Connie. Don't make a big deal about it."

"Okay, I won't." She took a step forward and put her arms around his waist.

After a moment, he returned her embrace. It was a brotherly sort of hug, comforting and undemanding. He was the first to step back.

"Do you want me to pick you up?" he asked.

She shook her head. "John will take me home."

There didn't seem to be anything left to say, so she turned toward the house. She heard the car start, then the scrape of wheels on the street as he pulled away.

All in all, Derek was beginning to confuse her; he'd never been undemanding before.

"One of life's great mysteries," she muttered. "Men!"

Her ankle gave her a little trouble as she maneuvered up the steps. Suddenly the door opened, spilling warmth and golden light across the porch, and John came out to help her the rest of the way.

"I waited all day for you to call," he said.

"I've been asleep all day. Derek and I didn't get back until after ten this morning."

He slid her jacket off her shoulders, his hands giving the simple gesture a bedroom intimacy. "Did you have any luck?"

"A couple of leads, but nothing you could call luck."

"I'm sorry, Connie."

"Yeah, me, too."

"What kind of leads?"

She shrugged. "We found a couple of kids who'd seen Jeff around."

"And?"

"And nothing. They'd seen him the other day, or a couple of hours ago, or got high with him somewhere. Why do you want to know?"

He stopped, turning her to face him. His eyes reflected nothing but the bright blue of his shirt. "It was only a friend's concern, Connie. No need to get tense about it."

"I'm not tense."

But she was; her back felt humped with it. John slipped around behind her and laid his hands over her shoulders. His fingers spread out across the line of her collarbones, an unmistakable male gesture of possession. He must have seen the hug, then.

His breath touched her ear. "Is that better?"

"Uh-huh," she murmured. "That feels great."

The motion of his hands slowed, then stopped. "Would you be jealous of your ex-husband if you were me?"

She considered that. Actually, the normal bounds of jealousy didn't apply to her relationship with John; their couplings had been hot and obsessive and all-consuming, completely unique to them.

"No," she said. "I wouldn't."

"Good." He took a step closer, raising the heat factor considerably. "I've never been a possessive man. But none of the old rules seem to apply with you. I want you all the time, Connie. Even now. If there wasn't a bunch of people in the next room, I'd do you right here on the floor."

People. Right. Connie took a step forward, disengaging from interesting thoughts of the contrast between cool tile and John's hot skin. *Down, girl.*

"How's Penny?" she asked, aware that he *allowed* her the distance; had he not, she might have been compelled to stay.

"She feels a lot better than yesterday. Don't be shocked when you see her, though; the swelling's gone down some, but the bruises are in full color."

He led her into the great room. Everyone had come: Hamilton Liu, with his impenetrable dark eyes and Margo wrapped around him like a wetsuit; Philip and Evvie, he with his pretty smile and pear-shaped frame, she with her broad shoulders and square, strong hands; Amy Cortez, gazing at John with adoring eyes while her daughter sat with crossed arms, obviously not wanting to be here; and last, Penny, who looked like a pin-up poster that some kid had defaced with magic marker. Somehow, bruises looked worse on that pale, delicate skin than they had on Connie's tawny hide.

Philip and Evvie decended on Connie, gracefully snaring her out of John's grasp. "We heard about the accident, dear," Evvie said. "It's terrible, just terrible. I'm so glad you came out of it all right."

"We heard your car was completely wrecked," Philip said. "We'll be glad to provide you with a replacement—"

"No, thanks. I couldn't."

"You could consider it a loan."

"No," she said, more firmly. "Thank you. I've got a rental clause on my insurance; I've just been too busy to do anything about it."

Philip's expression turned sympathetic. "Ah, yes. John told us you're trying to find your son. We're terribly sorry about the difficulties you're having. We've got a very good lawyer on retainer; you're welcome to use him."

Apparently they were as willing to lend human beings as cars or money. Connie sighed. Maybe they were accustomed to giving handouts to everyone around them. Everyone but Cullen, that is. They must have found him novel, with his prideful Balestier independence.

"Why were you so insistent that Cullen take your money?" she asked, diving right in.

"Because he was on the cusp of revelation," Evvie said. "New thought. Philip and I wanted to see him protected, nurtured, so he could achieve that. And when it happened, we wanted to see the word get out. Did you know he'd been attacked by certain religious groups?"

"My impression was that he'd gotten a few letters," Connie said.

Evvie spread her hands. "So far. But the more these people heard about him, the more attacks he was bound to receive. His boss, you know, was an Evangelical Christian; how long do you think he'd have his job once his philosophy became known?"

"Money provides a buffer from the world," Philip said. "The more money, the more effective the buffer. We ought to know. Now, here's the proposition, the same one we offered Cullen. We'll fund the corporation with five hundred thousand the first year, two hundred thousand a year later."

More than enough to kill for, Connie thought. But Cullen hadn't had control of the money; killing him had almost lost the Wahlfields for the group.

It didn't make sense. Cullen should have been worth more alive than dead. As D'Amato said, a killing born of anger, not planning. A crime of impulse.

Oh, please, not my son.

"We'd like for you to meet with our lawyer sometime soon," Philip said, holding out a business card. "Mike McKewn handles all our corporate affairs. He's very good. I've already instructed him to set things up per your requirements."

Connie took the card from her. Without looking at it, she thrust it into the pocket of her jeans. "I'll think about it . . . *if* the others agree to it."

"We're going to vote tonight," Philip said. "Democracy rules."

"I see."

Evvie laughed. "Don't worry, dear, we didn't call you aside to try to influence your decision. We just wanted to offer to help, and," she took her husband's arm, gazing up at him in open adoration. "To tell you how happy we are to have you with us. You remind us so much of Cullen, and it's a comfort."

Connie felt her mouth drop open. "Huh?"

"You don't resemble him physically, of course," Philip said. "Inside. You have the same drive, the same independence of spirit, the same disdain for convention."

"I'm very conventional," Connie protested. "I'm an—"

"Accountant," the older man finished for her. "That's your skin, the one you wear to fit into the mainstream. Inside, you don't, have never, believed the limitations accepted by other people."

Evvie nodded. "Even Cullen hadn't quite been willing to take the big risk. Only with us did he drop that outer skin; to his boss, to his mother, and to the rest of the world, he played a slightly wacky advertising man, a guy who dabbled in this and that, but who never truly settled. Playing at things doesn't alarm people; true belief does."

"You have his capacity to break down the barriers," Philip said. "If you dare."

They stood arm in arm, studying Connie like a pair of oversized vultures. There was nothing benevolent in their eyes, only need. They wanted her to replace Cullen for them . . . wanted her to *be* Cullen.

No wonder Cullen had resisted their money; it would have been a velvet-lined whirlpool. And the Walhfields waiting at the bottom, sweet and sincere and thoughtless as they sucked him dry.

I'll bet my eye teeth he would never have agreed to

take their generosity. Even Mom used to admit that while Cullen might be crazy, he wasn't a fool.

"Excuse me," she said, turning away. "I've got to talk to Penny."

"Of course, dear," Evvie called after her. "We'll be talking again soon."

Connie resisted the urge to look at them over her shoulder; she knew they'd be watching her with those hungry eyes.

Penny looked even worse close up, but it wasn't because of the bruises; her eyes held a shadow of betrayal and more than a little violation. "Hi, Connie."

"How are you feeling?"

"All right."

Connie reached for her hand but drew back when the other woman's face closed. "I wish there were something I could do. I'm sorry—"

"I don't blame you for anything," Penny said. "It's just that after Cullen died, everything began to come apart. And now this thing with Jeff . . . nothing seems to make sense any more."

If there's any truth in this craziness, that's it. "I know what you mean."

Penny's gaze focused more fully on her. It was an enigmatic stare, less tentative than Connie would have expected. "Your mother came by to visit today."

"Mother always does the right thing."

"Whether she wants to or not?"

Connie shrugged. "You've known her ten years, Penny."

"Phaedra." Her lashes and brow were almost invisible against the purple-black bruise around her left eye. "She didn't come here to see how I was, not really. I could tell she wanted to say something rather badly, but didn't have the nerve, maybe. So we made polite, inane conversation for about twenty minutes, then she left. Do you think she wanted to apologize for something?"

"Could be," Connie said. "But since I've never heard her apologize for anything, I can't tell you the signs leading up to it."

"I would have made it easy for her. Especially since she owed it to Cullen, not me."

Tears stung Connie's eyes. "I appreciate that."

"Is everyone ready?" John called out, over the murmur of conversation.

Penny rose, her attention shifting away from Connie so completely it was unnerving. "Yes," she said. "Let's go."

"Where are we going?" Connie asked.

Hamilton looked up. "We're firewalking tonight," he said. "You're in luck."

Connie felt as though she'd stepped into a hole—a big, deep, dark one. She met Hamilton's gaze. He knew exactly what she was thinking; amusement lit his impenetrable black eyes.

Do or die, she thought. Oh, hell.

Chapter Twenty-Two

The fog slid over Connie's face like a cool, damp hand. Every nerve in her body rebelled against it, and if John hadn't been holding her arm, she wouldn't have gone on.

A dull red glow ahead marked the bed of coals. She glanced over her shoulder at the house, the lights of which were the only other landmark in the swirling white blanket. No wind stirred the air, and no sound but for their footfalls and the quiet sussuration of the ocean.

Only the devil and the deep blue sea . . .

The red glow intensified, and she could finally feel the coals' warmth in the clammy, breathless air. John sat her down at the edge of the circle of heat.

"How's this?" he asked. "Comfortable?"

"Enough."

"Hamilton?" he called. "Come help me with the coals, will you?"

The other man seemed almost to materialize out of the mist. Moisture beaded his hair and laid a sheen on his skin. Connie drew in a sharp breath; despite the dark hair and eyes, he looked ethereal, almost as if he'd been created out of mist and sea-spray and a hint of fugitive moonlight. Then Margo appeared behind him, bringing reality to the scene with her smooth Yuppie good looks.

"Have a seat, Margo," he said. "I'll be back in a minute."

To Connie's surprise, the girl flopped down beside her. Then Amy and Lynn Cortez arrived and sat down on her other side. Philip and Evvie showed up next, easing down to the sand behind Connie.

She felt both enclosed and too vulnerable, unsure whether she'd rather have her back open to the fog. But moving didn't seem to be an option; she had allowed herself to be accepted, and it was too late to set herself apart.

"Isn't this fog great?" Lynn Cortez asked.

"Sure," Connie said. "Like starring in our very own horror movie."

"Oh, no," Amy said. "It's like the earth itself has wrapped around us. This is going to be a very special night. Can't you feel it, Connie?"

The only thing Connie felt was a trickle of moisture down her neck. But she wasn't about to spoil the mood, so she pulled her knees up to her chest and waited for the show to start. Slowly, she became aware that Margo was staring at her.

"What's the matter?" she asked. "Is my hair sticking up or something?"

The younger woman leaned closer. "I was just thinking that you're not like the rest of them," she whispered.

"Excuse me, but I'm having a hard time thinking you're a true convert," Connie whispered back.

"Not. I just happen to be a member of the Hamilton Liu fan club. He's gorgeous, isn't he?"

Her father ought to put a leash on her. "He's got an exotic appeal."

"Absolutely." Margo's expression turned pensive. "You're hooked up with John, right?"

"We see each other some."

"Is he, like, celibate?"

Completely astonished, Connie stared at the younger woman. "What on earth are you talking about?"

"Well . . ." Frustration lay stark and hard in her face. "I don't get Hamilton sometimes. He isn't . . . I thought it might have been something to do with the group's philosophy."

Two plus two suddenly added up to five. "He didn't stay with you the other night?"

"No such luck. He delivered me to my apartment, gave me a kiss that started my toenails smoldering, then took off. I thought I'd done something wrong until he called me today."

Connie turned to watch Hamilton work. He raked the coals with slow, graceful, economical movements. Waste not, want not. He was playing Margo perfectly, dangling the bait long enough to set the hook good.

"What time did he leave your place?" Connie asked.

"Time?" Margo frowned. "Oh, one, one-fifteen, maybe. Why?"

"Oh, nothing."

He'd had plenty of time, Connie thought. Everyone had heard John suggest eating at Denny's; Hamilton could have dropped Margo off, toenails and all, and made it to the restaurant in plenty of time to catch them.

But he didn't drive a Bronco.

That was problem number two. And then there was problem number one, which is why anyone would kill Cullen for money he didn't have.

Penny stepped out of a swirl of fog. She'd changed into something pale and swirly that seemed almost to float around her. Trying for the mysterious and mystical, Connie thought. Her battered face ruined the effect; bruises and black eyes held only reality, and an ugly one at that.

"We're ready," John said, holding his hand out to Penny. "Phaedra?"

She stepped to his side. After kicking off her shoes, she waited, eyes closed, while he spoke.

"We've shared this many times," he said. "And we've always found peace in it. Lately, though, we haven't had much in the way of peace. Tonight, we're going to reach out and touch the power within each of us, and we're going to set it free. Together, we're going to recapture the peace we lost."

He raised his hands, smoothing his hair back from his forehead. Seal-dark, seal-sleek, it lay close to his scalp, revealing the fine-drawn bone structure of his face.

"This fog is nature's gift to us," he continued. "Take a breath. Feel it. Smell it. There's only us, the fog, and the sound of the sea. Earth's heartbeat. Ours, too, if we can learn the rhythm."

"Cullen knew this," Penny said. "He always knew this."

Connie clenched her hands, not wanting to think. Not wanting to feel. And especially not wanting to be here. The sly, cool hand of the fog drifted over her clothes, settled like inevitability on her skin. She held her breath, but the time came when that ended and she had no choice but to take the mist into her lungs.

"From the beginning of time, fire has both fascinated and frightened mankind," John said. "It's the ravening beast that can't be contained, and the phoenix that rises from its own ashes. Destruction and creation. But here, in this time and place, we've learned to conquer it. In firewalking, we use our own power to *choose.* If we choose not to be burned, then the fire can't burn us."

"That," he pointed to the bed of ruddy coals behind him, "isn't your enemy. Fear is. It whispers in your ear, urging you to give up. If you listen to it, you have to fail. But if you trust your own strength, you can't lose. You can walk over these coals and not be burned, you can tap the forces all around us." His gaze, pale and depthless with a hint of the fire in it, fastened on Connie. "Give up the fear. Focus only on the strength we all have. Choose to believe not in the fire, but in yourself."

He closed his eyes, releasing her with a suddenness that made her heart drop down into her belly. He sat down with a smooth uncoiling of muscles, then folded himself into the lotus position.

Anticipation lay cold in Connie's guts, hung heavily in the quiet avid breathing of the people around her.

"Close your eyes," John said. "Connie, work with us. You can't know until you try."

She didn't want to. Oh, God, she didn't want to. But she closed her eyes, clasping her hands over her knees so tightly that it hurt.

"Relax," John said. "Breathe. In. Out. In. Take it slow. Think about your body, feel your heart beating, feel the air rushing in and out of your lungs. Center yourself around that and only that."

Breathing was easy. Shutting her brain down wasn't; Connie couldn't block out the coolness of the fog on her face. She opened her eyes for a moment, saw Hamilton cupping a large quartz crystal in his hands. The stone fascinated her; its smooth sides caught the light and cast it back in a copper glow, winkling at her with erie familiarity from between his fingers.

"Connie," John said, without opening his eyes.

She flinched, chilled by that unseeing knowledge of her lack of participation. Or maybe, whispered that cynical accountant's voice, he peeked. But she closed her eyes anyway.

"Breathe," he said. "Focus your attention on the center of your chest. In. Hold it. Out. Empty your lungs completely. Fill your body with life force. In. Out. Keep your body's rhythm. In. Out."

The sound of the breathing overwhelmed the quiet break of the waves. It surrounded Connie, and she felt her body take on the same rhythm. In. Out. Time hung suspended. In. Out.

John's voice slid like velvet across her mind. "Let it flow through you," he murmured. "The force of life is all around, in the air, the waves, in every grain of sand. Draw it in. Abandon yourself to oneness with it."

They breathed, nine people in unison. In. Out. The sound rose in counterpoint to the ocean, rhythmic and powerful. In. Out.

"Open your eyes, everyone," John said.

He took Penny's hand, lifted it as though offering her to the fire. She rose, her eyes rapt as she walked out onto the coals. Her dress seemed to float around her, the pale draperies mingling with the looping coils of fog.

Connie's gaze drifted back to John. He stood at the edge of the coals, his body limned in the burnished light, drops of moisture gleaming molten on his skin. His voice seemed to mix with the fog, smoothly sensual, irresistible and seductive, sliding over her skin in an almost palpable touch.

Demon lover.

His gaze locked with hers. Pale, pale eyes reflecting the light of the coals, reflecting his internal heat. And hers. It attracted her and repelled her, for it touched that dark and reckless place inside her.

The beast, as he'd said. Wild and raging, frightening and primitive, it was yet the most vulnerable thing about her.

He wanted it. And now, gazing into his eyes, she realized he thought he could have it. Tonight.

She found herself breathing shallowly, her body reacting as though he'd caressed her. This had gone beyond rationality, beyond control.

One by one, the others rose and walked the coals. John continued the mantra of trusting one's strength and believing that the fire wouldn't burn, couldn't burn. Connie, still pinned in the intensity of his eyes, didn't hear the words. She sat unmoving, scarcely blinking, locked in what might have been love—or might easily have been something else entirely.

He held out his hand. "Connie?"

With a start, she realized everyone else had returned to their seats.

It was her turn.

"Walk the fire with me," John said.

It was a powerful summons, fueled with everything they'd shared. That reckless part of her wanted to obey.

If you give him this, he'll take it all.

And what would she be giving up? A life that had become too squared-off and rigid, a computer program of an existence whose main component was loneliness?

He'll take it all.

Her gaze focused on his hand, extended toward her in a gesture both compelling and eloquent. No man had ever asked so much from her or had given so much in return. Soulmates, he'd called them. Destined.

To walk the fire, she'd have to break all the boundaries of her life. She'd have to set aside her absolutes, the equations that balanced and made the world make sense.

She'd have to believe.

She looked up, directly into her lover's eyes—and slowly, deliberately, shook her head.

Dropping his hand, he turned and strode across the coals. Connie stared at his feet, the way they moved over the embers with that quick animal grace she admired so much. God, she wanted him. But she wanted the man, not the mystic, and she wasn't going to give up her soul to have him.

He sat down again after walking the fire. His gaze, when it met hers, was as self-assured as ever. With a shock, she realized he'd misinterpreted her refusal. It jarred her, that inability; no matter how disturbing she might find his personal philosophy, she'd counted on it, somehow.

"Let's continue," he said, winding himself into the lotus again. "Get comfortable, everyone."

Connie thought about leaving. But a sense of incompleteness kept her there on the sand, her front too warm from the coals, her back too cool from the fog. The others, judging from their faces, expected some kind of revelation tonight. So she settled in, folding her legs Indian-style.

"Normally, our evening would end here," John said. "But this is a special night. We hang on the cusp of an exciting new future, but we have to be sure we don't forget our past as we move on."

"Cullen," Penny whispered.

"Yes, Phaedra," John said. "Cullen is part of our past and also our future."

Cullen's dead, Connie thought, closing her eyes.

John's voice swirled around her. "Philip and Evvie have offered to make our group a concrete entity, both to protect us from the outside world and to give us greater power to deal with it. Tonight, while we're so very much in tune with one another, I want us to make a decision whether or not to take their offer."

"Cullen turned it down," Hamilton said.

"Cullen hadn't made up his mind," John corrected.

Connie watched Hamilton's long, graceful fingers contract around the crystal. The stone glittered like congealed fire in his grasp.

"I'm against it," he said. "Cullen didn't believe in mixing money and the spiritual, and I agree with him. Our search should be pure, unfettered with ledger books and bank statements."

In a boardroom, someone would have pointed out that he was perfectly willing to mix *his* bank statements with his spiritual search. But John didn't. His gaze remained coolly impersonal, his body relaxed. Connie might almost have thought he didn't care.

But if nobody else realized what was happening here, she did. And it was nothing less than a battle for the leadership of the group.

"I, too, had doubts," John said. "The issue of money is a valid one. But just as we refused to let the coals burn us, we can refuse to let the money spoil us."

Raising his head, he looked at each of them in turn. "Cullen dreamed a big dream. He wanted to turn this beach into a place where people could come and find themselves, where they could fulfill their spirits and heal their minds. But big dreams need a lot of help. I believe that in time Cullen would have come to the realization that Philip and Evvie knew best, and I believe he would have accepted their generosity."

"I believe, too," Penny said.

John smiled at her. "Thank you, Phaedra."

"I want the dream," Amy said. Beside her, Lynn nodded.

"Connie?" John prompted.

She looked into his eyes. "No."

"Evvie, Philip?"

"Yes." Philip turned to Hamilton. "You know we think of you as our son. But in this, we have to disagree."

Hamilton inclined his head, his eyes glittering redly in the lurid light. "I bow to the majority."

"And now," John said. "I think we ought to say goodbye to our friend."

Shock stiffened Connie's spine. *He means Cullen. The king is dead. Long live the king.*

He closed his eyes, and everyone but Connie followed suit. She shifted position slightly, grateful for the gritty sound of sand in the aching silence.

"Breathe," John said. "Fill yourself with the force of life, draw it deep. Exhale. Hold the emptiness, ready yourself to be filled. In. Out. Again. Touch your center."

Connie felt her eyelids slide downward. She didn't want to do this, not again. But she was lulled by his voice and the gentle drift of fog-tendrils over her face, and her body just took over.

"We're going a little farther this time," John said. "Feel your center, concentrate on it. You're complete within yourself, focused on your own internal power."

"Yes," Evvie murmured.

They stayed like that for what seemed an endless time. Connie felt no urgency, however; the minutes ticked away beneath her skin, trapped, as she was, in the smooth, seamless cocoon of John's voice.

"Now," he said, "it's time to reach out. Extend through your skin until there's no difference between the outside and inside. Push farther. Through your feet, your hands, the top of your head. Connect. Feel. Be one with the wind, the ocean, the earth under your feet."

At another time, Connie might have laughed. But the world had taken a half-twist, somehow; here, with the fog pressing close all around, reality had changed. Something brushed lightly over her face. It might have been the wind.

"Cullen," Penny moaned. "Oh, Cullen."

The timbre of John's voice changed, becoming both smoother and higher. Connie's nape hairs rose.

Clovis.

"Cullen is in transition," he said. She said. Whatever. "He is the brother of my soul."

No, Connie silently protested. He's mine!

"Focus on your heart center," John/Clovis said. "Press your hands hard and concentrate. Yes, that's it. I can feel your life forces. Don't be afraid. You can't lose him; death is not real, and he remains all around us."

He drew in his breath with a hiss. "There is great sadness among you. You must heal yourselves of this. Let him go and the sadness with him, so that you can know his joy. Use the mantra. Akal . . . akal . . . akal . . ."

It seemed as though they'd all drifted into another world, these coals and this small patch of sand their desert island in an unfamiliar sea. Connie's nostrils flared. Something malevolent quested beyond the circle of light, waiting to snatch up any who strayed.

Pure, primitive fear thrummed along her nerves with neon jolts of adrenaline. She found herself breathing in time with the chant. *So this is Cullen's world. Did he ever feel this sense of . . . hovering presence, of eyes staring unseen at the edge of the darkness?*

She opened her eyes, no longer able to inhabit the darkness behind her lids. Around her, the others sat motionless, their breathing deep and even, their faces serene.

That damned Balestier imagination. Give it some fog and fancy, and it'll run away with you.

Then her gaze focused on Lynn Cortez. It was like looking into a mirror; her own primal fears were written upon the girl's face, stark in the deepening red light from the coals. Horror slithered up

Connie's spine, settled clammy fingers at the back of her neck.

"Can't you feel it?" Lynn cried.

Amy caught her daughter's arm, but Lynn shook her off roughly. Hamilton was the next to try; grasping the girl by the shoulders, he pulled her to her feet.

"What is it, Lynn?" he asked. "What's the matter?"

"You can't *feel* it?" Tears spurted from her eyes, ran in viscid streams down her face. "It's all around us," she sobbed. "All you have to do is look!"

"What?" Amy demanded.

Lynn wrenched free of Hamilton's grasp and leaped to her feet. She poised for a moment on her toes, her hair almost as wild as her eyes. "Somebody's going to die!"

Whirling, she ran off into the fog.

"Wait!" Amy shouted. "Lynn, wait!"

She hurried after her daughter. Hamilton went after her. Margo stared after him with a wide-eyed astonishment that would have been funny in any other situation.

Penny rose unsteadily. "Somebody help her," she whispered. "Oh, find her and help her!" Then she fainted, dropping to the sand in a flutter of gossamer fabric.

"Shit," John said, clearly and in his normal voice. "Philip, can you and Evvie get her to the house?"

"Of course."

John strode away. The fog closed around him with a sense of finality, shrouding even the sound of his footsteps.

The old man bent over Penny. But it was Evvie who took action, pulling the younger woman up off the sand and hoisting her over her shoulder in a fireman's carry.

"Come on, Margo, Connie," Philip said. "Let's get back."

Connie lifted her head, freed from the stupefaction that had held her since Lynn's first agitated words. Instinct screamed at her to opt for the safety of the house. Lights, furniture, straight walls and square corners . . .

But she'd felt the same brooding malevolence that had sent the girl screaming into the fog. Practical Connie. Two-plus-two-equals-four Connie.

As John had said, shit.

"You go on," she said. "I want to help out here."

"But—"

"I'll be all right, Philip."

He turned away. A moment later he and the other women disappeared into the arms of the fog.

Connie stood alone in the swirling whiteness, listening to distant voices calling for Lynn. She placed John as the farthest away, Amy next, and nearer the house, Philip and Evvie, calling at intervals.

Damn you, Connie, you should have known something was brewing with that girl. You're the one who played the quiet-kid role all your life.

Well, Lynn had certainly grasped her moment of drama. Connie lifted her head, suddenly aware that she could no longer hear the others' voices. Isolation—unfilled by the quiet murmur of the waves. As the fog caressed her face with cool, damp tendrils, it seemed as though she'd stepped off the edge of the earth.

And then she heard a sound behind her.

Chapter Twenty-Three

Rasp.

A small sound, the faint grit of sand beneath someone's shoe.

Rasp.

An innocent sound. The sound, perhaps, of someone coming to lead her back to the house.

Rasp.

So quiet. So very quiet. As though whoever made those footsteps didn't want to be heard.

This is silly, she thought. Just because some kid with an overactive imagination got carried away with the stupid breathing and the fog . . .

Rasp. Closer now. She had to choose.

Instinct made her decision for her: she stepped back, away from the coals. Once out of the glow, she found herself all but blind. She realized she'd been silhouetted against the light. Now, she'd become invisible.

The footsteps stopped. A soft exhalation of breath scored the silence as the other lost track of her. A terrible sense of *waiting* filled the night, and she felt the sour taste of fear sting her throat.

John would have called her name; in the fog, anyone would have called her name.

She crouched, glad she'd worn pale clothing tonight. The footsteps paused, then changed direction. Changed again.

He's looking for me.

Something moved through the fog nearby, almost seen, barely heard. She held her breath, pulling herself even closer to the ground. Mist distorted the other's image until it hardly looked human at all.

She wanted to run. Her legs ached with it; her heart already had the rhythm of flight, swift and hard and frightened.

Frantically, she tried to remember the path to the house. She hadn't paid much attention; it had been merely the way out to the firewalking spot, obstacles spotted by flashlight and avoided without thought. Branches, brush, an odd whorl of dune carved by the wind . . . any one of them could trip her up. She wiggled her ankle, gauging the chances of it holding out long enough.

Rasp.

She gathered herself, holding her breath as the footsteps moved away. One second, two. The far-off moan of a foghorn rolled in from the ocean, startling her. As the sound died away, she leaped to her feet and sprinted toward the house.

Every step sent pain jagging through her ankle But the hot pop of adrenaline took the edge off; pain was infinitely better than facing that unseen pursuer. Even through the rasp of her breath, she heard the other coming after her. Swift, gritting steps, another breath blowing in counterpoint to hers. She wasn't fast enough.

With a desperate spurt of speed, she doubled left, hurdled a clump of stiff dune grasses, then turned and plunged to her right. She heard a thump behind her as her pursuer fell, and a hissed profanity. Then the footsteps again. Instinct urged, *run, run, run.*

No! You'll never make it.

She leaped the crest of a dune, came down on all fours on the other side, and stayed. Tucking herself against the sand, she tried to think herself invisible. *Seeking fucking oneness with the earth.* She couldn't stop the thought, absurd as it was.

Footsteps grated toward her. She felt like one gigantic heartbeat as she hugged the ground, hoping the fog was thick enough. Surely he could hear.

Sand drifted down on her as the other ran along the crest of the dune above her. Panic sliced along her nerves, and she had to press her hands against her mouth to keep from screaming.

Then the footsteps went past, headed fast and hard toward the house. She let her breath out in a rush. Relief flooded through her, and she rolled over onto her back.

A scream ripped the air up ahead. Penny's voice, high and frightened, as though she'd seen the devil himself.

Maybe she had.

Connie surged to her feet and started in toward the house in a limping run.

"No!" Penny shrieked. "Get away from me!"

She screamed again, a wild ululation that made Connie's skin crawl. The sound cut off abruptly amid a crash of breaking pottery.

Connie's lungs burned with effort, her ankle with pain. She could hear other voices now, John's and

Hamilton's and the rest as they converged on the house.

The fog grew lighter and brighter, and she finally burst into the island of light surrounding the deck. Penny lay sprawled in the wreckage of one of the big planters, her hair mingling with the tumbled dirt.

"Oh, my God," Connie gasped, taking the three stairs in an awkward lurch.

She skidded to her knees beside her sister-in-law, groping for a pulse with shaking fingers. Penny groaned. Her eyelids fluttered, and she rolled over onto her back.

"Penny, talk to me," Connie whispered. "Where are you hurt?"

"I'm . . . okay."

Connie brushed dirt from the other woman's cheek. "Who did this to you?"

"It was Jeff," Penny moaned.

Connie rocked back on her heels. Jeff? Had it been her son stalking her out there on the beach, had it been Jeff whose hate had tinged the night with that brooding malevolence?

She jumped up as someone's feet hit the deck behind her. But when she turned, a shard of pottery clenched in her hand, she saw John. Hamilton ran out of the fog a few yards behind him, and then the others. They piled up behind John like waves behind a levee, staring at her with wide, frightened eyes.

"Connie?" John's gaze went from her to the shard and back again.

Penny struggled up on one elbow. "It was Jeff. H-he came running at me, and I just . . . it was like he came out of nowhere—there was no sound, no warning. I'm not sure he even saw me; his eyes were fixed and staring, and he ran right over me like I wasn't even there. I lost my balance and fell onto the planter."

Connie turned and hurled the makeshift weapon as far out into the fog as she could.

"Did you see which way he went?" John asked.

Penny pointed south. "That way, I think."

"Hamilton," John said. "Take a look around, will you?"

The younger man slipped back into the fog, and Connie heard him walking in the direction Penny had indicated.

"He's not going to find him," Amy said. She had her arm around Lynn, who looked like she'd been dragged, drained, and set out to dry. "If I were you, Phaedra, I'd find somewhere else to stay until the police find that boy."

Penny shook her head. "I can't leave."

"You can stay at our place," Evvie said.

"No!"

"I'll stay with her," John said. Then he glanced at Connie. "Hamilton and I can take turns in the guest room. She'll be safe with us."

He bent and lifted Penny to her feet. She clung to him, her grip so tight her fingers made white marks on his skin. He turned her gently toward the house.

"It's all right," he murmured. "Take it easy, Phaedra. It's over."

Vaguely, Connie registered the others walking past her. But her attention was focused out onto the beach. This couldn't be real. *That* Jeff couldn't be real—the one who beat helpless women and stalked his own mother through the fog.

"Connie?"

Startled, she looked up to see Philip standing in

front of her. Another man might have looked grim. But Philip's eyes showed only sympathy, a St. Bernard–puppy eagerness to help.

"You're shaking," he said.

She looked down at her hands, saw that she was indeed shaking. "I must be cold."

"Come on." Putting his arm around her shoulders, he turned her toward the house. "We'll warm you with some coffee, eh?"

It sounded so simple. But he had no son to turn his world upside down, no son to love through senseless acts, terrible acts. The love of a mother: desperate, bottomless, sometimes futile. Philip would never understand.

But she went with him anyway, unable to dredge up the energy even to disagree.

My son!

Connie sat on the hearth, unwarmed by the fire behind her. John sat cross-legged at her feet, the others in a half-circle around him.

He'd gone into a trance again. The whole set of his body had changed, his posture shifting, even his shoulders seeming to take on a slimmer, more feminine line. If it was an act, Connie thought, it was a damn good one.

"You must pass through the fear," he said in Clovis's lighter voice and more formal intonation. "The boy is working under a burden of karma that none of us could overcome without a great deal of help. You cannot hate him, nor should you pass judgment."

Connie watched the play of muscle beneath his shirt as he gestured with his hands; it was Clovis's habit, not his. Illusion or delusion, she couldn't tell.

Maybe it's the truth.

And that was the most frightening thing of all. Cullen had been nobody's fool. Could he have fooled himself, then, simply because he wanted to believe so badly?

Her gaze drifted to Lynn, who had retreated behind her usual adolescent's bored facade. There, against all the arguments logic could make, sat the anomaly. The unexplained, maybe the unexplainable.

And what does that make you? You felt it, too.

John leaned back against her shins, and she had to repress a sudden, swift urge to draw away.

"Clovis?" Evvie leaned forward. "Are we doing the right thing in forming this company?"

John/Clovis cocked his head to one side, obviously consulting some inner oracle. "I believe so. This alliance is vital and strong and will last beyond its individual members. You must nurture it while it is young, protect it, and help it grow."

His audience, with the exception of Hamilton and maybe Lynn, nodded agreement. Connie could have screamed; these people would accept almost anything that didn't come with the tag of the conventional.

She didn't understand why Hamilton didn't give John more of a challenge. He wanted to; she could see it in the flaring resentment in his eyes. But maybe he thought he'd lose more than he'd gain if the Walhfields pulled out.

Well, I've got a curve to throw you, fella.

"Clovis, can you reach my husband?" Penny asked.

John sighed audibly. "I've tried many times. But

there is a barrier between us I can't break. Perhaps the boy is holding him; there is something very strong between him and his uncle's spirit, something that has to be finished before either can find peace."

Connie stared down at his thick, fireshot hair, wondering who would yelp if she gave it a yank.

She'd had enough. More than enough.

"I've got to go," she said, standing up and away from him. "Excuse me, everyone."

His breath went out sharply, as though she'd punched him in the gut. His head lifted, and with a smooth and perceptible transition, he became John once again. "What are you doing, Connie?" he asked.

"Going home. I've got a big day tomorrow."

"I'll take you."

"I'll call a taxi."

"Don't be ridiculous," he said, rising. "Besides, I think we need to talk."

Connie nodded. "Maybe you're right."

"Hamilton, will you stay with Phaedra tonight?" John asked, turning to the younger man.

"Sure. Margo can take my car and pick me up in the morning."

Margo looked like she'd rather do anything but. Feeling as sour as the girl looked, Connie let John take her by the elbow and steer her toward the door.

John didn't talk much on the way to her apartment, however. He seemed subdued, almost drained. Finally, he pulled up outside the house and put the car in park.

It wasn't quite midnight. The porch light was on, as was the one in Mr. Ranke's living room. Upstairs, the notorious Sherrie must be having a party;

music belled out the open windows, underscored with laughter and shouted conversation.

"Just what you needed," John said. "Peace and quiet."

"I don't find peace anywhere these days."

His eyes caught the light oddly as he turned around to face her. "I'm sorry, Connie. I don't have children, but I can at least try to understand how painful this is for you."

"Yeah. Everyone understands."

"Are you angry that Phaedra called Detective D'Amato?"

"No. After all, what else could she do? I'm just . . ." she let her breath out in a harsh sound of frustration. "I'm trying to reconcile my image of the son I raised with that of this person who's doing these awful things. And I can't."

"You can't blame yourself."

"Who else then? A fifteen-year-old kid who doesn't know his backside from a truck tire? Come on, John. I feel like I'm being sucked straight to hell, and the more things happen, the faster I fall."

"I'll catch you," John said.

So graceful, she thought. So clever. Reaching out, she laid her fingertips against his lips. His eyes turned hot. So did she, in a disturbing mix of libido and bitterness. Libido because she wanted him now as much as ever, and bitterness because she couldn't be sure who he was.

"When I kiss you," she murmured, "who kisses me back, you or Clovis?"

"Me. Always."

She let her hand fall away.

"What's the matter?" he asked.

"I feel like half of me died when Jeff ran away,

and it seems like there's less of me every time I turn around."

Softly he stroked the back of his hand along her cheek. "Invite me in, Connie. I need you tonight."

She was tempted, more than tempted. But too much had happened tonight. She'd reached critical mass, mind and spirit and soul; she reeled with fear and loss and a foreknowledge of coming disaster that had nothing to do with the psychic.

"Not tonight," she said. "I need time to be alone. All I want now is to crawl into my hole and pull the cover in after me, and . . . you make me feel too much."

He smiled a bit crookedly. "That's the first time I've ever been turned down for being too good."

"When you hooked up with the Matthiases, you opted for the unexpected," she said. "I'm just living up to Cullen's promise."

He smiled, either not hearing—or choosing not to hear—the acid pain in her voice. "I hope you mean that," he said. "I like the unexpected. Now, let's get you upstairs. A hot bath and a good night's sleep will make things look a hell of a lot brighter."

He came around to help her out. She would rather have walked on her own. But with her ankle out, she had no choice but to let him carry her into the house. He negotiated the stairs through an almost physical wall of sound, then set her on her feet outside the door.

"Do you want me to go with you tomorrow?" he asked. "To look for Jeff."

She shook her head. "I'd rather be alone."

"Or with your ex?"

Instead of answering, she started looking for her keys. John grasped her wrist.

"I'm sorry, Connie. I wasn't making an accusation."

"And I'm not going to give an explanation."

"Okay," he said, always willing to be reasonable. Always willing to avoid disagreement, always willing to bend to the other person's needs.

But somewhere in there were *John's* needs, and they went far beyond the usual. He'd give her room in one aspect, only to take far more in another.

"Connie . . . what are you going to do if you *do* find Jeff?"

There it went, a straight, hard punch to the heart. The big question. She lifted one shoulder, let it fall. "I guess I'll help him any way I can, and do it while keeping him from hurting anyone else."

"Will you give him to D'Amato?"

"I don't think I'll have a choice."

"He's not responsible, Connie. His karma—"

"Stop," she said, holding her hands up. "I can't do this right now. Just let it be."

He stroked his knuckles along the curve of her cheek. "If you want."

She saw heat flare in his eyes and knew he was going to kiss her. It surprised her that she didn't stop him; she'd meant to. But the old, familiar arousal sparked to life deep in her belly and surged through her veins. It was always like this with him. Maybe it always would be.

But tonight, a kernel of cold intellect remained apart from the surging awareness of her body. She realized what had happened to her: she'd stepped over a threshold, to a place where sex and surcease were no longer enough. And it was that lack that brought her hands up to push him away.

"What's the matter?" he asked.

"Me. You. Oh, hell, John." She raked her hair back with one hand. "I don't have a problem with eccentricity. Look at Cullen. Shoot, look at my mother. But I'm having trouble with this Clovis business."

"Connie—"

"It's too far out for me."

"No," he said. "It isn't. I saw your face out there on the beach. And you looked as scared as Lynn did. I'd bet my soul you felt what she felt."

"I wouldn't bet my soul on anything."

"I would. But then, I've always been a risk taker."

There was an edge to his smile she found disconcerting; if she could have touched her soul, she would have clutched it to her chest to make sure it stayed where it belonged.

"I need my world to be defined," she said. "I need for equations to equate, for north to be the opposite of south, and for one person at a time to inhabit a body. Especially one I'm sleeping with."

"We're destined for each other. From the moment we met, I knew it and so did you."

"Tonight I'm destined for a hot bath and sleep, remember?"

He let it go, as she knew he would. Doing otherwise would have been unreasonable. She would rather have had a whopping good fight.

"Goodnight," he said, leaning forward to brush his lips over her eyelashes.

"Ahem!"

They sprang apart like guilty teenagers. Mr. Ranke stood at the top of the stairs, looking, in his plaid golf cap, rather like a skinny Jack Benny.

"Hi, Mr. Ranke," she said.

"Just a sec." The old man thumped on Sherrie's door, and the volume went down immediately. Then he turned back to Connie and John, his face radiating satisfaction. "There. She knows the rules. No loud music after midnight."

"What can we do for you?" John asked.

"Nothing. Just keeping an eye on things." The old man's gaze softened when he turned it on Connie. "You forget your key or something?"

"We were just saying goodnight," John said. "I'll call you tomorrow, Connie."

She nodded.

Mr. Ranke waited until the front door closed, then dug in his pocket and came up with a key ring. "Your ex came by tonight. Left his car, said you could use it for a couple of days. Said you weren't to say no; he didn't want you to have to be dependent on other folks for gettin' around."

"Thanks," she said, surprised and pleased by Derek's unexpected generosity. "He must have ESP; I've got something very important to do tomorrow."

"You ought to take it easy," he said. "You're looking worn out."

"It's all that wild living I've been doing."

"Wild!" He snorted, jabbing a gnarled thumbnail at Sherrie's door. "*That's* wild."

She smiled at him. "By the way, thanks for being discreet. About the car, I mean."

"I'm the soul of discretion."

"Mr. Ranke, please!" she said with a shudder of not-so-mock horror, "let's not talk about souls."

Chapter Twenty-Four

Jeff cupped his hands around his mouth to light a cigarette. The wind cut through his lightweight jacket, and he wished he'd been smart enough to run away in the summer. He wished he'd held onto his backpack. He wished for a lot of things.

"Hey, Jeff!"

It was a female voice, so he didn't run. Turning, he saw two girls walking down the street toward him. They looked familiar: one blond, one brown-haired. He'd seen them at a couple of parties this summer. Seemed like a lifetime. He strained for their names, smiled when he failed.

"Hey," he said. "Lookin' hot today, ladies."

They giggled. "Where have you been? You missed a great party last night. Dave scored some 8-balls, people were falling all over the street."

"Shit," he said, with real regret. "I was over at . . ." He let his voice trail off without finishing, because he couldn't remember where he'd been. He'd done a couple of downers and some rum with some guys early in the evening, but the rest was gone.

The blonde smiled. "Sounds like your party was better than ours."

"Yeah," he said, feeling lame.

The brown-haired girl tossed her hair back over her shoulder with a flick of her head. Her high-rise bangs didn't move. "Want to hang for a while? We got money."

"No kidding? Who'd you fuck for it?"

"Hey, everybody," the blonde said.

They all laughed then. Behind the laughter, Jeff felt his mind hanging as slack and empty as his pockets. "Sure, I'll do breakfast," he said. "Thanks."

"Where do you want to go, Jackie?" the blonde asked.

"Golden Arches, of course. Love those sausage biscuits."

Jeff would have gone anywhere it was warm and smelled of food. He played the gentleman, offering his arm to both girls. They loved it; all of them did. His mom had taught him well. He felt his smile twist, and unkinked it with an effort.

Later, full of coffee and sausage biscuits, he propped his feet in the swivel chair opposite. He'd heard these places were designed with not-comfort in mind: get 'em in, move 'em out. But he'd slept in places lately that made the hard chair seem like a Beautyrest.

"Did ya hear about Tick?" Jackie asked.

Jeff went very still. "No. What about him?"

"He's dead."

"Shit, no." He hoped his expression was the right one for the occasion; to him, his face felt like it was jumping all around. "Me and him used to hang a lot. What happened? Did he O.D.?"

"Nobody knows," the blonde said. "I heard some night watchman found him in a graveyard."

"Shit, he looked kinda like a vampire," Jackie said. "Maybe he got caught out in the open when the sun came up."

They giggled. Jeff stared at them, and suddenly their voices seemed to go all hollow in his head. He kept seeing Tick the way he'd been that night, his face chalky and dead, his eyes filmed over.

"What's so fucking funny?" he hissed, his throat stretching painfully around the words. "Me and Tick were *friends.*"

"Hey, look, I'm sorry," Jackie said. "Everybody knows Tick and you were tight. It's not really funny that he died, it's just that—"

"I don't want to hear this shit anymore," he snarled, shoving himself upright. "Thanks for breakfast."

He stalked toward the door. Just as he started to push it open, he saw a car go past. The driver turned to look at him, a flash of dark sunglasses, and he might as well have been wearing a badge on his forehead.

A cop. A fucking cop.

Jeff's hand went limp, and the door swung closed again. He watched the car slide into the nearest parking place. Damn. Had to find another way out of here. He ran back toward the counter and hurtled it, sending the order takers screaming in all directions. Faces loomed like big, flesh-colored balloons as he ran past. Then he slammed out the back door, running across the asphalt parking lot to dive into the anonymity of a townhouse development on the other side.

He kept moving, knowing the place would be crawling with cops in a couple of minutes. In one miniyard, clothes hung from a line. He filched a damp sweatshirt and pulled it on over his jacket.

The cops had arrived; he could hear at least two cars cruising a short distance behind him. The net was closing. Run. Climb one fence, then another. Run again. He did it until his lungs burned.

When he stopped to rest, he didn't hear the cars anymore. He propped his hands on his knees and sucked air into his lungs. But the burning didn't stop; it spread to his throat, to the back of his eyes. He reached up to rub them, encountered wetness.

I want to go home.

He didn't want his dad's tough love. He wanted his mom. He wanted to feel safe and warm, he didn't want to worry about cops or knives or finding dead people.

But his mom didn't want him. She'd closed the door, locked it, and pulled in the fucking welcome mat.

He sank to his knees, hugging himself as though to keep himself together. Tears and snot ran over his mouth and dripped down his chin. He couldn't do this anymore. Sleeping on the streets, cold and hungry and scared, running, hiding . . . was this all there was to the rest of his life?

He fell forward onto his hands, crouching like an animal while the breeze plucked at his hair and riffled through his clothes. Nobody cared. Nobody loved him.

I want out!

Yeah, right. There were only two options for him: sleeping on the streets, and sleeping in a cell. He knew what would happen to him in prison, a nice young thing like him. Shit, at least out here, guys *paid* you for it.

"I can't," he sobbed. "I can't."

He was tired of running, tired of running, fucking tired of being scared. Walls were closing in on him from all sides, and now the ceiling had started to drop, too. Head bowed, he stared down at the ground, wishing he could make everything stop.

The sun cast a glint off something in the grass. He blinked tears out of his eyes and refocused. Glass. A long, triangular piece of it, curved like it had come from a bottle.

He sat back on his heels. After a moment, he reached out and picked the shard up. It caught the light, reflected it back into his eyes.

Only one way out, Jeff.

His hand tightened around the shard. A drop of blood welled from his finger, traced a bright path through the dirt on the glass.

Scared of dying, still more scared of living. Shit.

"Only one way out," he said.

Connie checked the numbers as she drove through the Larchmont section of Norfolk. The houses got bigger as she neared the water. Philip and Evvie's place was a sprawling one-story that clasped the lot like a hand. A few hundred yards beyond, the Elizabeth River caught the sunlight, then cast it back again in a million dancing sequins.

Bigger and better than the house on the beach. Oh, yeah. Connie parked in the driveway and headed up the walk, which meandered pleasantly through well-ordered flowerbeds. A tiny fountain lay tucked in the lee of the wide porch, water tinkling over stones that looked like they'd been matched for color, texture, and shape.

She stepped onto the porch and the front door opened as though on cue. Evvie peered out.

"Hello, dear," she called, swinging the door open wider. "Come in, come in!"

The foyer was the size of Connie's apartment, not including the atrium. Light poured straight into the room, making Connie feel as though she stood in a giant fishbowl. Or maybe it was just Evvie's clear, avid eyes that made her feel that way.

"Would you like something to eat?" Evvie asked. "We have some heavenly blackberry pie."

"No, thank you."

"Herbal tea? Or coffee, if you'd rather. I'm afraid we drink only decaf."

Connie smiled. "Don't you have any vices at all? No, seriously, Evvie, I can't stay. I'm supposed to meet someone in less than an hour."

Evvie's disappointment was obvious, and it gave Connie a twinge of guilt. She nearly apologized, but the older woman had already turned away.

An archway led to another sun-drenched room. It was a hard, glittery place; crystals of every size, shape and description cluttered almost every surface. Even the furniture echoed the theme: a taut white leather sofa and loveseat, a coffee table created from a meld of marble and glass, a lamps made of black Lucite caught in a malformed teardrop. The only soft touch was the enormous white Persian cap sprawled in Philip's lap. It woke, fastening a baleful sapphire gaze on the stranger who'd entered its domain.

"Hello, Connie," Philip said, scooping the cat into his arms so he could rise.

"And this is Kira," Evvie said.

The cat jumped down from Philip's arms and

stalked over to Connie. Those sapphire eyes never blinked as she looked the visitor over. Suddenly, her inspection completed, she swiped herself along Connie's shin.

"Oh, look," Evvie said, beaming, "she likes you."

Connie bent to stroke the animal, paying special attention to the sweet spot just at the place where tail and spine met. The cat arched her back, breaking into a deep purr.

"She adored Cullen, too," Evvie said.

Uh-oh, Connie thought. "I used to have a cat who was very social. He used to make the rounds of the neighborhood, just visiting."

"Not Kira. She rarely deigns to so much as look at people."

Straightening, Connie sighed. "I just happen to like cats, Evvie. For some reason, animals always seem to know that."

"Of course, she does like Hamilton," Evvie continued. "But she's known him for years and years. You and Cullen are the only people she's ever accepted on sight like this."

"My mother always says that cats bond with people who wear clothes that contrast well with their fur," Connie said, looking down at her black leggings, which were now coated with long white hairs.

"I think your mother has a very cynical view of the world." Evvie smiled the brilliant, sly smile of someone who knew more than she was telling. "Don't you think cats have an ability to see below the appearance of a person? After all, that's why they've been chosen as witches' familiars all down the centuries."

"Well—"

"Auras, dear."

"Huh?"

"Cats can see auras. Yours and Cullen's are so much alike that Kira responded exactly the same way to both of you."

The beginnings of alarm shot through Connie's mind. Before she could think of anything to say, however, Evvie gave her another of those fey smiles.

"What was your cat's name?" the older woman asked.

"Barfly." A sudden wash of nostalgia hit Connie, memories she hadn't taken out and viewed in years. "He liked beer, you see. He adopted me, just walked into my yard and planted himself in my life. Twenty pounds of orange tabby tomcat. I don't know how old he was when he found me, but I had him for twelve years before he died."

"Why didn't you get another cat?"

She shrugged. "Jeff was getting into trouble then, and he took up all my time and energy."

"And love," Philip said. "A person shouldn't let the children consume his or her life; after all, they move on, and you should have something left when they go."

Slowly, Connie turned to face him. "I know you mean well, Philip, but you don't know—"

"But we do," he said. "We lost Matthew when he was nine."

"He drowned, you know," Evvie said.

"No," Connie said softly, "I didn't."

Philip's eyes were bright with tears; brighter, in a way, than all the crystals in the room. "Evvie had a number of miscarriages. Finally the doctors said she couldn't and shouldn't try to have any more, so when Matthew went, he took everything with him. It took a long time for us to find something else."

This is what Cullen saw. He didn't care about their money or their house; he saw the pain, the need for love, for belonging.

"I'm sorry," Connie said. She'd accepted the bright surface appearance of this couple, labeling them merely eccentric. But now she could understand their search for something meaningful, for something, anything, that might make sense of the pain.

"It was a long time ago," Philip said. "Come, sit down. We know you're pressed for time."

Connie took the seat beside him. Evvie perched like an oversized sparrow on the loveseat opposite, her eyes bird-bright and expectant. Kira jumped back into Philip's lap, and he stroked her slowly.

"Now, my dear," he said, "tell us what's so terribly urgent that you came all the way out here."

"Actually, I came to ask you a question."

"Fire away."

"Are you planning to make the company a beneficiary of your estate?"

He met her gaze directly. "How did you know?"

"Adding two plus two is my specialty, Philip. Was it your idea, or did somebody else suggest it?"

"It was our idea." Then he frowned. "I'm sure no one else mentioned it."

"Think hard, Philip. It's important."

He stared at her, surprise obvious in his face. Then he nodded. His gaze turned inward, turned blind. Silence hung in the room, tumbling slowly with the dust motes in the sunbeams. Connie didn't know if he was thinking, praying, or meditating, and didn't care as long as whatever answer he found did Jeff some good.

Finally, he looked up. "No. I'm sure it was my idea."

Connie sighed. "Have you discussed it with the others?"

"Not yet. But we'll have to—"

"Not now," she said, not having to try for the edge in her voice. "Please."

That got their attention; Philip stopped stroking the cat and Evvie leaned forward, her face creased with the beginnings of concern. "What's the matter, Connie?" she asked.

"Don't make any changes in your will," she said. "At least, not until I tell you it's okay."

Philip's brows soared. "Why not?"

"Because I don't think it's a good idea to muddy water that's already pretty dark."

"But I don't understand—"

"Neither do I," Connie said. "But there it is. I've been working this thing through in my mind, but nothing comes together. Add more money, and the tangle just gets worse."

Evvie rolled her shoulders, an indeterminate gesture. "We're not getting any younger, you know. We'd like to make sure Cullen's work carries on after we're gone."

"What about Hamilton?" Connie asked.

"Hamilton?" Evvie glanced at her husband. "I'm sure he'd be the first to say he didn't need or expect to be our sole beneficiary."

Oh, would he?

"Is he now?" Connie asked.

"Other than a few bequests to charities and such, yes," Philip said. "But Hamilton, I fear, is beginning to depend on what he *will* have and not striving to reach his potential in the here-and-now. It's not that we're breaking the promise we made to his mother to take care of him, but we want him to approach life with more . . . initiative."

Connie thought he'd shown a lot of initiative in getting himself a girlfriend from one of the wealthiest and most influential families on the East Coast. A nice safety net for a guy who thought his fortune might be flying out the proverbial window.

"Please don't change your will," she said. "If you won't do it for yourselves, do it for me."

Philip cocked his head, regarding Connie with that disturbing, bird-bright gaze. "Do you ever just run with your instincts, Connie?"

"No."

"Cullen did."

"Cullen had good instincts."

"And you don't?"

"Rarely," she said.

The sunlight hit one of the crystals just right, and rainbows bloomed to life on every wall. Connie drew her breath in sharply; it seemed almost as though someone had hurled a bucket of color straight into her eyes. And that she was drowning in it, green and violet and blue.

"It's beautiful, isn't it?" Evvie asked.

"If you like rainbows."

"Some cultures believe that the rainbow is a bridge between heaven and earth."

Connie knew what was coming next; it had to come, because the Wahlfields were what they were. She looked down, afraid that the sudden black anger might show in her eyes. "Are you saying that if I look hard enough, I'll find Cullen there?"

"No, dear," Evvie said. "I think that if you look

hard enough, you'll find Cullen inside you, where he's been all along."

Kira rose, stretched so that her claws made pulls in the fabric of Philip's pants. Then she leaped over to Connie's lap and settled in. That rasping purr cut the air.

Connie looked up to see the Walhfields studying her, rainbows in their eyes. She felt as though they were consuming her, pulling her apart piece by piece to make her fit their needs.

"You should have more faith in yourself," Philip said.

"Maybe," she agreed. "But my faith has been pretty badly shaken lately."

Evvie smiled. "That's because you've chosen to believe in the temporal instead of the spiritual."

"Maybe so. But what do you think Cullen's instincts would have said about changing your will?"

It was a deliberate low blow, all the more unfair because she knew they weren't capable of dodging it. She saw it register, saw it sink in. Good. She needed it, so she used it.

They exchanged a glance, and finally Philip said, "Why is this so important to you?"

"Because I hate to see anyone so vulnerable," she said, flinging her arms out in exasperation. "Good Lord, Philip. You don't try to protect yourselves at all."

Evvie picked up a big rose-quartz crystal and held it up in front of her eyes. Connie got the message. Then her gaze focused on the older woman's hands, and she noted how the flesh had begun to shrink from her fingers, a precursor to the old age that was coming.

And now that Cullen was gone, they had no one except Hamilton—and Connie wasn't about to believe he was in it for anything but the money. If he found out they were thinking about changing their will . . .

"Damn it," Connie snarled. "I came here because I *like* the two of you, okay?"

Philip grinned, looking absurdly like a mischievous little boy. "Oh. Well, in that case, I think we can wait a bit on the will. As long as you think it's that important."

"Thank you. It makes me *very* happy." Connie rolled her eyes. She didn't think she'd ever get used to this; no logical argument worked with them, but give them a simple statement of emotion, and they couldn't wait to cooperate.

"You've got the oddest look on your face, dear," Evvie said.

Connie glanced at her watch. "Oops, time to go." Feeling rather like a punch-drunk fighter, she got to her feet and bent to drop a reluctant Kira back into Philip's lap.

Evvie walked her to the door. Connie opened it, hoping to make her escape without further conversation, but she had to stop when she felt the older woman's hand on her arm.

"Kira's pregnant," she said. "Would you like to adopt one of the kittens?"

Connie blinked. "Kittens?"

"Yes, dear. To love, you know."

Refusal was the only option; she had more than enough work loving Jeff. Then she thought about

Kira's fathomless sapphire eyes, and said, "Sure, I'd like one."

She was still wondering what had happened to her as the front door closed behind her.

"It must be catching," she said.

Chapter Twenty-Five

Connie called D'Amato as soon as she got home. His voice sounded blurred, as though he'd gotten as little sleep as she had.

"What's the matter, Detective?" she asked. "Guilty conscience keeping you up at night?"

"You ought to know," he retorted, somewhat good-naturedly. "What can I do for you, Ms. Matthias?"

"Did you know that Hamilton Liu is the main beneficiary in the Wahlfields' will?"

"I figured as much."

"Did they tell you they were thinking about changing their will?"

"Don't be melodramatic," he drawled. "You know you've got my attention; just give me what you've got."

"I thought I'd make you beg."

"Ms. Matthias."

She smiled, because he'd know she was smiling. It was a pleasure dealing with someone truly predictable. "They wanted to make the new corporation chief beneficiary. And they were planning to do it before Cullen was killed."

Silence stretched for quite a while. Then D'Amato cleared his throat. "I know what you're thinking," he said.

"Do you?"

"Yup. Your theory is that Hamilton Liu found out about it and got worried that his nice little nest egg was getting ready to fly out the window."

"Twelve million *plus* real estate, Detective."

"Then why didn't he kill the Wahlfields?"

Connie snorted. "Like you don't know. Look, D'Amato. Hamilton is a smart guy, not one to miss the complexities of his situation. If he killed the Wahlfields, you'd take a real hard look at the beneficiary of all that money. By killing Cullen, he thinks he can break up the group. No group, no threat to his security."

"I've got to give you credit, Ms. Matthias. You're tenacious."

"So are you. And so, despite the fact that you'd jump off a bridge before admitting I might be right, I have faith that you'll check it out. Because you—"

"Always check everything out," he finished for her. "You're a hard woman. I'll let you know if I hear anything interesting."

He hung up on her. She didn't mind, because she knew she'd had the best of *that* conversation. At another time, they might even have been friends; she liked his tough, hard-edged mind with its firmly established parameters.

The phone rang under her hand, startling her. She picked the receiver up again. "Hello?"

"Connie?"

For a moment, Connie didn't recognize the voice. Then, with a shock, she realized it belonged to her mother. "Mom? Is something wrong?"

"Connie, I . . ." Sandra gasped for breath. "I'm sick. Can you come? I . . . need your help. Please."

"I'm on my way."

Connie didn't know what pulled her out of her apartment at a run. Maybe it had been that hint of desperation in her mother's voice. Or maybe it was the fact that Sandra had never asked for her help before. Never.

"Be home, Mr. Ranke," she muttered, sliding to a stop at his door.

He answered on the first knock. "What's up, Connie? You look—"

"My mother's ill," she panted. "Derek's due here in about fifteen minutes. Will you watch for him, tell him what's going on?"

"Sure. Leave it to me."

Prompted by the sympathy on his face—or maybe by her own need—she went up on tiptoes and kissed his cheek. Then she whirled away, calling a thank-you over her shoulder.

The drive to Sandra's seemed to take forever, every red light her personal enemy. But she made it at last. Something nagged at her as she drove past the front of the house, something subtle that didn't quite register. Then she got it: the living room curtains were still closed, and the door hung ajar an inch or two.

Connie's heart kicked into high gear. Sandra opened the living room curtains at 9:00 A.M. sharp, rain or shine, sick or well, weekday or weekend. And she never, *never* left a door unlocked, let alone open.

"Jesus, Mom," she whispered.

Her tires squealed as she turned into the driveway. Then she was out, her footsteps jarring as she ran down the walk and took the porch steps two at a time. She didn't remember pushing the door open, but it banged shut behind her with a force that rattled the picture window.

She ran from room to room, her alarm rising when she found each one empty. "Mom!" she called. "Mom!"

A moan drifted from behind the closed door of the guest bathroom. Connie tried to open it but met resistance on the other side.

"Mom, let me in."

Sandra moaned again. Truly frightened now, Connie jammed her shoulder against the door and shoved. It gave an inch, then stuck. She grunted and tried again. Another inch. Grunting, she forced it another couple of inches. The smell of vomit rolled out in a choking wave.

Connie could see a foot in the opening, and realized that Sandra herself was the obstruction. Somehow, she'd gotten herself wedged between the door and the toilet. "Mom, can you hear me?"

No answer. Crouching, she grasped the foot and gave it a sharp tug. "Mom!"

Sandra gave another of those low moans. "Connie?"

"Mom, you've got to do something for me. I can't open the door anymore without hurting you. You're going to have to move." Getting no response, Connie tugged the foot again. "Mom!"

"Yes."

"Slide away from the door so I can get to you. Toward the tub."

Sandra's foot moved. Not enough, but it moved.

"Come on," Connie urged. "Just a little more."

She could hear the rasp of her mother's breath,

the swish of fabric against the tile floor. Sandra's foot disappeared from the opening.

"Thank God," Connie muttered, pushing her way in.

Sandra lay between the tub and the toilet, her body curved in a fetal position. Vomit streaked the commode, the floor, and Sandra's face, hair, and hands, and lay in clumps in the fluffy pink bathrobe she wore. Her skin looked green in the harsh bathroom light.

Connie dropped to her knees and checked for a pulse. Some of her panic eased when she found her mother's heart going steady and strong. "What's the matter, Mom? Did you fall?"

"Mmh." Sandra's eyes fluttered open. "I'm just . . . ill. I've been . . ." Her abdomen heaved visibly, and she grabbed Connie's sleeve with convulsive strength.

"Okay, I've got you." Connie lifted her to a sitting position, then held her as she vomited into the toilet. Sandra moaned with each heave, as though her guts were going to come up with the bile.

"It's okay," Connie murmured. "It's okay, Mom. I've got you."

The spasm ended. Gently, Connie raised her mother's head and propped it against her own shoulder. Sandra began to cry weakly.

"Was it something you ate?" Connie asked.

Sandra nodded. "Brunch . . . at Norma's. Crab."

"Well, there's none of it left in your stomach, that's for sure. I'd better get you to a doctor—"

"No! I'm fine. Tired."

"Mom—"

"As you said, there's nothing left in my stomach. Just . . . stay with me for a while. Please?"

The note of desperation had returned to her voice. "Of course I will, Mom."

Sandra relaxed so completely that for a moment Connie thought she'd fallen asleep. Then Sandra said, "Thank you. I'd like to clean up now."

That sounded more like Sandra, Connie thought. Then she laid her hands on her mother's shoulders and realized just how fragile the older woman had become in the past few years. Even the bones seemed to have lost mass.

Emotion tightened Connie's throat; Sandra had always seemed indestructible. Bigger than life, somehow, a force to be respected, admired, envied, but loved only at a distance, because she could give out a lot more punishment than Connie could take.

"Let's get you cleaned up," she said.

She levered her mother up out of the awkward space and half-carried her down to the master bathroom. Then she sat Sandra down on the toilet and washed her like a baby.

"Feel better now?" she asked, patting a few last drops from Sandra's face with a clean towel.

Sandra nodded.

"I'm not sure I got all the soap out of your hair, but it's better than the alternative. Later on, when you're steadier, you can take a shower." She turned away to toss the filthy robe and nightgown into the hamper.

When she turned back, she saw that her mother's face was wet again. Tears. Connie stared at her, dumbfounded. She couldn't remember when she'd seen Sandra cry before. Even at Dad's funeral, Mom had been tragic but calm, the source of strength for everyone around her.

"Oh, Connie," she sobbed. "I wish you didn't hate me!"

Hate you? Connie's brain seemed to have been disconnected, thought and action suspended by shock. She saw how her mother's lax breasts quivered as she cried, saw the wrinkled skin of her abdomen and the webbing of blue veins in her legs.

This shouldn't be happening, not like this. Sandra sitting naked on a toilet seat, sobbing her heart out. . . . There had to be more dignity, even in catharsis.

Connie turned away abruptly, walking into the bedroom to fetch another robe. Behind her, she could hear Sandra crying, great, jagged sobs that hurt the soul. She paused, crushing the garment between her hands as a sudden, powerful urge to run swept through her. *Don't look, don't listen, don't feel what's happening here.*

She went back into the bathroom, because it was the only thing she could do. Gently, she eased Sandra's arms into the sleeves and belted the robe around her.

"I don't hate you, Mom," she said, again because it was the only thing to say.

Sandra only cried harder. "He was my son, and now he's dead. Do you know, can you imagine how it feels? Can you understand, even a little, how much it hurts to bury your own son?"

"Yes," Connie said. "I understand."

She laid her hands on the older woman's shoulders. Sandra pulled away. It hurt more than it should have for something that had been expected. Connie dropped her hands to her sides, watching her mother's tears dry into arid despair.

"I loved him so much," Sandra said. "He was so

alive, so full of himself. He . . . made me feel alive, too. Oh, we argued. He and his dolphins, his rainforests, and the stupid little bird that the loggers hated so much. And then the crystal-gazing and astrology, the ridiculous fortune-telling cards and the weird friends—"

"Mom, don't."

Sandra bowed her head. "We argued over everything. I think he enjoyed even that; his spirit was so sunny that he even argued good-naturedly. But not me." Doubling her hand into a fist, she pounded her chest once, twice. "I was mean about it. I made fun of his beliefs, his life-style, and his friends. And the more tolerant he was about it, the nastier I got. I don't know why he bothered coming at all."

She paused for breath, and Connie opened her mouth to say something, anything, to stem the tide. But Sandra overrode her; in a way, she wasn't speaking to Connie at all.

"I thought he was throwing his life away on this New Age nonsense. He just . . . took a half-step away from the real world, and I'd have given my eye teeth just to have it be dolphins again. I tried to talk sense to him, I tried to make him see how silly the whole thing was."

She drew a deep, shuddering breath, that fist pounding again in a steady rhythm of pain Connie could feel in her own body. "And now he's dead. My son, my beautiful son. I'll never see him again, never hold him. And I'll never have a chance to ask for his forgiveness. I should have been more accepting. Oh, God, I just should have believed in him."

Connie closed her eyes.

"I didn't get the chance to tell him I loved him," Sandra continued, obviously determined to punish herself still more. "I never got to tell him how I admired his fire and commitment and intelligence. I never told him how very proud of him I was. And you—"

"Don't!" Connie flinched away from that, both physically and spiritually.

She jumped again as her mother grabbed her forearm, fingers digging deep.

"I was jealous of my own daughter," Sandra said. "You and Cullen together . . . no one could intrude on your special twin world, no one could really understand. From the moment you were born, I was left out. I was glad when you went to California. *Glad!* Because I thought I'd finally have one of you all to myself.

"But then I hated you for that, in the end, because it hurt Cullen so much. He missed you every moment you were gone. I think that's why he started in with this mumbo-jumbo, trying to replace you—"

"Don't say it," Connie hissed. "Don't you *dare* blame me! I missed him just as much."

"You left him."

"I left *you!* I left because I couldn't stand listening to your harping on how you'd told me not to marry, to get an abortion so I wouldn't be *burdened* with—"

"And wasn't I right?" Sandra shrieked. "Isn't he the mistake I told you he was?"

"No!" Connie shouted back. "He's my son! He's a living, breathing human being with good and bad all jumbled up inside him, just like the rest of us. And as long as I live, I will never, ever give up on him!"

"You're a damn fool, then. And if he calls here again, I'll turn his sorry—"

"What did you say?" Connie's voice dropped to a whisper.

Desperation shot through Sandra's eyes, and she let go of Connie's arm. "I—"

"He called here?"

"Well—"

"He did. He called looking for me, didn't he?" Connie leaned close. "What did you do, Mom?"

"I, ah . . ." Her voice trailed away.

"What did you do?"

Sandra's chin went up. "He wanted your phone number. I told him it was unlisted, and I refused to give it to him. For your own protection."

"For *my* protection?" Connie drew in a breath, let it out again in a sharp exhalation of fury. "Who are you kidding, Mom? You're just jealous—again. After all, if you can't have your son, you're going to make damn sure I can't have mine, right?"

Connie didn't see the slap coming. Then her cheek felt as though it had exploded, and the sound of flesh on flesh echoed in the room. Sandra gasped, covering her mouth with both hands. Her eyes showed wide and frightened over her fingers.

"I'm sorry," she said. "Oh, I'm sorry!"

Without a word, Connie turned and walked away. It was too late for apologies . . . too late for everything.

"Connie!"

She kept walking, shrugging Sandra's hand away when the older woman tried to stop her.

"Connie, wait! We have to talk."

"I think everything's been said between us that needs to be said—ever."

Sandra's shoulder slammed into the back of her legs, and they both went down in a tangle of limbs. Connie scrambled onto her hands and knees only to go down again beneath her mother's weight. They pitched around there in the hallway, a lying-down shoving match that was none the less ferocious because it was silent.

"You're not leaving here until I talk to you," Sandra panted.

"Let go of me!"

"No!" The older woman's face was mottled with effort, but she let up for a moment. "I've got something to say to you, damn it! Once I'm done, you can walk out of here forever, but by Heaven, you're going to hear me out."

Connie stopped struggling. After a moment, Sandra let go of her and pushed up to a sitting position.

"You're awful goddamn active for somebody who couldn't hold her head up a couple of minutes ago," Connie said.

"I've lost my son." Sandra's eyes were stark and terrible. "And now I'm fighting not to lose my daughter."

Connie met that raging, desperate gaze, wishing she didn't understand so well. She felt stripped bare, scoured dry by things she wasn't equipped to feel. But she'd lost a brother and maybe a son, and found that she wasn't willing to lose anything else if there was the slightest chance of working things out. So she sat up and pushed the tumbled hair back from her face.

"All right, Mom. I'm listening."

Sandra nodded. "I don't hate Jeff; after all, he's the last of us. But I do hate what he's doing to you. Do you think I feel nothing when I see the pain in your eyes? Don't you think I can understand what this is doing to you?"

"I don't think you understand anything but your own needs. You never have. Neither Cullen nor I could ever hope to compete with your clubs and caucuses."

The older woman chopped the air with the edge of her hand. "It was always you. You were the one I admired, the one whose respect I always wanted."

Connie drew a breath that hurt. "What?"

"You were the one I could depend on. The one we *all* depended on. Cullen never got over your leaving. But you managed to get along just fine without him. You always manage. While Cullen flailed around, doing this and being that, you were making a good life for yourself and your son."

Connie tried to hold onto her rage, for she needed it as a shield against the rest of her emotions. But it drained away in the face of the despair in her mother's eyes, leaving Connie awash in things she didn't want to feel.

"Cullen knew," Sandra said. "In his heart, he knew you were my favorite. And he spent those fifteen years trying to fill the void you left when you moved away."

Connie couldn't have been more astonished if the bed had gotten up and walked. "Me, your favorite? You've got to be kidding! You never let up on me. 'Connie, you're ruining your life.' 'Connie, you choose the wrong men, the wrong cars, the wrong clothes.' 'Connie, you had the wrong son.' All my *life,* Mom. And it seemed that Cullen could do no wrong. You and he just sort of tootled along together, not always agreeing, but without the bitterness that colored all *our* arguments."

"You were always ready to believe you couldn't beat Cullen in anything. And we fought, you and I, two alpha females in the same household. Sure. But I respected your independence and your grit, even when you infuriated me. God, Connie, you fought me all the way down the line on everything. I resented that. I resented the *hell* out of that."

"Because you couldn't control me?"

"Maybe. Maybe that was it. You drove me nuts. Once you'd made a decision in that logical brain of yours, you simply didn't listen. You'd inform me that I was being unreasonable, that you'd examined the risks and accepted them. And that was that. In a way, I understand Jeff's wild, screaming rebellion; there were times when I felt like doing the same myself."

Connie leaned her back against the wall. "Is that why you turned him away when he called?"

"Oh, damn, Connie. He caught me flat-footed. And then he started in with his snottiness and his demands, and I reacted impulsively. Of all people, you should understand; he's just like his father—or like Derek used to be—and that used to send you into screaming frustration. Remember?"

"More than I'd like," Connie admitted.

"I know I should have been more mature than he. I was wrong."

Connie closed her eyes, seeking anger inside. She should feel it, plenty of it, enough to help her walk out the door and never come back. But there was only sadness for all the things she and Sandra might have been to each other.

"I'm so sorry," Sandra said. "I know I haven't been the most attentive of mothers, that I'm not warm and cozy and supportive . . ." She bowed her head, and tears splashed down on her tightly clasped hands. "Please try to forgive me," she whispered.

Slowly, Connie gathered her mother into her arms. Sandra broke down completely then, crying with fierce, unrestrained abandon.

"Shhh," Connie murmured. "Shhh. I forgive you."

She wasn't sure it was true yet, but something inside her told her it might be some day. For now, it would have to be enough.

And there, in the hallway, they clung to each other, two women who'd lost so much: father, husband, brother, sons. Joined in love and loss and an uncertain future, they gave what comfort they could.

Chapter Twenty-Six

Jeff turned the glass shard edgewise to his wrist. It felt cold against his skin. He wondered if it would hurt to bleed to death. How long would it take—a minute, two?

He pressed down, flattening the veins. The blood pounded a frantic tattoo in his head, wanting to be set free. One quick slash, and it would all be over. A violent rush of sensation poured through him: the urge to live, the urge to die. It rocked him, sent him spinning through the wasteland of his memories.

"No!" he moaned. "No!"

Blood on his hands, blood on his clothes, Tick's dead eyes staring up at him. Uncle Cullen, his mouth open in pain and astonishment, listing to one side. The knife stuck out of his chest, its handle twitching with the rhythm of his heart. A bloom of red around it, a starlight-shot sheen of wetness on the hilt. Fear and horror, no-don't-do-it even with the knowledge that it was already too late. His own hands reaching out to catch the man as he fell to the sand, his breath rasping as he watched Cullen's fingers move in spasmodic little jerks. Then came the sound of ripping cloth as his uncle's shirt was torn off.

Jeff didn't try to understand the shirt; he could only watch the knife hilt go twitch, twitch, twitch.

And then the voice. "See what you've done, Jeff? You've killed him."

I killed him. *The words echoed through his brain, quiet screams that sank straight into his soul.*

"I'll help you," the voice said. "I'm your friend. Run away, Jeff. Go somewhere where no one is going to see you. Don't tell anyone. I'll take care of things here."

The man took his wrist, turned his hand upward and placed a square of paper in it. "Take this. It will help you forget what happened here. Forget what you did."

Jeff stared down at the gift. Acid vision distorted its outline and changed the texture of the skin below. Pores as big as foxholes, hairs looking like dark iron spikes.

And nothing else.

No blood.

No blood.

Blood on the shirt, blood on the hilt.

"Jesus *fucking* Christ," he said aloud.

No one was going to believe him; he couldn't be sure himself whether that memory was true or not. But goddamn, it had felt *real.* And there sure as hell wasn't a whole lot of other hope for him.

He dropped the shard onto the ground and levered himself to his feet. Time to get some help. There was only one place where he wasn't going to be locked in either a jail cell or a padded room. Genuine nondenominational help.

It took him a couple of hours to walk to the Redemption Mission. He tried hitching, but he didn't look like the clean-cut all-American boy anymore.

Nobody stopped for dirty, ragged street kids, and that was what he'd become.

He found Rick in the mission office, sleeping with his feet on the desk and his chair tipped back against the wall. Sunlight flooded the room, picking up the gold lettering on the battered Bible beside his feet.

His eyes opened, pinning Jeff with that too-understanding stare. "So you came back."

"My name's Jeff."

"What can I do for you, Jeff?"

"I'm in trouble, and I need help."

Dropping his feet to the floor with a thump, Rick pointed to the metal folding chair on the other side of the desk. "Have a seat and tell me about it."

It took awhile. Dusk began to fall, throwing shadows into the room. Rick didn't move to turn the light on; he hadn't moved since Jeff had started talking, as though he feared it might end the conversation. But Jeff was on a roll; he couldn't have stopped now if he'd wanted to. And Rick just listened, studying him with that gritty blue gaze that looked tough and unrelenting and sympathetic at the same time.

Jeff didn't cry, didn't raise his voice. But when he finished his story, he sat slumped in the chair, completely exhausted. The silence stretched on and on, then finally Rick got up and turned on the light.

"I believe you," he said, propping one hip on the desk.

"You do?"

"The Lord gave you that memory for a reason, Jeff. He wanted to save you."

"You're not going to start with the preaching, are you?"

"No. But I want you to understand the gift you were given today, and to use it to do something with the rest of your life. You have to believe that these problems can be made right."

"How?" Jeff demanded. "The cops are going to lock me up and throw away the key. Or if I'm lucky, I might spend the next fifty years where they put the dangerous nutcases. And my parents . . ." he paused, getting his voice under better control. "My parents have just thrown *me* away. They figure I'm the bad seed, or something."

"Your parents were here," Rick said.

Jeff could only stare.

"They've been looking for you," Rick continued. "Your mother said to tell you they believe in you."

"They were here?"

"They love you, Jeff."

"They've got a goddamn strange way of showing it."

"You're not perfect. Don't expect them to be."

"You're preaching."

Rick ran two fingers down his nose, which looked as though it had been broken and fixed more than once. "You're right. Sorry."

"How long were you on the street?" Jeff asked.

"From the age of nine until twenty-five, when I hit rock bottom."

"Why?"

"I took to the streets because I had a dad who alternately screwed us and beat us. I hit rock bottom because I was a junkie." He rolled up his sleeves, showing Jeff the scarring of old tracks. "I'd be dead by now if I hadn't found a better way." His hands trembled as he rolled his sleeves back down. "Did your parents abuse you?"

"No!" Jeff was surprised by the sharpness in his voice. "My dad rode my ass constantly, threatening military school if I didn't straighten up, shit like that. Mom just plain drove me crazy."

"Why?"

"If I climbed out the window, she nailed it shut. If I sneaked out the back door, she put in a deadbolt. One time she found out I was skipping, she went to school with me for a friggin' month. Haunted me like the Angel of Death."

"So they care what happens to you."

"She thinks I killed her brother."

"Give me a break. *You* thought you killed her brother. Be reasonable about this."

"Would you be reasonable if you looked into your mother's eyes and knew she thought you were capable of murder?"

Rick's eyes hardened. "Don't give me that hard-life shit. My mother sat in another room and pretended nothing was wrong while my old man screwed my sister. And I lay in my bed waiting for my turn. Look, Jeff. You came to me for help. I'm willing to give it to you, but don't come on with self-pity or an attitude."

"I wasn't—"

"Are you tired of running?"

Jeff sat stiffly, wavering between punching the guy and walking out. Then the tension ran out of him all of a sudden. He leaned forward, elbows on knees, and bowed his head. "I was gonna kill myself today. Yeah, I'm tired."

"Do you want to go home?"

"Yeah. No. I don't know."

With a sigh, Rick got to his feet. "My place is only a couple of blocks from here. Why don't you come with me, grab a shower and something to eat, and we'll hash this thing out some more?"

"Yeah," Jeff said, giddy with a rush of relief and gratitude. "Thanks."

"Come on. We'll go out the back way; it's shorter."

Jeff followed him down a hallway, past the kitchen and a storage room full of boxes. The back door opened onto a narrow street lined with trash-cans that leaked the smell of garbage into the cool evening air. It had started to mist, a not-quite rain that filmed the skin with moisture.

"I appreciate this," Jeff said.

"No problem."

"Is this part of your religion—helping people you don't even know?"

"Part," Rick said. "Part of it is that you remind me an awful lot of me a few years ago. I was so damned angry at the world that I did everything in my power to destroy myself."

"You should have destroyed the ones who did it to you."

"It occurred to me." The man sighed. "I struggle with the hate I feel for them sometimes. And then other times, I can forgive them. As the years go by, the forgiveness comes more frequently."

They turned the corner and Rick started diagonally across the street. Jeff kept pace with him.

"Did you ever go home?" he asked.

"No."

"Do you ever wonder what would have happened if you had?"

Rick turned a glance on him that had become hooded and dark. "All the time."

"Would you have killed him?"

"Before I found the Lord, yes, I think I would have. But now—"

An engine roared to life nearby. Then headlights bloomed, spearing straight into Jeff's eyes. Blind, he stood pinned in the sudden, searing illumination, while the engine bellowed like a great animal, growing louder and louder behind the glare.

"Look out!" Rick shouted.

Too late.

Jeff opened his mouth to scream as the car loomed in front of him. Then Rick appeared between them, his arms outflung against the headlights.

The impact sounded like a melon being smashed with a hammer. Rick slammed back into him, a boneless mass of flesh that splashed hot and wet across his face and chest.

His head hit the pavement, hard enough to stun, but not hard enough to knock him out. He lay helplessly as the car screeched to a halt in front of him.

He could hear the drip of blood from Rick's shattered body, the purr of the engine and the sharp click of the car door as it opened. Someone stepped out. Jeff could only see the man's feet and legs up to the knees. Blue jeans, nice, clean running shoes—*he's gonna get those dirty*—

"Hello, Jeff. I've been looking all over for you."

He knew the voice. *That* voice. Had to get out of here, had to run. . . . He tried to pull his arms and legs under him, but nothing seemed to work.

"You killed him," he croaked.

"I couldn't let him identify us, could I?"

"You *fuck!* He never did anything to you!"

The man pulled Jeff to a sitting position. "Now,

Jeff, you're not exactly in the position to be nasty, are you?"

The movement sent red lances of agony shooting through Jeff's right side. He cried out.

"Hurt?" The man felt along Jeff's arms and shoulders. "Oh, well, looks like your collarbone's broken. Maybe a rib or two. I don't think you're going to be doing any more running, hmm?"

He grasped Jeff's arms and pulled him up and over his shoulder, then dumped him into the back seat of the car. Jeff would have screamed if it wouldn't have hurt too much. He held his right arm close to his side, trying to find some space between the red jags of pain.

The car surged forward. Jeff used his legs to brace himself against the movement. Tears puddled in his eye sockets, overflowed in twin rivulets to his temples.

"I need a doctor," he said between clenched teeth.

"You need help," the man agreed. "But you can't go to a doctor, Jeff. You're wanted for murder, remember?"

"I didn't—"

"Of course you did." The man turned a corner at a speed that sent Jeff into a jaw-clenching sweat. "We're going to discuss that in detail later."

Fear shot through the haze of pain. He wished he'd turned himself in to the police. At least then he'd have had a chance. Had to do something. Mom and Dad, had to let them know . . .

"Where . . . ah, shit!" he gasped, as the man swung into a sharp right turn. "Where are you taking me?"

"To the beach, Jeff. I've been saving something special for you. Trust me, you'll like it."

Trust me. Sure. Jeff tried to get up, but the pain battered him back down again. So, it had to be something else. Anything, no matter how lame. Slowly, panting with effort, he eased his jacket off his shoulders.

"Oh, God," he whimpered softly, even as he forced himself further into the agony.

He peeled the jacket down and off, then cradled it against his chest like a baby. *Just give me a second, God. Just one shot at it.* He reached over his shoulder with his good hand and slid the lock up, then fumbled at the door handle.

Easy, easy.

The car swung right again. At the crest of the turn, Jeff opened the door and tossed the jacket out. The sound of rushing air seemed to bellow in his ears.

"What the fuck—" the man shouted.

The car fishtailed to a halt, throwing Jeff against the back of the front seat with enough force to make him scream. He torqued in and out of consciousness until the man slapped him into focus.

"Don't try jumping out again, Jeff," he said. "Or I'll have to break your other collarbone. Among other things."

"What the hell difference does it make?" Jeff panted. "You're going to kill me anyway."

"You wound me. Actually, I have no intention of killing you. I only want to help you. See, it's important that you remember the truth about what happened to your uncle. And don't forget your friend. You have to remember that, too."

He held up a tiny square of paper. "Time for your treat."

Jeff shook his head, refusing it. But the man grabbed his chin, fingers digging in cruelly. "Come on now, Jeff. You know you want to."

The pressure increased, forcing Jeff's mouth open. He gagged as the man thrust the paper in and held it, gagged as he felt the acid dissolve on his tongue.

"See?" his captor said. "That wasn't so bad. In a little while, we'll give you another. And then another, until you finally remember what happened the night Cullen was killed."

Jeff closed his eyes. *No, no, no, nonononono. I just learned to remember. I know the truth.*

But now the forgetting was about to begin again.

After leaving her mother, Connie decided to drop in at the Redemption Mission. She found the place closed, the only light coming from a side window.

"What the . . ." She glanced at her watch. Six-forty, right in the middle of the hours in which dinner was served . . . or should have been.

She knocked on the door. When no one answered, she walked around to the side window and knocked there. The blind opened so suddenly that she gasped.

A man peered out at her, a tall, wide man who all but blocked the light. He slid the window upward. "I'm sorry, ma'am, but we're closed tonight. If you need something to eat, you can go down to the church on—"

"I'm not looking for food," she said. "I'd like to talk to Rick."

His face crumpled. "Rick . . . was killed in a hit-and-run just an hour ago."

Connie felt as though the world had dropped out from beneath her. She reached out, supporting herself on the window frame. "He's . . . dead?"

"Yes."

"I'm sorry," she whispered.

"So are we all," he said. She noticed that he held a Bible in his hands, one that had seen a lot of use. "Is there something else I can do for you?"

"My son had talked to him the other day, and I was hoping that maybe he'd come back—"

"What's your son's name?"

"Jeff. Jeff Matthias."

The man shook his head. "Rick said nothing about your son, I'm sorry." Then his eyes softened. "Rick was your only link to the boy?"

"Yes."

"I'll pray for you, that you find another way."

"I've never been much of one for prayer," Connie said.

"Then I'll believe in it for the both of us."

He closed the blind, and the sound ran like sharp fingernails along her nerves. She walked back to her car. Instead of driving away, however, she slowly leaned forward until her forehead rested against the steering wheel.

"Oh, God, why?" she whispered.

Until now, she hadn't realized how much hope she'd placed in Jeff coming back to this place. Until now, she hadn't been quite so afraid she'd never find him.

She straightened, reached to start the car. Derek had to know. Somehow, somewhere in this mess, they had to find another way.

The drive to Derek's passed in a blur; she drove like an automaton, relying on experience and reflexes while her mind did something else. To her relief, the Toyota sat in the driveway.

She rang the bell, rang it again when he didn't answer. A moment later, he opened the door. He must have just gotten out of the shower; his hair was wet, slicked back from his forehead, and his well-worn sweats looked like they'd been put on in a hurry.

"Sorry to bother you," she said, although she wasn't. "Can we talk?"

He studied her closely for a moment, then stepped away from the door. "Sure. Come on in and I'll make us some coffee or something."

Connie followed him into the kitchen. It was a pleasant enough room, only so-so clean, but judging by the number of pots and pans hanging in an overhead rack, he'd progressed from the hamburgers and scrambled eggs of his youth.

He followed her gaze, and one side of his mouth turned up. "I can do chicken, baked, fried, and broiled, pot roast, chicken-fried steak, not to mention stir-fry and meatloaf."

"Everybody can do meatloaf," she said, turning toward the table.

He caught her by the arm and swung her back around. "What's up, Connie?"

"Rick was killed tonight. Hit-and-run."

His breath went out in a rush. He let go of her arm and turned to brace his arms on the counter. Connie watched the muscles tighten beneath the sweatshirt, and her throat ached with repressed emotion.

He knew. He felt what she felt. Impelled by something she neither understood nor resisted, she took a step forward and put her arms around his waist. He stiffened, then relaxed a bit as she laid her cheek against his back.

"Kindness for the ex-husband?" he asked.

"Let's call it a return for that hug the other day. Besides, I need it."

"Fair enough," he said. "Now we've got to figure out what we're going to do about Jeff. I'm not giving up, Connie."

"Neither am I." Tears welled in her eyes. Not now, damn it, she thought, blinking them away. But they kept coming, silent and hot, and dripped onto the sweatshirt beneath her cheek.

"You're crying," Derek said.

He started to turn around, but she tightened her hold. "No," she said, "don't."

"There's nothing to be ashamed of."

"I know that." She drew a breath, fighting for control of her voice. "I've spent most of the day crying with Mom. I guess this is just a . . . continued reaction."

"What's with her?"

"Guilt. She made fun of Cullen's beliefs and now he's dead, and she turned Jeff away when he called her looking for me."

"God damn!"

"I forgave her."

He made a noise that was half-sigh, half-growl. "So why can't you forgive me? My only sin was being married to you a hell of a long time ago."

"I *have* forgiven you."

"Could've fooled me."

"I fooled myself. Until today, I didn't think I had any forgiveness in me at all."

He loosened her grip, turned around so that he

faced her, then put her arms back around his waist. "So what happened to that nice, safe, ordered little world where no one could touch you enough to *earn* your forgiveness?"

"Life intrudes," she said.

She knew the kiss was coming. He gave her time to refuse, but she went up on tiptoes to hurry him along. It was an explorative kiss, one that quested rather than demanded. But then it deepened, becoming not so much a demand as a melding. Young love, hot and fierce and wild, a marriage, a son, all those years of fighting and compromising, all the new fear and pain and desperation . . . all in all, one hell of a kiss.

Derek broke for air. He had the look of a man who'd been taken apart and put back together a whole new way. "Holy shit, Connie."

"Kinda unexpected."

"Yeah. What about John?"

"I've put him on hiatus."

"Does he know?"

"Do I ever pull punches?"

He smiled. "That's something even I haven't been able to accuse you of." Then his expression turned serious. "Before we go any further with this, how about making that hiatus permanent?"

"Hmmmm." It wasn't a hedge, just a delay; this had happened so fast and so powerfully that she wasn't quite sure what to think about it. "Is this a return to selfishness?"

"Yes," he said. "I'll share my books, my Weed-eater, and to a very, very good friend, my favorite fishing pole. But I don't want to be kissing you and wondering if some other guy's doing it tomorrow."

She reached up to stroke her fingertip across his

bottom lip, and saw the reaction in his eyes. "And what will you give up in return?"

"Monday night football," he said. "Hey, I like these stretchy pants. I can just—"

"Women," she corrected, making a decision purely on instinct for one of the few times in her life.

"Okay."

"That was too fast, Derek. You must be between lovers."

"That makes me all the more amenable to compromise."

Connie drew her breath in sharply as he slid his palms down the curve of her buttocks, then lower, deeper. He'd always had nice long fingers . . . "It still works for us, doesn't it?"

"It never stopped working for me," he said. "In a way, you shadowed every relationship I had after our divorce. Every time I touched another woman, I couldn't help thinking about what it had been like between you and me, and nobody ever fared well in comparison. I knew it, and eventually they did, too."

"And what was it like?" she murmured against his mouth.

"Making love to you was like riding a roller coaster in the middle of an earthquake. I always felt poised over the abyss, knowing that if I got a fraction of an inch deeper and hotter, I'd go plunging off into—"

"Hell?"

"Mmmm." His eyes unfocused for a moment. "Maybe. But it sure felt like Heaven."

"And now?"

"Now it's worse. 'Cause I want you more."

He wasn't wearing anything under his sweats. "Yes," she said. "I think you do."

Things started happening quickly then. Once they'd gotten down to bare skin, however, Derek changed the pace. Oh, the fire was still there; Connie felt as though her body had become one big heartbeat, tuned only to the touch of his hands. But the impatience had gone. Now they could concentrate on the touching, the tasting, the sharing.

It was good. Oh, it was good.

Connie arched her back as he kissed his way down her belly. Suddenly, a thought speared through the sultry haze in her mind. Something important still needed to be settled, and settled now. Grasping Derek's hair, she stopped his downward movement.

"Wait," she gasped. "I've got to ask you something."

"Make it quick," he said. "I'm busy."

"Do you want my soul?"

He looked up at her, his eyes tawny and hot and incredulous. "What the hell would I do with your soul?"

Reaching up, he disengaged her hands from his hair. Connie closed her eyes as he went back to what he'd been doing.

"Oh, good answer," she murmured, arching her back again.

Chapter Twenty-Seven

Connie almost woke up when Derek kissed the back of her neck and said, "I've got to go to work. Make yourself at home. If I find you here when I get back, I'll consider it a bonus."

"Un-huh," she murmured, instantly drifting off again.

The phone woke her again hours later. She fumbled around, lost in an unfamiliar room, and finally found the telephone on the floor by the bed. "Hello?"

"Uh, Ms. Matthias?"

D'Amato. Caution drove the dregs of the fog from her brain. "In the flesh, Detective."

"I thought I dialed your ex-husband's number."

"You did." After a moment, she added, "Don't ask, D'Amato. Do you want me to leave Derek a message?"

He cleared his throat. "Actually, he was second on my list. I've been trying to reach *you* for hours. We need to talk. Face-to-face."

A cold little knot formed in her belly. "Tell me now."

"Can't. I've got something to show you."

"Where and when?"

"I've got a couple of stops to make," he said. "Why don't I meet you at your place in, say, an hour?"

Her hands started to shake as she hung up the phone. Something was up, and it wasn't good. She found her watch on the bedside table and peered at it. Four-thirty, and not A.M.; she and Derek had been *very* busy when dawn had rolled around.

"Damn," she muttered.

There'd been no escape from the world, not really. They'd just chosen to ignore it for a while, and events had just ground along without them.

She rushed home and took a quick shower, feeling shaky and scared and off-balance. D'Amato knocked on her door just as she finished her makeup. She paused to brush powder across her nose—a sort of laying on of armor against the unexpected that was as irresistible as it was absurd.

D'Amato knocked again. She swung the door open, her eyes widening when she saw that he held a large plastic bag under one arm. Her heart started beating in time with her apprehension.

"What's up?" she asked.

He came in, closing the door behind him. His eyes weren't quite so hard this evening, which scared her even more. "Let's sit down."

She took one end of the sofa, he took the other. Almost on cue, they turned to face each other across the no-man's-land of the center cushion. Then D'Amato opened the bag, pulling the snap-lock closure apart with a sound Connie knew she'd never forget.

"Do you recognize this?" he asked, laying a heavy denim jacket on the sofa between them.

Her pulse chattered in her ears. She'd bought that for Jeff in California. Reaching out, she traced the peace sign he'd drawn on one sleeve, then the hole where the bottom snap had been. Jeff had ripped it out in one of his rages. Connie could see him now, his face red, his mouth distorted as he'd torn his jacket open and hurled it across the room.

And then there was the blood. The denim was stiff with it, from collar to mid-chest. She curled her fingers into the fabric, wadding it between her hands.

"Do you recognize it?" D'Amato asked, his voice gentle.

She nodded.

"Is it Jeff's?"

She nodded again. "How did you know to come to me?"

"Because a denim jacket, with a peace sign on the sleeve, was in the description of the clothes your ex said he took when he ran away. Look, don't make assumptions from this."

Connie looked up at him. Her chest felt too tight, her breath inside her a solid column that hurt. "What shouldn't I assume, D'Amato?"

"The blood might not be his. He could have given the jacket to someone else, anything. We won't even know if it's human blood until we hear from the lab."

"Where was this found?"

He disengaged her hand from the jacket, then folded it neatly and slid it into the bag. "A jogger found it in the gutter near the intersection of Thompson and Little Creek. We're searching the area now, but it's going to take a while."

She clasped her hands in her lap to keep from

snatching the jacket away from him. It might be the last she'd ever have of Jeff. "You mean you're looking for a body."

"We're looking for anything."

"Right," she said, squeezing her hands together. Squeezing and squeezing as though it was her only hope of keeping herself from flying apart. "*You* think he's dead."

Blunt. Brutal. She didn't know any other way to deliver it. Or to take it. D'Amato studied her with those merciless, honest eyes, and gave it to her straight.

"Your son isn't living a life-style that generally makes for a long life," he said. "But I'd love to be wrong."

Connie met his gaze, saw honest regret there. My son, she thought. She tried to imagine him lying still and cold somewhere, his hair falling forward over a face that would have looked just like Derek's one day.

She started to rise, impelled by the unbearable vision. Then the world spun and the coffee table flew up toward her face.

"Ms. Matthias? Connie?"

She clawed her way upward to consciousness as something cold and wet touched her forehead. D'Amato's face swam into her field of view and she realized she lay on the floor, a pillow wedged behind her head.

"You fainted," he said.

"I was hoping you'd tell me it was all a dream."

"I'm sorry."

She held out her hands. D'Amato grasped them

and pulled her to her feet, then steadied her as he helped her to the sofa. Her skin felt cool, her guts as leaden as her mind.

"You're in shock," he said. "I'm calling someone to stay with you. Who do you want?"

"I don't need anyone."

His mouth thinned. Taking a notebook out of his pocket, he went to the phone. Vaguely, Connie registered the sound of him dialing.

My son.

She pulled the bag into her lap and took the jacket out again. How many times had she seen him wear this? Dozens, hundreds. She raised it to her face, rubbing it slowly across her cheek. It smelled of sweat and old blood, but there was something indefinably *Jeff* about it.

Outside, the huge red ball of the setting sun sank beneath the horizon. Darkness claimed the room. Connie welcomed it; with her sight dimmed, she could almost imagine this was only a jacket.

Strange, she thought. Jeff didn't *feel* dead. Not in her heart, where it counted.

D'Amato came back to crouch beside her. "I couldn't reach either your ex or your mother. But I got hold of your sister-in-law, and she's on her way over to pick you up. Said she'd take you to her house for a while."

Connie didn't care. She rubbed the denim along her cheek, over and over. *My son.* "You'd think I'd be able to *feel* that he was gone," she said. "A mother is supposed to know these things."

"Only God knows these things," he said, switching on the lamp.

Dazzled by the sudden brightness, she looked up at him. "A man died last night. His name was Rick, and he worked at the Redemption Mission. Hit and run. He knew Jeff. He was going to try to get Jeff to come home. Maybe if he hadn't died—"

"Life is full of what-ifs," D'Amato said. "You can make yourself crazy thinking about them. Or believing them."

He tried to pull the jacket out of her hands, but she resisted. With a sigh, he got up and went to sit at the other end of the sofa. Holding vigil, she supposed. Maybe expecting her to cry. But this was too big for crying; she wanted to crawl in a hole and pull the cover in after her. In a way, she managed it, cocooning herself in broken shards of memories. Jeff, a tiny, impossibly ugly scrap of humanity, howling in protest as the doctor laid him on her stomach; Jeff, his plump, four-year-old face beaming beneath a mop of sun-bleached hair; Jeff, his twelve-year-old body all bones and awkward angles, scowling into the camera. Jeff, with his eyes leavy-lidded and hazed from whatever he'd smoked or taken . . .

Even that. She rubbed the denim along her cheek, wishing even to have that Jeff back.

Beneath it all, D'Amato made small talk, apparently not caring that she didn't respond. She sort of drifted along on the ebb and flow of his voice and her own memories.

After a while, D'Amato got up. Then Penny came to sit beside her. The stark pain in her eyes mirrored that in Connie's soul.

"I've come to take you home with me," she said.

Connie didn't respond. Couldn't, actually. It astonished her, this silence on her part; she'd thought her estrangement from the present to be self-imposed.

Penny glanced up at someone behind her. "Come

with me, Connie." Then her voice went down to a whisper. "Trust me, this is the best thing for you. Of all the people in the world, I understand."

So she did. Connie drew her breath in a sigh that hurt going down, hurt going back out. Then she nodded.

"I need the jacket," D'Amato said. "It's evidence."

It took an effort of will for Connie to loosen her grip on the jacket, a greater one to hand the garment over.

"Go on, take her out," he said. "I'll lock up here and tell the landlord to keep an eye on things."

"Thanks," Penny said. She put her arm around Connie's shoulders and urged her forward. "Don't worry, Detective. I'll take care of her."

The drive to the beach was a silent one; Connie didn't feel capable of talking, and was grateful the other woman respected that. As they pulled into the driveway, the tang of the salty sea air roused her, kicking her brain back to some semblance of function.

She got out of the car and stood looking toward the ocean. Waves broke silver upon the sand, and the moon and stars hung cold and glittery against the backdrop of the sky. Clouds piled upon the horizon, reaching slow, inexorable tendrils that would soon drown the moon.

An unmerciful sort of night, she thought. Even the house seemed alien here, a thing of hard edges and unnatural angles that had come to lay squatter's rights on the beach.

"Come on, Connie," Penny said. "I'll make us some tea."

Her voice pulled Connie out of the fanciful and

back to the real world. The view returned to normal. A house, the sea, and the sand. That was all.

Inside, the house seemed to echo with too many memories and too few inhabitants. Connie stood in the doorway as Penny set the teapot on to boil.

"How can you stand it here?" she asked.

Penny looked up, her brows raised. "What do you mean?"

"It feels so lonely."

"Ah, but it isn't, Connie. I have such good friends to keep me company." Her mouth curved in a smile. "Why don't you go sit down by the fire? You look cold."

Yeah. Cold to my soul. No fireplace was going to be able to generate enough warmth to penetrate that. But she went into the great room and stood before the fire, close enough so that the flames cast orange-yellow reflections around her feet.

"Cullen, I could really use you right about now," she murmured. "You were the optimistic one."

"I talk to him, too."

Connie turned. Penny stood beside the sofa, a delicate china cup and saucer balanced in each hand—company china to perk up a guest. No food, however, which was odd; Penny had always been proud of her manners and hospitality. *There goes the old add-'em-up mind again. Clickety-clack. But Penny's in the same boat you are, Ms. Accountant; the rules no longer apply, the little things no longer matter.*

"Here you go," Penny said, setting the cups down on the coffee table.

Connie sat down in front of the nearest cup. Steam rose from within porcelain so thin it looked translucent. She ran her finger along the graceful curve of the handle. "It's pretty."

"Evvie gave me these. They were her grandmother's, I think." Her spoon made ladylike tinkling sounds as she stirred her tea. "Detective D'Amato told me about the jacket. I know it seems bad, but we should focus on the positive. As long as they haven't found Jeff's . . . ah . . ."

"Body," Connie said.

"You shouldn't assume the worst. That jacket could have gotten there any number of ways."

"D'Amato thinks he's dead."

"Well, in his line of work—"

"There was blood all over it. In it. A lot of blood."

"Oh, Connie, I'm sorry. But you still can't be sure that he's . . . dead. There are so many other possibilities." Penny raised her cup to her lips. "Drink your tea. It will settle your nerves."

Connie took a sip, grimacing inwardly when she tasted sugar. She didn't like sweet tea. But it was warm and felt good going down, so she finished it.

"I'm glad you came tonight," Penny said. "Sometimes it's comforting just to spend time with someone who feels like you do. We don't need to hide our grief under company manners." She folded her hands in her lap. "I don't have children, so I can't empathize with you about Jeff. I know it must be awful. Especially the not knowing. Hoping, yet not quite daring to hope too much . . ."

"You've got the gist of it," Connie said, forcing the words through a throat gone suddenly tight. She got up and went to stand before one of the big oceanside windows.

"More tea?" Penny asked.

"No. Thanks."

Tears blurred her vision. She pressed the heels of her hands against her eyes, afraid that if she started crying she'd never be able to stop. Behind her, she could hear the rattle of crockery as Penny took the cups into the kitchen.

A door opened and closed nearby, and a moment later she felt the weight of someone's hand on her shoulder.

"Connie."

John. She lowered her hands, clasped them in front of her to keep them from shaking. He turned her to face him. His eyes shone in the firelight, and his hands were gentle as he pulled her into his embrace.

"I heard," he said. "I'm so sorry."

She stood stiffly for a moment, then slowly relaxed against him. The need for comfort was stronger than the boundaries she wanted to draw between them.

"It was only his jacket," she said. "They haven't found *him.*"

"What if they never do?"

"Then I'll keep looking. For as long as it takes."

He pulled back, enough so that he could look into her face. His thumbs stroked her cheeks as he brushed some stray hairs back into place. "Sometimes you just have to let go."

"You let your keys go, or your wallet, or maybe your dog. Never your child."

"So bright," he murmured. "So full of life that you burn with it. Dark fire, Connie. Full of anger and self-doubt and tenacity. Far more interesting than Cullen's goodness."

She pulled away. "We're talking about my *son,* not some damned auras."

A soft sound brought her swinging around. Penny stood in the doorway, one hand braced on the jamb. She looked like a pretty porcelain doll, all smooth, pale skin and empty eyes. Not unusual, for Penny.

"I didn't know you'd come in, John," she said.

"I had to see Connie, of course."

"Of course."

Suddenly, Penny looked straight at Connie. An emotion welled into those long-lashed model's eyes, a deep, dark tidal wave that came straight from the soul. Connie recognized it, even as she took a step backward from it.

Hate.

Bottomless, black, feral. It glared at her from her sister-in-law's eyes, a stark, ugly contrast to the beautiful face in which it was housed. It hit, clung like thick, hot acid.

She hates me!

The knowledge sent Connie back another step. Her back came up against John's chest, and she welcomed the solid human comfort of the contact. It anchored her against the buffeting stormwind of Penny's hatred.

"Penny, what's the matter?" she asked.

"I'm tired of sharing with you," the other woman said. "All Cullen ever talked about was you. Connie, Connie, Connie. How great you were, how wonderful things would be for him if you ever came back to stay."

"It didn't mean he loved you less," Connie said. "We were twins, after all—"

"I *know* you were twins." Penny stepped forward,

into the shattered firelight. It played along her skin, warming it to match her eyes. "Twins this, twins that, pieces of shared soul, things no one but you could understand or appreciate, and all the rest. Ten years of it."

She smoothed her hair, a gesture that should have been unremarkable, but which was anything but; it pulled her skin back tautly, giving her an eerie look for a moment. "Do you know what he said to me the day before he died? He said that he stood poised on a threshold of the spirit, and now that you were back, he felt free to take the step over. I'd been with him ten years, I'd helped him, supported his dreams, followed along like a good little wife, and all he could think about was taking that step with you."

"Penny—"

"*He* didn't know you as well as he thought he did, did he, Connie? But I knew. Here he'd hung his hopes and dreams on sharing his new frontier with you, and never guessed for a moment that you didn't give a shit about any of it. You were his twin, so he couldn't be 'complete' unless you played the big role in his little play."

"I never once told him I shared his beliefs," Connie said. "You're being unfair, Penny."

"Phaedra!" she screamed. "Phaedra, Phaedra! You and that goddamned bitch of a mother never say it right!"

Connie's temper flared. "Now, just one minute—"

"No!" Penny overrode her, both with fury and the blazing intensity of her eyes. "I shared my husband with you for ten long years. But I will . . . not . . . share . . . John."

"John?" Connie wasn't sure she'd said the name or thought it; her mind spun frantically, searching for a handle in a world gone mad.

And then she got it. Oh, she got it. But when she started to take a step forward, John slid his arm around her waist and held her in place.

"Sorry, Connie," he said.

Chapter Twenty-Eight

Connie held tightly to herself, pulling in, consolidating her strength against the chaos that had overtaken her world. Everything seemed preternaturally vivid. She could see the play of light on Penny's face as the flames leapt and danced, smell the faint scent of soap on John's skin, She could feel her own blood pumping through her veins, her lungs moving air in and out, in and out.

But strangely, she felt no fear. And no hope. She knew they'd kill her after they'd finished playing the game. Oh, yeah. The prize was already forfeit; all she had left was her anger, and it was a cold, passionless thing.

When she finally spoke, her voice held no emotion; that was private, not to be shown to . . . these. "Which of you killed my brother?"

"I did," John said. "Phaedra had to stay here in case you decided to join Cullen on the beach."

Connie stared at her sister-in-law, for the first time seeing the crabbed, selfish soul that lay below the beauty of her face. Penny had always been weak, a reed bending before whatever breeze was blowing at the moment. Lovely, adoring, biddable.

The perfect accompaniment to Cullen's dramatic spirit, the perfect accomplice to his murder.

"It was the money, wasn't it?" Connie asked.

"As you know, your brother wasn't much of a businessman," John said. "He had the Wahlfields begging to give him money, and he wouldn't take it. Said it didn't mix with things of the spirit, and that was the problem with most organized religion, et cetera, et cetera."

"He never thought about the rest of us," Penny said. "With his talents, Cullen could have been anything. People have built empires on less. But all he wanted was to go meditate on the beach somewhere."

"He confided in us," John said. "He always confided in his wife and his best friend. He'd decided against the corporation."

"So you killed him."

The firelight flickered in Penny's eyes. "He never once thought about me, what I wanted, what I needed. The Walhfields all but forced this house on him, they were so eager to be a part of the Matthias grand plan. They'd have given more. All he had to do was give them his answer to life in twenty-five words or less, and they'd have handed him a fortune in return. Those old fools have so much, they wouldn't even notice."

"And you figured that once my brother was dead, John would just step into his shoes." Bitterness edged her voice. "In more ways than one. The king is dead; long live the king. And the queen doesn't even need to change her sheets."

"You make it sound so ugly."

Connie was startled into laughter. "Ugly? You want ugly, let me paint you a picture: Cullen sitting on the beach, his eyes closed, and John here sneaking up to stick a knife into his chest."

"Cullen didn't suffer," Penny said.

"Didn't suffer!" Connie surged against the restraint of John's arm. "No wonder you see him everywhere you go. If it were me, I'd haunt you into the next life and beyond."

"See him?" John echoed. "Don't you get it? Cullen's dead; nobody's going to see or hear from him again. That other was a nice little drama put on to impress the Wahlfields."

Penny smiled. "I took drama in school."

Connie pushed forward again. John's fingers closed around her throat, not hard enough to hurt, but hard enough to bring her back onto her heels. She drew her breath in with harsh little rasps, unmoving but defiant beneath his hand. And even now, her mind took the facts and added them together, coming up with the answers that had tantalized but remained unfocused until now.

"You set my son up," she said. "All the way around, you set him up."

"He was perfect," John said. "Actually, it was his coming here that gave us the chance we'd been looking for. It isn't every day that the perfect, ah, pigeon drops into your lap."

"Damn you," Connie whispered. Only for him.

His hand slid to the base of her throat, a touch as loverlike as it was threatening. But right now, she dared anything, for she knew the end of the game hadn't come. Reaching up, she gripped his wrist, digging her nails into the skin.

"Jeff didn't beat Penny," she said.

"No," he agreed. "I did. She tried to kill you that night in the fog, you know. I was upset and got a little carried away. Blaming Jeff was just icing on the cake."

His fingertips traced the spot where her pulse throbbed. A wave of nausea hit Connie along with the memory of how aroused he'd been the day after the accident. Their lovemaking had been wildly erotic, at times on the edge of control.

"And I thought you were glad I didn't die," she said, her voice bitter.

"But I am," he replied. Then, as though he'd read her mind, he added, "All that was yours. It had nothing to do with Phaedra, believe me."

Penny reached up to touch her black eye, then dropped her hand to her side. Slowly, her fingers curled into a fist. Connie watched emotions play across her face, anger and shame and raging jealousy twisting her features into something much less than lovely. The weak link was Penny. Easily used, too easily misused.

"It was a shock for you to find out about us, wasn't it, Penny?" she asked. "Is that what set you off that night? You followed us, waited while we ate, then took your shot at me in the fog."

"I saw you on the beach," Penny said, her eyes stark with pain. "I watched from the window upstairs."

"He's quite the lover, isn't he?" Connie smiled, watching her sister-in-law through narrowed eyes. "Exciting and innovative. And flexible. Very flexible. The kind of lover you want to keep around."

"He *had* to seduce you." Penny all but spat the words. "He had to distract you, make you think about something other than Cullen's death."

Connie leaned back against John, felt his body's immediate response. Outrage congealed in her soul.

Dark, powerful, without restraint. At that moment she truly was capable of murder. And he knew it. She could feel the awareness in the way his hand spread out on her waist, in the ragged little catch in his breathing.

And why shouldn't it excite him? This is the dark side he always wanted to set free.

"Is that right, John?" she asked. "Did you make love to me to distract me from Cullen's murder?"

"No," he said. "I did it because I wanted to. From the moment I saw you, I wanted to possess you body, mind, and soul. I would have killed to get my hands on you."

A kind of madness gripped Connie; she wanted only to strike out, use any means, any weapon, to hurt these people who'd taken so much from her. "Did it feel good, that night on the beach?" she asked.

His breath slid hot across her ear. "You know the answer. I felt as though I'd fallen off the edge of the world. No one has ever made me feel the way you do. And I know it was good for you, too; you loved the violence and the freedom, loved the storm and the wind and me inside you."

"Yes," Connie said. Damn her, damn him, she'd given him a piece of her soul that night, touched things in herself she kept secret, even from herself.

Penny seemed to curl in on herself, tears glittering on her cheeks amid the flickering orange reflection of the flames. And Connie was glad, glad. She could feel John locked tight against her, her mate in this execution of Penny's psyche. And still it wasn't enough.

"You said you loved me," she said, letting her head fall back against his chest.

"I do love you. You're the mirror of my soul, Connie. We were destined to be together."

"Dregs of another life?"

"Maybe." He leaned his cheek on the top of her head, and she knew he was looking at Penny. Probably smiling, for he was enjoying this nasty little game. "Maybe our souls have been entwined since the beginning of time, maybe they will be until the end."

"No," Penny moaned. "You love *me.*"

"Cullen loved you, Phaedra," he said. "And don't fool yourself about being in love with me. I merely gave you what you wanted: a not-so-gentle lover and a shot at the big time."

He slid his hand from Connie's throat to her hair, combing it with his fingers. A lover's gentleness, a lover's touch. Penny's mouth twitched. Then she whirled, stumbling away as though she'd been blinded.

"Is that what you wanted, Connie?" John asked.

"Yes."

He laughed softly. "The beast is roaring tonight, isn't it?"

"Isn't that what you wanted?"

"Oh, yes."

Sinking his hand into her hair, he pulled her around to face him. Then he kissed her. Connie rebelled at last, not for the violation; he'd taken much more from her than the sanctity of her body. No, it was the sheer possessiveness of his caress, and the certainty of it. He knew she was his. Life or death at his whim.

"Damn you!" she gasped, tearing her mouth away from his.

She brought her knee up. His reactions were

faster than hers; he shifted his hips, catching the blow with his thigh. Then, using his grip on her hair, he slammed her against the wall.

Stunned, she sagged forward, only to be knocked back again as his body came against hers. He was hard, his erection straining the front of his pants.

"I know where you spent the night," he murmured.

She clawed for his eyes. He caught her wrist in a grip that numbed her arm to the elbow. "Was it good for you, Connie?"

"Go to hell."

He dragged her hand down between them. She closed her hand into a fist, but he squeezed her wrist until her fingers went lax from pain. She cried out.

"Come on, Connie. Don't be shy. Did you enjoy fucking your ex-husband? Was it like old times?"

An answer, any answer, would be a victory for him. She clenched her teeth, remaining silent as he held her hand on his erection, remaining silent as he bucked his hips, stroking himself against her palm.

"I'd pull it out for you," he whispered, "but I think that might be taking too much of a chance."

"Let go of my wrist, and I'll castrate you *through* the pants."

His pale irises almost seemed to whirl in the flickering firelight. Slowly, he forced her arms wide, pinning them against the wall. "That's what I love about you," he said. "Even your hate excites me. It takes courage to hate, Connie. Hate makes you strong, gives you the guts to look me in the eye and tell me to go to hell. That's what Cullen lacked. There's got to be something wrong with a man who likes everybody, don't you think?"

"Cullen—"

"Shone like the sun," he finished for her. "Shit. Cullen was a fool. His wife and his best friend were fucking almost under his nose, and he couldn't come down from the clouds enough to see it."

"Yeah. He should have looked down long enough to see the mud under his feet."

John's mouth thinned, and she knew she'd made a hit. "Do you know what happened that morning?" he asked, his voice silky. "I found him meditating, sunk so deep that I had to call his name several times before he noticed me. Then he stood up, and I nailed him with the knife. Bang, dead center."

"Bastard!"

"Your son watched."

She gasped, the air driven from her as if he'd punched her.

John's smile had the casual cruelty of a wolf's as it tore into its prey. "You should let the boy go. He was a loss to society long before Cullen died. Useless to throw your life away on someone who doesn't appreciate it."

Fear hadn't blunted her mind; it worked with utter clarity, setting the last few pieces into place. "And then what? We live happily ever after?"

"We could build that empire together, you and I. With your brains, my charisma, and the Walhfields' money, we could be the New Age answer to the fucking TV evangelists. It's a huge concept, bigger than anything Cullen could have imagined. Think about it."

She wanted to live and knew she wouldn't be able to. "Stop playing games, John. You know you're not going to let me walk out of here."

He sighed. "You're right, I'm afraid. You'll never

give up that part of yourself I really want, and I told you once that I'm unwilling to settle for less than everything. It's a shame, really; there have been other women besides Penny who threw their all at me, and I never gave a damn about any of them."

He cocked his head to one side, a strange, birdlike gesture that sent a frisson of fear up her spine. "But you . . . I would have loved you forever. I would have given you my soul."

"It's all bullshit, isn't it? The channeling, the trances . . . you used Clovis like you used Penny. The shortest route to the nearest dollar bill."

"It's all bullshit, Connie. The Father, the Son, the Holy Ghost, crystals and cards and the great life force, all a con to keep the sheep bleating to the shepherd's tune. Nobody's going to find power by looking within; power comes from money; the only Nirvana is what we make right here."

Looking into his eyes, Connie could believe in Satan. The proof was right there, in those wide-open pupils ringed with pale blue iris. "However offbeat Cullen's beliefs might have been, they were *real.* The Walhfields, Amy and Lynn, even Hamilton, came together out of faith."

John chuckled. "You don't believe in any of it."

"I don't have to. *They* do, and that makes it real. You and Penny are the only frauds here."

"Such fire," he murmured. "Another woman would be frightened."

"I don't have enough to lose to be scared."

"Ah, Connie. You know that's not true." His lips curved in a smile that was both tender and mocking. "In a way, I wish you'd come here before we decided to kill Cullen. If I'd had you, it might almost have been enough."

"You only wanted me because I *didn't* love you. If I had, you'd have been as bored with me as you are with Penny."

"That may be true. I'm a predator, and we prefer the chase to the capture. But then," he leaned forward to run his tongue along the curve of her cheekbone, "you've got a lot of the predator in you, lover. You just might have been able to hold me."

He moved lower, seeking her mouth. Connie turned her head to one side, straining the tendons in her neck to avoid his kiss. He laughed, then pressed his open mouth to her skin and sucked heat to the surface.

Putting his mark on her before she died.

When he raised his head again, she looked straight into his eyes. Death resided there for her, and not an easy one; he'd dish out every bit of torment, punished her body, mind, and soul because he couldn't possess them. She took a shuddering breath, fighting to keep her voice under control.

"What have you done to my son?"

"Figured it all out, have you?" he asked.

"Jeff was the perfect patsy for Cullen's murder, but he didn't quite react as planned, did he?"

Smiling, he shook his head. "Neither did you. I didn't expect you to go out to the beach that morning and certainly never dreamed you'd steal the candles I so carefully planted. But it turned out that I didn't need them after all, not with Jeff acting as his own worst enemy."

"You murdered that boy, didn't you?" He didn't answer, but the look on his face was enough. "He was Jeff's friend, and you killed him the same way you killed Cullen, hoping Jeff would be tagged for that one, too. But he ran, and inconvenienced you by not getting caught. You had to do something. So you tracked him to the mission. I don't know why you ran Rick down, other than the fact that he was trying to help Jeff."

"He was just in the wrong place at the wrong time," John said. "You've got a lot of things right, Connie—but not everything. You see, I didn't track Jeff to the mission; I tracked *you.* And I appreciate the help."

She flinched away from that. "Where is my son?"

"Has anyone told you that you have an appallingly one-track mind?"

"Go to hell."

He freed her hands so suddenly she didn't have time to react before his fingers sank into the hair at the nape of her neck. She stiffened, swallowing her automatic cry of pain simply because he wanted to hear it.

"Hurts, doesn't it?" he asked.

She pressed her lips together. He tightened his grip, pulling her back into an arch. "Say yes, Connie."

"Owww," she gasped. "Yes, damn you!"

"You don't give an inch, do you?" With a jerk that nearly pulled her off her feet, he propelled her toward the door. "Come for a walk on the beach, sweetheart. There's a storm brewing tonight. Your favorite."

Chapter Twenty-Nine

Jeff was coming apart, pieces of him shredding away like rotten bark. He'd become trapped in the abcess of his own mind, unable to move or speak, unable even to hold the memories that kept spinning away from him.

Too much acid. This was a trip he wasn't coming back from.

Hold on, keep as much as you can. Then, *What for? This is it, the grand tour. Nobody goes home.*

One small piece of him left. He held it tight, digging in. It fought him like a frightened animal in a panic to get free. The acid beat through his veins, white lightning of dissolution. And it was winning. All he had to do was let go; it would take him away and never let him come home again.

Then he heard his mother's voice. It gave him strength, firmed his grip on the struggling bit of his soul still left to him. And it brought him back to the world. Marginally, and in shattered bits, but he was there. He concentrated on little things, the grit and wet-seaweed smell of the sand beneath his cheek, the all-encompassing sound of the ocean to his left.

But the acid hovered close, setting up a dark little

chamber of horrors in the back of his mind. Dark. Black velvet wrapping him close, sliding across his mouth and nose with a suffocating touch. He found himself drifting away in it, brought himself back, drifted away again. And again.

Breathe. In. Out. In. Lose touch with the rhythm, and it would stop. He knew how close he was to stepping into that darkness forever. *Breathe, Jeff. Breathe.*

He could hear footsteps now. His mother's voice again. And his. The enemy. Jeff pushed at the looming darkness, holding on. Hoping it would be long enough.

Dear God, if you don't give me anything else ever again, give me this. Help me.

He hadn't prayed in a long time. Hadn't realized he could.

Mom.

Connie resisted John's pull on her hair, fighting him every step of the way as he hauled her out onto the deck.

"Don't," he hissed.

She reached up, clawing at his hand. He gave her hair a jerk that sent her to her knees. Agony radiated down her neck and across her shoulders, and she couldn't repress a cry.

"Behave," he said. "Or I'll tear it out by the roots."

"I . . . can't walk like this," she gasped.

He let go of her hair, and the cessation of pain almost made her pass out. But he only shifted his grip to her arm. "Let's go, Connie."

"You'll never get away with this."

His teeth flashed as he smiled. "Come on. No fooling around, or it's back to the hair."

He hauled her off the deck and onto the soft sand. She stumbled deliberately, testing his grip. No give there; she nearly dislocated her shoulder when she went down.

The clouds had suffocated the sky, bringing with them the hazy sparks of far-off lightning and a wind to whip the ocean into whitecaps.

It was the kind of night that kept people at home, safe behind their glass and wood and plaster. Only the predators were out . . . and their prey.

"It's going to be a hell of a storm," John said. "Do you feel it?"

"Yes," she said. "I feel it."

Something lay on the beach just where the waves died on the sand. For a moment, she thought it was a piece of driftwood. Then a flare of lightning lashed the beach, and she saw that it was human. Male. Young.

"Jeff," she gasped. "Jeff!"

She lunged forward. Inexplicably, John let her go. Or maybe not so inexplicably; he had the best of insurance against her running away. She went down on her knees beside her son, scooping his upper body into her arms. He was breathing, if shallowly. His tee shirt rode up on his belly, and she could see terrible bruises staining his skin.

She looked up at John with eyes that burned with hate and fear and a wild rush of tears. "What have you done to him?"

"He was in a car wreck." John's mouth twisted in something that didn't resemble a smile in the least. "Hit-and-run."

"Jeff," she whispered, brushing sand from his cheek.

"He can't hear you," John said.

"What did you give him?"

"A ticket to dreamland, lover. Don't worry about him; it's not like he hasn't taken this trip before."

Connie leaned down and touched her lips to Jeff's forehead. His skin was hot, his muscles lax. As she raised her head, however, she saw his lashes go up, revealing a sliver of eyeball. He wasn't completely gone, then. She let her hair fall across both their faces.

"Fight it," she whispered.

John's hand fell on her shoulder. She shook it off reflexively, as though brushing away an insect. He made an ugly sound, half-laugh and half-snarl, and slung her backward onto the sand.

She rolled over and up to her feet and found him smiling at her. Instinct brought her up on her toes, ready to fight; reason kept her in place.

"Go ahead," he said. "Run. I'll kill him if you do."

He placed his foot on Jeff's throat. Pressed. The boy gurgled softly, his hands twitching with an abortive struggle for breath.

"I wasn't going to run," she said.

"Ah. The beast is rearing its ugly head again." He smiled. "It might work, if he could get away while you attacked me. But not now. You'd lose, and then I'd kill him as punishment."

"You're going to kill him anyway," she spat.

"Now, that depends. I may decide he's more useful alive. After all, he's got to tell D'Amato just how he killed Cullen and that boy. I've given him enough acid that he won't remember what happened from what he imagined."

"That's what happened before, isn't it? You gave him drugs, then told him he killed my brother."

"And he believed me, of course. I'm his buddy, the guy who gives him the good shit."

The wind whipped Connie's hair into her face. She dragged it back, her mind whirling with the possibilities of living and dying. Funny, now that she'd found Jeff again, she wanted to live more than ever. It didn't add up, both of them getting out of here.

"How do you plan to get away with another killing?" she asked. "Don't you think the police are going to look real hard at a brother and sister being murdered so close together?"

"But I'm not going to kill you," he said. "You're going to do it yourself."

She gaped at him. "You're insane."

"Not at all." He took a pill bottle out of his pocket and tossed it on the sand at her feet. "Even D'Amato knows how distraught you were at losing your son so soon after losing Cullen. You came here, found Phaedra's sedatives, and just gave in to an irresistible compulsion. It happens all the time. You've already taken the first dose."

The tea, Connie thought, calculating absorption rates. Damn. She hadn't eaten anything since lunch; she'd been too upset by seeing the bloodstained jacket to think about eating dinner. It wasn't going to be long before she started feeling the sedative's effects.

"You're going to write a suicide note," John continued. "I've even composed it for you: 'I can't live without Cullen and Jeff. Please forgive me, Mother.' Short and sweet and right to the heart. Characteristic of you to think of your mother at the end, don't you think?"

"I'm not going to do it."

"Yes, you are."

"Screw you. I'm not making it easy for you."

The air lay thick and close, an almost palpable touch upon the skin. But no rain fell. It seemed almost as though the clouds held their collective wet breath, saving their load for the end of the drama. Lightning stroked the sky's low-hung belly, and thunder groaned and muttered in its wake.

Connie stood frozen, unable to run or fight because of the boy lying so still and helpless beneath John's feet. She stared at the man as the storm rolled toward them. His eyes glittered in the searing illumination of the lightning flashes, and she knew he was riding high.

"You'd kill me if you could, wouldn't you?" he asked.

"Don't judge me by your standards."

"It's too bad you don't have what it takes to tap into that darkness inside you. We could have made quite a team."

She dragged a strand of wet hair back from her face. "Why don't you cut the crap? You were going to kill me all along. You just didn't know when. That's what turned you on so much."

"True. And you felt the danger, deep in that shrouded little soul of yours. That's what turned *you* on."

She hated the truth of it. "Did you make love to Penny after beating her? Did that turn you on?"

"Actually," he said, "it was the thought that she'd kill for me that excited me most. But I *did* have to make sure she didn't do it again."

"Why, because you wanted to kill me yourself?"

Smiling, he slid his foot beneath Jeff's shoulder and flipped him over onto his stomach. Then he stepped on the back of the boy's head, pressing his face into the wet sand. A wave darted up to foam in around the depression.

Connie started forward, but then John looked up, pinning her in place with his storm-mad gaze. "Being with you was like riding the whirlwind," he said. "Dangerous, obsessive, just this edge of frightening, but too damn exciting to get off. There were times when I came to your place fully intending to kill you. And then something would happen. That fucking landlord would be sitting on the porch, watching me, or I'd take one look at you and just go crazy wanting to be inside you. Your eyes go all creamy when you want—"

"Let him up!" she screamed. "He can't breathe!"

John blinked. But he lifted his foot, letting Jeff's face up out of the sand. The boy coughed water out, sucked air in.

John tossed a notebook into the sand beside the pill bottle. "Write the note, Connie."

She didn't respond until he poised his foot on the back of Jeff's head again. Then she stooped and picked the notebook up. Its leather cover felt coolly reptilian in her hand; this was her death warrant, hers and maybe Jeff's.

"Open it," John said. "There's a pen inside."

Slowly, she obeyed. The wind riffled the pages teasingly, and she laid her hand over them. "I don't remember what you wanted me to write."

"I can't live without Cullen and Jeff. Please forgive me, Mother."

Connie got the words down in convulsive little

jerks that didn't resemble her normal handwriting at all. Her fingers felt leaden; the sedative Penny had given her was beginning to kick in.

"Sign it," he said.

She scribbled her name across the bottom of the page, then hurled the noteback back to him. He caught it and tucked it away in his pocket.

"Now the pills," he said, pointing to the bottle at her feet.

"Let my son go."

His brows went up. "Where's he going to go, Connie? He's too fucked up to move."

"Then leave him here. We can go back to the house—"

"The pills, Connie."

"Damn you!" she screamed. "Let him go!"

He pressed Jeff's face back into the sand. The wind pushed the water up in eager little wavelets, turning the boy's tawny hair dark.

"As I see it," John said, "the name of the game is risk. Who's willing to take the most, you or me?"

"Oh, God, let him up!"

He reached around to his back, came around with a wide-bladed hunting knife. "This isn't the same knife I used on Cullen; Jeff screwed that up along with everything else. But I doubt the cops are going to know the difference. Or care, as long as they get the paperwork off their desks. Now, you've got a choice here. You can run, and take the chance that I'll stop to cut his throat before coming after you. Or I might let him live, and go after you. He can take the rap for your murder, too. Not as neat and pretty as my original plan, but I'm a guy who can flex with the situation."

Connie stared in horror at her son. The water was

deeper now, foaming up around his ears, and his hands made aimless clutching motions at the air.

John's voice cut through her paralysis. "Take the risk, Connie, or take the pills."

Her pulse beat a counterpoint to the thunder. She shifted her weight to her right foot, weighing her chances. No. Not *this* risk. Not her son's life. She couldn't do it.

Cullen would have. Cullen would have found a way.

"All right!" She bent, snatched the pill bottle from the sand. "Let him up."

Crouching, John used the boy's hair to pull his face up out of the water. For a moment, Connie thought Jeff was dead. Then he moaned, water and sand dribbling out of his mouth.

John looked up at her, his smile full of smug pleasure. He'd known what choice she'd make. He'd known she wouldn't dare.

"Open it."

Her hands shook as she fumbled with the plastic top, shook even more as the capsules rolled out into her palm. "I can't swallow them without water."

"Chew them," John said, shifting his foot on Jeff's head.

She lifted her hand, took one of the capsules onto her tongue. The gelatin clung to the moisture, already beginning to dissolve. It had the same coppery taste of blood, or maybe it was the flavor of her own fear.

"More," John said.

"Give me a chance," she said. "You don't want me to choke to death before I finish committing suicide, do you?"

How many? she thought. How many would it take?

"More," John said.

"Let my son go."

"Still trying to bargain?"

Desperation lay hot at the back of her eyes. "He's worth more to you alive than dead."

"Is he?"

"Even if he remembers anything, the police aren't likely to believe him. His death might raise more questions than it answers."

Still watching her, John pressed the boy's face back down. "More, Connie."

Sobbing in frustration, she put another capsule in her mouth. Chewed. Swallowed. John brought Jeff up for air, then pushed him back down again.

Another capsule. And another. She could feel her limbs growing heavy, her mind working more slowly. Then John pulled Jeff up again. Her son turned his face toward her, and she saw awareness in his eyes. Awareness, and something else.

He knows what's happening. He's going to try something. To save me.

No, she thought, black terror rushing through her mind. Don't! But there was nothing she could do to stop it.

So she waited. She watched. And she felt her son gather himself, husbanding his strength. Pride tightened her throat. He was stubborn, just like his father. No one ever took a Valle down without paying for it.

Overhead the thunder raved. The wind tore at her hair, whipping it around her face. Its violence roused her, brought rage popping like soap bubbles in her mind.

Not my son.

Damn him. *Damn him.*

Rain began to fall, big, fat drops that made dark Rorschach patches upon the sand. One splashed on her hand. She opened her fingers, let the pill bottle fall.

"Pick it up," John had to shout over the thunder.

She went down on one knee, scooping up sand along with the bottle. Jeff's right arm slid beneath his body, bracing him. Time seemed to stand still as she waited for him to make his move. Sound faded. She could feel her heartbeat, and his.

Jeff heaved himself to one side, catching John just below his knees. Off-balance in his crouch, the man sprawled backward. He was up again a moment later, his teeth glittering to match the knife.

With a shout, Connie flung the handful of sand straight into his eyes. Then she took off at a run, pausing only to haul a floundering Jeff to his feet and pull him after her.

Rain started pouring down in torrents, closing around them like a curtain. It seemed almost as though the earth and sky had reversed themselves, sending the ocean crashing down in one vast cascade. Connie would have offered up a prayer of thanksgiving if she'd had time; if she couldn't see John, then he couldn't see her. She turned to look over her shoulder. The rain pounded their footsteps out of existence almost as fast as they made them. Good. Maybe they had a chance.

"Come on, Jeff!" she shouted in his ear.

He staggered, his arms and legs moving in uncoordinated jerks. Connie pulled his arm over her shoulders. A hundred steps. A hundred more. His teeth were bared with effort, and she knew he didn't have much left.

Finally, his legs stopped working entirely. She

dragged him along on sheer adrenaline, clawing her way up the slope of a dune before his weight pulled her down.

"Sorry, Mom." His eyes started to glaze. "Can't keep . . . straight."

"Don't leave me now," she panted, shaking him.

"Get . . . away."

His eyes drifted closed. She shook him again, but he didn't respond at all. He'd made that single heroic effort on sheer guts.

And you tell me he's lost!

But time had run out. The sedatives she'd taken had begun to kick in heavily, pumped through her system, maybe, by exertion and adrenaline. Even the rain slacked off, taking away their cover. Off to her left, a single light shone like a malevolent yellow eye through the thinning veil of water.

She went down on one knee beside her son and tried to look at her options. Every one held risk. Every one took away as much as it offered. *Damn* John, with all his big talk about taking risks. Easy talk when he'd never had this much to lose.

She forced herself back to her feet, and somewhere found the strength to drag Jeff into a hiding place between two dunes. His eyelids twitched as he made some internal journey through the world into which John had pushed him. If he lived, would he remember her?

"I love you, baby," she said.

She stroked his hair back from his forehead, wishing she'd been religious enough to deserve a miracle. Then she set off, drifting from cover to cover.

Straight toward the house.

Chapter Thirty

Connie slid into the shadows in the lee of the deck. Her breathing sounded too loud, even with the shrouding noise of the rain.

"Connie!" John's voice drifted in from the beach, well down from the place where she'd left Jeff. "You can't get away," he called. "Make it easy on yourself."

She pressed her body against the railing and peered at the house. A shadow crossed the window, and a moment later she saw the curtain twitch aside.

Penny. What was she thinking, alone there in the house?

"Connie!" John called, his voice smooth and malevolent. "Connieeee!"

He was still playing with her; the field had become just a little bigger and uneven, but the advantage was all his, and he knew it.

Inside, the curtain twitched again. Penny's shadow moved again, this time toward the door. A moment later she stood framed in the doorway, her backlit hair a golden aureole around her head. Connie held her breath; would Penny help him or betray him?

"John?" she called. "Is something wrong?"

"Get me the big flashlight," he shouted back. "And Cullen's gun."

"All right."

She turned back into the house, and Connie's long-held breath went out in a sigh. As the proverb went, the leopard wasn't going to change its spots. John needed, John wanted, and Penny gave.

He'll kill her, too, someday. He's already murdered her soul.

Connie felt the seconds ticking away, each taking a part of her strength with it. Her vision was starting to blur.

Go, go, go!

She slid beneath the rail and headed across the deck toward the door. *Just give me two minutes and the telephone, Lord.*

Something moved inside the house. Connie ran to the edge of the deck and vaulted over the railing. The drug ruined her coordination, however, and she sprawled heavily on the sand. She scrambled back to her hiding place.

Click. The back door opened. *Click.* It closed. Footsteps marked Penny's progress across the deck. Now she was passing the table, now the flowerpots; now she was approaching the steps. Now she'd entered Connie's limited field of view.

She held the gun like she knew what to do with it. Sure; Cullen would have made sure she learned to use it safely. The weapon gleamed evilly in the fitful light. And Connie could hear John moving around out there in the darkness. He'd begun searching the beach now, knowing they couldn't have got far.

Time had just run out. Everything had run out. Connie leaned her shoulder against one of the deck's supporting poles and listened to Penny's footsteps. Drowsiness washed over her in black-velvet waves, each pushing her farther into the fog.

She lost track of the footsteps, then realized she'd nodded off between one and the next. Her mind felt as though it had been wrapped in cotton.

Where is she? What have I missed?

Panic spiked through her, holding back the encroaching oblivion. Where had Penny gone? Then the flashlight came to life almost overhead, sending rays of golden light pouring through the spaces between the boards.

"Come on, Penny," John called. "Hurry it up, will you?"

His voice came from the left, near the spot where Connie had left Jeff.

That thought sent her scuttling along the edge of the deck toward the stairs even as her brain shrieked caution. This was stupid. Dangerous. Impossible.

There's only one way to win.

It wasn't her thought.

This is it. All or nothing.

Win or lose. Live or die. Not just for her, but for Jeff. The big gamble. She slid into the wedge of shadow cast by the stairs. Hesitating. Searching for a surer way. What if she chose wrong? What if John was on his way back to the house? What if . . .

Penny reached the top of the stairs. The oval of light darted across the ground, swift flashes of spiky grass that looked spectral in the glow. She took another step down, her shoe crunching on the sand.

Connie jerked as someone called her name. No, didn't call exactly. . . . And then she felt an overwhelming touch of *presence.* A familiar presence, warm and vital and twin to her soul. Cullen. She couldn't see or hear or touch him, but she knew him.

Go for it, Connie. Toss the coin. The big risk for the biggest prize of all.

She lunged forward in a sort of half-scramble that hit Penny behind the knees, knocking her backward upon the sand. The gun flew from her hand, went skidding off to come to rest in the cone of the flashlight beam.

They grappled for it. Connie lost it then, intellect rolled beneath a tidal wave of terror. She went after Penny with everything she had, teeth and nails, feet and elbows. And finally grasped the hard, cool barrel of the gun.

She slammed it against the side of the other woman's head. Penny went limp beneath her.

Connie lay gasping for a moment. Then something snagged her hair and pulled her upright. She cried out from the pain of it, cried out again because she'd dropped the gun.

"Hello, Connie," John murmured in her ear. He forced her to her knees, then down into a sitting position on the sand. "I found Jeff just over there. Too bad he couldn't make it any farther."

"You bastard—"

A sharp tug on her hair brought her gasping to silence.

"I didn't touch him," he said. "Yet. It's important that he survive you for a few hours. He's going to kill you, as he threatened to do. Then he'll just walk out into the ocean."

"You're crazy." She could feel the hard bulk of the gun beneath her leg. "You'll never get away with it."

"Of course I will. I have Jeff to count on. Everyone knows he's whacked out, especially the police."

He dragged her head back, bending her throat into a taut arc. Her eyes widened as he brought the knife around in front of her; the blade gleamed platinum in the flashlight's illumination.

"Don't fight it," he whispered. His tone was that of a lover, sleek and caressing, in stark contrast to the brutality of his grip. "I'll make it easy on you. You won't have to be afraid anymore."

Rage swept through Connie, cold and utterly clear. It burned through her, white-hot and powerful, leaving only recklessness in its wake. With a convulsive effort, she wrenched the revolver out from under her leg and fired it, upside-down and blindly, over her shoulder. Fired again. Again. She lost count but kept squeezing the trigger long after the gun was empty.

Her field of view narrowed, in the end encompassing only the knife. It hovered just in front of her throat, quivering, like a beast thirsting for blood. John's knuckles turned white, as though he strained to move the knife forward against an invisible barrier.

Crazy, Connie thought. Or maybe not. Too many things had happened tonight to question this.

"Cullen," she said. "Thank you."

"Wha . . . ?" John muttered.

He groaned, low and harsh. Then he let the knife go. It spun downward, tossing the light in a kaleidoscope flare before being extinguished on the wet sand. Connie reached behind her, unhooking his fingers one by one from her hair. Freed, she tottered to her feet and turned to look at him.

He swayed on wide-braced legs, staring at her as though she'd grown an extra head. Three dark spots marked the front of his shirt. They grew and spread, running into one another until his torso was covered.

"I took the risk," Connie said. "But it wasn't *your* kind. It was mine. Mine and Cullen's."

John touched his shirt, brought his fingertips away red. "I don't believe—"

"You should have." She smiled. "We're twins, you know."

He stared at her a moment longer. Then he took a staggering step toward her, bloodstained hand outstretched. Connie crossed her arms over her chest and watched him come. One step, two.

Teeth bared, he strained forward another step. Then he went down. He hit the sand hard, not even trying to protect his face. His back heaved as he struggled for breath.

Connie leaned down. "You should have had more faith, John."

He turned his face away. She straightened slowly, pushing with knees that had suddenly gone soft, and headed for the house.

She made it to the steps before her vision went fuzzy. She kept herself pointed toward that single beckoning light ahead, realizing with vague surprise that she'd been crawling for some time.

Had to reach the phone. For Jeff. For Cullen.

The open door loomed ahead, a fun-house shape that yawed and narrowed crazily. But she made it through, her hands and knees registering the change of texture beneath them.

She reached the phone at last, hauling herself up hand over hand on the curtains. It took a couple of tries before she managed to lift the receiver. The numbers felt too small for her fingers, or maybe it was the other way around. 9 . . . 1 . . . Her hand slipped off, fell like wet dough to her side.

For Jeff. For Cullen.

Tucking the receiver beneath her chin, she lifted her right hand with her left. Pointed, touched. 1. A woman's voice came on the line. Connie lost the words amid the roaring in her head.

"Help," she croaked. "Need . . . ambulance. D'Amato. Call . . . D'Amato."

She fell to her knees. The phone slithered away from her, still issuing words she didn't understand. She reached for it only to knock it farther away. Tears of frustration stung her eyes.

And then she felt that presence again, touching her like a benediction.

It's over.

Over. Connie let the phone go. She leaned back against the wall and watched a moth spiral around the overhead light. The insect fluttered wildly, falling away from the heat only to return and try again. She wished she could speak, to warn it away from its immolation.

It's his great truth, Connie.

But it's going to kill him.

It's only a doorway. One that must be passed through before the next step can be taken.

What step?

She could feel him smile. And she could feel him go.

"Cullen," she whispered.

The roar swelled and grew, bringing darkness with it.

Chapter Thirty-One

Connie became aware of sound and movement around her. She fought the darkness, struggling to make her vocal cords work. Somebody had to look for Jeff, see if he was all right, help him, help him . . .

A warm hand gripped hers. She clung to it, striving to raise herself above the current of drowsiness. There were things that had to be said, had to be known.

"It's me, D'Amato."

His voice brought her further into awareness; she opened her eyes a slit and saw him leaning over her. "Jeff," she croaked.

"We found him."

A man leaned between them, blocking her view of the detective. "We've got to get going, Joe. They're waiting for her in the ER."

Connie rolled her head to one side. "D'Amato."

"Wait a sec," he said. "I've got something to say to her." After a moment, the paramedic moved away. "Jeff's alive. He's way off in drugland, but he's alive. They'll be bringing his stretcher up in a minute. Now, just relax—"

"No." With an effort that brought sweat beading her face, she reached out and grasped his hand. "John . . . killed Cullen. She helped him. Penny. They tried to kill me, make Jeff take the blame."

"What?"

"Money. Wanted . . ." She knew the word, couldn't get it out.

"Walhfield money?"

She nodded. "Made me take the drug. Suicide note . . . his pocket. Made me write, ah, used Jeff—"

"To force you?"

"Yes."

"What happened to your sister-in-law?"

"Penny . . ." Talking was becoming harder. The darkness pushed at her, small, insidious tendrils seeping through her mind. "She . . . had the gun. I took it, hit her. Shot him. No choice, D'Amato. Do it or die."

"Shee-it," the paramedic said. "Look, I got to get her out of here."

"Okay." D'Amato leaned closer, his eyes glittering with an emotion she didn't understand. "I'll look into it, Connie. All of it."

She closed her eyes. A moment later, she felt herself being lifted, and then the thud of the ambulance doors closing. Her hearing seemed to draw in, furling itself like the petals of a flower. The men's voices faded away.

After a while, she even lost the siren.

"Good morning, Cinderella."

Connie opened her eyes to find Derek standing in the doorway of her hospital room. His face looked calm enough beneath the all-night stubble of beard, but emotion raged in his eyes, a wild, supercharged current of relief and outrage, frustration and anger.

"You're not going to start squeezing necks again, are you?" she asked.

"Not yours."

He rushed forward then, scooping her up and hugging her hard. She closed her eyes, breathing in the smoke-tinged male smell of him.

"I came as soon as I could," he murmured. "I was working a fire and didn't get D'Amato's message for a while."

"Have you seen Jeff?"

"Yeah."

"They told me he's going to pull through."

"They told me the same thing, so it must be true."

He set her back onto the pillows, although he looked like he'd rather hold onto her awhile. Connie grasped the front of his shirt and pulled him down to the bed beside her. He slid his arm beneath her shoulders—not a sexual touch, but a very comforting one.

"I talked to the doctor," he said. "He told me Jeff's high tolerance for drugs probably saved his life. It's a hell of a comfort, isn't it?"

Connie shrugged; what some people called irony, others called a miracle. "Has he come out of it yet?"

"Not yet." Derek raked his hair back with his free hand. "He was carrying a load of sedatives along with the hallucinogen. There might be some long-term effects, the doctor said."

"We'll deal with it. Anything's better than dying."

He nodded. "Speaking of dying, they operated on John Bruycker last night. Looks like he's going to make it."

"John?" For a moment, she had trouble catching her breath. "I thought he was—"

"Dead? Nope. He took one in the shoulder, one in the upper arm, and one in the abdomen. That one hit the small intestine. Must have been excruciatingly painful."

"Thanks for passing that on," Connie murmured.

"Remind me never to get you really mad."

She glanced away. "Tell that joke a couple of days from now, okay?"

"Okay." He grasped her chin and tilted her face upward. "Did you love him?"

There could be no evasion here, nothing false. She owed it to him and to herself. So she went back over her relationship with John, the laughter, the steamy sensuality, the obsessive need, the poised-over-a-cliff feeling that he wanted more from her than she'd ever be willing to give another human being.

"No," she said. "It was a lot of things, but never love."

"What about us?"

She touched his cheek with her fingertips. "I'm willing to give a shot at finding out. You?"

"There were times when I hated you," he said. "But I don't think I ever really stopped loving you."

"What about Jeff?"

"What about him? I've been through the fire for that kid, and I'd do it again if I had to. But I'm not running my life to please him. I've proved everything a parent should have to prove."

"I agree."

His breath went out in a long sigh. "You know, I didn't expect that from you even now."

"Maybe I've been through enough with him that I'm no longer willing to be held an emotional hostage. And maybe I just want you enough so that I'm no longer willing to let a kid play us against each other."

Things got muddled then. The pillow slithered off the bed, and Derek somehow managed to kick the phone off its support, but those were minor inconveniences in a kiss that started out as impetuous but soon settled into something that promised to go on and on and on.

At least until the nurse came in. She cleared her throat loudly more than once before Derek finally raised his head.

"I see you have a visitor, Ms. Matthias," she said, grinning at them both.

"This is my ex-husband," Connie said. "We were discussing, ah, future plans."

"I could see that. I wouldn't have intruded, but the station downstairs called to say your son is beginning to awaken. I thought you'd like to be there. Would you like me to bring a wheelchair around?"

"No," Connie said. "I'll walk."

Derek levered himself upright, then reached down to pull Connie to her feet. She swayed for a moment before getting her balance enough to walk.

"By the way," Derek said, steadying her with one hand on her arm as he led her down the corridor, "how does it feel to have your stomach pumped?"

"I think I'd rather be shot or stabbed."

"John would have been willing to accommodate you."

She jabbed the elevator's down button, her stomach lurching as the car started to move. "That bastard. He made Jeff think he killed Cullen, and made *us* think it, too. You should have seen the man's face when he was telling me about it." The scope of her hatred frightened her; had John stood here with her, she would have cheerfully shot him all over again.

"Problem?" Derek asked.

She sighed; he'd always been too good at reading her. "Just trying to remain civilized."

"What for?"

He understood. But then, Jeff was his son, too. With another sigh, she leaned her head against his shoulder.

The elevator doors snicked open. Derek's expression smoothed, shutting away the beast so no one would see. Connie could only hope her control was as good.

Jeff's room was full of sunlight. It slanted across his face without remorse, showing the thinness, the purple-shadowed eyes, the signs left by fear and exposure and death too closely seen.

The perfect tool, John had said. She could hear his voice, smooth and rich and malevolent, and she could see his eyes, pale irises sparked with reflected lightning. The memory was soul-deep, visceral. Maybe it always would be.

A doctor came into the room, moving soundlessly on rubber-soled shoes. "Mr. and Mrs. Valle?"

"Close enough," Derek said. "How is he?"

"He's beginning to respond, but slowly. It would do him good to hear your voices."

Connie laid her hand on the boy's wrist, comforting herself with the slow, steady throb of his pulse. "Jeff? Jeff, It's Mom. Can you hear me, son? We'd like you to open your eyes."

His eyelids twitched, but that was all. Connie

looked up at the doctor. His expression remained noncommittal.

"What is it?" she asked. "Why isn't he responding?"

The doctor picked up the chart and made a notation. "He's been through a lot—"

"Give it to us straight," Derek said.

"I have. We have every reason to believe he'll recover. There may be some memory loss, but he's young and despite the abuse he's put his body through, surprisingly healthy."

"Oh," Derek said. "I thought you were preparing us to hear the worst."

"From what I've heard, Mr. Valle, you've already experienced the worst." For the first time, the doctor smiled. "Just be patient. What Jeff needs most is time."

"Time is something we have plenty of," Connie said.

Once again Connie laid her hand on Jeff's wrist, again comforted by the throb of his pulse. It had been three days now. He'd been sleeping less, talking more, and making more sense each day.

"You okay?" Derek asked.

She looked up at him and smiled. "Yeah."

Jeff stirred, sliding his arm out from under her hand. "Mom? Dad?"

"Right here," Derek said.

The boy's eyes opened, and he looked at each of them in turn. "I . . . guess I let you down pretty bad."

Connie drew her breath in sharply; this was the first time Jeff had been willing to talk about what had happened. "So, I let *you* down. I should have believed in you more."

"I didn't know myself, Mom," he whispered, stark pain shadowing his face. "For a long time, I was sure I'd killed Uncle Cullen."

Connie stroked the hair back from his forehead, glad to see something besides defiance in his eyes. "You came through. Did the right thing at the right time," she said.

"So did you."

"And so did your father," she said. "Did you know he half-strangled your friend Henry to get information about you?"

"No s . . . kidding?"

"No kidding. Jeff, changes have to be made."

He glanced from her to Derek and back again. "I can't live like that again."

"Will you agree to go to counseling with us?" she asked.

"Yeah."

"And abide by the rules of the house?" Derek added.

"Whose house?"

Derek slipped his arm around Connie's waist. "Your mother's. For now. But I warn you, she and I are going to be working together on the rules. Is it a deal?"

"Yeah." Jeff's gaze lingered on his father's hand. "As long as you agree to try to understand that I'm not exactly a kid anymore. I've seen stuff most adults never have to deal with, seen it and lived it."

It was too true; looking into his eyes, Connie could see no trace of the fifteen-year-old innocence that should have been there. He'd been touched by murder, guilt, and betrayal, and whatever was left of his childhood had been lost.

For one brief, awful moment, she thought Derek was going to be stubborn about it. Then he nodded. "Okay, son. You do the counseling, go to school, and try to learn something, and we'll see about giving you more freedom. But the next time you screw up, it's military school for you."

"Deal."

It was a man's promise, born of knowledge that the world required compromise if one was to survive. She watched Derek register that and saw respect come into his eyes.

And for a moment, father and son looked so much alike that her heart ached. A threshold had been passed, a rite of manhood that had taken her little boy and put a man in his place.

Surprisingly, it felt good.

"So, Dad," Jeff said. "Do you still want to kick my butt?"

"Well, put it this way," Derek replied. "Your butt is lower on the list than some other butts."

It wasn't perfect, Connie thought, but it was a beginning.

Epilogue

The all-too-familiar hospital smells enveloped Connie the moment she walked into the waiting room. D'Amato had scorned the comfortable-looking sofa in favor of a molded blue plastic chair. If he'd done it to stay awake, he'd failed; his eyes were closed and a half-empty coffee cup teetered precariously in his hand.

Her shoe scraped the carpet. He woke with a jerk that sent the chair sliding back a couple of inches. The coffee cup slipped. He caught it, righted it, and set it on the floor without spilling a drop.

"Policeman's reflexes?" she asked.

He shook his head. "New shirt."

"The desk sergeant said I'd find you here."

His gaze flicked to the gym bag she carried in her left hand. Silently, he gestured to the chair beside his. She slid into it.

"What can I do for you, Ms. Matthias?"

"I owe you something," she said. Placing the gym bag on her lap, she unzipped it and took the black candles out one by one. They looked oily in the sunlight.

He looked at them for a moment, then at her. "It's a little late, isn't it?"

"You could arrest me for withholding evidence."

With a sigh, he picked up one candle and turned it over and over in his hands. A pair of scratches marred the surface, marks made by Cullen as he died. "I wonder what the odds are that Bruycker used gloves when he planted these?"

"He's not stupid," Connie said.

"Yeah. He had a real pretty deal going, didn't he?" Something that almost looked like humor came into his eyes. "Your ex had him pegged right. If it hadn't been for the fact that your sister-in-law had tried to kill you while he was driving the car behind yours, somebody else might have pegged him, too."

"Don't count on it, D'Amato. Hell, I'd been sleeping with him. If I didn't suspect him, who else would?"

"Only a jealous man," he murmured. "You really have a way with people, you know; I can't think of a case I've seen where someone had two people trying to kill her for two different reasons."

"It's my charm. And after today, you might be able to add Hamilton Liu to the list of hopeful assassins."

His brows went up.

"The Walhfields have decided to make me executrix of their estate. Hamilton's legacy will be put into a trust, managed by me, until he shows himself capable of some occupation other than seducing society girls."

"You agreed to this?" D'Amato demanded.

"I suggested it. They're too nice, and simply too

trusting. Oh, and they're making a rather large contribution to the Redemption Mission."

D'Amato grunted, but under the whiskers, looked more pleased than not. "Can I borrow the bag?"

She nodded. He slipped the candles back in, then slid his forearm through the bag's handles.

"Am I under arrest or not?" she asked.

"Not. I've got bigger fish to fry." He shot her a glance. "Do you want to see Bruycker?"

"Not really."

"Do me a favor."

Connie blinked. "He thinks I'm dead, doesn't he?"

"Hey, this ain't Perry Mason. I don't expect him to break the moment he sees you. But right now, he happens to think the only witness he's got to worry about is your sister-in-law, and I've been content to let him."

"What about Jeff? He's willing to testify."

"The most incompetent lawyer in Virginia would crucify him on the stand. With his history, he's got zero credibility. And your sister-in-law's not much better; the DA's ordered a competency hearing for her. But I want to shake that self-assured SOB. I want him to worry. How about it?"

She sighed. "I owe you for the candles."

"Yes, you do," he said, rising.

She fell into step beside him. He walked with that steady tread, a man sure of himself and his world, of black and white, true and false, good and bad. She envied him.

"What's Penny saying?" she asked.

"She says everything was his idea, that she was so

completely under his sway that she lost all sense of right and wrong."

Connie remembered how Penny had fled upstairs, crying after John had professed his love for another woman, and how a few minutes later she'd come out, gun in hand, ready to help him again.

"I'll buy that," she said.

"Well, Bruycker says that she was in it up to her eyeballs, and that she was the one who planned and did the killings. After all, wasn't he with you when she ran you into the path of that truck?"

"That bastard. He thinks he's got it all figured out, doesn't he?"

"He's done pretty good so far. He even used your sister-in-law's Mercedes to run down that guy at the mission. We found traces of blood matching that on Jeff's jacket."

"I wish I'd killed him."

D'Amato didn't look shocked. But then, he'd probably met a lot of relatives of murder victims who felt the same way. "Be glad you didn't. If your sister-in-law hadn't talked, we might still be looking at your son."

"What about the kid in the cemetery?"

"No physical evidence to tie Bruycker in. We'll do better pursuing the other charges."

"No justice for Tick, only a grave," Connie murmured. "Poor kid."

"They're all poor kids. They come, they die, nobody mourns them."

Wrong, Connie thought. She'd never again go to sleep in her safe, comfortable bed without thinking about those children running the streets. Giving strangers blow jobs for a few dollars, dying from overdoses, dying from AIDS, dying by the hand of one of those strangers.

"Here we are," D'Amato said softly.

Her skin tingled. Anticipation, perhaps, or maybe only the remembrance of fear. D'Amato went in ahead of her, shielding her from view for a moment. She registered the uniformed officer sitting in a chair beside the door, but then all her attention focused on John.

He was sleeping, a dark, sleek figure amid the tubes and bandages. Even that hadn't dimmed his vitality. Memories washed over her, powerful remembrances of touching, of sharing.

He'd appealed to her in the most primitive and powerful of ways and awakened something that would never entirely leave her. Gone was the Connie who'd held herself inviolate, apart even from her lovers. Gone was the Connie who'd stepped back, allowing Cullen to be the central figure, the one who'd taken the spotlight and also the heat.

I'd thank you, if you hadn't tried to kill my son. Now, all I can do is hate you.

As though hearing that thought, he opened his eyes. Her soul lurched as he stared at her, his eyes reflecting her own memories back at her. He still wanted her. Then his expression changed as he registered the consequences of her presence here.

"Hello, Connie," he said. "Have you come to pick my bones?"

"Yes," she said.

His gaze wavered, shifting to D'Amato as though he were easier to look at. "You could have told me, Detective."

"You didn't ask."

Connie stepped forward, trying to pull John's

gaze back to her. But he kept his face averted. She wished she could think he felt shame, but she knew better.

"You know," she said, "you shouldn't have spent so much time gloating that night on the beach. I guess even fake New Age mystics tend to lean toward the overdramatic."

"You would have taken a more practical approach?"

"I did," she said.

He smoothed the sheet with those graceful, long-fingered hands that had so fascinated her. Fascination. Her galloping pulse slowed, and it felt as though her body cooled with it. Her mind absorbed everything around her, smell and sight and sound, filing it away in that space marked "John Bruycker, lover." And closing it.

When he looked at her again, she no longer shared the past in his eyes. He'd become only her brother's killer, a man she hoped to see in the electric chair. Reality: harsh, unforgiving, definitely not Cullen's. But all hers. And now that she'd faced it, she could let it go.

John Bruycker had become a job that had to be done. After all, she'd always been the efficient one of the family.

"I really did love you," he said.

She drew in her breath sharply, realizing that he hadn't perceived the sudden encompassing change that had occurred. What might have been a poignant declaration now seemed merely absurd.

"See you in court," she said, turning away.

D'Amato followed her out, laying his hand on her shoulder to offer comfort she didn't need. "Are you okay?" he asked.

"Just fine."

He studied her for a moment, then nodded. "I believe you are. Come on, I'll walk you down."

Outside, it was one of those bright, brittle Tidewater fall days. Connie filled her lungs with the piquant air. "Well, I guess we're finished for a while," she said, holding her hand out.

D'Amato didn't take it. "Remember that conversation we had once about kids?"

"Is this a trick question?"

"My oldest daughter is pregnant."

She dropped her hand to her side. "I'm sorry."

"I was a righteous fool, wasn't I?"

"So, who hasn't been with their kids?"

He laughed, a harsh sound. "I figured you'd understand."

"Are you going to throw her out?" she asked.

"I can't. She's my daughter. I love her too much to turn my back on her."

Connie smiled, a genuine one this time. It almost hurt. "You know what I've found to be the only useful tool when dealing with kids? Endurance."

"You might be right," he said.

"Well, I wish you luck." She turned away again, but he caught her by the arm and turned her around.

"Answer me something," he said. "By all accounts, your brother was a smart guy. Why didn't he see his wife and Bruycker for what they are?"

"Because Cullen was for real, and I guess he just didn't see the falsehood in those he loved."

D'Amato snorted. "Next thing you'll be telling me you believe in this karma stuff."

"Sorry," she said. "My faith lies in another area."

"Phew! You had me worried there for a minute. This case has been a bitch from the beginning, what with all the mystical crap. Damn hard to pick the truth out of all the flim-flam. I'm relieved it turned out to be good old human sex, ambition, and greed."

Connie wondered what he'd say if she told him about Cullen coming to help her that night on the beach. She opened her mouth to tell him, then closed it again.

It had been a genuine miracle, life stolen right out from under Death's cold hand. Now, she believed in a much different agent for her miracle than the one Cullen would have chosen, but that didn't tarnish the gift.

She didn't know why it had happened to her; she'd never considered herself miracle material. But it was hers.

And she rather thought she'd keep it for herself.

"See you, D'Amato," she said, turning away again. "And good luck. Remember, babies are a whole lot better than other things your kids could inflict on you."

"You're sure about this endurance thing?"

"Positive," she said, without turning around. "Sooner or later they grow up, and move away, and God will finally have mercy on your soul."

She paused to glance at him before getting into her car. He'd tossed his head back and spread his arms in supplication.

"Take me now, Lord," he said.

Oh, yeah.